I0628966

DUSK OF DEATH

AN ARMEN LEZA, DEMON HUNTER NOVEL

BOOK I OF THE ARMAGEDDON TRILOGY

BY

N.L. GERVASIO

Just Ink Press. LLC

A Just Ink Press novel

eBooks are not transferable. They cannot be sold, shared or given away as it is an infringement on the copyright of this work.

This is a work of fiction. Names, characters, places, and incidents either are the product of the author's imagination or were used fictitiously, and any resemblance to actual persons, living or dead, business establishments, events, or locales is entirely coincidental.

Just Ink Press, LLC
1016 S Roosevelt Street
Tempe, AZ 85281

Dusk of Death: an Armen Leza, Demon Hunter novel
Book I of the Armageddon Trilogy

Copyright © 2016 by N.L. Gervasio
Edited by Sharon Gerlach and C.J. Obray
Cover design and interior images by Jinxie G

ISBN-10: 0-9916214-7-6
ISBN-13: 978-0-9916214-7-7

All rights are reserved. No part of this book may be reproduced in any form, without the prior written permission of the author, except in the case of brief quotations embodied in critical articles and reviews.

First publication: August 2016

For information, address:
Just Ink Press, LLC
justinkpress@gmail.com
www.justinkpress.com

TABLE OF CONTENTS

Acknowledgements

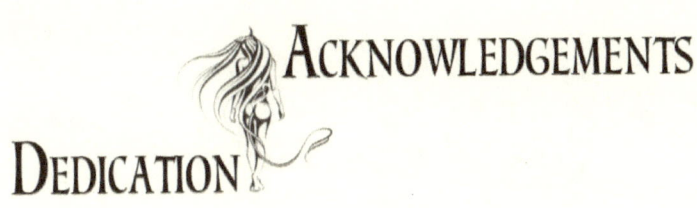

Dedication

To You.

For your patience, a quality we both know I don't possess.

I'd like to thank Sharon Gerlach for being such a remarkable editor during this beast of a book that I'd started many years ago when we were still on Writer's Café. Your strong guidance has undoubtedly shaped it into the story it finally is today. Thank you, my friend. Truly.

I'd also like to thank CJ Obray for the final line edit and counseling near the end, and for understanding exactly what word I mean to write regardless of the word I may have chosen.

To David Jones and Cindy Harper, two of the most wonderful Beta Readers I've encountered. Thank you for your fabulous input and time. And Diana "Dee" Holliday, my dear old high school friend, I'm so glad you enjoyed Armen's story and I thank you for the feedback.

And James Mayfield. You, sir, are the reason this book exists. Thank you so much. I'm glad we found each other once again and I wish only the best for you, always.

Dusk of Death

Demons, detectives, and a forensic scientist who has fallen from Hell.

Hell wants her back.

Let the demon hunt begin.

All hope is not lost.
—Origen

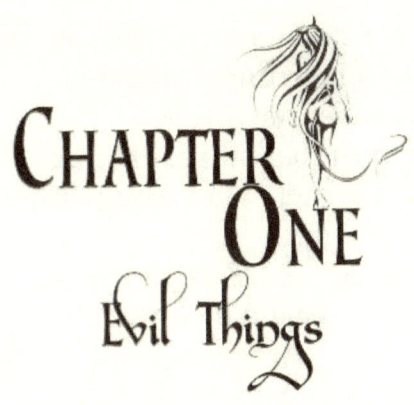

Chapter One

Evil Things

ARMEN LEZA SHOULD BE DEAD.

A hazy cloud of nothingness fogged her mind from when she had become flesh a few years ago. One moment she'd been a demon; the next, human skin graced her ancient bones. All that had been in between was missing.

When she'd fallen from Heaven, cast out by her Father, her memories hadn't faltered.

Not.

One.

Moment.

She had fallen into the Darkness while screaming for her murdered child.

The Darkness changes people, makes them go cold inside. She had forgotten about her child. She'd forgotten about the pain. One day, someone pulled her from the dark and gave her purpose. The pain flickered to life again, but it had focus.

Being a demon had taken some getting used to. Growing accustomed to her human shell was slow-going at best, but she'd get there. That wasn't to say she liked it very much. Something about being human didn't feel . . . right. Of course, neither had the demon form.

She sat in her usual spot on the sofa staring at one of the centuries-old paintings, ruminating on events she could never change, clawing after the past and holding onto the memories that stirred the fire within her, until the phone's ring scattered her thoughts like dust particles escaping a ray of light.

Several moments later, dusk settled as the last few beams of daylight snaked their way through the edges of worn shades. Terry Armstrong had hung up on her—again. In truth, Terry was never much for goodbyes; he didn't give the send-off to someone until they were dead, so he never said the farewell to the living. Of course, she never heard the word itself uttered from him. Armen assumed he thought saying that one little word invited bad luck, and she found the quirk rather entertaining, even if his calls usually weren't.

She set down the phone and shuddered, the chill running up her spine and into the nerve center of her brain having nothing to do with the night air. As she was the medical examiner who specialized in the occult, work calls usually meant bad news, even if they were rare, but something in Terry's voice this time made the hair on her arms stand on end. She thought she had picked a quiet profession to live out her human existence. She'd much rather return to her ruminating thoughts. The emotions at play within her human form bounced around, back and forth between her millennia of experiences and her current situation with a certain detective. The emotions were distracting, to say the least, since they were quite different from angelic or demonic, or warrior emotion, or the lack thereof.

Right. She'd been a warrior once. A beautiful flaxen-haired badass warrior, not unlike the Valkyrie.

The memory blinked away and she made her way to her bedroom, changing into a pair of old faded jeans, tank, and a hoodie, and reached for a pair of shoes—some no-name brand of black and white sneakers she'd bought dirt-cheap at one of the big retail stores. Armen knew the family behind the stores quite well. They had been on her list in the days of old, before her flesh. The List of the Damned.

Armen had seen Hell; fire and brimstone were nothing compared to the Darkness—a plane that sat on the edge of Hell.

Hell was comparable to a metropolitan city much like New York but surrounded by a river of fire. It was the outskirts a person wanted to steer clear of, the other planes of existence just outside the ring of fire. That was where the real monsters lay in wait. And Armen would know, for she'd been sent there in the beginning, before she became demon and was allowed to ride the flames.

Far worse than the Bottomless Pit of Abaddon, or Sheol, the Land of the Dead, was Gehenna—a place all feared. The Darkness there would consume you.

She pulled on her socks and shoes with a shudder of remembrance, fetched her car keys from the table, and jogged down the stairs to her Jeep. The sky bore several shades of purple that turned midnight black as she sped off into the darkening twilight toward Terry's new case, hoping she'd reach her destination before the captain arrived.

Armen climbed out of her Jeep, disgruntled and shivering. "Is *he* here yet?"

"Good evening, sunshine," the man greeting her said with a lop-sided grin. A homicide detective with the

Phoenix Police Department, Terry Armstrong had been a pain in her ass since the day they'd met. Unfortunately, she enjoyed it entirely too much.

"Why's it so freakin' cold?"

"It's wintertime, Armen."

"It's a desert!"

"Where are you from again?" The comical grin spread across his face, suiting the twinkle of jest in his eye well. He was tall with a close-shaven head. Tattoos covered his muscular arms and, Armen suspected, other places as well. She thought he was insane for wearing only a T-shirt under his Kevlar vest.

"Hell," she said harshly. Calling it by any other name would only confuse him.

Terry laughed. "With that snippy attitude of yours, it wouldn't surprise me." He stepped closer, his six-foot-three frame towering over her. "Where's your coat?"

"I left it at home. I didn't think it'd be this damn cold. I mean, shit, a hoodie should be enough in a desert wasteland."

He withheld his laughter, though a small snort escaped him. "Wait here. I'll get one for you." He came back to her and held out a coat dangling from his fingers. After she slipped it on, he handed her a cup. "I thought you might like this, too."

The scent of the brew reached her nostrils before her hand took the cup. "Thanks, Terry."

"Anything for my favorite medical examiner."

She narrowed her eyes. "What are you buttering me up for?"

"Nothing. I can't say you're my favorite medical examiner?"

She cocked her head to the side and sent him her best 'you can't be serious' look. "Why in the world would I be your favorite medical examiner? Better yet, why would you even *have* a favorite one?"

He laughed again. "My, you're touchy tonight. Didn't sleep well today?"

Shaking her head, she replied, "The days are too short," then sipped her coffee. She crinkled her nose as the burnt caffeinated beverage slid over her tongue.

He nodded. "Then you must love summer."

Again, she shifted her head from left to right, her long blonde ponytail swishing as though it were a pendulum. "The nights are too short."

His boisterous laugh echoed in the surrounding area. "A no-win situation for you, then?"

"Pretty much," she replied. "I'm screwed either way."

"Come on," he said. "If you want to see this before *he* gets here, we'd better hurry." He took her by the elbow and started to lead the way.

She jerked her arm from his grasp. "I am not a child who needs to be coaxed into the mouth of Hell, Terry."

He gave her a blank stare, his eyes completely devoid of emotion, before continuing forward. "Your choice of words always amazes me, you know," he said as they neared the building. "I mean, who says something like that, really?"

"I guess I'm alone in my vernacular."

Terry chuckled. "Is that your word of the day?"

She grinned. "No, actually the word of the day was *wisenheimer*, and amazingly, it had your picture next to it."

"Ah yes, well, I am quite photogenic," he replied with a toothy grin.

Armen fought the urge to roll her eyes. "So, tell me what I'm about to see."

He shook his head. "Nah, I'd much rather see the look on your face when you see it without prior description."

"Damn, it must be bad." Especially if he wasn't telling her; he really got a kick out of watching her face twist into different expressions. According to him, the more grotesque the description, the higher her brows went.

"No, *unique* would be a more appropriate word." He stepped through the door.

That did not make her feel any better about the prospect.

She followed him but stopped short in the doorway, wrinkling her nose as she caught a familiar odor. The squalid scent slithered uninvited into her nostrils, and she had to force herself to move forward, despite the inclination to purge her last meal.

Terry paused, a quizzical expression morphing his features momentarily. "You okay?"

"Fine." She took another sip of the singed coffee, mostly to have the brew's aroma dominate the other odor.

"He's in here." Terry headed for a bulky, steel sliding door standing partially open on the west wall of the warehouse. He pulled on the large handle. The door creaked and screeched as he heaved it open.

The scent of copper filled her nose and coated her tongue in a thick slime, and she gagged on the rancid air before barely stopping herself from turning tail and running away.

"Jesus Christ," she whispered when the scene paraded before her. She winced; using the divine name could bring trouble, given the scent she'd picked up moments ago. The real world of cops and robbers and twisted murderers wasn't ready for supernatural of the religious variety yet. Not that they ever would be, unless they were fans of a certain television show.

"Told you it was unique," Terry said. "Some damn weird occult shit, though, eh?"

Right, that's what we'll call it. She shifted her eyes from the scene to Terry's face. "That's an understatement."

The man hung on the freestanding wall, pinned by nails piercing his stretched skin. He still lived, if one could call it that. As Armen stepped toward the door's track, the victim shrieked; startled, she spilled hot coffee over her hand, cringing as the liquid scalded her skin.

This skin . . . .

He stopped suddenly, and Armen studied the wall.

Ancient symbols, drawn in blood, surrounded his crucifixion pose. Razor wire encircled the entire scene so no one could go near. The man's head dropped forward, but he wasn't dead—yet.

"He keeps doing that," Terry said. "But he's not talking. We've tried. Makes noises, though. Maybe they cut out his tongue?"

"Perhaps." It wouldn't surprise her one bit; the symbols told her what kind of evil was at play. "Why did you call me? He's not a corpse."

He cast a glance down at her. "The occult shit. You have a knack for it. I figured you would know what all this meant."

She turned her attention back to the hanging man and sighed. "The symbols, they're demon script."

"See what I mean?"

"Terry, this is a very bad situation."

"Oh, you don't have to tell me that. We need to figure out how to get him down."

"He's not meant to come down. If you attempt it, he'll most likely die, and horribly, as well as anyone who attempts to remove him."

"What could possibly be more horrible than what he's already been through?" He abruptly raised a hand as she opened her mouth. "Wait, don't answer that."

Armen shook her head. "I take it no one's searched the area?"

"Nope. Didn't know what would happen," Terry replied. "Barnes started to head straight for him, but I stopped him. I remembered that one, you know, a few months back, where you told me about the trigger that set it off and killed that woman?"

She remembered it vividly. The first officer on the scene had made the mistake of trying to rescue the woman and ended up in the psych ward after losing his right arm and watching the woman and her unborn child die. Half of the fetus had landed at the officer's feet.

A veteran officer like Terry wouldn't have been so easily broken, but then again, there was something different about him. She just couldn't put her finger on it.

"Yeah, well, I figured this one might be the same. I was hoping to find a way for the vic to *not* die this time." His right brow hitched upward. "Any ideas?"

She thought about it, clicking her tongue a few times. "Not unless I can walk in there and look around."

"You just told me— "

"I know, but I'm not stepping near that." She pointed at the razor wire.

He chewed on his inner cheek. "If Captain finds out, he'll kill me."

"If I don't, the victim will hang on that wall until he's dead, and then you can set off the trigger into a corpse."

Terry sighed heavily. "I trust you. Go . . . but don't set the damn thing off!"

She grinned and set down the coffee. "What, do you think I'm an amateur at this?" She carefully stepped forward, eying the entire room for any type of trigger based on motion.

"And be careful," he added.

Armen nodded in silence. The concern in his voice was too much for her to deal with. Terry liked her, she knew that, but she wanted nothing to do with anything remotely resembling a relationship outside of work. She just didn't have the time, or the interest, in such pursuits. The last one destroyed everything she'd known. She wasn't about to make that mistake again.

Finding nothing that would set the trap off if she stepped inside, she took a step over the door's track. When nothing happened, she exhaled and circled around to the right, where she noticed a small gap—an inch or so—between the wall and the floor. She crouched and put her head to the floor to see underneath. The wall appeared to be floating. This had dark magic written all over it and there was nothing she could do to reverse the multiple spells she sensed. It was too much and would take too long—

"See anything yet?" Terry said loudly.

She nearly jumped out of her skin and placed her finger to her lips to shush him. He said no more as she stood and walked around the back of the wall, carefully avoiding the razor wire.

A skittering sound behind her traveled rapidly toward the small elevator shaft to her right. She pivoted in time to see a distinct trail of red smoke winding around and into the shaft.

"What was that?" Terry shouted, nervousness layering his voice.

Armen peeked around the wall and glared at him, pointing at him and then cupping her hand around her ear.

He nodded and waggled his hands in a gesture that virtually screamed how nervous she was making him.

Armen smiled at him. She hadn't thought anything could make Detective Terry Armstrong nervous, but she had detected it in his voice before she'd stepped away from him. She turned her attention back to the scene, trying to determine how the contraption would work if triggered and just where in the hell the trigger was.

From the corner of her eye, she saw a stocky man walk up to Terry.

"Armstrong."

"Johnson," Terry replied and crossed his arms over his broad chest.

"What's she doing?"

"Trying to figure out what the trigger is."

"Ah, letting your woman do your work for you, huh?"

Terry twitched at Johnson's comment. Armen slipped behind the wall again. She was no man's woman.

"Well, she's probably the only one who can figure it out, Johnson," Terry's voice bounced off the empty walls. "Unless, of course, you have some clue as to how to get this man out alive?"

Silence.

"Are you sure? I'd be happy to let you have a go at it," Terry said. "You could walk in there yourself."

Armen headed to the right, following the fading red smoke.

"Nah," Johnson answered with a shake of his head.

"I didn't think so."

A short, sharp whistle pierced the air, and Armen stopped to look back at Terry. She hated it when he did that. She furrowed her brow and nodded in the direction of the shaft. Terry shook his head, and Armen wrinkled her nose in a mock growl. He couldn't see the red smoke.

"ARMSTRONG!" The shout came from behind him, and Terry and Armen both jumped.

Armen threw her hands up. "Damn it!" Why bother staying silent anymore? She was the only one doing so.

It's not like any of them knew what they were dealing with, right? Of course not, because they're *human.* "Idiots."

"What in God's name is *she* doing here? I'd recognize that damn Jeep anywhere! Unless you've got a damn corpse on your hands . . . ."

"Shit," Terry said and waved Armen over to him as he turned to face his boss. "Captain, you got here damn fast. I thought the freeway was closed?"

"You're full of shit, you know that?" Captain Brian McNeil walked up and quickly scanned the scene. He froze when he saw Armen standing near the shaft. She barely refrained from waving. "Get her out of there. She's cluttering up the crime scene."

Armen crossed her arms over her chest and rolled her eyes. Opening her mouth was not a good idea when it came to the captain.

"She's trying to find the trigger so we can save this guy," Terry said.

"The hell she is." Brian took a step toward the scene, past the track of the sliding metal door.

The hanging man screeched in agony. He slammed his head back against the wall.

An unseen force grabbed Armen's arm, her flesh beneath sizzling like it had been touched by the fires of Hell, and yanked her backward into the shaft. She hit the steel elevator cables, and a loud twang echoed as she descended into darkness. The victim's screams followed her down in a garbled mess as she struggled to control her fall. Her leg banged against the side, and a scream of her own ripped from her throat before she landed hard at the bottom of the shaft.

A dust cloud mushroomed around her. She coughed out a moan and covered her mouth and nose, keeping her eyes closed until the dust could settle.

She could hear the captain's shouts. "For Christ's sake, what's happening to him?"

Terry's voice sounded over some racket she couldn't quite place, like metal rapidly moving against a hard surface. "I'd step back if I were you. We don't know the razor wire's purpose."

It was too dark to see past the opening she'd fallen through. She attempted to stand, but her leg wouldn't hold her. Not wanting to risk the elevator car rushing down to crush her, she pulled herself out of the shaft, dragging her bum leg out of the doorway.

"Armen," Terry yelled.

She felt along the floor, crawling to a nearby wall and leaning against it, rocking her head back, and biting her lower lip to keep from screaming again from the pain shooting down her leg. Rattling from a metal gate reverberated down the shaft before she heard Terry's voice. "Shit."

A beam of light penetrated the darkness of the elevator shaft, sweeping its walls. For one heart-skipping moment, the beam hit red scales.

"ARMEN!"

Armen gasped, stunned by the revelation of what had pulled her down.

"Son of a . . . ."

"Get everyone back," Terry shouted.

A flashlight clattered out of the shaft, bouncing and spinning, offering glimpses of her surroundings. Large square columns, three across and at least four deep, marched across the cavernous cellar.

A growl, a shout, and a curse later—and a large shadow detached itself from the darkness.

Chapter Two

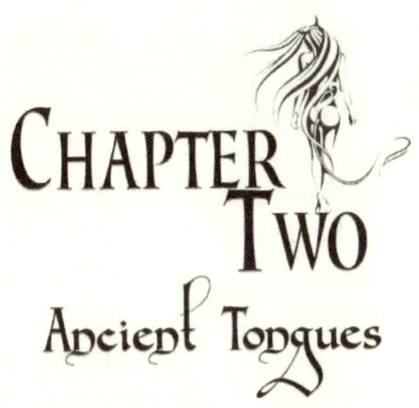

Ancient Tongues

"ARMEN!" TERRY'S SHOUT CAME FROM within the shaft this time, the cramped space emphasizing her name like a bullhorn.

Armen closed her eyes. *Idiot.* As much as she'd like to, it would be a mistake to tell him to shut the hell up. She knew *what* had pulled her down here, but not *who.*

She surveyed the landscape around her in the small amount of light the flashlight emitted. Each brick column was two feet wide and nine feet tall, spaced about thirty feet apart. Their shadows created an impenetrable pool of darkness in the windowless room. Dirt and debris littered the stone floor. The decades-old building reeked of urine and feces, along with that distinct scent she'd smelled upstairs.

The skittering faintly sounded from a far corner to her right. She tensed. Given the distance of the sound, the cellar had to be about half the size of one of those super stores owned by the family on her List.

"Azel," a whisper came in an ancient tongue. The voice surrounded her, coming from everywhere and nowhere. Staying quiet didn't matter anymore. It knew exactly where she was, and apparently *who* she was.

Armen scanned the darkness to no avail before replying in the same language. *"Who speaks such a name?"*

Azel was her last name in reverse, for the reversal that had taken place.

"Forsaken one," the voice whispered in her right ear.

She turned her head to the right.

"You have become flesh," it said in her left ear.

She cocked her head back to the left. "No shit. Tell me something I don't know."

"Armen?" Terry emerged from the shaft.

A sibilant hiss quivered through the air and Armen slapped around her ears. *"I have come to claim you."*

But Armen knew demons lied. *"You cannot claim me. I am in the Light now."* Or so she thought. It was the only explanation she had for her flesh.

A giggle, then a sigh. *"You think one insignificant deed places you in the Light?"*

She could be wrong. *"If it were insignificant, I would not be flesh."*

"Yet, the flesh shall make it easier to take you, my sweet," the voice answered.

"Sariel," Armen growled. No one else called her that. *"I should have known it was you behind the torture of these humans. What is your purpose?"*

Laughter filled the room. Terry picked up his flashlight and shined it around, hitting Armen in the face with the light.

She squinted. "Damn it, Terry," she said, raising her left arm to block the light. "Are you trying to blind me?"

"Sorry," Terry replied and lowered it. "Are you okay?"

"Fine," she answered. "Stay where you are. I'll come to you."

He complied, though confusion crossed his features. His compliance wouldn't last long, however. Shock from whatever happened upstairs still held him. Once it wore off, he'd try to play hero again.

Armen leaned forward and whispered to the demon. *"Leave this place, Sariel, or I shall be forced to banish you!"*

"You no longer hold such power, Azel."

"Who are you talking to?" Terry asked, shining the light around.

"No one important."

Bright red light flashed through the room. Sariel's red demon flesh glistened in the light, his scaled face right in front of hers. *"No one important just saved your life, forsssaken one."*

Yep, she'd upset him. But why would he save her if he was there to claim her? The hint of a smile curved her lips when she looked him in the eye.

"Is that so?" The sight of demon flesh had never bothered her, nor had looking into Sariel's ancient red eyes. She'd done so on many occasions, some of which she wished had never happened. "I think you're lying, but then, that's what you're good at. Isn't it?"

"What the hell is that?" Terry's voice was too calm. He aimed his weapon at the creature.

The demon spun to look at him, and he hissed again.

"Lower your weapon, Terry," Armen said. "It's of no use now."

"You can't be serious," he said, voice still steady. Curious.

The demon took a step forward.

"Lower your weapon, Terry," Sariel mocked Armen's voice, but in an inhuman tone that did *not* belong to Armen. She hoped Terry picked up on it.

"Why don't you shut the hell up?"

"Poor human, your life is so fragile." It moved away from Armen and slipped around one of the large columns. *"It must pain you to know that your lifespan is but a blink to me and mine."*

"I'm sorry, are you comparing your eternally damned life to my meager human existence?" Terry asked with a grin. "I'll take the meager existence, thanks. At least I have a chance for salvation."

The demon jutted its head forward, mouth open, sharp, pointy teeth glistening in the low light. On the bright side, Terry was keeping him distracted. On the not-so-bright side, Terry may get himself killed before she had a chance to banish the pest.

Armen chanted in an ancient tongue, whispering words that hadn't passed her lips in ages. Terry's distraction wasn't good enough as the demon whipped around and slithered toward her, slashing its clawed hand across her face. She flung up her left arm to block too late, and its talons scored gashes down her cheek. Blood began to trickle and she covered the burning wound as an unexpected shriek shot from her mouth. Terry fired multiple times, the gunshots deafening in the empty echoing space. The demon disappeared in a burst of fire and smoke.

"Terry!" Her own voice sounded muffled in her ears, and she finished off her spell in a whisper of tongues before the demon could return. She tried to push to her feet and growled in anger when she fell to the floor again, a bolt of pain shooting down her right leg.

"Sorry, it's instinct." He ran to her, holstering his gun. "Let me help you up."

She slapped at his hands when he reached forward. "You've done enough, thank you."

He pulled her to her feet. "You're hurt," he said as she stumbled.

"And you yanking me to my feet isn't making it any better. I'm deaf now, by the way. Thanks."

"Hardly, if you can still hear me."

She scowled and pulled her arm from his grasp, wobbling as she teetered away from him.

He grabbed her arm again. "Sometimes I love your stubbornness, Armen, but not tonight."

"You shouldn't love anything about me." Armen tried to push his arm away as it snaked around her waist to support her.

Terry took a deep breath. "What was that?" He jerked his head in the direction where the demon had been. He probably hoped the subject change would subdue her anger.

"A demon, what did it look like?" Sarcasm froze the edges of her words. She was never at her best when pain took hold.

"That's the answer I didn't want to hear."

"Then you shouldn't have asked." She looked up at him and he angled his flashlight toward the ceiling. He'd at least learned one lesson tonight. "You normally wouldn't be able to see them, but you interrupted something and he decided to show himself."

"That's who you were talking to?" he asked, and she nodded. "What language was that?"

"The language you saw written in blood up there."

He gave her a sharp look. "Do I want to know why you would know such a language?"

"I'm guessing my expertise in the occult isn't going to satisfy that question."

"Not when you were talking to the thing like you knew it."

"Then probably not, and I'm not in the mood to discuss it." Armen really didn't want to tell Terry what she had once been not so long ago.

"How about discussing what you were talking *about* with a demon?"

Armen shook her head. That wasn't up for conversation, either.

"Very well, then. Let's try to get back up there." He moved toward the shaft to see if there was a way to get up to ground level. His flashlight lit the area, moving from side to side, scanning for openings before he finally brought it down and shined it on her face.

"That looks pretty nasty. You need medical attention, but I don't know how I'm going to get you up there. I don't think there's any other way up." He swept the light around the room again. "I'm not sure what this damn room was used for."

"Storage," she replied. "I think, other than housing the homeless for a while."

He gave a short nod and walked her to the wall. "You stay here. I'm gonna go see if there's another way out."

Great. She was by herself, injured, perfect prey for a demon who wanted to get her back to Gehenna. But why? What did Sariel want with her? She didn't have a clue and she couldn't have meant that much to him; certainly not enough to pull her back. But apparently enough to save her life? She shook her head lightly. *Nah.*

Terry's footsteps grew closer, the flashlight's beam sweeping across the floor back and forth, occasionally hitting a column. "No other way out. This place should be condemned." He stepped up to her and looked down. "You all right?"

"Good as can be for the moment."

"We'll have to climb up."

Armen looked up into the shaft. "My hands and arms are fine. I can climb the cable." Hands and arms weren't the problem. Her skin burned where the demon's talons tore through, and it took everything she had to withhold the scream.

"You'll need a leg to support you."

"I still have one good leg."

He frowned. "You have a damn answer for everything, don't you?"

She half-smiled, though it hurt like a bitch. "Usually."

Terry looked over his shoulder into the darkness. "That thing's not coming back, right?"

She stared at him for a space of three heartbeats, raised a brow, and blinked. "You just walked through the underbelly of this building in near pitch black and you're asking me that *now*? His work is done here . . . for the moment."

His glare lingered a moment. "Christ, Armen, what the hell is going on?"

"I assure you, *He* has nothing to do with it."

"You and I need to have a long talk." It was a stern demand, not a request.

"You're hurt." She reached down and grabbed his wrist, turning his palm up. "How are you going to climb up with this?" The skin on his palm was shredded.

"Don't change the subject."

"Answer the question."

"I'll manage it," he said. "But you and I are still going to have a long talk." He gently pushed her forward, toward the cable, and aimed the light up the shaft. "Climb."

Armen hopped from her good leg and hoisted herself up the cables. She damn near dropped onto Terry when her bad leg hit one of them too hard, but she gritted her teeth and powered through. One hand up, then the other, her good leg wrapped as best she could around one of the cables. Terry's climb would be much more difficult. She could already hear the strain in his grunts. The fact that he climbed up directly behind her didn't help her grasp on the cables much.

"Stop moving so damn much. You're going to make me fall on top of you."

"Go," he commanded, and let her get to the top before moving again.

He *would* be a gentleman about it. Asshole.

After making her way up the cable, she shimmied her foot onto the landing and pulled herself free of the shaft onto her good leg. Terry caught up and soon he stood next to her, supporting her once again with an unwelcome arm around her waist. They stood motionless, staring at the carnage. Blood and body parts had splattered the warehouse. Armen wished she still had the coffee to subdue the scent of blood.

"What the hell set it off?" Armen surveyed the aftermath, careful not to get too close.

"I'm not sure, but I think it was the captain," Terry replied. "He stepped inside right when you went into the shaft. Next thing I knew, the razor wire unraveled."

Armen blew out a frustrated breath. "Utterly brilliant." It was a mortal trigger; when a human stepped inside, the trap engaged. Armen wasn't exactly *born* human, so it wouldn't go off for her. But she couldn't tell Terry any of that.

"Last I saw, the razor wire nicked his arm," Terry said. "That should make you happy." He moved forward with her. "Watch your step."

The floor was slick with bodily fluids the human eye should never see. They moved near the wall and sidled along to the open door. A horde of officers stood slack-jawed at their appearance. None dared to enter in case the carnage wasn't over.

"Any paramedics here?" Terry asked, helping Armen through the doorway and away from the horrific scene.

"Yes, sir," one young officer replied.

"Fetch 'em, please." The officer darted off and Terry helped Armen sit down on a crate. He looked at her face again, inspecting it briefly. "Jesus, Armen, that looks worse up here."

She eyed him. "Would you please stop using His name in conjunction with mine?"

Terry frowned. "Who, Jesus Christ?"

"Yes."

"Devout, huh?"

Armen sighed. "Not quite, and you're actually cursing with His name."

He just blinked at her. She bit the inside of her cheek, not knowing any other way to explain her relation to the man they called Jesus Christ.

The paramedic approached. "What the hell attacked you, a big cat?"

"More like a dragon," she mumbled.

"Well, whatever it was, he got you good." He inspected the wound and cleaned it.

"Her leg's hurt too," Terry said.

Armen growled when the paramedic straightened her leg to inspect it.

"Watch out, she bites." Terry's jaw tightened as another paramedic cleaned his hand. He didn't make a sound, though, tough macho cop that he was.

The paramedic continued his inspection. "Think I can pull this pant leg up? Or do I have to rip it?"

She yanked the pant leg up; just the idea of having the paramedic looking her over annoyed the hell out of her. She'd fix everything once she got home. Well, maybe not the leg. That would have to heal normally. Damn, sometimes she hated being human. Though she healed a bit faster, it still took time.

"Gonna be a nasty bruise," he said, inspecting the reddened area. "Can you stand?"

"Not without help. But at least I didn't break it."

"You should probably get an X-ray. Could be a fracture. You're gonna need stitches too, unless you want nasty scars," he said. "But they aren't too deep, lucky you. Looked worse before I cleaned them up. I did the best I could, though. You wanna go for a ride?" He nodded back to the ambulance with its flashing lights.

"Not particularly," Armen said.

"You sure?"

"Armen, you probably should go," Terry said.

"I am not sitting in an emergency room for seven hours!"

Terry looked at the paramedic. "Told you she bites." He returned his gaze to her. "You'd go straight back if the ambulance takes you."

"Terry can take me home," she said to the paramedic.

"What? Why?"

"Somebody has to help me up those stairs, and I can't shift with a bum leg."

He turned to the paramedic. "Does she *have* to go to the hospital?"

"No, but she should do something about those lacerations."

"I'll superglue them, how's that?" She gave him her best smug grin, though it hurt like hell.

The paramedic cocked a brow at her. "It's called Dermabond, but if you think that'll work, sure, go for it," he replied and pulled a small tube from his pocket. "Here, I have an extra."

"Thanks." Armen smiled as she caught the tube. "Don't worry, I have those little stitch bandage thingies at home."

He arched a brow at her. "How about you don't do that and get stitches with the Dermabond?"

"No."

"It's your face, lady." The paramedic laughed, picked up his case, and walked away shaking his head. The other paramedic soon joined him.

Terry frowned at her stubbornness and looked around again. "Hey, Johnson, where's Captain?"

"Outside," he answered. "He'll probably want to see you."

"I don't doubt it," Terry replied.

"I don't know what happened down there with you two, but he heard it. Thought you should know."

"Thanks. Come on, Armen, let's get you home."

"Don't we have to do a report or something?" she asked when he helped her to her feet. She winced when her weight shifted briefly to her injured leg. "Ow."

"I'll take care of it." He tossed his keys to Johnson. "Take my car in, would ya?"

"Sure thing," Johnson replied, tossing the keys into the air a couple of times. "If you can get past the captain."

Terry nodded at him and helped Armen hobble along. People scuttled about outside the warehouse, discussing what had happened and how to go about inspecting the scene. Terry did his best to sneak away.

"Armstrong," Captain McNeil said just loud enough for Terry and Armen to hear him.

His arm was bandaged. Armen had to hide her smile; it served the man right for not paying attention and for not letting her or his officers do their jobs.

"Is it over?" His voice was shaky, a fine tremor underlying his normal deep tone.

Terry's eyes met Armen's with a question. She nodded before he could ask out loud. "Yes, it's over. You can collect evidence now, although I doubt you'll be able to convict anyone."

The captain nodded. "I heard that. Go home and rest. Give me a report later."

"Yes, sir." He continued to move Armen along to her Jeep and helped her climb in to the passenger side.

"He's shaken up," Armen said. "He didn't even yell at you."

"Damn miracle, if you ask me," Terry said as he climbed in and started the Jeep.

He backed out and headed toward Armen's condo a few blocks away. She remained quiet throughout the short ride. Terry would again question why she spoke to the demon like she knew him. The sad fact was that she did indeed know Sariel quite well, and for a time far longer than Terry could fathom.

But she had a few questions for him too, like how he remained so calm in the face of a demon. Most humans would have frozen or run, neither of which was a good idea when a demon was involved. It made for great prey.

And they loved a good chase.

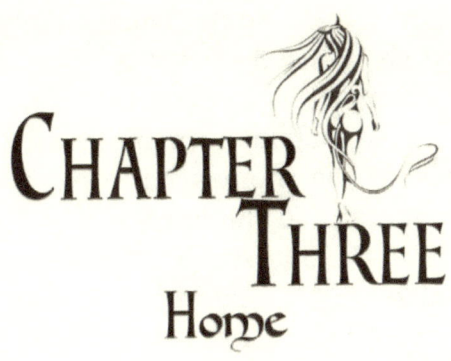

CHAPTER THREE
Home

TERRY HELPED ARMEN CLIMB TO the second floor and handed over her keys. She opened the door, limping inside at a slow pace, clutching the wall as they entered her living room. He followed close behind her in case she fell, which annoyed her.

Her living room, kept dark because she liked the darkness, was furnished simply with just a small sofa and chair, both deep burgundy to match the heavy drapes that shut out the daylight. A petite bookshelf in the corner held vintage prints, and the few paintings scattered across the walls complemented the gloomy décor, and her wary nature.

Upon entering, Terry made a sound so indefinite in its possibilities that she couldn't decide if it was in appreciation of her décor or against it.

"How are you getting home?" She made her way into the kitchen to make some tea, shrugging out of the borrowed police coat and throwing it over one of the chairs.

"I can call a cab." He sat down across the counter from her. "You should take care of your face first, Armen." He stood again and made his way around. "I know how to make tea."

She gave him a weak smile. The bandage on her face tightened, and she winced. "Thanks." She moved aside, grabbing the counter for support. It was unsettling that Terry knew she was about to make tea, but she didn't mind so much at the moment. She eyed the distance between the counter and the kitchen table, and hobbled forward. Once there, she studied the distance between the kitchen table and her bedroom. It was a long shot with nothing much to hold onto except wall.

She felt Terry's eyes on her. When she aimed for the wall by her bedroom, she stumbled and fell to the floor. He ran over and hooked his arms beneath hers.

"Chri–, Jes–." He blew out a frustrated breath. "Here, Armen, let me help you."

She struggled against him. "I don't need any help. I just aimed poorly."

"Well, obviously you *do* need help; otherwise, you wouldn't be on the floor." He pulled her to her feet and leaned her against the wall. He palmed the wall near her head, and leaned close to her. "Armen, you're hurt. There's nothing wrong with needing a bit of help now and then." His green eyes focused intently on her.

And he was too close. His warm breath fluttered over her lips. She tried to hide the gasp and hoped the heat rushing to her cheeks didn't give away how she felt at the moment.

"I'm sorry," she said softly. "I'm just used to doing everything myself."

"I know you are. But that stubbornness of yours has to give sometime."

She closed her eyes and gave a short nod. "Can you help me get to the bathroom?" She opened her eyes to Terry's widening emeralds and a smile stretching across his face.

"Wow! That must've hurt."

Anger soared back into her. "Are you going to help me or not?"

He chuckled. "Sure, come on." He moved his hand down to her waist, and with her arm around his shoulders, he helped her walk to the bathroom.

Once there, he lifted and set her down on the edge of the granite counter. "Where do you keep those 'stitch bandage thingies'?" He only half-attempted to hide the grin as he drew quotation marks in the air.

"Funny, *wisenheimer*. I told you that was the word of the day. They're in the medicine cabinet."

"Indeed, you did." Terry searched through the cabinet and found the butterfly closures. He set a few on the counter and stepped in front of her.

She lifted her brow. "What are you doing?"

His eyes met hers. "Helping you."

"*That*, I can do myself."

"Nonsense," he said. "It'll be better if I do it for you."

"Oh, and you have a medical background, do you?"

He smirked. "I've been through EMT training, so yes, I have some medical background. Plus, half of my friends are firefighters and paramedics."

Her smug smile slid off her face. *Shit.*

"Thought that'd get you." He reached up to pull the bandage off, and she slapped at his hand.

"I'll do it!"

"Damn, you're grouchy when you're hurt."

"Wouldn't you be?" She pulled at the bandage on her cheek, wincing as the tape yanked tiny hairs from her face.

Terry looked at his left hand wrapped in gauze and held it up in front of her. "No."

She ignored the fact that he wasn't complaining, which pissed her off, and stared at the blood already seeping through the dressing. "You should probably change that. There's some first aid supplies in that cabinet down there."

He crouched and searched through the cabinet. When he stood again, Armen had ripped the bandage completely off. From the way he stared at the wounds, she knew it must look bad. "Does it hurt a lot?"

She shook her head, but stopped short. "It burns a little," she replied, which was the understatement of the year. "Does yours hurt?"

"It doesn't seem to hurt much now," he said. "I think I lost all my fingerprints, though."

She smirked. "You could commit a crime one-handed."

"Or red-handed, at that," he replied.

She let out a groan, but then laughed. "Oh, that was bad."

"You laughed," he said.

"Because it was *bad*."

"And still, you laughed." He eyed her wound more closely. "Looks like it only got you with two fingers. The third is just a scratch."

Armen waited for the questions to begin. She'd been dreading the moment he'd start asking about what he'd seen and why she could speak a language not known to man. The dread settled into the pit of her stomach, making her feel queasy.

"Where's that Dermabond?" He yanked an exam glove from his vest pocket and pulled it over his right hand.

She pulled the compound from her pocket and handed it to him.

"Ready?"

She drew in a deep breath and nodded, waiting for more pain to hit her face.

"You sure you want to do this? The lacerations are awfully close together."

She glared at him. "Make it work."

"Here goes." He applied the Dermabond to the first wound and attached a butterfly closure above the cut. Then he pulled the skin together and attached the other end of the closure below the cut, smoothing the Dermabond in place as best he could around the closure. He continued the process until the gash sealed.

Armen breathed through the pain, turned, and looked in the mirror to see Terry's handiwork. "Not bad." Although the gashes were worse than she thought. *Damn.*

"Thanks," he replied. "No medical background...."

She turned back to face him. "Shut up and finish it."

"Oh, now I'm qualified, am I?"

"Terry—"

He chuckled again and worked on the next laceration. "Why does it burn?"

Here it comes. "Because of the nature of the creature."

"Demon, huh?" His fingers worked deftly at closing the second gash, which wasn't easy considering he had one hand wrapped in gauze. That had to be painful for him, too.

"Yes." She stared at the wall while he worked on her wounds.

"A demon you were talking to in a language I've probably never heard before."

"I'm sure there are several languages on this planet that you've never heard before."

"Perhaps so, but you said it was the same language as the demon script written in blood."

Armen sighed. "Why do you have to have such a damn good memory?"

"It gets the job finished." He stood straight and looked at her. "There, all done." He snapped off the glove and tossed it in the trash can.

She turned to look in the mirror again. He'd done a pretty good job. She slowly turned back to him, waiting for that question—the one asking *why* she knew demon tongue.

Terry held up his hand. "Mine now?"

The man was always full of surprises.

She took him by the wrist to undress his hand. Round and round, the gauze slowly came off until she reached the square covering his entire palm and those wrapped around his fingers. Terry winced and drew in a breath between his teeth as she pulled the gauze back, exposing the torn flesh to the air.

"Hold still," she told him and inspected the wounds. "Damn, Terry, you've ripped off an awful lot of flesh."

"Steel cables will do that when sliding down at fast speeds without gloves."

"You're insane for doing so."

"Didn't have much of a choice. I fell into the shaft when the razor wire started moving. I think I'd rather fall and shred my hand than get sliced up by that shit."

Armen's heart sank. "This is my fault. If I'd been paying attention—"

"Don't start that. I'm the dumbass who couldn't keep his footing. Besides, Captain set the damn thing off, remember?"

Terry clenched his jaw as she cleaned the wound. When she reached toward the medicine cabinet, she nearly fell into the sink.

He caught her with his right hand. "What do you need?"

"That jar there." She pointed to a small jar containing a blue jellied compound.

He plucked it from the shelf.

"Thanks," she said and unscrewed the top. "This may feel a bit odd."

"What is that?" She applied a glop of it to his hand. "It tingles."

"It's a salve I made. Works great for pretty much anything."

"Special herbs and whatnot?"

"Something like that."

"Why didn't we put that on your face?"

She smoothed the salve around his hand. "It won't work on my wound because it was made by a demon. I'll have to grin and bear it." She replaced the dressing pads with new ones and reached for a new roll of gauze. As she unrolled it around his hand, her eyes met his again. "Why didn't *you* go to the hospital?"

Terry grinned. "I didn't want to sit in the emergency room for seven hours, either."

Armen laughed. "Nice excuse."

"Wonder where I got it from. Besides, I knew you'd take care of me." He looked at his hand when she finished wrapping it up. "There isn't any pain at all now."

She smiled. "Special herbs and whatnot."

He chuckled, and his hand dropped to her thigh. "How's your leg?"

She sucked in a breath from the touch. "It aches," she replied. "Probably ache more tomorrow, but I'll manage."

"Like you always do."

She turned away because his eyes held that caring crap she didn't want to consider.

An uncomfortable silence settled over the room. Terry stood too close to her. He leaned forward, slowly gliding his uninjured hand to her ear and cupping the side of her head. He combed his fingers through her loosened hair and held it suspended.

"You want me to help you wash this out?" His voice held a softness too personal for two people who just worked together.

She looked from the corner of her eye, seeing the blood and dirt caked in her blonde locks. "Damn," she said. "No, I think I can do that. Just help me over to the tub." She carefully pulled off her hoodie and saw the seared claw print on her arm. "Shit. I was wondering why my arm hurt." The wound wasn't open, having already started to heal, which it would do much faster than the gashes in her cheek since her flesh wasn't ripped open.

Terry lightly touched the burn marks. "He grabbed you there. I remember you were chanting something when it happened." He looked around the room. "Don't you still have that cane from the last time you got hurt?"

"It's in the closet."

Terry helped her off the counter and to the edge of the tub. "I'll get it for you." The teapot began its whistle. "And then I'll get that."

Armen leaned forward and turned on the water, adjusting the temperature. She reached up for the showerhead, but it was too far.

"Damn it," she mumbled.

The light flipped on in her closet. She eyed the showerhead's distance, braced her left leg, and grabbed the wall for support to climb up and grab it.

"Holy hell, do you have enough shoes?" he shouted from within the small walk-in.

"No, I don't," she returned.

As she made her way slowly up the wall, her foot shifted and she started to lose her balance. She sat back down on the tub's edge. "Fuck."

The teapot's whistle grew louder. She heard him hit the light, and then he walked back into the bathroom to find her attempting to reach the showerhead again.

"For the love of God, can't you just ask for help?" He placed the cane next to the tub and grabbed the showerhead for her.

"The last time I asked, you mocked me."

He walked out of the room shaking his head. "I'll make the tea."

"You do that," she replied and soaked her hair.

Armen hobbled out with her cane and a wet head a few minutes later to find the teabags steeping. She sat at the table where Terry placed a cup for her.

"You used the green tea, right?" When he nodded, she asked, "Could you get the honey for me, please?"

He picked it up from the counter next to the toaster. "Here you go, honey," he said and handed it to her.

She eyed him and he grinned when she shook her head. "You're so not funny."

"Yes I am." He sat down and circled both arms around his mug. "So." He paused intentionally so she would look at him. She'd become accustomed to this tactic after working with him a few years. "Have dinner with me tomorrow night."

She blinked in surprise, shock throwing her for a loop. "What . . . why?"

Terry grinned. "Because I want to see you in that little black dress I saw in your closet."

"Oh God, Terry," she said. "Do you really think that's a good idea?"

He remained stone-faced. "Why wouldn't it be a good idea?"

Armen stared at her cup. "Because I really don't want a relationship."

His mouth twisted up on the right side into a half-grin. "Who said anything about a relationship? I'd just like to take you to dinner."

"Dinners lead to movies and lunches and picnics in the park," she replied. "And relationships."

He laughed, shook his head, and drank his tea. "You crack me up sometimes. Paranoid about getting close to someone?"

"I'd rather not discuss it."

He raised a brow. "You don't seem to want to discuss much tonight."

"Not everything is up for discussion, Terry," she said. "I mean, hell, getting close to someone equals dependency on them."

"Somehow, Armen, I doubt that you would ever depend on someone."

"Of course I wouldn't. It's ludicrous to put yourself in that position."

Terry set his cup on the table. "Is that a bad relationship talking? A good relationship has no dependency; it has compromise and partnership. Y'know, like how we work together."

"And why exactly would I tell you such information?"

"I don't know." He shrugged. "I thought we were at least friends."

Armen sighed. "You *are* my friend, Terry. I'd like to keep it that way."

"So, we can never go to dinner, or have lunch together, or have a picnic in the park, huh?" he asked, his grin reappearing.

She picked up her teabag and tossed it into the trash can. "Don't be ridiculous."

"You just said—"

"I know what I said. I meant those as dates!"

"Ah, and so I asked you out on a date, then?"

"When you refer to dinner and me wearing a little black dress, yes."

He chuckled again. "Why do you have the little black dress, Armen? I doubt you wear it around the house. I'm just giving you the opportunity to wear it out."

Her annoyed gaze locked on him. Too bad she wasn't truly annoyed with him. Fact of the matter was that she *was* attracted to Terry, but that just couldn't happen. Not in a hundred million years or when Armageddon hit, whichever came first. "You really annoy the hell out of me sometimes, you know that?"

The corners of his mouth curved upward. "I think you love it when I do that."

She sighed heavily. "Whatever."

He leaned toward her. "Just go to dinner with me. You know you want to wear that dress."

Armen shifted her eyes back to his. "Do you ever give up?"

"No," he replied. "I'll keep bugging you until you say yes."

"Isn't that harassment?"

He shook his head slowly. "Nah, just a man trying to get a woman out in the real world, which he thinks she desperately needs."

She finished off her tea and set the cup on the table. "The woman thinks the man needs to call his cab."

He laughed. "Ah, I love avoidance. And you're *so* good at it." He pulled his phone from his pocket and skimmed through the contacts list. Once the cab was on its way, he turned to her. "It'll be here in twenty minutes. That gives us some time to talk about other things."

"I'm not in the mood."

"Why do you know a demon language?" he asked, ignoring her comment.

"I told you I don't care to discuss it at this time."

"And I told *you* that you and I were going to have a long talk."

"You only have twenty minutes," she said with a grin. "It'll take much longer than that."

"Give me the short version."

"There is no short version," she said. "It's all or nothing."

"Very well," he said and hit the 'send' button on his phone. "Yes, I'd like to cancel that cab I just ordered. Terry. Thanks." He hung up the phone and looked at her. "Would you like some more tea before we begin?"

She stared at him, mouth agape. It took her another minute to shut it and gather her thoughts before speaking. "Are you kidding me?"

He shook his head. "I am not letting you off that easy, Armen. Some weird shit happened down there. Who's this *Sariel*, and what the fuck does he want?"

She sucked in a breath through clenched teeth and slammed her hand on the table. "Don't say his name!"

He ignored her warning. "If this *Sariel* is killing people, I want to know why."

"No, you really don't, and if you insist on saying his name like it's just a name, I'll have to ask you to leave. Oh wait, I already did!"

He stared at her for a long moment. Too long, in her opinion. "Talk to me. Tell me what it wants. How do we fight it?"

A chill seeped into the kitchen. "I guess you're about to find out."

Terry shivered and ran his hands over his arms. "Why is it suddenly cold in here?"

"Don't take notice of it," she whispered. "Call your cab and go home." She certainly couldn't fight the bastard with Terry around. Of course, the bum leg might be an issue.

"I am not leaving you here alone after what happened tonight."

God, the man was just as stubborn as she was. "Just go, Terry," she said softly, shivering. "Leave, now." A faint cry from the depths of Gehenna made Armen jump in her chair. She hadn't heard a cry like that since she became flesh.

"What was that?" Terry turned in his chair, scanning the rooms.

Armen gaped again. "You heard that? How could you?" It suddenly dawned on her that, because of what he witnessed earlier, he would now hear and see things usually undetectable to the human mind. "Shit." Wonderful, she'd inadvertently brought a human into her screwed up world.

"Azel," a faint whisper came.

"Fuck off," she said, and her head snapped to the side. "Go away!"

"What the hell's going on?" Terry moved closer to her.

"Forsaken one." The voice grew stronger.

"Not in my home," Armen demanded.

"Armen, you need to tell me what's happening." Terry forced her to look at him.

She stared into his eyes, unblinking. "It's him. He's back."

"How?"

"You said his name."

"What? It's just a—"

"Name? Really?"

"If just saying their name summons them, why doesn't it happen more often?"

She grabbed his wrist. "Because you're aware of them now. Otherwise, you'd have to do an actual incantation spell."

"So does the other name—?"

"No. That one doesn't work the same." She rose to her feet to face the demon entering her home. "Good job, brilliant actually, except we're not ready for him."

"Not here, not you, not me," Terry growled.

"Oh yes here, yes her, and yes you." Sariel materialized in her living room. He took on a more human form this time, long black hair cascading down his back and fire red eyes. His flesh seemed surreal, unearthly, and didn't shift right when he moved to look at one of her paintings. *"Oh, I do love Goya. He captured Death so well."*

"Sariel, I'm warning you," Armen threatened as she grabbed her cane and stepped forward, pulling herself from Terry's grasp.

"Armen, no." He stepped up behind her. His voice was too calm for a man facing a demon for the second time in one night. It made her wonder what exactly Terry had seen in his lifetime.

Sariel craned his head around to view them, and with one swift motion, his entire body turned to face them. He smiled. Even that held pure evil within it.

"Warning me?" Sariel asked lightly. *"Oh, you amuse me, Azel."*

"Get out of my house!"

"I shall not. Your protections are not very strong, Azel. You should take better care of them." With a snap of his fingers, her protections vanished.

"Believe me, as soon as I get you out of here, I will."

"That is to assume I shall leave this place," he replied. *"And that you shall still be in a position to do so."* His lips twisted, baring teeth not of human form, sharp and

pointy—every damn one of them. *"How is the gift I gave you?"*

"It's just fine, thank you," Armen said.

Sariel laughed. *"It will not be for long."*

The cuts burned. Deep. She tried to take the pain he gave her, tried to push it back. Armen shrieked, her hand flying to her cheek. Her knees buckled, and she dropped to the floor. Terry knelt beside her to help her, and she didn't bother to slap his hands away this time. The pain consumed her.

"Where is their precious Savior now, Azel? Where has He been when I have claimed those souls? Where is He for you, if you are within the Light once more?"

"Go back to Hell," Armen seethed through her pain.

He laughed again. *"Do you like the pain these humans endure? I, myself, find it rather intriguing how much one can bear. It has been quite . . . entertaining."*

Terry struggled to pull Armen up. "Leave her alone."

Sariel searched his eyes. *"Ah, you have a knight, my sweet. Is he willing to take your pain from you?"*

Terry sneered at the demon. "You heard the woman, go back to Hell."

Sariel's laughter echoed around them.

Armen forced herself to sit up, glaring at Sariel as he made a move to harm the man at her side. "You can't touch him." She bit back the pain that burned through her flesh.

Sariel's eyes brightened as he studied Terry. He lifted his arms and said, *"I do not have to touch, Azel."* Flames erupted over his body and spread to the floor.

Armen struggled to get to her feet, pushing herself up with the cane. "You bastard." She grabbed Terry and pushed him backwards. "Outside, *now*!"

Terry stumbled back and grabbed her arm, opened the front door, and pushed her out as Sariel's flesh melted away. For a brief moment, when Armen looked back, she saw the same demon from the warehouse. Then Terry yanked her out the door and carried her down the stairs as her condo went up in flames.

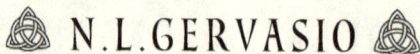

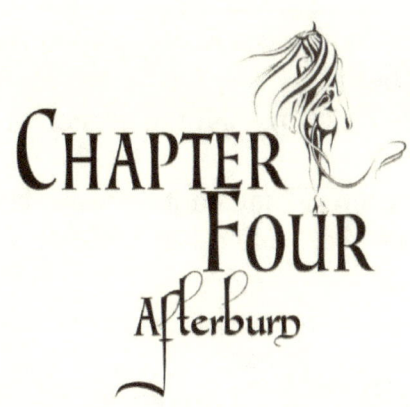

Chapter Four
Afterburn

RED AND YELLOW LIGHTS LIT the surroundings of the condominium complex. Firefighters encompassed the area around her condo. *It* was the only one damaged in the fire. Terry stood holding a shivering and injured Armen while others looked on. She, likely along with Terry, wondered just how in God's name they were going to explain what happened. No one was going to believe a demon set the damn place on fire.

"Ember from the fireplace?" Terry asked softly.

Armen looked up at him, her jaw quivering. "I don't have a f-f-f-firepl-l-l-lace."

Terry looked around. "Hey guys, does one of you have a coat or blanket for the lady? She's freezing."

A rough-looking man with piercing blue eyes walked over to them and handed Terry a blanket. "Sorry 'bout that."

Terry nodded and wrapped the blanket around Armen's shoulders. "Thanks, Greg."

She looked up at Terry again when the firefighter walked away. "He looks like he'd be a bi-k-k-ker under all that gear."

Terry chuckled. "He's got a hog. I ride with him sometimes."

"You have a motorcycle?" She pulled the blanket over her still damp head.

Terry looked down. "Not a motorcycle, sweetie, a chopper."

Armen frowned. "That's not a motorcycle?"

"No and yes." He pulled her to him and wrapped his arms around her.

"What are you doing?" She shivered, a chill racing down her spine, and looked up at his chin.

"Keeping you warm." He adjusted his arms to a more comfortable position at her waist, and then moved his hands briskly up and down her back. "Is it working?"

She shifted her eyes to meet his. "I think you're just using it as an excuse."

Terry chuckled softly. "You *would* think that." He lowered his forehead to hers. "Looks like you'll be having dinner with me tomorrow night after all."

"Why's that?"

"Well, you certainly can't stay here anymore."

"And where do you think I'll be staying?"

"I have an extra room."

"I can stay at a hotel."

He jerked his head once to the side and abruptly snapped it back in his classic short 'absolutely not, flat-out no' response. "Not with all this weird shit going on."

He couldn't be serious. "Come on, Terry—"

Another firefighter walked up to them. "This your place?" he asked Terry.

"No, it's hers."

"Sorry, ma'am," he said. "One painting survived. Didn't have a mark on it; not even smoke damage far as we can tell. Thought you'd like to hang on to it."

"Goya, I'm sure," she mumbled. "Can I go in and look around?" She pulled the blanket tighter after Terry stepped back.

"No, ma'am," the firefighter replied. "Not for a couple of days. There's still some hot spots in there. Wouldn't want you getting hurt more than you are."

"I understand," she said. "But I can definitely go in and look around in a few days?"

"Shouldn't be a problem," he said. "Do you know what started it?"

"Not a clue," she answered.

He looked at Terry, who shook his head.

"We were having tea in the kitchen," Terry said. "Burners were off."

The firefighter nodded. "You can go now. We've got your number?"

Armen nodded while shivering beneath the blanket. "Yes, I gave it to s-s-s-someone."

Terry spoke up. "If not, you can call me to get hold of her." He passed over his card. "I ride with Greg sometimes."

The firefighter studied it. "Oh, Detective Armstrong. I thought you looked familiar." He pocketed the card and held out his hand. Terry took it with a firm grip. "Have a safe night now. We'll call if we have any more questions." He took a few steps away, grabbed something, and returned. "Here's that painting."

"Thanks," said Armen as Terry grabbed for the canvas. The firefighter walked away again, and she looked at the painting. "Burned the damn frame right the hell off, but the paint and canvas weren't touched."

Terry studied it. "That's insane."

"Fucking asshole."

He nodded and looked at her. "The keys to your Jeep were in the kitchen, weren't they?"

"Yeah, but I have a spare," she replied. "Near the driver's side back tire."

"Brilliant," Terry said with a grin. "You're going to freeze on the way to my house, though."

She glared at him. "I don't remember determining where I would be s-s-staying."

"Don't argue with me. You don't have any place else to go and no identification now."

She sneered. "Damn it." He was right. Her bag was in the kitchen.

He pulled her over to the Jeep. "Get in."

"I should hit you with my cane," she said, trying not to smile while she climbed into her Jeep.

"It'd be much more interesting to see you hit that son of a bitch demon with it."

She laughed. "I don't think it'd have much effect on him, even with its gifts. The bastard is evil enough."

"Probably not," Terry said as he climbed into the driver's seat after retrieving the key. "But we need to find something that will." He turned to her as he started the engine. "Any ideas?"

"I'm working on it." Right now, she was more concerned with freezing to death on the ride to Terry's house, which was in the historic district of downtown Phoenix. "Why were you at a case in Tempe?"

"Technically, it was Phoenix, on the west side of 48th Street." He pulled onto the road.

"Hmm." The wind swept around her face and into the blanket, freezing her to her core as Terry drove toward the freeway. *I'm never going to make it.*

He must have seen her shiver. "Don't worry, I'll make it quick."

"That's what I'm afraid of," she replied. "I'm going to be a Popsicle by the time we get there." After sundown, temps dropped close to freezing, depending on the time of year and global warming. It didn't help that her hair was still wet or that she was getting wind-blasted, or that she only had on a tank under the blanket.

He laughed and drove up the on-ramp of I-10, heading west into Phoenix. "Seriously, ten minutes, tops," he shouted as he sped up.

"More like twenty in this 3-speed," she yelled, and then pulled the blanket tighter around her head. When she looked at her speedometer, it read 75 mph.

Ten minutes later, they pulled into Terry's driveway. "H-h-h-how m-m-many l-l-laws did y-y-you break g-g-getting here?"

He hopped out of the Jeep with a laugh and came around to her, unlatching the seatbelt because she wasn't moving. "Come on," he said softly and slid an arm beneath her knees, the other around her shoulders. "I *do* have a fireplace."

Terry carried her to the door and struggled to open it, but quickly got her inside and sat her down on the sofa. He shut and locked the door before returning to Armen's side.

"It's going to be all right, Armen," he said softly, his hand running down her back over the blanket. He got the fireplace going, disappeared a moment, and returned with a large quilt from the linen closet. "Come on, get closer to the fire."

"My cane."

"Shit, it's in the Jeep," he said, helping her to the chair. "I'll get it."

She craned her head around and watched him walk out the door.

The hairs on her arms stood on end, sending goose bumps in a wave over her body. Something was off. She pushed herself out of the chair slowly and hobbled over to the front window. Terry stood a few feet from the front door, staring up at the stars. When she saw his eyes close, she figured he'd seen a shooting star and made a wish, but that couldn't be true because if there was one thing she knew about Terry, it was that he didn't believe in wishes.

The gashes on Armen's face burned, and she hissed.

Terry pulled the cane and the painting from the Jeep and turned to come back to the house. Something blocked his path.

Sariel. The demon stood between Terry and the front door, wearing a black suit. She strained to hear the conversation between the fragile human and the high-level demon.

"Your domain holds much better protection than hers," Sariel said with an evil grin and lit a cigarette by merely sucking on the end. Its tip flickered to life in bright red embers. He blew out a ring of smoke. *"I see something other than the two of you survived the fire."*

"On purpose, I'm sure." Terry reached into his t-shirt and pulled out a trinity knot pendant attached to a silver chain. He clutched the top of the painting tightly. Part of Armen wished he'd break the damn thing over the demon's head.

Sariel sneered at the pendant. *"You think your little pendant is going to keep me from you?"*

"Well, it looks to me like you aren't too fond of it." Terry looked down at the demon's black leather shoes. "Feet hurt yet?"

Smoke drifted upward from his soles. Sariel frowned. *"Consecrated? How?"*

"My father was a priest," Terry said. "When I bought the house, he blessed the entire property for me."

"A holy man, how divine," Sariel seethed and lifted his right foot and placed it back down.

"Yes," Terry said. "I wasn't sure if it would actually work, though. Never had a need for it before. Cool plus in my favor."

"Except that priests are not allowed to marry, so your father broke his vows to . . . ." He looked up briefly before setting his eyes on Terry again.

"*God*? Is that what you're getting at?" Terry said. "He asked *God* for His blessing, and *God* gave it, so no, he did not break his vows."

Sariel sneered again, lifted his left foot, and placed it back on the ground. *"Your human father spoke to Him? I doubt it so."*

"Sure as I'm standing here talking to *you*," Terry replied. "Now, if you'll excuse me, I have someone to take care of." He swung the cane at Sariel, who grabbed the end of it.

"Has she told you yet what she once was?" Sariel yanked on the cane, bringing Terry a step closer to him. His hand sizzled against the wood.

Armen cringed at his words. She didn't want Terry to know.

Terry smirked. "I've figured it out, demon. It's not all that difficult a puzzle." He looked at the demon's hand. "This is blessed too."

Sariel hissed and withdrew his hand with a jerk. *"Wait until the next show. I shall make it special for you."*

"Leave my property, demon," Terry commanded.

Sariel cringed and took an involuntary step back. He hissed at Terry, who took a step forward and pushed the end of the cane to his chest.

"*Goodbye*!"

Sariel screeched and vanished in a cloud of red smoke.

Armen gasped, covering her mouth with her hand. *So that's why he never says goodbye to anyone.*

Terry turned toward the house, and Armen hurriedly hobbled back to her chair.

"Bloody bastard," he muttered as he shut and locked the door, and leaned the cane and painting against the end of the sofa. He stepped over to Armen and knelt beside her. "Warmer now?"

She peeked from around the edge of the blankets that covered her and nodded.

"Good. Would you like some cocoa or tea?"

"Cocoa," she whispered hoarsely.

He stood and went to the kitchen. When he returned, she'd pushed the blankets down to just below her shoulders. "Here, this will help warm you," he said and handed her the cup.

She looked down into it and smiled faintly. "Marshmallows."

Terry pulled a chair next to hers and sat down. "Give me some of that blanket, would you?" He scooted his chair closer.

The corner of her mouth curved upward. "Are you expecting to get shot in your own house?"

He looked down and laughed when he saw he still had his Kevlar vest on. "Think I should with demons showing up everywhere?"

"Wouldn't work anyway," she replied.

"True," he said and shrugged. "Guess I'll take it off, then." He stood, unfastened it and pulled it off, dropping the vest to the floor next to his chair.

Armen tried very hard not to stare, but it was extremely difficult when muscles bulged beneath his tight white t-shirt. Before he could notice her distraction, she handed him her cup and pulled the blankets from underneath, rearranging them so that they could cover them both. "I heard voices outside."

Terry's brow rose. "Oh, yeah, I was talking to a neighbor."

"Liar." She took a sip of her cocoa.

He chuckled. "You have good ears then."

"Yes, it's frightening sometimes, the things I hear."

"I'll bet." He took a sip of his drink and looked at her. "Do you feel like talking?"

She sighed. "I suppose. It's now or never, right?"

"It doesn't have to be now. You've been through a lot tonight."

She swallowed the sob wanting to escape. Demons don't cry. "I've lost everything, Terry." Her eyes watered and she reached up to wipe one of them. There was so much more to her statement than he would ever know or understand. "All I have now are the clothes I'm wearing and my Jeep." Not to mention losing every piece of humanity she'd procured in her three years of flesh. Except the Goya. "What am I going to do?"

"You can stay here as long as you need to, you know."

"I don't want to burden you."

"Nonsense. *You* would never be a burden to me, Armen."

She stared at the flames, not sure what to think of that. Again, Terry's blatant interest in her brought on a level of anxiety she wasn't used to. But the flames comforted her, reminding her of what she had once called home. Armen decided that her next home would have a fireplace. After an eternity of staring into the orange hues and watching embers float up into the chimney, she turned to Terry, who sat cozy in the blanket and sipping his cocoa.

"What are we going to put in the report?" They certainly couldn't report that they'd encountered a demon. That was a quick ticket to a psychological evaluation, regardless of what the captain had heard, or thought he'd heard.

Terry shrugged. "Let me sleep on it. I'll think of something."

"You have to have a reason for firing your weapon."

"I know," he said. "I'll figure something out. Captain trusts me."

"Why is he so hard on you?"

"Keeps me on my toes."

"Then why does he hate me so much?"

He looked at her, flames reflecting in the green of his eyes, turning them almost brown. "Says you give him a bad vibe."

She certainly couldn't hold Terry's honesty against him, no matter how much the truth stung. It was one of his defining qualities. "How so?"

Terry shrugged again. "Not sure what he means."

"Do I give *you* a bad vibe?"

He lifted his mug to his lips. "Would you be in my house if you did?"

"I suppose not," she said softly and moved her eyes to focus on him again. "So, your father was a priest, huh?"

Terry smiled around his mug. "Yes."

"So that means you probably know the bible like the back of your hand."

"And then some." His eyes flicked back to hers. "Yes, the parts that didn't make it into the final book."

"Really?" Her usual tone had returned now that she'd warmed up.

Terry nodded. "I know who that surly bastard is. And yes, I know your name too."

Armen stiffened. "How long have you known?"

He glanced at her briefly before his eyes returned to the flames. "I've been piecing it together for a while now. What I want to know is why you've been forsaken."

Armen looked into her cup, swirling her finger around the edge. "Which time?"

Terry laughed. "Well, at least you still have your sense of humor."

"It helps me sort through all the bullshit."

He smiled. "Something tells me you've seen a lot of bullshit."

Her eyes met his. "You have no idea."

"So tell me. I recognize your name and have picked up on the hints you've dropped, unintentionally, I'm sure."

"On one condition."

"What would that be?"

"You tell me why you're so damn calm around a demon."

He shifted toward her in his chair and leaned on the arm. "My father."

Armen cocked her head. "What about him?"

"Well," he began and took a drink, "he wasn't just a priest."

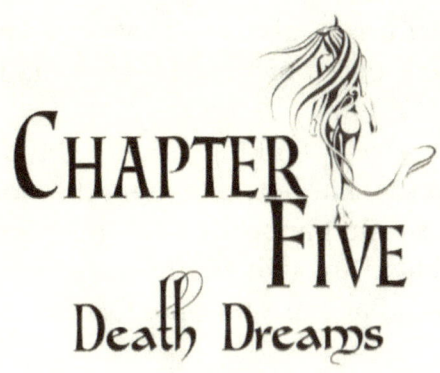

Chapter Five
Death Dreams

A DEMON WRANGLER. HAD SHE heard that correctly? Terry nodded when she asked for clarification, and she sat for some time, staring into her mug.

"So he hunted them?"

"Yeah." He took another drink. "Some of 'em were pretty nasty too; he'd come home all beat up."

She remembered hearing about the wranglers and was told to steer clear of them, but she'd never run into one.

Painted ivy grew up the sides of the stone and stucco fireplace. The wall was painted Navajo white to blend in with it. At least it wasn't a bright white; otherwise, Armen would have to seriously reconsider Terry's sanity. At this point, however, she started questioning her own.

"You okay?" Terry asked as he finished off the last of his cocoa.

Armen nodded, still deep in thought, staring into the flames. "Fine." He continued to talk about his father, the demon wrangler-slash-priest-slash-father. Then, silence. She looked up.

"What?" She studied his face, which held a grin not suitable for the topic.

"What'cha thinkin' about?" That was a bit more than friendly or on the topic of 'Hi, my dad's a demon wrangler'."

"What am I *not* thinking about would be a much better question." Like how mundane her job used to be where demons didn't appear out of thin air, or how hard it can be to blend in with the humans, to mimic them, especially now that she was one. Or about the day she fell . . . .

"I'm exhausted. I think my entire body hurts."

"You should get some rest."

Armen set her cup on the table. "Which room am I staying in?" She carefully stood.

"Last door on the left." He held a hand out to catch her in case she fell, which she apparently needed because she stumbled. "I think I'll help you."

"It's just because I'm so tired."

"Mm hmm. I take it this conversation is over."

She looked up at him as he slipped an arm around her waist. "Would you mind if we continue it tomorrow?"

"Sure, that's fine." He walked her down the hall and into the small guest room, depositing her at the bed. "You need something to sleep in?"

After wondering what his comment would be if she told him she didn't wear anything to bed, she shook her head and gave the mattress a small bounce. "Ever sleep on this?"

"Why?" he asked, his lips separating enough to show his pearly whites.

She cocked an eyebrow at him.

He laughed. "Yes, it's fairly comfortable. You'll sleep well on it." He walked to the foot of the bed and opened the cedar chest. "Blanket?"

"Please."

He extracted a deep red plush blanket and laid it on the bed. "There you go. Anything else I can help you with?"

"I don't think so."

"You sure?" he asked, brow arched.

"Terry, all I have left is to undress and climb into bed," she said. "You most certainly aren't helping me with that."

He chuckled this time and grabbed the doorknob. "Okay, fine." He half-turned as he stepped out the door. "Goodnight, Armen."

"Night, Terry." After he closed the door, she turned down the bed and kicked off her shoes. Terry was milling around in the room next to hers, and she wondered if he wore anything to bed. "Ah." She slapped a hand to her forehead. "What's wrong with me?"

Finally undressed, she crawled under the covers and pulled them up to her chin, but her mind kept wandering back to Terry and his oh-so-perfect muscular body. Why did humans still have such primal urges? She blew out a frustrated breath, turned off the light, and turned over. "Bastard," she whispered and closed her eyes.

Blood seeped from every pore of the middle-aged woman's face, pushing its way out as her face swelled until the skin cracked from the pressure and she let out an agonizing, shrill scream. Armen blinked at the sight, unable to believe what her eyes were showing her. She turned away. A man with black bile trickling slowly from his mouth, nose, and eyes came into view. Another man, with dark hair, his face twisted in pain, his flesh peeled off one long strip at a time by fingers that didn't exist. Just the heads showed, like at a carnival walking through the House of Horrors; nothing else. She scanned for Sariel's presence, knowing this sideshow was his style, but she couldn't find him.

With a gasp, she struggled to force her eyes open. Dark shadows swirled above her bed in and out of her vision, mixing with the nightmare. Still caught between waking and dreaming, her body couldn't move except to shiver. A weight on her chest pinned her to the bed, robbing her breath. She was trapped like a fly in a web.

Early morning light swept through the small house in the Historic District of Phoenix. The sound of Terry stumbling into the hallway reached her ears. He opened her bedroom door and gasped. Then a language damn near as ancient as the one she'd used the night before passed his lips.

"I banish you back to the darkness from which you came, demon."

Why hadn't he said 'goodbye' to it? A hiss shuddered through the air. What he'd said had some effect on the beast above her. Armen broke out of the dream world and swung her right arm.

"Leave this realm!"

The dark shadows swirled about and flew up through the ceiling, leaving a mocking giggle to echo in the room until silence fell.

Terry ran over and sat on the edge of the bed. "You okay?" His bandaged hand reached for her arm, but stopped short of gracing her flesh.

She nodded and flopped back down on the bed.

"You forgot to shield yourself before you went to sleep," he said softly.

She opened one eye. "And you didn't shield the house," she replied. "I was distracted. What's your excuse?"

He chuckled. "I guess I was distracted, too."

"Yes, well, let's take note to not be distracted ever again."

He looked down at his hand, resting on his leg. "That's rather difficult around you."

She closed her eye. "Please don't start with the date thing again."

"I'm not," he said. "I'm just concerned for your safety."

She flipped an eye open again. The longing in his eyes was ever-present. "Liar."

He smiled and closed his eyes briefly. "Was that Sar—*him* again?"

"Several of his minions, the little bastards," she replied. "I'm never going to get any sleep now, not until he's burning."

Terry frowned, confused.

"In the fires of Hell, Terry," she added. The confusion left his face. "Or maybe I'll just throw him into the Pit. Got any calendula around here, since mine's all burned up?"

He shook his head. "Never needed it here."

"Because daddy blessed the place?"

He nodded. "Yep. Good ol' Dad."

"I think it's wearing off," she said. "It needs to be repeated now and then."

"I'll call him later," he said and shifted on the bed next to her. "I saw you struggling. I didn't quite know what was happening or what to do."

Armen blew out a breath, tucked the blankets around her chest, and propped herself up on one elbow. "I was being pressed. Ever heard of that?"[1]

"Is that when it feels like someone is holding you down while you're sleeping?"

Armen nodded. "And it's not a fun feeling, either."

"I think that happened to me once when I was a kid," he said. "I remember my father freaking out about it and going through the entire house with his sage and some other herb."

She smiled. "Calendula. Smart man." Armen looked around the room. "I feel like I got only a few hours of sleep?"

"About that."

She dropped back to the bed on her left shoulder and closed her eyes. "I need more."

"Me, too," he said. "Want company?"

Armen opened her eye. Terry's handsome face held a devilish grin and that damn twinkle. "You really don't ever give up, do you?"

He leaned forward. "Not when it comes to you."

Armen then realized he was shirtless, and she could see every tattoo running up his could-lift-a-small-car strong arms and across his breaks-the-mold amazing chest. She barely contained the urge to run her fingers over his skin. "Nice tats," she said in attempt to distract her thoughts. Totally didn't work.

"Thanks." He leaned closer and waggled his eyebrows. "Got any?"

Armen nodded and she pushed her head back into the pillow.

"Where?"

"Someplace I don't intend to show you right now."

"Ah, but that means you'll show me someday." Damn if that grin didn't reach his ears.

"No, it means that I'm naked and you'll see everything if I show you right now." She cursed herself immediately.

"Real-ly?" he said, dragging the word out as his brow jumped.

"Oh, Terry, go back to bed." She slapped his arm.

He chuckled. "I really frustrate the hell out of you, don't I?"

"Yes, you do. Now get out."

He laughed, leaned forward, and kissed her forehead. "Night, Armen."

She watched him walk away and grinned. "Nice *chonies*, Terry," she said with a laugh. "Are you getting into the festive season?"

He stopped in the doorway and looked down at his boxers, which had little Christmas trees all over them. "Nah, I just haven't done my laundry yet. Besides, these are boxers, not *chonies*. Get the lingo right." He shut the door. "Shield yourself if you don't want me in there again!"

Armen laughed, took a deep breath, and closed her eyes, hoping for at least a few more hours of uninterrupted sleep. She chanted softly as she drifted off to sleep, shielding not only herself, but the house as well.

The next demon to set foot on Terry's lawn would burst into flames. She hoped it was Sariel.

Chapter Six
Amore

ARMEN ROLLED OVER IN BED and looked at the clock. She blinked a few times before viewing it again. Noon. She glanced over her shoulder to the other side of the bed, wondering where Terry was. She heard him faintly singing somewhere in the house. The blankets hadn't been pulled off the bed. She hadn't fallen to the floor. Terry hadn't come to her rescue. *What the hell?* Her memories of Terry holding her in his strong arms and telling her she'd always be an angel to him regardless of her demon past were nothing but the fading eclipse of a dream.

"Figures."

She sat up and carefully slid her legs over the edge of the bed. The bruise looked nasty, all black and blue and soon to turn several disgusting shades of yellow. The cane rested against the nightstand instead of the dresser like in her dream, and her clothes were missing. She frowned, and then saw a robe lying neatly over the blankets.

"Oh, that's sweet." She pulled the robe on and took great care in rising from the bed, reaching for the cane. She fussed with her hair a moment before opening the door and stepping into the hall.

Terry was in the kitchen, clad only in faded jeans, a towel draped over his bare shoulder as he washed dishes. Armen's muffled laugh caught his attention, and he spun around, startled.

"Sorry." She limped over to the kitchen table and sat down.

"It's fine," he said. "I just didn't expect you to be up this early."

"Eight hours of sleep, I guess," she replied with a shrug.

He smiled and stepped in front of the stove. "Coffee or tea?" he asked, turning back to her.

Or me. She smiled. "Coffee's fine."

He pulled a cup from the cabinet and reached for the coffee pot. "So, how was that bed? Did you sleep well?"

"Like a dream after that crap this morning." *Especially with the dream I had.* "Where are my clothes?"

"I'm washing them. Hope you don't mind." He turned around with a full cup of brew. "I figured you'd want clean clothes, since you don't have anything else. We can go shopping for you later, if you'd like."

She thanked him and took the cup. "Don't you have to work tonight?"

He shook his head. "It's my night off. Sent the report to the captain about an hour ago."

"I can't believe he let it go this long. It's not normal for the man."

"I know," he replied. "That shit really shook him up."

"That shit would shake anyone up—except you, for some odd reason."

"It's not all that new to me, Armen." He sat down across from her with his own cup of coffee. "Remember, my father's a demon wrangler."

She held up a finger and shook it as she took a drink. There had been a demon wrangler present when she became flesh. Agares had nearly killed the wrangler, prompting Armen's sudden attack of compassion and righteousness. "Yeah, I want to talk about that." She lowered the cup to the table. "Are all demon wranglers former or current priests?"

"Yes, why?"

She'd stepped into the blade's path and took Agares' sword to its hilt for a demon wrangler—a man of God. What. The. Hell? The moment that the blade's hilt touched her stomach played out and froze in time inside her mind.

Even Angels and Demons could die, but only if killed by one another. And she should have been dead. Something brought her back. But why?

"Just curious," she replied and picked up her cup again. She thought back to the moment before she'd stepped into the blade's path, struggling to recall the demon wrangler's face. Oddly, he hadn't been frightened; he was ready and willing to accept his Fate, trusting it to her Father.

"Then why do I get the feeling there's more than mere curiosity there?"

Armen shrugged. "Maybe because you're always reading into things." It was damn near impossible to throw him off, even if she had tried to hide it. His muscles tensed noticeably. "Could you please put a shirt on?"

Terry smirked. "Why?"

She huffed. "Fine, never mind, then."

He chuckled. "My being shirtless is upsetting you?"

"Shut up!"

"Wow, it *is* upsetting you," he said. "I had no idea I had that effect on you."

"Oh, please don't think you have any kind of effect on me," she snapped.

Terry's eyes brightened. "I have an idea. When we go shopping later, you can buy another little black dress so I can take you to dinner tonight."

She let out an exasperated sigh. "You're impossible!"

"Actually, I'm very possible, but only for you." The dryer sounded its finish. Terry rose from the table and headed for the laundry room. "Lucky you; saved by the buzzer."

Armen shook her head and sipped her coffee as her mind jumped back to the demon wrangler. Surprisingly, there had been no fear in his vibrant green eyes, and his strong-jawed face had been calm and determined. Armen's eyes widened, and her gaze slowly swung to Terry, who had just come out of the laundry room with a bundle of clothes in his arms.

He dropped them on the table and looked at her. "What's that look for?" He sorted through the clothes, pulling his out and placing them in a separate pile from hers.

She stared into her cup. "Nothing."

He abandoned the clothes. "All right, what's got you so on edge this morning with the stares and wide eyes and getting upset about me not wearing a shirt?"

Armen slammed her cup to the table, spilling the coffee, and stood. "I am *not* upset that you're not wearing a shirt!" She snatched up her clothes, grabbed her cane, and turned to head out of the kitchen.

"Well, you're certainly upset about something." He seized her arm, jerking her to a stop. Her clothes fell to the floor.

She growled, wrenched her arm from his grasp, and carefully knelt to pick them up.

He followed her to the floor. "Did you just growl at me? Armen, seriously, I want to know what's going on inside that head of yours."

She picked up her tank and threw it over her arm. "Terry, please, I am *not* a morning person." She reached for her jeans, but he grabbed them first.

"You're not a morning, afternoon, or evening person." He yanked the jeans away from her.

"Give me my pants!" She reached for them again, but he pulled them out of reach. "You're lucky I don't bite your head off!"

"Then talk to me!"

"I don't feel like talking." She took the rest of her clothes and stood, holding out her hand as she precariously balanced on one leg. "Give me my jeans."

"Friends talk, Armen," he said, holding the pants behind his back.

"Friends don't hold clothing hostage." She jerked her hand forward, fingers spread, waiting for the jeans.

Terry gripped her arm with his right hand and pulled her to him, his arm quickly snaking around her waist to keep her from falling. He looked deeply into her eyes. "I am not holding your jeans hostage."

She arched a brow.

"Okay, maybe I'm holding your jeans hostage, but it's only because you won't talk to me."

"We were talking just fine a while ago."

"That's not what I meant and you know it," he said.

She lowered her head. "Terry, you want to know things I'm not ready to reveal to anyone, least of all you."

Terry's hand slithered away from her, and he took a step back. "Ouch." He held out the jeans. "Here, take them."

Armen could see the hurt in his eyes as well as hear the fine tremor in his voice. She took the pants. "Terry—"

He shook his head and went back to sorting his clothes.

Armen stepped forward. "I didn't mean—"

"No, no, if there's one thing I've learned about you, it's that you're perfectly clear on what you mean."

"Please don't misunderstand—"

"How could I possibly misunderstand that?" The hurt in his eyes tripled. "*Least* of all, me. Not much misunderstanding in that one. I am at the bottom of the list of people you'd be likely to confide in. End of story."

Armen stared down at the clothes on her arm and wanted to shrink away. Learning the English language's nuances was one of her greatest hurdles, and she apparently needed a refresher. Terry continued to fold his clothes in silence. Finally, she turned to leave the kitchen.

"I think it's best if I stay somewhere else."

Chapter Seven

Admit No Thing

Armen dressed and pulled her hair back into a ponytail. She ran her tongue over her front teeth and wrinkled her nose. A toothbrush would be in her immediate future. She limped to the door and opened it, finding Terry leaning against the wall, waiting, arms crossed over his burly chest. He'd actually put a shirt on.

"Two things," he said, holding up two fingers.

She leaned on her cane. "What's that?"

"Was it my father you saved?"

"I'm not certain," she replied. "He looked like he could be an older version of you."

"Probably was." He straightened, pushing away from the wall, and placed his hands on either side of the doorjamb. "I don't think any others have ever been saved from that fate. Thank you." The last two words were a mere whisper.

Armen shrugged. She had no clue what to say. "You're welcome" didn't seem fitting.

"He never knew your name."

"It wasn't important for him to know." She wasn't sure she liked the idea of Terry knowing her true self. She leaned away from him.

"So, you've been forsaken from Heaven *and* Hell?"

Armen nodded. It wasn't entirely correct but close enough.

"You weren't kidding, then, when I asked you where you were from."

Her ponytail swished along her back from the quick head shake.

"Damn," he said softly.

They stood in silence for a while, and then Armen looked up at him again. "Is that all?"

"No."

She waited, but he didn't continue. "Well?"

Terry smiled. "You're attracted to me, and it's killing you to admit it."

Her jaw dropped. "You can't be serious!"

"See what I mean? You fight it. I've seen you struggle when you look at me. That's why you were so damned upset that I wasn't wearing a shirt."

"Oh, you've lost it." She pushed him out of the way. "Do you have a toothbrush I can use?"

"Yes, there's one in the guest bathroom." He pointed at her. "And I have not lost it. You were all cheery when you came into the kitchen, and now you're pissed."

She stopped in the hallway and turned to the side. "I'm pissed because you're being an ass."

"And I'm being an ass because you're getting all bitchy on me." His grin grew seven times too big. "Or maybe it's just frustration."

She growled again and walked into the bathroom, slamming the door.

Terry chuckled. "Come on, Armen, just admit that you have feelings for me, and everything will run more smoothly," he said from the other side of the door.

"I'll admit to nothing," she replied with a mouth full of toothpaste. She leaned over and spit into the sink. "You're delusional."

"Oh, I am so not delusional."

The world suddenly went deathly silent on the other side of the door. She hated silence.

"Did you have a dream about me?" His voice had deepened and was much closer to the door.

Armen stared into the mirror, wide-eyed, and suppressed a cough after she'd sucked back toothpaste with a gasp. She was quite glad he couldn't see her face at the moment. She turned on the faucet and rinsed her mouth before she choked. "No!"

"Oh, I think you did. That was an awful long pause."

"It's called a mouthful of toothpaste, you jackass." She could just see the look on his face. "You're reading into things, as usual."

"Hey, I'm only listening to my instinct, which is generally correct, I'll have you know."

"Well, it's wrong this time." She leaned over the sink and splashed cold water over her face, hoping it would drown out the sound of his voice if he continued with the topic.

"I doubt it. You're just being stubborn, as usual. Seriously, Armen, would it be that bad?"

She flung the door open. "You *know* what I was! Your *father* is going to know what I once was. He'll remember me, Terry. He's a *priest*!"

"He *was* a priest," Terry corrected.

"It doesn't matter. Do you really think he'll be happy if his son starts dating an ex-demon?"

Terry's eyes brightened. "Does that mean you've considered it?"

"No, it doesn't mean anything," she said, frustration grinding out her words. "Will you drop this already?"

He pushed away from the doorjamb and stood in front of her. "No, I'm not going to drop it."

"Now you really are pushing the boundaries of harassment."

He moved fast, his hand hooking behind her neck. He pulled her to him at the same time, cradling her face with his bandaged hand. And the son of a bitch kissed her, his lips colliding into hers. She thought about pushing away, but he turned out to be her weakness, and she slipped her arms over his shoulders, effectively pulling him closer to her. His lips worked against hers, and she ended up returning the kiss with a moan. He slid his hands down her sides and gently lifted her from the back of her thighs, crashing her back against the wall and pressing himself against her. The cane fell to the floor. He rested one hand on her ass while the other slid up and cupped her breast. She moaned into his mouth. He bit her lip and worked his way down her jaw line.

Armen fought for her sanity in the sea of hormones, but it was long gone.

He pulled back and rested his forehead against hers. "Just thought I'd get that in before you start shouting harassment."

"Bastard," she whispered, slapping his shoulder.

"Actually, no, my parents were married."

Armen growled again but didn't make any attempt to lower her legs.

"You know, that growling thing you do is a major turn-on." He gently kissed her forehead.

"It figures."

Terry's cell phone rang in the living room and he gently set her down before he moved away from her. "Aren't you a lucky woman today? Saved by the bell again."

Armen let out a short laugh. "I doubt luck has anything to do with it."

He chuckled as he answered his phone. Soon after, his face went stone-cold serious. "Where, Dad? I'm on my way." He looked at Armen, who still stood in the hallway. "Come with me?"

She shrugged. "If you think I'd be of any use."

"Yeah, I do. I wouldn't have asked otherwise."

She turned to go back to her room, but remembered that her hoodie burned up in the fire. "Do you have a coat I can borrow, or something so I'm not freezing in just a tank?" Something in the sound of his voice gnawed at her, but she couldn't quite place it, and she glanced back at him. Perhaps one of the churches had been attacked and that was why his dad called him.

"Yeah." He pulled his sweater over his head and yanked the bottom down to his waist, then headed her way, going into his own bedroom. "You want a shirt, too?"

"Please."

He tossed a long-sleeved jersey at her and walked back down the hall.

She joined him in the living room, pulling the shirt over her head. He'd grabbed a pair of boots and was wearing his gun.

"There's a coat in that closet over there," he said, nodding to the door near the front door.

"Thanks. So much for a day off, huh?"

He bent forward and tied his boots with short, sharp yanks. "To be honest, I didn't really expect to have the day off with all this shit going on." He jumped to his feet. "We need to hurry."

"Why?" She selected a pea coat and pulled it on.

Terry snatched his keys from the coffee table and walked to the front door. "Because I have a feeling this one is *special*."

Armen froze in place. "What do you think it is?" Sariel's words from the night before rang through her mind and sent a shiver down her spine. *Wait until the next show. I shall make it special for you.*

He just shook his head and opened the door.

Outside, Terry moved Armen's Jeep, parking it on the outside of the garage before opening the garage door. "Thought you'd be much warmer in this," he said and disappeared inside.

An engine rumbled to life. Terry backed out his black '65 Lincoln Continental and stopped in front of her.

"Cool car," she said as he closed the garage door.

"Thanks. You gonna get in, or just stare at it?"

"I'm getting in." She opened the passenger door and slid onto the leather seat, closing the door behind her. "Wow, Terry, I had no idea you had such a vehicle."

Terry turned to her. "If I'd known cars were your thing, I'd have brought it out sooner." He put the car in gear, giving her a once-over from the corners of his eyes. "You look good in my coat."

Armen smiled and clicked the seatbelt into place. "Thanks, it's warm."

Terry headed down the narrow street to their next destination, and most likely another face-to-face meeting with Sariel. Worry gnawed at her. What was it going to be this time? She prayed that if it was Sariel's little show, it didn't involve anyone close to Terry.

CHAPTER EIGHT
The Grigori

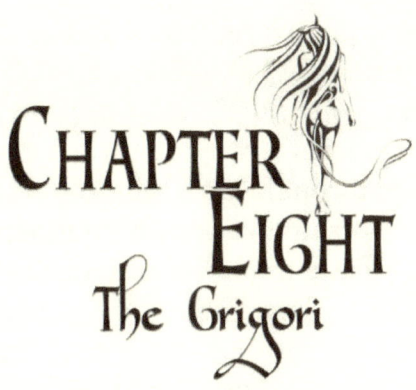

"TELL ME SOMETHING," TERRY SAID as they drove down the interstate. "Why were you there, with my dad that day?"

Armen stilled at the query. "Someone summoned me."

He hummed a reply before falling silent for a spell. Then he suddenly sprang to life again as he took a turn. "So, if asshole demon is an angel of death, where do you fall in the . . . levels . . . the ladder—"

"Tier?"

"Yes," he said. "The tier, where were you in that hierarchy?"

"What's that got to do with anything?"

"Just answer the question, Armen."

She snapped her head around to glare at him. "Where I sat doesn't mean anything here."

"I'm just trying to figure something out. Don't cop an attitude."

"What the hell are you trying to figure out?"

"Who summoned you," he said. "It might have been my father, Sean, but if he didn't know your name, he may have known your title."

She sighed heavily and turned to look at him. "I really don't want to get into this discussion, Terry." Her eyes fell upon the approaching houses and the emergency vehicles he couldn't yet hear.

"Just tell me your title," he said, growing impatient. "It might be important."

She peered through the window again, listening carefully, before turning back to him once more. "When I was a demon, I made the lists and had one of my own to cover. I didn't really have a title other than Captain." She wasn't about to tell him her true title. "When I was an angel, my title was Grigori, the eleventh of the twenty chiefs of tens. Happy now?"

Terry's mouth gaped. "You're . . . you're a Watcher, *and* a chief at that? *That's* what got you cast out of Heaven?"

She swallowed the sorrow stuck in her throat. "Yes."

Terry was taken aback by her revelation, she was certain, but he eventually found his voice again. "So, does that mean you were once male?"

"No, I've always been female."

"But the Grigori took the daughters of man as their wives."

Stabbing pain pierced her heart, millennia-old wounds still fresh, buried under the sands of time. "Yes, they did, and I took a son of man." She steeled herself before turning to face him. "Why do you ask these questions?"

He shrugged. "Just trying to find out more about the woman I . . . care about."

She slapped his arm. "Don't you dare start spouting that L-word, Terry."

"Yes, ma'am," he replied with a salute as they rounded the corner and onto a street filled with flashing lights and people scurrying about. Inside the car, silence reigned.

"Shit," he said in a soft voice.

Armen wrinkled her nose in a mock growl when she saw the captain of the Phoenix P.D. standing next to one of the Rural Metro fire trucks.

"Does he not ever sit behind that ginormous fucking desk of his?" The agitation in her voice was unmistakable, but she didn't care. "Is this even his jurisdiction?"

"Not technically. It isn't mine, either." Terry climbed out and headed for the captain. "What's going on?"

He was worried, which concerned Armen. *Oh, Sariel, what have you done now?*

"Armstrong," Captain Brian McNeil greeted in monotone. "You shouldn't be here. This isn't police business for you."

Terry looked sternly at his boss, his hands balled into fists to keep from shaking. "Of course it's not. This is my parents' house."

His parents? Armen's eyes widened. *Oh no.*

"What's happened? I just talked to my dad."

Brian looked surprised. "When? We've been on the scene ten minutes."

"We left about fifteen minutes ago, Terry."

He stared at her a moment, and Armen was pretty sure he was calculating some serious shit in his mind. In fact, she was damn certain of the moment everything clicked because he blinked before turning back to the captain. "Has anyone gone in yet?"

"Shit," she spat.

Brian ignored her, as usual. "They went in, and they came right back out. This one isn't like the others." When Terry frowned, Brian added, "There's no trigger."

"Are you sure about that?" Armen asked.

Brian's left eye twitched; he was obviously irritated by the sound of her voice. "Pretty damn sure, Ms. Leza." Loathing seeped from every syllable.

Armen grinned slyly. "You just can't call me doctor, can you?"

Brian turned to face her directly. "Not that I would ever consider *you* a doctor."

"Look, you . . . ." Armen wagged a finger at him.

Terry stepped between them. "Enough!" His entire body shook.

Armen felt horrible; she'd argued with Brian just to get one more jab in while Terry's parents were in danger. "I'm sorry, Terry. Let's go take a look." She started toward the house, but Brian stepped in her way.

"Oh, no you don't," he said. "I can't have either one of you going in there."

Terry pushed Brian aside. "I'm going in," he said forcefully. "You can fire me later."

Armen followed closely, giving Brian a smug grin as she passed him. "Terry, really, you probably shouldn't go in there. Let me go in first and have a look."

"No," was his stern reply, as though his stubbornness would assure he found his parents alive and well. "What would you do if it were your parents?"

She arched her brow.

"Never mind." He stopped at the door. "I *have* to go in."

"Sounds like you're trying to convince yourself more than me."

He closed his eyes and took a deep breath.

"Emotional ties."

"I know," he said softly, his voice trembling. He gave her a very weak smile.

"If he's in there . . . ." She drew in a deep breath, choosing her words with care. "I know you have a strong will and a good heart, and that this shit doesn't affect you like it would most people, even if it is your parents. But if he's done something really terrible, I'm afraid that even *your* mind will break. I *know* him, Terry."

Terry steadied himself. "Neither one of us can go in alone. It has to be together. Team effort, right?"

Armen nodded reluctantly. She didn't have much choice but to let him go in with her. She was hardly in a position to stop him.

"You ready?"

"To face *him*? Never," she said honestly. "You may recognize his name and say that you know who he is, but do you really *know*?"

"Enlighten me," he replied. "Quickly."

She leaned forward. "He's an angel of death, only he doesn't just write and erase in a book for eternity."

Terry's eyes widened. "That's real?"

She pulled her head back. "Considering your father's professions, you should know this shit. Look, he is not just an angel of death; he's the Morning Star's angel of death. It's entirely different."

His brow creased as he stared at the welcome mat on the front stoop. "The death befits the sins?"

"To a certain degree, the punishment is fitting," she replied. "Your life dictates your death, and if *they* want you, you can't stop it, even if you've tried to turn your life around. Contrary to what some religions like to believe, there are some things that you just can't come back from. The more evil there is within the human soul, the darker the army they will build. Those people we've found so far? They tried to find God, were born-again. I know the pregnant woman did."

"So you're saying finding God won't help you?"

"What I'm saying is that if you don't find God through the correct process, it won't work. You can't just walk into any church and be reborn."

His brow pinched in concentration. "Then why my parents? My father was a Catholic priest."

Armen could tell he didn't really want to know the answer, but it was likely he already did. "What does your father do?"

"Demon wrangler," he replied softly, lowering his head.

"And how many has he sent back?" She touched his arm again.

"Dozens, maybe hundreds, even thousands. I don't know," he said, unsure of anything now.

"Something's going on, Terry," she said, touching his arm. "This isn't just payback from demon-boy to you. It's a game—a big game—like chess, and if you don't know how to play it, you'll die."

"A game of what, Armageddon?"

Armen shook her head. "Not fire and brimstone like it says in the Bible. Not Judgment Day, as you all like to call it. It won't be like that."

"Then what will it be?"

"Hell on Earth," she replied, but still pondered whether she should tell him more. That was the simplest explanation she could give.

"If you ask me, it's already Hell when I have kids killing each other and rapists and murderers out on the streets."

Armen unintentionally let out a short laugh. "You think that's bad? I've *seen* Hell, Terry. That's just the icing on the cake."

"Beautiful." He looked at the front door again, which stood ajar. "How do we send him back?"

"Did your father ever teach you anything?"

"Some," he replied, looking down at his hands. "But I'm no demon wrangler. They have training for that."

Armen smiled. "Oh, I think it's inherited, sweetie."

Terry's eyes brightened a little as he gave her a small grin.

"Let's do this." She pushed the door open and stepped inside.

He held onto her arm as if his life depended on it. "Don't let me do anything stupid."

"Of course not," she replied, and reached over to cover his hand with hers.

"Should I know more?" He was likely worried that even after everything his father *had* taught him, it wouldn't be enough. And it was entirely possible that it wasn't.

She turned to look back at him. "You're not ready yet."

"Why did I know you were going to say that?" He stepped up next to her. "I mean, you couldn't just lie to me or something?"

"You know me entirely too well, and what would be the point of lying?" she replied. "At least you're trying to keep your humor, though."

"I think it's the only thing that'll help me here"—he clutched her shoulder—"besides you, because right now I want to tear through this house to find them."

"Oh, you can't do that. Then I wouldn't have anyone to hit on me all the damn time." She stopped talking then; there wasn't anything good to say in this situation, and she couldn't fully comprehend how Terry felt at the moment. Her Father could never die and she would never be in this position, but for one fleeting moment, she held concern for Him. If Armageddon had truly begun, could her Father survive it? Could the man these humans called God die?

"I know. We'll find them."

Armen smiled because she didn't have to say those possibly false words "everything's going to be okay." She hoped they were true.

The house was eerily still. Corners were oddly dark despite the time of day. She proceeded cautiously through the foyer, looking into the dining room on her left, and then into the living room on her right, where a large cross hung on the wall. Neither room had been disturbed. She stared at the cross a moment, contemplating whether He would hear her if she prayed. She decided against it. Why would He answer her prayers? They hadn't spoken in so long. She drew in a long concentrated breath and picked up Sariel's scent, and she immediately blew the breath back out, trying to rid the noxious smell from her nose.

"You okay?"

Armen nodded. "Can you smell him?"

Terry took in a breath and instantly wrinkled his nose. "That's him?"

"Yeah, disgusting, isn't it?" She focused on the kitchen and the stairs. Apprehension ran through her when she looked at the stairs. "I think we need to go up."

"You think he's up there?"

Armen nodded again. Fewer words were best.

"Wait." He took off through the living room and around a corner. Armen tensed, wondering just what in the hell he was doing, and how dare he run off on her like that! He came back with a Bible in one hand and a golden cylinder in the other.

Armen eyed the Bible, though the other item caught her attention. "Are you serious? That's not going to help."

"Says you," Terry whispered.

Her eyes moved to the cylinder. "What's that for?" It looked familiar, but she couldn't recall where she'd seen it before. Certainly not the day she died.

Terry looked down at it. "I've seen my dad use it. It's a weapon. Has special powers or something."

She put a hand on her hip. "This isn't some sort of magic show, Terry."

"Armen, my father uses this when he's hunting demons. It's a weapon."

"I don't remember seeing that."

"That's because he didn't have it with him then." Terry looked up, worry stretching across his face.

"He went hunting without his *weapon*?"

"No, he was *hunted*. Were you there or not?"

"I showed up in the middle of it." She kept her voice low.

"Well, I've seen him use this and it does hurt them." He moved toward the stairs.

"Not arguing that; just concerned that you're not prepared for this because you're bringing a book and a tin can to a demon fight." She proceeded to move up the stairs, dread weighing heavy on her as she climbed the first few steps.

"Ye of little faith," he said, outstretching a hand toward the stairs, signaling for her to pass him.

"Books don't kill demons."

"I think we should stop talking," Terry suggested, and pushed past her once they'd reached the top.

"Why? He already knows we're here."

He spun around. "He does?"

"Of course he does. You don't think he'd go to all this trouble and not expect us, do you? If that were the case, we wouldn't be having this conversation at all."

Terry looked down the hall. "Master bedroom?"

"Jackpot."

He looked at her. "That's just plain eerie."

"Not half as eerie as what you're about to see," she said and winced. "Sorry."

"You're keeping me grounded, so I'll let it pass," he replied. "Otherwise, I'd be running in there like a damn fool and getting myself killed."

"We can't have that." She walked past him toward the Master bedroom doors. "Take a deep breath, Terry. I'm not entirely sure what he's done."

"A large part of me does not want to go in there to discover my dead parents."

She sensed him directly behind her. It made her feel safe. What lay in front of her was another feeling altogether. "We don't know they're dead. Don't think the worst."

"Considering what I've seen these last few months, I can't help it."

Armen stopped and turned to the side. "I think you've seen a hell of a lot more than you're letting on."

"Maybe I have."

She frowned. "That's why you're not freaking out, isn't it? I mean, if I had parents and they were in there and I'd never seen this shit before, I'd already be dead."

"If you're trying to help, stop. It's not working." His eyes fell to his hand that held the Bible as he raised it. "Look at me; I'm shaking like a leaf."

"Try to remain calm, if you can," she said and laid her hand over his. "We need to get out of this."

"Let's pray that this isn't the worst thing I've ever seen."

"You and I need to have a longer talk."

"If we make it out of this mess, you bet'cha." He attempted a smile, but failed.

Armen turned back to the doors. A red glow surrounded the edges, and a low hum beat against them.

Chills ran through her, making her shiver. "Hell, it's *him* that makes me so damn cold."

"I'd think he would have the opposite effect."

"Oh, I wish. I miss the warmth." She flinched at how that sounded. "Damn it."

"It's okay, Armen. I know what you meant."

She shifted her weight to her good leg and raised the cane, pushing the doors open. A soft moan seeped into the hall. A crack like a whip sounded, and movement at the corner of her eye. Armen screamed.

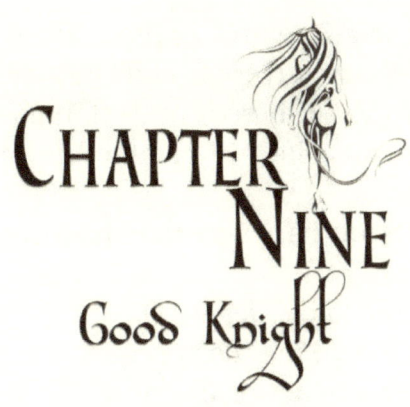

Chapter Nine

Good Knight

"TERRY, NO!" ARMEN IMMEDIATELY RAISED her arm to stop Terry from entering the room. "I know you really want to go in there, but don't forget that he can mimic sounds, and I don't think you're in the frame of mind to distinguish between his voice and theirs, which I believe is the reason we're here." He nodded slowly, acknowledging her silent query regarding the call from his dad. The last thing she needed right now was for Terry to attempt some heroic deed and get himself tortured or killed.

Terry growled softly, but stood back and waited for her to examine the room. "I hate it when you're right. Sometimes."

"Stay put." She slipped inside and around the corner. "And don't shoot me."

He snorted.

The room's décor held the repulsion of Ancient Religion with accents of Medieval Torture, like a black sunrise. Blood, deep red in the otherworldly glow, splattered the bedspread and walls. Tattered bits of cloth lay strewn about the floor and furniture, some stuck to the walls, blood serving as the adhesive. Terry's mother lay on her side, her face hidden in the curve of her tortured body; his father Sean lay on his back, deep gashes scoring his face and arms. Both were tied down with a rope that quivered and moved. When Sean shifted, the rope slithered and tightened its bonds, making him groan. Life still breathed from him, but just barely.

She felt eyes on her from the shadows the red glow didn't reach. Sariel.

"Armen. You know I hate it when I can't see you. Seriously, you're making me nervous." Terry.

"Stay put. You're not ready for this."

"That doesn't help!"

Sean's eyes opened and fixed on her, just like when she had appeared before him that fateful evening she became flesh. The phone receiver lay near him, still on but emitting only dead air. Had Sean called the authorities and Terry, or had it been Sariel? Sariel would never have created a disturbance great enough to attract the neighbor's attention. Sean's eyes suddenly flicked to her right. She turned too late.

Sariel flew out from the shadows, knocked her cane to the floor, and gripped her arm in a hold she'd never escape. A short-lived scream burst from her mouth. Though she struggled against him, as was her instinct, in human form she was no match for the demon. He twisted her around until he had her arms locked down and held her against him, immobilized.

Terry stormed into the room and froze upon seeing Armen held captive. His eyes took a quick sweep of the room before he focused on the center of attention.

"Oh, good knight," Sariel said, his voice slithering past her ear. *"Come to save your maiden, or those who gave you life? I shall let you have the choice."* Sariel ran his demon-flesh fingers across Armen's wounded cheek. She shrieked and fought against him, the excruciating burn inescapable.

Terry took in more of the scene, calculating his next move. Armen hoped it wouldn't be a stupid one.

His gaze shifted to Sariel's fire-lit eyes. "How about you let them all go, and I won't send you back to Hell?"

Armen blinked in surprise as Sariel laughed. *Stupid, it is.*

Terry studied him, how he held Armen. "If I banish you, you can't come back."

Armen shook her head subtly as Sariel's haunting laughter filled the room. *"I can come and go as I please, princely knight. But you are more than welcome to attempt it."*

Sean groaned. Terry held the Bible in his bandaged left hand and raised it in front of him.

"I banish thee, Sariel, back to the – "

With a quick jerk of Sariel's head, the book burst into flames. Terry dropped it and slapped his hand against his jeans to extinguish the bandage. He growled and eyed Sariel menacingly, stepping on the burning book to squelch the flames. Sariel snaked his tail across the hardwood and whipped it around, knocking Terry off his feet before Armen's warning could leave her throat. The scepter clunked to the floor and Terry landed on his mother's side of the bed. When he rose, the anguish pouring from his eyes upon realizing his mother no longer lived choked off the oxygen to Armen's lungs.

"Mom," he whispered, reaching out tentatively. He withdrew without touching her. Anger filled his eyes, and he got to his feet and picked up the cylinder.

Sariel laughed again. *"Oh, I so enjoy playing with the humans, Azel,"* he whispered in her ear. *"Tell me you enjoyed it as well."* Armen shook her head. *"Liar."*

"Reversal," Sean mumbled. "Grigori o' the . . . South Tower."

"That is correct, Wrangler, she was once Grigori," Sariel said with a fang-filled grin. *"How sweet, Azel, he knows who you are."*

"He should," she gritted through her clamped jaw.

"Enchantments . . . resolver," Sean whispered.

Sariel gasped with delight. He grabbed her face and turned her to him. *"Is he the one who brought you to flesh, my sweet?"*

Armen closed her eyes. Sean didn't bring her to flesh, per se, but he was the reason she wasn't a demon any longer.

"Oh, he is. What joy!"

Sean shrieked as Sariel whipped him with his tail.

"You shall be punished, Wrangler, for taking my sweet Azel from me."

"Leave them be, Sariel, please," Armen begged, her voice shattered. "He didn't make me flesh. No human has such power."

Terry slowly edged around the corner of the bed, his demon weapon in his right hand, thumb searching the metal shaft furiously as Sariel spoke to her. Sariel didn't notice Terry's presence, or just plain ignored him. If Sariel just wanted to take her, she could allow it, and then kick his ass once they were equally matched on the other side again. She would willingly die to stop Sariel's massacre.

Sariel looked at Armen curiously, a wicked grin stretching across his scale-covered face. *"Do you think if you sacrifice yourself this time, you shall return Home?"*

A tear fell down Armen's right cheek and she shook her head. "It doesn't matter. I can never go Home. *You* know that."

"'Tis nae . . . true." Sean forced the words from his throat.

"That is correct, Azel," Sariel said softly. *"You cannot go Home."*

Armen agreed as Sean shook his head. He struggled with the bindings on his hands. Sariel had done well with the spell, a binding of physical and metaphysical means. It was not rope that held him, but a fleshy creature that constricted every time Sean attempted to loosen it. Armen couldn't recall the creature's name.

"Armen?" The metal in Terry's hands clicked. Twelve-inch blades shot out at both ends. "Tin can, my ass."

"But you can return to me," Sariel told her, his long fingernails hypnotically caressing the side of her face. Another tear made its way down her cheek, and she nodded again as she closed her eyes. *"I have missed you so."*

"Armen, no," Terry growled.

"Armen," Sean said hoarsely. "He still loves you."

She opened her eyes and focused on Sean. "How can He?" Her voice filled with sorrow and she nearly choked. "He told us that we would never obtain peace or return Home."

Sariel chuckled. *"He cannot love a demon, Azel. He has tossed us all aside for the love of these humans."*

"She's not a demon anymore, asshole," Terry said. "He has not tossed anyone aside."

"Be that as it may, we no longer hold the Light," Sariel replied.

"You don't hold the light for reasons other than what she's done," Terry responded. "Let her go!"

Sariel tilted his head and grinned at Terry. *"Why, so you can have her? My sweet Azel; would you take her from me?"*

"A thousand times, yes."

Sariel laughed. *"Here then, take her."* He pushed Armen toward Terry. She stumbled across the floor, toward the blade's sharp point. A gasp, followed by a scream. She grasped Terry's shoulders, her mouth and eyes wide.

Sariel's hideous cackle traveled around the room.

Terry reached around to catch her. He moved his mouth closer to her ear. "I L-word you."

A tear rolled down her cheek. "Terry," she whispered, shaking her head.

He winked at her and kissed her forehead. "You worry too much." He slowly took her to the floor, pulling the scepter away as he did. Once she lay prone, he rose again, fury building in his eyes as he faced Sariel. "You've taken two women I love in one day."

Sariel gave a short nod. *"I think that you, good knight, took that last one, but I shall take credit for the first. If it makes you feel better, she put up a good fight."*

"You bastard," he shouted and lunged at Sariel.

"Son, do nae fight with anger," Sean choked out as Sariel ducked and turned out of Terry's path.

Armen heard Sean's cry of pain again as the creature—*what the hell was its name?*—tightened, its flesh rough against his skin, cutting, tearing it open. His heavy breathing from the struggle reached her ears, a wheezing she couldn't remove from her mind, and she feared for his life.

"Oh yes, son, do fight with anger," Sariel replied, mimicking Sean's voice when Armen heard the blade slice through the air. Sariel's tail whipped above her and lashed back out of sight. *"I have been waiting for this day, to kill two demon wranglers. What pleasure it shall bring my lord."*

Terry attempted another strike, the blade cutting through the air, displacing molecules, yet not quite reaching its target or she would have heard it slice Sariel's flesh. "I'm not a wrangler, demon."

"So you think." The blade hit the hardwood, chopping Sariel's tail in two. The flesh sizzled. Sariel roared. Armen felt a smile trying to stretch her lips, but she was still attempting to play dead.

"Silver. Shit!" Terry's hesitation cost him when Sariel charged. His feet hit the wooden floor hard two feet back from where he'd been, and he lost traction, landing on Armen's cane. He crashed to the floor on the other side of Armen. The blade struck the floor. "Dad!"

She didn't know what to do, what she *could* do to help him, and didn't understand why he wanted her to play dead in the first place.

He grasped the weapon with both hands and tugged, his muscles rippling even beneath the sweater. Sariel took two steps toward him, stepping over her legs.

She tried not to cringe and move away, fear of his cloven feet cracking bone.

Terry pushed himself up on one knee and kicked at the demon. Sariel fell back. Terry dropped back to the floor to free the scepter from the wood, not risking a glance at her.

Gaining his footing, he twirled the blades over his head and crouched low as Sariel advanced, stepping over Armen once again. Terry tried to lure him further, and kicked her cane in what looked to be by accident.

Armen knew better. Terry didn't do anything by accident, and the cane spun toward her. The whip-like crack split the air again and his dad screeched once more.

Sariel stood just out of reach of the blades. Terry lunged forward. Sariel fell back a step, his foot bumping into Armen's leg. When Terry didn't advance, the demon glanced at Armen, seeming perplexed.

She held herself perfectly still, watching him through slit eyes.

"Dad, you still with me?"

"Aye. Tell Him to get this beast out of here."

Sariel turned back to Terry and laughed. *"He shall not help you."*

"We'll see about that." He raised the blades horizontally before him. *"By the power of God, I cast you from this home, demon.* You are *not* welcome here!" The metal glowed white.

Armen grabbed her cane, pulled it apart, and swung its blade at the demon's legs as she sat up.

Sariel screamed and twitched before backhanding her, sending her several feet behind him.

"Now and forevermore, your entrance to this home is blocked."

Armen found herself praying for Terry's safety as she tried to sit up again. She looked up to find Terry barreling down on a shrinking Sariel. The red glow in the room faded. Sariel hissed his discontent in his final moments. She flashed a smile, waiting for Terry to finish. Now she recognized the weapon in his hand, the scepter. It had belonged to her Father.

"The one I taught you, son," Sean said.

"Per solem et lunam et stellas, mare malum miseris ad infernum." Terry bellowed the final part of his chants. Sariel shrieked, cringing into a ball on the floor.

"*Vale, Dæmon,*" he shouted. Sariel disappeared in a cloud of red smoke.

Armen sat frozen, shocked by her sudden epiphany: Terry didn't give goodbyes to the living, but it sure as hell worked wonders on demons.

Chapter Ten

A Time to Grieve

WHEN THE LIGHT FROM THE scepter dimmed, Terry jumped over to Armen, touched her face briefly where Sariel had struck, and moved toward his parents after she gave a nod. He climbed onto the bed and knelt before his father, cutting through the bindings that tied his hands and legs and wrapped around his waist. They slithered away, screeching.

"Dad?"

Sean gave a silent nod. "Your mither." He rubbed his wrists and turned to her.

Terry looked at his mom. "Dad . . . ." A tremor of emotion cracked his voice. He shook his head, indicating his mother's fate.

Sean stared at his wife. "Lucille?" He shook her gently, tears welling in his eyes. "Lucille . . . ." The name came soft as a whisper across his lips and he closed his eyes.

Armen felt completely out of place, as she always had since she became flesh. She didn't belong in this world, and she didn't belong during their time of grieving, either. She turned to leave.

"Armen," Sean said.

She stopped, looking back at him. Terry craned his head around.

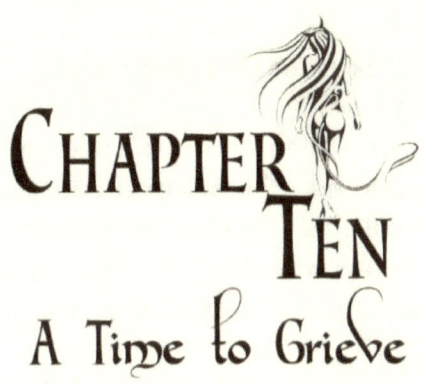

"Yes?"

He cleared his throat. "What ye did . . . before an' now . . . thank you."

Armen nodded silently and turned to leave the two grieving men behind. She stepped into the hall, out of sight but not out of earshot in case something else happened and she was needed. Although, after seeing Terry wield his father's scepter, she realized they might not need her help.

In the short time she'd known Terry, she'd never imagined that the reason the word *goodbye* never passed his lips was because of its power to vanquish. She'd never met a human who held such power.

"Dad," she heard Terry sob. Her heart ached. She'd never once called her Father by such a name. But then, they weren't that close.

"I'm all right, son," his dad replied through his own sobs. "I'm okay, but let's pray for your mither."

"Medical attention, Terry," Armen said from the doorway as gently as possible and turned toward the stairs. While she had once been Grigori, meaning she could pass for human and intermingle with them, she'd always had trouble with emotion. There was something about it she couldn't quite grasp, even now that she was human. She wore their flesh, could feel the emotions, but she didn't understand them and didn't feel comfortable in her own skin. Most people she met thought she was a bitch, and that suited her just fine. She wasn't here to make friends. To be honest, she didn't know what her purpose was—why she had died as a demon and been reborn as a human. Until recently, she hadn't really considered it. She had just accepted this fate as she had the last one.

"Armen," Terry called to her. She stopped and went back to the bedroom. "Could you help me, please?" His voice was torn, and she felt a deep sorrow welling up from depths unknown to her for millennia.

"I was going to bring them up," she replied. "I think it would be best that your father not move just yet."

"She's right, son," Sean said. He looked at Armen with tears in his eyes. "Go get 'em, please." His shirt was soaked with blood at its ragged ends. Luckily, the creature's thorns hadn't gone as deep as Armen knew they could.

"Bring Greg," Terry said, his voice choked with grief.

Armen turned away once more with a nod, recalling seeing a familiar firefighter before entering the home. As fast as she could, she descended the stairwell.

> *Then sware they all together and bound themselves by mutual imprecations upon it. And they were in all two hundred; who descended in the days of Jared on the summit of Mount Hermon, and they called it Mount Hermon, because they had sworn and bound themselves by mutual imprecations upon it.*

"Enoch, you bastard." When she opened the front door, brilliant sunlight shone in and warmed her, making her flesh tingle, quite the contrary to her descent so long ago. She squinted until her eyes adjusted. All who stood outside the house turned their attention to her. Armen never liked being the center of attention. She spotted the firefighter whom Terry had talked with when her condo burnt down.

"Are you Greg?" He nodded. "Terry needs you. His father's badly hurt."

Greg picked up a med box and jogged over to her. "Where are they?"

"Master bedroom," she replied, letting him go by her and into the foyer.

"What about his mom?" Greg asked when they reached the stairwell.

Armen looked up at the burly man and shook her head. He nodded and climbed the steps silently with her.

"Go left at the top of the stairs. It's the last set of doors." Greg jogged up the steps, leaving Armen to climb at a slower pace behind him. Before she could reach the top, the captain walked through the front door with two paramedics. They followed her up, and she pointed the way to the paramedics when they reached her. Brian slowed his pace and walked with her down the hall.

"What happened in there? We heard some pretty horrible things." Brian kept his voice low so it wouldn't travel down the empty hallway.

"Is that why you didn't come in?" There was a hint of satisfaction in her voice.

Brian threw a glare at her, but quickly regained his composure. "It is. Along with the fact that no one else has any damn experience with this shit but the two of you."

Armen kept her head low. "Do you really want to know what happened, Brian?"

"Yes, actually, I do."

She stopped halfway to the bedroom's doors. "A demon, Brian, the same one from last night. It killed Terry's mom. His dad has multiple lacerations, and that's just from the visual I got from several feet away."

"Jesus," was all Brian could manage to say.

"No, Brian," she replied. "The man you call Jesus would not have allowed any of this."

He frowned. The way she spoke was probably part of what bothered him about her. "How'd you two get rid of it?"

"Not me. Terry."

"Terry?"

"Yes."

"Did he kill it?"

"Unfortunately, no. He just sent him away." She wondered why Terry hadn't dispatched Sariel with the scepter. It was made of silver, so it should have been able to destroy him.

"Where?"

"I honestly couldn't tell you." She walked away, toward the bedroom. Brian followed. Greg was already tending to Sean with Terry hovering nearby. She peered around the corner as Brian stepped inside the room. One of the paramedics examined Terry's mom. *Lucille,* Armen reminded herself of her name. *I hope you make it Home safely.* But an unsettling feeling shredded through her.

Terry turned to look back at Armen again, who stared directly at him. She gave him an uncomfortable smile, and he looked down and turned back to his dad.

"Dad, how did this happen? How'd he get in here?"

Armen wondered the same. Certainly, if he had blessed Terry's home, he would have blessed his own.

"The devil has his ways, son."

Armen arched a brow after catching the fine tremor laced in his words. Sean was lying.

"Armen said . . . there's some sort of chess game in play," Terry said. "Something to do with Armageddon?"

Sean agreed with a nod and looked directly at Armen. "But it is nae me they're truly after."

Terry blinked once, twice, three times before he could form a question. "Who are they after?"

"I've sent back hundreds of them over my lifetime, son; I dinnae doubt they want me oot the way. But I believe they want the one who saved me. The one who is the key to their quest." He stared at Armen before suddenly switching his view to his son. "And the one who uses words as weapons."

Terry gave Armen a worried look. "Meaning Armen and me."

His dad slowly nodded and looked up at Terry with tears in his eyes. "I'm sorry, son. I tried to keep you oot of this."

Chapter Eleven

Apocrypha

ARMEN STEPPED UP BEHIND TERRY and peered around him. "Excuse me, sir, where do you keep your sage?"

Sean looked to Terry. "Show her, son. She'll need more than sage."

Terry nodded and stood up from the bed. "It's downstairs. Come on."

Armen followed Terry down the stairs, through the now-bright living room, and around a corner into the family room, which also had a large cross on the wall. Terry opened a set of double doors leading into a room lined with bookshelves and glass cases filled with ancient-looking relics. An old mahogany desk stood in the room's center, piled high with paperwork and other artifacts. One particular item in a glass case caught her eye, and she moved closer to get a better look at it. The piece was Roman.

"Is that what I think it is?"

Terry let out a snort. "No, it's just a replica. The real one is . . . somewhere else." He moved his eyes from the piece to her, and abruptly turned to one of the bookshelves.

Armen looked at him curiously. "You don't trust me with the information, do you?"

"It's not that." He searched the book titles, dragging his finger along the worn spines. "You don't work for the Church."

"Neither do you, and yet you seem to know about it."

Terry reached up and touched the top of one of the many old books. "I'm the man's son, Armen. Of course I know about it."

"Being his son shouldn't make you privy to the knowledge," she replied, crossing her arms. "Just who in the hell is your father? Or perhaps you've proven yourself somewhere along the way."

"Perhaps."

"Is that the Book of Enoch?"

Terry half-smiled. "Yes." He pulled the top of the book toward him.

"Why would a Catholic priest have"—a noise like a bolt coming loose stopped her mid-question—"apocrypha!" She grinned. "Your father is brilliant."

Terry was solemn-faced. "Not so brilliant if he let a demon in his home." The bookcase depressed into the wall and slid to the right, revealing a doorway. He peered into the darkness. "Let there be light." Lights came to life, illuminating their passage down the stairs.

"Seriously?"

"I know, but it works," he replied distantly. "Come on."

She followed him down into a small chamber with two wooden doors. He opened the door to his left and stepped inside, hitting the light switch on the way in.

"Shit, this looks like an apothecary." Dried herbs and powders and oils lined the walls of the room. How could she pass up this amazing opportunity? Humans had their way of creating medicinal salves and whatnot, and Armen had hers.

He went to a counter, pulling open drawers and bringing down jars from the shelf to view their contents.

"Your dad never had a congregation, did he?"

Terry only half-turned his head to her, continuing to inspect the jars. The only answer he gave was silence.

"Did he work at the Vatican?" She stood beside him to see what he was searching through. "Marigold AKA Calendula, yes, I'll need that." She took the jar from his hand and removed a small amount. Terry remained quiet and pulled another jar down. Armen looked over the shelves, searching the names. "Does he have any coconut oil or comfrey oil?"

Terry pointed his thumb over his right shoulder. Armen studied the oils on the shelf behind them.

"Ah yes, there it is." She snatched the coconut oil off the shelf, carrying it back to the counter. "I'll need a bowl."

He slid one across the counter to her.

"Thanks." She poured a measured amount of oil into the bowl. Heating it up would be a problem normally, but since Terry knew she was a damn demon once, all bets were off. "You're awfully quiet."

"I don't have much to say right now." He grabbed another jar from the shelf. "Sage." He handed it to her.

She took the jar. "I understand."

He abruptly turned to her, slamming his hand on the counter. "Do you? Have you ever lost your mother to a demon? Oh, that's right, you don't have a mother and you *were* a demon."

Armen dropped the jar of sage on the counter. It spun a few times before settling. She tried to contain her fury because, after all, he'd just lost his mother. It certainly wasn't a good time to rip him to shreds.

"Have you ever read the book that unlocked the door to this place?"

"Of course." He sneered. "Growing up with Dad, I've had to read everything."

"What happened to the children of the Grigori, Terry?" She kept her voice as even as possible, though her temper flared.

"The Nephilim were slaughtered. They were an abomination, a mix between humans and angels. They were giants."

"Giants." Her voice shook with anger. "My son stood as tall as you, and he was not deformed. He was perfect and yet, they killed him. Gabriel himself pushed his sword through my son's chest while I watched helplessly because they held me back. So yes, I *do* understand. The only difference here is that my son was killed by the word of God—my own *Father*—which in my opinion is far worse than being killed by a demon, having been one and all." She turned back to the bowl. "I did not kill your mother, Terry. Direct your anger elsewhere."

From the corner of her eye, she saw him slump in defeat.

"I'm sorry," he said softly. "I don't know how to deal with this."

"Well, I can't have you arguing with me right now. You didn't kill the bastard." She reached down the counter for the pestle and mortar and pulled them to her. "He'll come back."

"How in God's name am I supposed to kill him?"

"The scepter. Did you not notice what it did when you cut into him?" She grabbed another jar from the shelf and pulled a sprig from it, ripping off the leaves and dropping them into the mortar.

He shrugged. "I figured that was normal."

She vigorously crushed the herbs. Better the herbs than some part of Terry.

"The only time I saw my dad use that thing, it had the same effect, but when he forced the blade into the demon's chest, the demon didn't die."

"You are not your father." She opened a drawer, unable to find what she was looking for. "Spoon?" He pointed one out to her and she grabbed it, and then poured the crushed herbs into the bowl.

"What's that supposed to mean?"

"You're a detective, figure it out." She bit her lower lip. "I'm missing something."

"I'm not a demon wrangler, Armen. I don't know what the hell I'm supposed to be doing."

"Oh, you're no wrangler, that's for sure. Not after what I saw and heard." She turned to the shelf of oils again. "What is it? Damn." She tried hard to recall the recipe. Her book of shadows burned up in the fire.

"What did you see and hear?"

She waved him off and studied the jars. Seeing the beeswax, she reached for it, but still searched the shelves, moving to the powders.

He grunted. "What are you looking for?"

"I don't remember," she said, frustrated and growling softly.

"Well, what are you making?" He reached forward to touch the mixture, and she slapped his hand away. "Hey!"

"The salve I put on your hand? I'm making something similar. I figured since I have access to this wonderful apothecary, I'd make it for your dad, given his wounds." She turned to the shelf behind her again and searched.

"But I thought it wouldn't work on wounds caused by a demon."

"Not all of your dad's wounds were made by that bastard. Most were by that creature, the zeelu." Her eyes brightened. "A-ha! There you are." She snatched the jar from the shelf and opened it. "Wonderful medicinal properties."

"What the hell did you see and hear?"

She crushed the herbs and poured them into the bowl. "The *goodbye* thing. I've always wondered why you never say goodbye to anyone. You just hang up or walk away." She turned the spoon over, stirring the contents together. "I even found it amusing at times that you didn't say it, but I never realized *why* you didn't say it."

"Because it expels," he said flatly.

Her eyes flicked up to meet his. "Do I want to know how you found out?"

"Probably not."

"Tell me anyway." She stirred the mixture, gradually heating the bowl with her hand and then slowly cooling it before heating it again. Its color changed from yellow to green. She continued stirring, waiting for it to change again.

Terry sighed heavily. "I was five."

"Five is awfully young to discover such a gift." She reached for one of the many essential oils on the shelf in front of her, cracked it open, and added a few drops.

"I wouldn't necessarily call it a gift."

"I can't believe those words just came out of a priest's son's mouth."

He traced a circle on the counter with his finger. "Yeah, well, you're not the only one who has issues with Him."

"I suppose." The mixture showed signs of turning blue, the color she needed it to be. Totally not normal when humans made it, giving the salve her signature, so to speak. "So, what happened?"

Terry sighed again. "I said—that word—to my grandfather."

Armen dropped the bowl. "Oh my . . . Terry! It works on humans? Oh, dear!"

Terry picked up the bowl and stirred the mixture, his eyes glistening as he tried to focus, not commenting on the warmth.

Armen pulled the bowl from him and set it on the counter. "Terry." She grasped his arms. He shook away and went for the bowl again. "Terry, stop!"

"No! Give me the damn bowl." He growled.

"Why, so you can force it all inside?" She yanked the bowl away once more and pushed it out of his reach. "Have you ever talked to anyone about this?"

Terry nodded, but stared at the floor. "The priests tried to help me, but there was nothing they could do. They simply didn't know how. Just told me not to say it to anyone ever again."

"Then talk to me," she said softly, her hand caressing his face.

His eyes met hers, a tear rolling down his cheek. "You don't like to talk."

She brushed the tear away. "I'll talk, if you will."

He opened his mouth, but before he could speak, Greg yelled for him. He wiped his eyes and cleared his throat. "Down here."

Greg ran down the stairs and stopped abruptly in the doorway. "Your dad, Terry. He's missing."

"What do you mean he's missing? Did you leave him alone?"

Greg nodded. "He asked to be left alone with your mom for a minute."

"Shit, Greg, all the man needs is a minute. How'd he get out?"

"Balcony," Greg said. "And Terry . . . the scepter's gone too."

Armen grabbed the jar of calendula she'd spotted in her search for other herbs. She stuffed a handful in her pocket. "Where's he going?"

"To find Sariel." He pushed past Greg. "Come on, he can't have gotten far."

"Does he have anything else you can use?" Armen hobbled as quickly as possible up the stairs behind him. Greg followed her, no doubt watching her closely in case she fell.

"I am not running down the street with a damn sword in my hand," Terry shouted from the office and bolted for the kitchen and back door. "Shit!"

Armen and Greg hurried behind him. Armen came to a sudden stop by the desk, forcing Greg to side-step so he wouldn't barrel into her. She picked up a small box of bullets off the desk.

"What are you doing? Come on, he's moving fast."

"Go! I'm coming." She pocketed the box and limped as fast as she could behind him. Right now, she really hated having to use the damn cane, but she was certainly faster with it than without.

"Leza! What the hell is going on?" Captain McNeil. Great.

She stopped. "Do you have your gun on you?"

"Of course I do, why?"

She threw the box at him. "Put these in it and come with me." She burst out the door and headed for the gate along the back fence.

"Would you care to tell me why?" He ran up behind her, turning the box over in his hands.

"They're silver," she said. "Silver will harm a demon."

"You've got to be kidding me." He held the gate open for her.

"I don't kid about shit like this, Brian." She looked down the alley and could see Terry in the distance. "I'm never going to make it down there."

"Come on. We'll take my car."

He dragged her along, back through the yard and house, and out the front door. Brian opened the passenger door, and ran around to the driver's side and hopped in. He started the car and threw it in gear.

"You really shouldn't be running around with a bum leg." He hit the brakes and his horn. "Get the hell out of the way!"

"Don't get me killed, Brian," she said as he drove through the small crowd of firefighters and police officers.

"Shut up, Leza." He stomped on the gas pedal once the road was clear, and turned the corner at the end of the street.

Armen held on for dear life. "Holy hell, you drive like a madman." Terry suddenly came into view in front of them. "Stop the car!"

Brian hit the brakes again and Armen braced herself against the dash. Once the car stopped, she opened the door and jumped out. "I can't believe they gave you a damn license." She limped up to Terry. "Where'd he go?"

"I don't know. I can't find him. Shit." He turned back to the alley. "DAD!" Terry ran down the alley again. He passed Greg, who slid to a stop in the gravel and turned to chase after him.

"Mr. Armstrong," Greg shouted, cupping his hands around his mouth to amplify the sound.

Armen drew in a deep breath and sighed. "All right, I'm doing this my way."

She closed her eyes and took another deep breath, then started walking down the alley. When she opened her eyes again, her vision altered. Everything alive was a brilliant white. She could see Terry and Greg searching, a cat perched on the top of someone's back fence, and Brian when he passed her to join the others. But there were dark spots, as well. Now that they weren't in the house, Terry's incantations couldn't protect them from the shadows within the brightness.

"Oh, this is bad," she mumbled. *The scepter. Focus on the scepter.* She hobbled down the alley toward the others, shadows slinking along the sides, following her. The hair on the back of her neck rose to attention. She stopped to see if the shadows would stop too. They did. Nervous was an understatement for how she felt about it. Sean's theory about the demons' quarry would seem correct.

Chapter Twelve

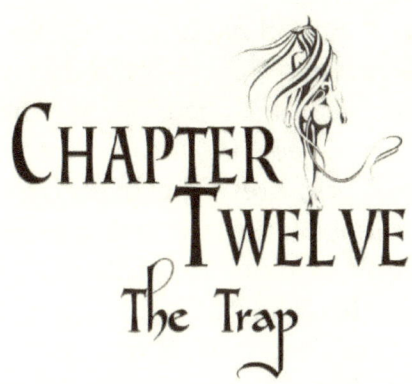

The Trap

A CRY, FAINT AND DISTANT like it came from the depths of Hell, sounded as Armen took two steps forward. A shadow slid along the ground toward her, rising from the rock.

It struck.

Armen sidestepped and swung her cane at the intruding shadow. The cane sailed right through it. She wobbled, attempting to maintain her balance on her good leg. Another shadow rose from the gravel.

"ARMEN!" Terry sprinted toward her.

Greg spun wildly in attempt to see what was happening. Brian took the box of bullets from his pocket and fumbled it open because he never could listen to reason when it came from her.

Armen swung around to her right when Terry drew near. He glided through the rising shadow and took her into his arms. They stumbled, but Terry maintained his balance and lifted Armen off her feet. He turned in a circle and set her down gently.

His eyes smiled at her, wide and sparkling. "Sorry about that."

She touched his arm. "Terry, are you okay?"

"Yeah. Your eyes—"

"Oh, sorry." She blinked and her vision returned to normal. "Are you in die-hard-cop mode yet?"

"Of course." He snatched up her dragon cane with both hands, twisted its head and body opposite directions, and withdrew the blade from inside. "You keep getting into trouble."

Surprise took Armen. "How'd you know it did that?"

He swung the blade at the oncoming materializing demon and sliced it in two. "I'm a detective. I figured it out." He slipped an arm around her waist to support her. "Besides, I just saw you use it upstairs. Hang on unless you want to fall."

She gripped him tightly. "We need to find your dad."

He forced the blade through another demon's stomach as it materialized. "Tell me about it. I have no idea where he may have gone, though." His eyes met hers briefly before skimming the corners and spotting another demon. "What about you? Do you know where he went?"

"I might have an idea."

"Well, spit it out. We don't have all day!"

She hesitated. He cut another demon in two and met her eyes. "He's in the house."

"How? We were just in there." They hurried down the alley to his parent's backyard again.

"There were two doors downstairs," Armen said. "What's the second door for?"

"I don't know. He'd never let me in there." He turned his head to find the other two. "Greg, Brian, back to the house."

Greg trotted up to them. "What for?"

"Armen says Dad's there," Terry replied.

"And the scepter," she added. A shadow slunk up on Terry's right. "Look out!"

Terry swung at the beast, taking its head and shoulder. Its shriek filled the momentary silence on a decibel level the other two men could hear.

"What are you swinging that thing at and what was that noise?" Brian asked from Greg's other side.

Terry threw him a wild look of confusion, and Armen squeezed his arm. "He can't see them, Terry."

"You're kidding. How could he not?" They reached the gate and Terry edged through it sideways with Armen.

"He hasn't been given the knowledge yet. He only sees the after effects when it involves humans, and he apparently heard that shriek."

"Obviously," Terry mumbled and made his way to the back door. He stopped before opening it. "Okay, we need a plan here."

"There is no planning when it comes to *him*."

Terry looked her sternly in the eye. "You are *not* going to try to sacrifice yourself again." When she didn't respond, he squeezed her arm. "I mean it, Armen."

"All right," she said.

"Armen," he said, his tone fatherly, as if He spoke to her.

"I said all right!" Was he kidding? After what'd happened up there, she wasn't about to attempt that again. Damn Sariel and his way with words; she'd almost fallen for it. "Even I'm not immune to his words."

"You'd better mean it," he said, and turned the doorknob. "Otherwise, you can just stay right here with Brian!"

She sneered.

"Me?" Brian said. "Why can't I go in?"

Terry eyed his captain. "Because you can't see a damn thing and that makes you a liability." He pushed the door open and peered inside. "Go around front, Brian, and don't let anyone else in the house." Brian pushed through the door to head to the front of the house, pausing as Terry turned back to Greg. "Tell me what you saw in the alley."

Greg nodded slowly. "I guess that makes me a liability too. I'm going. Be careful." He moved through the kitchen past Brian and headed for the living room.

"Well?" Terry asked Brian.

Brian put the bullets on the island counter. "She says silver bullets will harm them." He nodded in Armen's direction. "You know, just in case."

"Thanks."

Brian leaned close to Terry, his face stern, and voice matching it. "You'd best come back from this shit."

"I'd like that as well, Captain."

Brian gave him a short nod and headed for the front door.

Once the door closed, Terry turned to Armen. "It's just you and me, sweetie."

She shook her head. "Oh, I never should have called you that."

His brow arched. "Honey bear?"

"Shut up."

Terry looked at her more seriously, knowledge of the things he'd seen in his lifetime returning in his eyes, along with his cop sense. "How do I kill him?"

"You need the scepter."

"Push it through his chest, take off his head? What exactly do I need it for?"

"Either of those will work."

Terry slid the cane back together and handed it back to her. "Take this back. You'll need it." When she shook her head, he practically pushed it into her hands. "I'd feel much better if you had a weapon."

She took the cane without another word.

He withdrew his weapon. "Silver, huh?" He pressed the release and slid the magazine out, emptied it, and refilled it with the silver bullets. Once finished, he armed the chamber with a silver round. Then he led her through the kitchen and stopped in front of the office to check the room before entering. Once cleared, they carefully headed inside.

They both stared at the bookcase with its hidden passage. Armen felt the cold seep into her pores. Sariel was definitely nearby.

"After all of this is settled, I'm buying you that little black dress and taking you to dinner, whether or not you like it."

"If we make it through this, I won't argue with you."

He chuckled. "Now that would be a switch, *you* not arguing with *me*."

"Frightening thought, isn't it?"

Terry peered down the small stairwell. The light was out. "Let there be light," he whispered, but nothing happened. "Shit."

Armen suddenly shivered, and Terry looked down at her.

"Well, we know he's here, now don't we, Miss Shiver?"

"What I want to know is how in the hell he got back in the house."

"Yeah, I sent him away, didn't I? And banned him from reentering," Terry said, contemplating the thought. "My dad's been up to something."

"Do you think this was all a trap?"

Terry searched for something to light the stairwell. "I don't know. My mom—" He reached for a candle. "If it was his doing, I doubt he intended to get us involved."

"You can't get any more cliché than walking down a dark stairwell with a damn candle."

"Well, I didn't wear my utility belt with the flashlight." He looked around the shelf. "And of course, I have nothing to light the damn thing with so the point is moot."

"Give me that." She took the candle from his hand and blew a breath across the wick. A flame flickered to life.

Terry blinked twice. "That's interesting."

"Enchantments, hello?" she replied and handed the candle back to him.

"Can you give me the winning Lotto numbers?" He took the first step inside the doorway.

"It doesn't work that way, sorry." She lowered her voice to a whisper. "Shush." She pointed down the stairs, and then put her fingers to her head, mimicking horns, and made an evil face.

Terry stifled his laughter. "You're weird," he mouthed. "But I L-word you anyway."

She wrinkled her nose in a mock growl. "Don't say that." she mouthed in return.

Terry shook his head and walked slowly down the stairs, never more than a step ahead of Armen as he guided her. At the base of the stairs, two wooden doors stood before them. The one to the left led to Sean's apothecary. Neither had a clue where the other led. Armen trembled violently again and clamped her mouth shut to stop her teeth from chattering. Sariel was near. Terry handed her the candle, held his hand up with three fingers, and pointed to the doorknob.

Armen licked her fingers and pinched the wick, extinguishing the flame, then set the candle on the floor by the wall. Her vision altered once more. Terry was searching in the darkness for her. She took his free hand and guided it to the doorknob, then tapped his hand three times.

Terry opened the door.

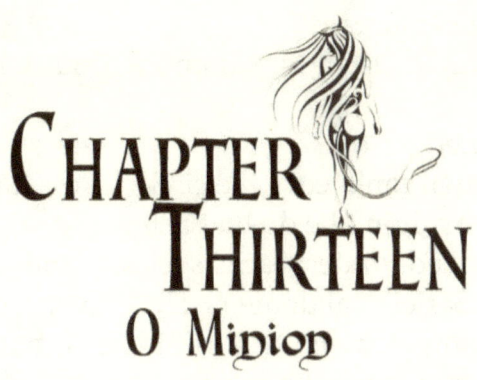

Chapter Thirteen
O Minion

RED SMOKE FILTERED THROUGH A space already filled with grunting, feet scraping in calculated steps across the stone floor, a blade slicing through the air, and a soft demonic cackle. A draft from above pushed past them and through the door, clearing the smoke. Sean and Sariel were locked in battle in the center of a large stone room.

"What the hell?" Terry glanced around the room, awestruck.

Neither entity acknowledged them.

Terry seemed more stunned by the revelation of a hidden dungeon beneath his parents' home than he was by finding his father battling a demon.

Armen thought it looked like something that belonged in the bowels of an old castle rather than in the basement of a fine old Arcadia home. Not enthralled by the room's ominous feel, she pushed past Terry to study the scene.

"Your dad has him trapped in the circle," she whispered.

Terry moved quietly next to her and leaned over. "What circle?"

She pointed out several lines drawn on the stone floor. "*That* circle."

"That's a pentagram."

"It's a circle used to summon. Could be a smart move."

He frowned. "How?"

"The demon can't leave the circle unless it is opened."

"Then why didn't he do that before?"

Sean ducked under Sariel's claws and twirled the blade into Sariel's abdomen. The silver cut into the demon, hissing as it slid across his flesh, but it was not enough to bring down the beast.

"Maybe he didn't have time before." She winced when Sariel knocked Sean to the floor. Terry took another step forward and she stopped him. "No. You can't break the circle."

Sean jumped to his feet and held the scepter before him.

"I am not burying two parents today!"

His shouts caught the demon's interest, as well as his father's.

"Terry, ya eeejit, gettae," Sean said sternly, his deep Scottish dialect decimating the English language.

Sariel's deep laughter echoed through the room, and Armen froze.

"Come to play again, my sweet?" Sariel walked to the edge of the circle, keeping a close eye on Sean. He tested the circle's edge with his hand. His fingertips sizzled, sending sparks flying, and he swiftly retracted them. *"Not fair, Wrangler. Come now, play nice."* He sliced through the air with his hand when he turned, and Sean ducked and rolled to the other side of the circle.

"As if *you* would ever play nice," Armen said.

Sariel thrashed the severed end of his tail at the edge, sending flickering flames and sparks across an invisible wall of protection.

Armen shivered uncontrollably.

He peered over his shoulder and grinned. *"Come, my sweet, I shall warm you again."*

"Only in death," she replied.

"Of course," Sariel purred. *"Something I thought I had achieved with you earlier."* He grinned, showing several pointy teeth. *"Well done."*

She withheld the urge to react to the rare compliment.

Sean lunged forward, attempting to stab Sariel in the chest, but the demon moved out of the way.

"Stay back, son!" He swung the blade around, catching Sariel on the arm. Once again, the demon's flesh sizzled when the silver sliced into him. The deep cut didn't slow him, however.

"Sean, I do wish you'd come out of there," Armen pleaded, worried. She knew what Sariel was capable of.

"Dad, listen to her. Please."

Sean continued his attack. Sariel suddenly shifted, taking on his more human form, and stood before them in his black suit.

"Tsk, tsk, Wrangler, you should not have summoned me into your home." Sariel walked the edge of the circle, his sizzling fingertips trailing along the invisible wall, leaving red sparks behind him. His long black hair caught on a breeze not felt by Armen. *"I have more power here now that I have taken your wife."* He leaned forward with the last word and hissed at Sean, eyes ablaze and forked tongue snaking its way out.

Sean roared at him and lunged forward, certainly not heeding the advice he'd given his son upstairs.

A chilling breeze wrapped around Armen. It meant only one thing. "Sean, get out! You need to leave the circle!"

Terry grabbed her arm. "How do you open the circle?"

Armen looked at him like he was crazy. "You can't, Terry."

"Bullshit."

"Sariel will get out."

"If I don't open it, my father will die." Sorrow swept his eyes. "Please, Armen."

She shook her head. "I can't . . . ." He pulled her up to face him directly. "It won't matter anyway."

"What are you talking about?" But then his eyes shifted; he noticed the shadows moving along the walls. "Shit. What the hell is that?"

"His minions. What do you think chief of tens means? It sure as hell doesn't mean TEN demons. We're in big trouble here, Terry."

He watched the shadows slithering toward the circle where Sean and Sariel still battled. "Are they going to open it?"

Armen nodded.

"Do we need to stop it?" Everything about his voice said he didn't like that option.

"Not if you want your dad out of there alive."

"And then we'll have more than Sariel to fight, right?"

She nodded again. "This may only be a few. If the circle opens, it could be thousands."

"Shit." Terry raised his gun.

"Wait until they're flesh," she said, hoping he'd listen. "The silver can't harm them when they're just shades."

He sighed heavily. "Oh man, do we need to have that long talk."

"Kill Sariel and we can have it." She turned the head of her cane and withdrew its sword. "Oh, and you can't kill *him* with the bullets. It has to be the scepter."

"Of course it does."

They watched the shadows carefully, waiting for the first one to turn flesh.

"Don't miss," she added. "I don't want to get hit with a ricocheting bullet."

"I don't miss, Armen. Watch our backs." One of the shadows snaked its way over to the circle and began to materialize. He fired when the demon completed the transition. It screeched and fell to the ground, writhing on the floor. Its flesh bubbled and seeped with fluids before it exploded. He turned his face away. "Well, that's disgusting."

"Tell me about it," Armen said. "It gets worse."

"How could it possibly—" He aimed and fired a round into the next one that materialized. "Jesus."

A chorus of hisses rose above the clamor of Sean and Sariel fighting.

Armen threw a hand in the air. "Oh fucking hell, why don't you just *shout* His name if you want to attract their attention?"

Terry looked bewildered. "What'd I say?"

"Hell, Terry, it may be common for you to use, but it's a Divine name!"

"What, Jes—"

"DON'T SAY IT AGAIN!" She slashed at the demon materializing before her. "Fuck! Now they know we're here!"

"Sorry."

"Shut up and shoot," she yelled over the echoing screams. A swarm descended upon them. "You're not going to have enough bullets for this so make them count. Hit the big ones first."

Armen swung her blade down upon a demon. Terry fired his weapon at the largest ones. The echo of the gunshot reverberated in her ears, and she was certain she would be deaf after this. Déjà vu of the dark, creepy warehouse basement took hold. Armen ran her blade through the minions that were certainly *not* small, yellow, and cute, taking a head from one, cutting another in two at the waist, and bayonetting a third. Some recognized her and hesitated, making them easier to kill. She relished in it. *Oh, to be fighting again!* She'd forgotten the feel of it. But it was different now as adrenaline pumped through the veins of her human body.

The gunshots stopped with a click of the hammer.

"I'm out," Terry yelled and ducked when a demon swiped at him with its claw. "Armen!"

Only a few to go. "Duck!" She turned on the heel of her good leg and brought the silver blade over Terry's head, taking off the head of the demon about to attack him. "Reload."

Terry fumbled for the box he'd stuffed in his pocket and scooped up a handful of bullets. He released the magazine and quickly popped the bullets in as Armen fought off demon after demon surrounding them. He punched the magazine back into place, pulled the slide back, and released it.

"I'm good," he said and aimed at a rather large beast approaching him. He fired once, twice, three times before it fell to the floor shrieking in agony.

Armen cut through the last minion and froze when the chilled wind swept through the room. Sean screamed, and when she spun around, she saw him fly through the air and land about twenty feet away. The circle had been breached. The scepter rolled to the wall. Neither moved.

"Terry," she whispered.

He slowly stood, trembling, his father's motionless body too far away to be able to check him.

"Get the scepter," she said softly.

Terry raised his gun, ignoring her. Armen turned her head, closing her eyes.

A giggle unbefitting a human drifted toward them on the pungent air. Armen opened her eyes; Sariel approached slowly, a red glow surrounding his human form.

"Azel, tell your knight his little silver bullets shall not work on me." He cleared the edge of the circle and continued on. *"And that he does not have enough to destroy my legions."*

Armen tugged on Terry's arm. "He's right. He has tens of thousands more. You need to get the scepter. I'm not quick enough right now."

Terry still ignored her and kept his aim on Sariel.

"Emotion is such a curious aspect of the human species," Sariel continued, still walking forward at a leisurely pace. *"I must say that after all of these years, it still intrigues me. Would you not agree, Azel?"*

"Personally, I never understood it," she replied, hoping to distract him. Terry stood perfectly still. She'd had enough of being ignored and whacked him on the back. "TERRY!"

A shot fired and hit Sariel in the chest. The demon only laughed. He placed a finger where the bullet entered. *"A remarkable sensation."* He reached inside his chest with his thumb and forefinger to retrieve the bullet, pulled it out, and held it up to view the slug closely. Smoke rose from his fingertips, the silver scorching his flesh.

"The scepter," Armen whispered to Terry and pushed him. He stumbled a couple of steps and turned his head to her. She growled at him.

The giggle sounded again. *"Oh, do not anger my sweet Azel, good knight."* Sariel still inspected the bullet he held between his fingers. *"She does tend to bite, but then, that was always one of her endearing qualities."*

"At least I don't claw and scratch."

Sariel dropped his head back in a laugh. *"But you most certainly enjoyed it, Azel."*

Terry frowned. "What's he talking about?"

"Now is not the time, Terry." She tipped her head toward the scepter.

"Have you figured out what she likes yet, good knight? She is a tricky one."

Terry growled. "No, I think it is," he said sternly as he turned back to Armen.

Sariel laughed. *"It would seem I am not the only beast in the room."*

"Can it, freak-show," Terry shouted and pointed the Glock at him again.

Sariel's mouth popped open in mock surprise, and he held his hands up as if to show he held no tricks up his sleeves, no hidden cards.

Armen knew better.

She drew in a deep breath to compose herself before she lost control. "Terry, do what we need to do and we can talk about *everything* later," she said surprisingly calm. The day's events were catching up to him; his face twitched.

Armen took a step forward. "Terry, sweetie," she cooed, capturing his attention. He turned his head in her direction again. "Do what you need to do. Get the scepter and do it. Focus, Terry."

"Dad," he whispered.

Sariel stood with his hands still in the air. Armen wondered just what in the hell he was up to. His eyes shifted to meet hers.

"Azel, my love, when will you stop this madness and come home?" His voice was filled with flawless devotion. A hint of a smirk curved his lips.

Armen quirked a brow at him. "You're a bastard, you know that? While you're spouting false professions of love, Sariel, why don't you explain exactly how I was pulled away from your side and changed to flesh?"

"I would know no such thing, my sweet," he replied, his fangs appearing between his separating lips.

Armen growled and balled her left hand into a fist. "I hate you!" She raised the cane's blade and threw it at him. It sailed end over end toward Sariel, who only laughed as it approached. At the last second, he jerked his head to the right and the blade whistled past his ear.

"Hate is all I have ever expected of you, my sweet Azel," he replied. *"As we are the Fallen and do not have the ability to truly love any longer."*

Armen pounded her fist against her chest. "*I* have the ability to love," she shouted. "HE made *me* that way."

"Yes, so He did," Sariel replied. *"It is what makes you so special, my sweet."*

She frowned, confused. "What are you talking about?"

He covered his mouth with his hand, as though he'd given away a secret. That incessant laughter of his annoyed her to no end. *"Your compassion has never faltered, Azel."*

"What are you up to?" She placed her left hand on her hip. "Terry, get the damn scepter already."

Terry was already halfway there. He grunted and snatched the scepter from the floor, thumbing the button, forcing the blades out, and after checking his dad, he took a few steps toward Sariel. His upper lip curled and he glared at the demon in human form while clutching the scepter tightly in his right hand.

Terry's face held sheer anger and determination to kill the angel of death.

"Stay away from her," Terry growled, and walked toward the demon.

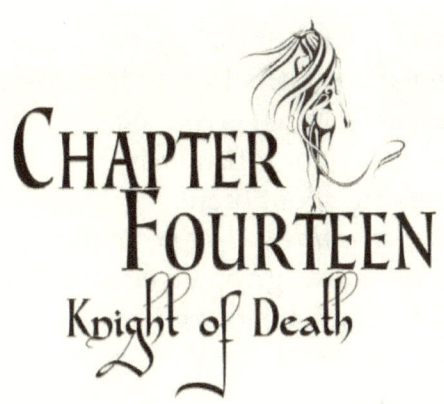

Chapter Fourteen

Knight of Death

Armen had never before heard Terry sound so . . . pissed. If she hadn't thrown part of her cane at Sariel, she'd have been able to move toward him. She leaned on the sheath but it bit into her palm. Sariel twirled toward her like a tornado. She stumbled away from him and would have fallen to the floor if not for Sariel's arms encircling her from behind.

"And what shall you do if I do not stay away from her, Wrangler?" Sariel pressed his face against Armen's cheek. His tongue slithered out and he licked her.

Armen jerked her head. "Stop that!" She fought to free herself, but he held her too tightly.

"Come now, Azel, the wrangler wishes to play knight," he said. *"Let us give him the opportunity."*

"I told you I'm not a damn wrangler." Terry studied Sariel's moves and how he held onto Armen.

"Oh?" Sariel laughed. *"What was that display outside your home, then?"*

"He's just a homicide detective," Armen said.

"Shush, love, the gentlemen are speaking," Sariel replied to her.

Armen growled and struggled again to get out of his grasp. Sariel easily held her in place.

"What display?"

"Your power with words." Sariel pressed his head against Armen's. She leaned away from him as far as she could, which wasn't much given the tight quarters.

Terry held the scepter firmly in his grasp. "Not sure what you're talking about there."

"The effect your words had on me in front of your home, as well as upstairs." Sariel gripped Armen tighter than she thought possible and she gasped for a breath. She knew better than to let Sariel know it hurt. He would only make it hurt more.

Terry scowled at the demon as though he could see her pain. "Let her go."

"Come, come, say that word once more."

"No," Terry replied.

"Is it because I hold her, and she would dissipate as well?"

Terry shook his head.

"Then say it. You claim to not be a wrangler, yet you stand before me, willing to fight me, and hold a wrangler's weapon in your hand. What is it, pray tell, that stops you from the command of words?"

Terry let out a chuckle. "You're stalling." He paced to the side, twirling the scepter in his hand and keeping the demon within sight. "Tell me something, demon. What is it that you fear?"

Sariel jerked against Armen. *"Fear?"*

"Yes, what do you fear?" Terry repeated.

The demon laughed. *"I fear nothing, good knight. That question would be better suited for a human."*

Terry paced in the opposite direction, still twirling the scepter. "Ah, yes it would, under normal circumstances. But our situation isn't normal, is it?"

Sariel's lips moved closer to Armen's ear. *"A bright one you have found, Azel."* His breath floated across her flesh.

"Don't be so hasty to judge." She wasn't about to tell him that Terry was one of the more intelligent men she'd encountered during her time on Earth. She made a futile effort to free herself, needing to get to her pocket, but Sariel had her arms pinned at her sides, and he stood as still as a statue and was just about as heavy as one.

"Judgment is not my calling, Azel. Or have you forgotten such things with your feeble human mind?"

Terry continued to pace. He slowly made his way in a circle, forcing Sariel to move with Armen. "I think you fear something all men fear."

"And what would that be?"

Terry stopped and looked at him, his grin spreading. "Death."

The demon laughed loudly, making Armen wince. *"Death? Have you forgotten what I am, knight? There is no death for me!"*

"What about non-existence? Does that play into your pathetic little rules?"

His boldness shocked Armen. Was he *crazy*?

"Non-existence, hmm," he said softly. *"I do not believe it possible."*

Armen knew better. After all, angels and demons could die. No one knew what happened after that, though, much like how some humans felt about their afterlife.

Terry moved again, twirling the scepter a few times. "So, you're saying that if I were to force this blade into your chest—"

"Nothing would happen." Sariel flicked a glance at Sean. *"Your father has already attempted so."*

"Ah, yes, but I am not my father." Terry stepped forward.

Sariel snaked an arm around her neck, the other hand sliding down to grip her left arm. Her right hand was now free. And Sariel smelled like fear.

"And I am no wrangler, demon." Terry took another step forward and to the right.

"So you claim. What exactly would you be, then?"

Terry shrugged. "Don't know, really, other than human. What would you be exactly?"

"I AM THE LORD'S ANGEL OF DEATH!" The red glow surrounding him intensified. He thrust out his arm in a display of power.

"Not *my* Lord's."

Sariel hissed at him. A ball of fire engulfed his hand. *"Your Lord is nothing compared to mine!"*

His grip loosened. Armen whirled around and threw crumbled calendula into his face. She broke free of him and fell to the stone floor. Sariel shrieked, as the herb burned his face. Armen crawled away from him and Terry lunged forward with the scepter. He plunged the blade into Sariel's chest, and the demon screamed, his human guise bubbling and melting away. The red scales beneath it burned. Sariel roared in agony as Terry thrust the blade deeper and trapped him against the wall.

"Angels are pawns, demon. Knights outrank you."

Armen dragged herself across the floor to Sean, who stirred into consciousness, and made a mental note to ask Terry just how in the world he knew a knight outranked an angel. Because they did, with exception of the archangels.

"Sean, are you okay?" She stopped him when he attempted to sit up. "Don't. Just sit still for a bit."

"I'm fine, Armen." He pushed himself upright and leaned against the wall next to her. "My head sure hurts like the dickens, though."

"I can see where Terry gets his stubbornness. I hope he can hold on. That's not going to be pretty."

Sariel's human flesh was now gone, leaving only the demon's red scales, but even those were disintegrating now.

Terry wrenched the blade to the side. Sariel's scream became lost in a gurgle as his throat opened. "I believe you wanted me to say a certain word, Sariel, but I don't want to do so because I'd rather you leave existence altogether." The fire disappeared from Sariel's eyes. "Something you didn't think was possible, remember?"

"I suggest you step back noo, son," Sean shouted after Armen nudged him.

Terry pushed the scepter down, the other blade pointing to his feet. "Welcome to non-existence, demon." He shoved the blade up, forcing it through Sariel's head from inside his chest, then yanked it out and jumped back several steps.

Sariel's head whipped back and forth rapidly as his body shrank. If he had been able to scream, it would have been loud, ear-piercing. Armen thanked her Father that she didn't have to suffer his cries. She paused a moment, realizing that she had prayed earlier for Terry's mom, and for Terry's safety—the first time she'd prayed in millennia. She redirected her attention to what was left of the demon before the revelation could become too forthright in her mind. Fiery embers moved like a brush fire over his body as he writhed in agony, destroying his flesh and bone, and soon he was nothing but a pile of ash.

"Amen," Sean said with a breath of relief.

"Yeah," Armen whispered and looked up as Terry walked over to them.

He crouched in front of them and placed the scepter on the floor. "Are you two okay?"

"We'll live," Armen said, and Sean agreed with a nod. "And you?"

"Good as can be. Dad, you need to close this place off." Terry craned his head around to look for something. He headed across the room.

Sean pushed himself up. "Aye, will do." He started toward the altar hidden behind the glow of a torch. Terry leaned over to pick up part of Armen's cane. Sean stopped when Terry grabbed his arm. "Well done, son. I'm very proud of you."

"We have to talk," Terry said, his voice monotone.

"We will." Sean continued on his way.

Terry picked up the other part of Armen's cane, slid the two pieces together, and walked over to her. He held out his hand and when she took it, pulled her to her feet.

"Don't be too hard on him," she whispered. "You don't know what happened."

"We're not going to have that discussion right now."

She lowered her head. "We'll have to at some point."

He lifted her chin with his fingers and leaned forward, resting his cheek against hers. "I thought I'd lost you for a moment there. When he had you in his arms, I didn't know if I could save you again."

She cupped his cheek. "I'm fine, Terry. It's not like the last time."

He slipped his arms around her waist and pulled her to him, nuzzling his face into her neck. "Tell me it's over."

"I can tell you that I hope it's over."

He pulled back and looked at her. "I thought you had an answer for everything."

"I said 'usually'."

Sean's chanting floated to her ears—some ancient rite of closure. The murmurs bounced off the stone in an echo, surrounding them in ancient Latin. Before long, she heard the sounds of straw brushing the floor. She turned to look. Sean was sweeping up Sariel's ashes. When she looked back at Terry, she could see the question in his eyes.

"He needs to do that. It will help cleanse the home."

Terry closed his eyes briefly before focusing on her again. He moved his lips closer to her ear. "What was his name?"

"Whose?"

"Your son's." He looked her in the eye once more.

She paused, staring into his deep green eyes, and her breath hitched before she could speak the name that hadn't passed her lips in an eternity. "Ezerah," she finally answered, blinking back tears.

Terry nodded and held her tightly. "I'm sorry you lost your son. He'll be in my prayers."

Armen swallowed the lump in her throat as grief, an emotion she hadn't felt in millennia, engulfed her. She opened her mouth to say something, anything, to him, but her voice failed her. Terry held onto her, and her eyes swam with tears. She fought hard to push it back, but it became a losing battle.

"It's okay, Armen," Terry whispered, his own grief rising from the depths with the tremor in his voice. He held Armen close as she wept for her son who had died so many years ago. A soft cry left her lips and soon, she became limp in his arms. "It's okay." He held her up. The side of his neck and part of his sweater were wet with her tears, and his own tears marked a trail down his cheeks.

"Come on, you two," Sean said and gently placed a hand on Terry's shoulder. "We need to get upstairs noo."

Terry nodded and pulled his head away from Armen's shoulder and neck. Armen wiped her cheeks as Terry set her on her feet. He held her steady until she had the cane ready, and then moved to her good side and took her hand. They climbed the stairs together, behind his father, and walked to the front door of the house, where Brian, Greg and several others were waiting outside.

Armen had never felt more wrecked in all her lives.

CHAPTER FIFTEEN

Dismal Days

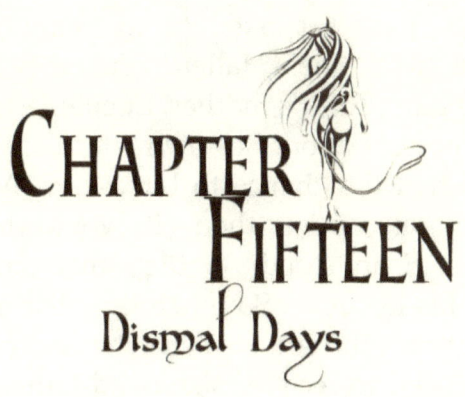

ALWAYS A PREREQUISITE FOR A funeral, clouds loomed overhead. If it were summertime, the sun would be shining and Armen would be dying of heat stroke in the black get-up she wore. Sometimes, the sun burned more during the winter months, but the Arizona weather was fickle. One day it'd be in the 60s, and the next it would soar near the 80s. She tugged on her collar to let some air in at the mere thought of the heat, though it was only 68 degrees. Warmth, however, was a blissful reminder of Sariel's absence, though a sorrowful one for the reason she stood in a cemetery. The demon had bound her to him when he pulled her from the Darkness so long ago. As a result, she would feel cold when in his presence unless he touched her. It was a great internal warning that he was near. Now she would never feel his presence again. She was about ninety-nine percent certain she'd not miss a moment of his pathetic existence, but that lingering one percent missed the warmth of his touch, which she knew was batshit insane.

Terry stood next to her in his black suit with his head hung low, eyes red and puffy. He stared at the hole in the ground where the coffin hung suspended. They had already attended the service. If she never had to attend another of those, it'd be too soon. All the praying to someone she hadn't spoken to in years was a keen reminder of why she'd fallen, and they now stood graveside to bury Terry's mother, Lucille.

Armen thought about her own son, Ezerah, and how she'd never had the chance to bury him. Well, burying wasn't really an option then—it would have been a funeral pyre. Sean stood on the other side of Terry, sobbing for his lost love. So much time had passed since Armen had taken the son of man who had helped create Ezerah. She tried to recall if she loved him—really, truly loved him—but she was powerless to bring the memory forward. She struggled to recall even his name.

She supposed that answered her question.

Another prayer, and Terry closed his eyes and murmured with the crowd. He held tightly onto Armen's hand and squeezed every so often. It pained her to see him like this because she now understood losing someone dear to the heart. The feeling had been buried so long. While she'd never met Lucille, she stood at Terry's side for support, and it helped her deal with her own loss. Terry had brought the memory and grief out of her in those final moments in the altar room under his parents' house. He still hadn't spoken to his father about the whole episode, and she wondered if he ever would, or if he would just suppress the anger she could feel emanating from him. Terry's situation was not all that dissimilar from her own situation with her Father.

"Amen," he said softly and squeezed her hand once more.

Armen returned the squeeze.

The casket lowered into the ground. Once it rested at the bottom, a man walked over to Sean and Terry, handing each of them a white rose—Lucille's favorite—and then stood before Armen with a rose held out to her. She stared at him until Terry nudged her with his elbow.

"Take the rose, Armen," he whispered and held up the one in his hand.

"Oh, sorry," she said and took the flower. The man moved on after blessing her. She wrinkled her nose. The right corner of Terry's mouth turned up just enough for her to see he caught her reaction to the blessing. It wasn't that she didn't accept the blessing. She knew the childishness of her actions, but couldn't let go of the past. Not yet.

Sean stood in front of the grave, murmuring under his breath, before tossing the rose inside. Then Terry walked to the edge, whispered just loud enough for Armen to hear him, and he dropped the rose in the grave. Armen was next.

She walked to the edge of the grave and closed her eyes, holding the rose to her breast. *With this rose of purity, Lucille, I show you the Light you have yet to find.* In her mind, a beautiful woman stood before her, hand stretching toward the rose. Armen held the rose over the grave. Lucille's fingers wrapped around the stem, but Armen didn't let go. *Tell my son I love him.* Lucille nodded once, looked at Terry, and then returned her gaze to Armen. She dropped the rose onto the coffin and opened her tear-filled eyes, then shuffled off to stand beside Terry and his father.

Terry's hand went to her shoulder and he leaned forward. "Are you okay?"

Armen looked up at him, and he wiped a tear from her cheek. "Your mother is a very beautiful woman."

"Yes, she was."

"And she loves you."

A smile graced his lips as tears welled in his eyes again, and he pulled her into a hug. "Thank you."

"You're welcome." His suit muffled her voice as it enveloped her face, but she held onto him firmly, not wanting to let go. As people filed alongside Lucille's grave and tossed roses in, they made their way to Terry and Sean, forcing Armen to remove herself from Terry's arms and stand at his side again.

A rather large man with striking similarities to both of the men at her side made his way over to them. He embraced Sean, whispered a few things in his ear. Sean nodded and wiped his eyes. Then he turned to Terry.

"Your mither," he said, his deep Scottish brogue stronger than Sean's. "She was a guid woman, son." Terry nodded and the man's eyes settled on Armen. "And who's this lovely young lass?"

"This is Armen, Uncle Seamus," Terry replied, placing an arm around her shoulders.

Armen held out her hand. "Nice to meet you."

Seamus brushed her hand to the side. "I'll nae shake your hand when my nephew has his arm around you like that. C'mere." He wrapped his burly Terry-like arms around her in a tight hug. "Welcome to the family."

Armen choked on her words and attempted to play it off as laughter. "Thank you." She didn't know what else to say to him.

A long line formed behind Seamus, and Terry touched his arm. "Do you think you could take Armen away from this, please? I don't think she's up for it."

"Aye," Seamus replied, took Armen's hand, and placed it on his arm. "Come, lass, let's wander over here and see how many spirits we can disturb, shall we?"

The laugh forced its way out, and Seamus led her away from the crowd. She quickly covered her mouth.

"Noo, noo, lass, there's no need to be ashamed of a little laughter," Seamus said. "I'm a right funny man anyway."

She chuckled as he led her to a stone bench and offered her a seat before sitting next to her.

"Noo, Armen, tell me what you do fer a living, besides making my nephew a very happy man."

Armen looked up at him. "How in the world can you see that right now?"

Seamus' thin lips parted, baring age-worn and coffee-stained teeth. "I can see the sparkle in his eye when he says your name, deary. Come, come, what do you do?"

"I'm a medical examiner," she replied and waited for the jokes to begin, but thought they would be inappropriate, given the setting.

"Ah, you play with dead people. Nice," he said with a grin. "Ever had anyone come back to life on you?"

"Um, no," she replied, and gave a small laugh at the crack he'd made. "They're quite cold when they get to me." She held up a finger. "Although, in the field, it's a bit touch and go with that."

Seamus' loud laughter had a few people turning their heads. "A sense of humor, I love it. You'll do well in this family."

"Um, yeah," she said softly and looked away.

Seamus shifted on the bench, turning more toward her. "Are ye nae dating my nephew?"

Armen looked at her hands. "Well, we haven't really been on a date yet, sir. We just work together a lot."

"I never would've guessed it from the way he looks at you."

"Yeah, I know," she said with a sigh and looked over to Terry, who had person after person hugging him.

"You look at him the same way, y'know, but there's something a bit different about it. Like you think you don't deserve him."

She shifted her gaze to Seamus. "Is it that obvious?"

He shook his head. "I'm a bit keen on those things. Besides, Terry has mentioned you."

"He has?" She was shocked, though she shouldn't be. She'd known about Terry's feelings for some time.

"Of course, you're a braw lass. Why wouldn't he mention you?"

"I'm sorry, braw?" Armen had heard a lot of terms in her lifetime, but that one wasn't familiar.

"Guid," Seamus replied with a wink. "Ye met on the job?"

Armen gave a short nod. "It was a while back. Well, technically he saw me two months before we ever conversed."

"Ah, well, Terry can be a bit shy. Can't blame the man after what happened with the last woman he cared about."

"Last woman?" She never heard him mention a girlfriend or wife. "What happened?"

"If ye dinnae know already, I'll nae tell you. Terry'd have my hide for divulging such information before he has the chance to."

Armen had the distinct impression that it was something really bad, considering the grim look on Seamus' face, no matter how brief. "That's fine. I can wait a pretty damn long time."

"You must have the patience of a Saint, then," he said. "Because it'll take a pretty damn long time before he'll tell you."

She cringed. "Hardly."

He chuckled softly. "Your name, Armen, it sounds familiar. Might I ask where your mither came up with such a name?"

She stiffened and cleared her throat. "I don't have a mother."

"Oh, I'm sorry, deary," he said. "Forgive me."

"It's okay. It happens a lot."

"'Course it does. Anyone who's had both parents in the mix is bound to assume at some point in their life that everyone else has the same thing. It was rude and I apologize."

"You already apologized. It's fine." She now felt incredibly uncomfortable. Armen didn't care to discuss her parent, which was where that conversation always went to next.

"What about your father?"

Yep, there it is. "Oh, He disowned me."

"What in God's name for?" Shock morphed his face. "From what I can tell, you're a wonderful young lass."

She chuckled. "It's a really long story. But thank you." She was quite certain he knew a good portion of the story, considering he was Sean's brother and if he was any sort of a religious man.

Armen watched Terry walk toward her and Seamus. The suit he wore hid his bulk well, making him look like a sleeper—a person others misjudge in their ability to defend themselves. And boy, could Terry ever defend himself.

He helped Armen to her feet and brushed his hand across her cheek. "Has my uncle been keeping you entertained?"

"Oh yes, he's a right funny man."

Seamus laughed as he stood. "I like her, boy."

"Yes, he can be." He looked down at her legs. "Still doing okay down there?"

She no longer needed the cane, telling her the injury wasn't as serious as she'd thought. "It's not hurting as much."

"Good." He looked to Seamus.

"We'll be heading back to the house noo." Seamus turned and walked off.

"Right behind you." Terry led Armen to the car slowly. His father was ahead of them and climbed into the limousine in front of his Lincoln. He helped her into the car and they had to wait a few minutes for everyone to get into their vehicles. Seamus and his wife climbed into the limo with Sean.

Terry slid his hand over hers. "Did you see her?"

Armen only nodded once, her throat closing with emotion as the image of Lucille appeared in her mind.

"Was that all she said, that she loved me?"

She met his eyes. "She didn't speak, Terry. She couldn't."

He frowned. "Why not?"

"The dead can't speak." She stared out the Lincoln's front window. "At least, not to me."

He turned his entire body toward her. "Then how do you know she said that?"

Armen sighed. "I told her to tell my son that I love him. She nodded and looked at you and then back to me. It was understood."

Terry looked down at their hands. "Did she look...happy?"

"She's happy now." She covered his hand with hers. "I directed her toward the Light."

Terry quickly raised his eyes to hers. "She wasn't in the light before?"

Armen shook her head. "She hadn't found it yet."

"Really? How?"

Armen's heart threatened to choke off her air flow as it leapt into her throat, and she pushed back the tears and swallowed to clear her airway. "It only happens when one experiences that type of death."

"What do you mean?"

How can he not understand this? "Terry, Sariel.... Look, I don't know what happened, how he killed her exactly, but whatever he did, he trapped her." She studied his expression, determining how much she should tell him, but decided to just tell him the end because in the short time she'd been flesh, she'd learned that humans couldn't handle hearing the details of a loved one's death and afterlife. That they couldn't deal with hearing the truth. "I released her."

Terry opened and shut his mouth a few times. Realization dawned of the torture Lucille had endured and eventually succumbed to. "Oh my God."

Giving in to a demon's torture, especially one of Sariel's standing, bending to his will, was comparable to submitting yourself before the Morning Star. It explained why his father reacted the way he had, why he went after the demon on his own, even though he never would have been able to destroy him. Sean Armstrong, the ex-priest now demon wrangler, would have sacrificed his own soul to save his wife's.

And Sariel knew it would happen.

Armen understood that quite well. In a way, she'd done the very same thing for Sean a few years ago.

Chapter Sixteen

On Faith

THE DRIVE TO THE HOUSE remained quiet aside from the rumble of the Lincoln's engine. Terry didn't even turn on the radio. Armen sat still and stared out the window, leaving her hands to fidget. She had a good pull on a long black thread in the side seam of her skirt when Terry said her name and she nearly jumped out of her skin.

Concern washed over his face. "Are you all right? You seem a bit jumpy."

Armen looked down at her fidgeting hands and flattened them against her legs. "I'm fine. You just caught me off guard, that's all."

"Looks a hell of a lot more like something's got you on edge."

She turned to face him. "I'm. Fine. Terry."

"Oh-kay." A long silent pause filled the air while Terry tapped his fingers against the steering wheel to a tune only he could hear. "Thank you for helping my mom." He looked back to the road for the umpteenth time, but Armen could tell he didn't believe for a second that she was *fine*.

"You're welcome," she replied softly.

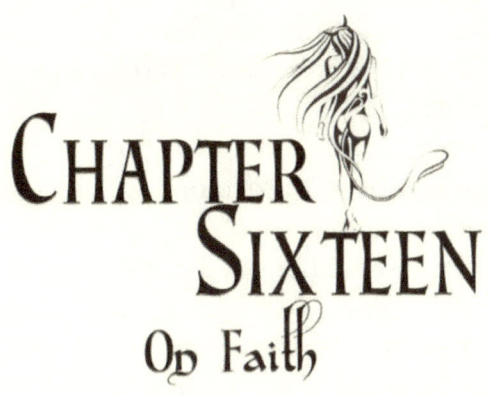

"Knowing that you released her from her fate means more to me than you'll ever know, more than I can express in words."

"I was only doing what was right." She turned to gaze out the window once more. "She doesn't deserve their tortures."

Again, Terry was silent as he followed the limousine to his parents' home. He had voiced that he didn't like the idea of having anyone at the house just yet. They'd barely cleaned *and* cleansed the home.

Armen turned her head in his direction again, her eyes studying his face once more. He seemed to age over the last few days, lines creasing around his eyes and mouth, the strain evident. Neither of them had slept much, and the dark circles under Terry's eyes showed it. She was pretty damn certain she looked like shit too, and didn't bother to check the visor for a vanity mirror. She doubted there was one in this classic beast.

"You need a good rest." She turned back to the landscape.

"We both do, I think." His reply was soft, gentle. "Maybe tonight."

Armen nodded silently. "Maybe."

"I don't know if I want to leave my father in that house. What if . . . something happens?"

"Sariel's gone, Terry." She shifted her head and eyes to his face again. "You took care of that."

"But what if another one comes?"

"Sariel was the cause of everything. All should be quiet now." *For a while*. Exactly how long that while would be, she didn't know. Demon time was much different than human time. Shorter, yet longer. Longer, yet shorter. It all depended on which level one was standing in and with whom they were dealing. Sariel tended to make things last as long as possible, but worked quickly to get a jump on whatever torture he had planned.

After a few miles, he spoke again. "Did you love him?"

Armen damn near snapped her neck, and certainly cracked a vertebra or two, she turned her head so fast. *"Who?"*

"Sariel?" He tightened his grip on the steering wheel, veins popping up on the skin, knuckles bulging and turning white.

"You can't be serious." Her anger surfaced at the edge, her blood boiling just beneath the layers of her skin. She couldn't believe Terry had fallen for Sariel's ploy. She wanted Sariel back just so she could shove that damn scepter through him herself.

"I *am* serious. The things he said—"

"Demons lie, Terry." She bit back the anger so she wouldn't scream at him, or slap him upside the head. "You of all people should know that."

"Okay, how about the things you said back to him?" His right cheek twitched, telling her that he also withheld his anger as much as he could. "Am I supposed to accept *demons lie* for that, too?"

Armen sat in mouth-agape silence as Terry pulled into the driveway. She blinked a few times. Closed her mouth. Opened it again.

"This is why I *never* tell anyone what I once was, you fucking bastard."

As soon as the car stopped, she was out faster than Terry could put the car in Park. She slammed her door. Terry jumped out yelling. Sean was already at the door, and Armen bolted for him, even though she probably shouldn't be running. However, she was quicker now that she'd rid herself of that damn cane.

"Answer me, Armen," Terry demanded, jogging up the walkway to the front door.

She was already inside with Sean. "No! I am not answering such a ridiculous question." She ran through the kitchen.

"Damn it, Armen," Terry shouted, but his father stopped him in the kitchen. "Dad, move!"

"What in the devil are you two goin' on about? She nearly tackled me to get inside."

Terry stood before him, attempting to look around the corner. "I see you."

Armen flipped him off and ducked out of his line of sight. She opened Sean's office doors and closed them behind her most of the way. She wanted to listen in case Terry got past his dad.

"Terrance!"

"It's nothing, Dad."

"Well, if it's nothin', drop it. Guests'll be arriving soon and I'll nae have you running about your mither's house swearing at the top of your lungs!"

"Pa—"

"If ye cannae discuss it calmly, you'll chase her away." Sean peered into the kitchen, catching sight of Armen in the doorway of his office. "Which you've nearly done with whatever you've said to her."

"He called me a *demon,*" Armen shouted from the study. Emotions bubbled up inside her, wanting out in a bad way, and she damned Terry for bringing them to the surface again after she had closed them off for so long.

Sean slapped him upside the head. "What'd ye go and do that fer?"

"I didn't call her a demon."

"Bullshit," Armen shouted. Their voices were more distant now, as she moved toward the bookshelf.

"Son, God's given her a second chance. It is nae fair of you to throw in her face what she once was."

"She loved him, Dad. Sariel said—"

"I heard that demon's tall tales. What you fail to understand here is that one, demons lie to get their way, and Sariel got his way by enraging you through your jealousy. And two, what happened between them was in a time long before you and me, and long before she became flesh, before she *sacrificed* herself for me. You were wrought with emotion at the time, so I dinnae expect you to pick up on the voice patterns of demons in such an instance, but you'd best learn how to keep emotion at bay when dealing with 'em. Armen, from what I can tell, cares for ye a great deal, and she played the game so you could destroy him. Who are you to judge her when He has already passed His judgment?"

"Shit," Terry said.

"Watch your mouth," Sean replied, and Armen heard the light slap of a hand against skin. "Armstrong men dinnae act like wee boys. Noo, go talk to her, like a man."

"Crap," Armen said and pulled back on the book of Enoch. The bolts moved and the shelf slid to the side, exposing the surprisingly non-drafty stairwell. "Let there be light."

She ran down the stairs and opened one of the doors.

His footsteps hit the stairs loudly and his shadow darkened the space beneath the door. She turned toward the counter before he opened it. He found her sitting on a stool in front of the counter where they had been three days prior, where she'd started to make her healing salve for his father. She rested her head on her crossed arms on the countertop, attempting to ignore him, but Terry always had such a strong presence. It may even be reason for her attraction to him. If she didn't know better, she'd swear he had divine lineage.

He gradually made his way to the counter and stood next to her. He reached for a jar and pulled it down from the shelf, then sat it in front of her. The glass clinked against the tile, and Armen raised her head to look at it.

~ *Calendula* ~

She pushed herself up and turned away from him.

Terry sighed softly. "Personally, I thought it was brilliant. I never would have thought to throw *that* in his face."

Armen swiveled on the stool, turning her back completely to him, and stared at the doorway.

"Look, I'm sorry. I'm an idiot." He laid his right hand on her shoulder, but she shrugged it off. "I deserve that. I deserve much more than that." He moved to the side and held up his bandage-free left hand. "Look, your salve completely healed my hand. You can't even tell it was shredded four days ago."

Armen sat perfectly still and silent.

Terry closed his eyes and took a deep breath. "Armen, please say something to me. Anything. Yell at me, if you need to. I don't care. Just talk to me. You said you would talk to me."

Armen hopped off the stool and turned around to face him, arms crossed. She steadily drew in a deep breath. "The trouble with humans is you don't appreciate the reflection of silence. You *have* to fill it with needless chatter." Terry blinked rapidly. "Yes, I said I would talk if you would, but the problem is, Terry, *that* wasn't talking, *that* was accusing, *that* was assuming you know everything about me and my past, which, might I remind you, is *in* the past. There's a reason they call it the *past*."

Terry stared at her. "I didn't call you a demon."

"No? You asked me if *demons lie* was appropriate for what I said to him." She wagged a finger at him. "*That* is calling me a demon. For fuck's sake, I was an angel once."

"Christ, Armen, that isn't what I meant," he replied, his voice just above normal speaking tones. "I mean, I didn't mean for it to sound that way . . . Oh, to hell with it. You're pissed at me and you have every damn right to be. I'm an ass, okay?"

"You're an ass, all right. And I told you not to use His name in conjunction with mine."

"Jesus Armen Christ!"

She crossed her arms over her chest again. "Oh, now you're being juvenile."

"Am I? Really? I'm not the one who has an issue with His name being used with mine."

Armen growled and glared at him. "See, I knew this would happen." She waved a finger, pointing at Terry and then at herself.

"You knew *what* would happen?"

"This . . . what we're doing, arguing because you threw my past in my face." She motioned with her hand again. "*This* is why I didn't want to get close to anyone, Terry. *This* is why I didn't want to tell you about myself. I told you I didn't want a relationship. You just had to kiss me, didn't you?" She balled her hands into fists and hit her thighs to stop the tears from coming. If there was one thing in the world Armen hated, it was being vulnerable, and boy, had she opened herself up for that one.

He lurched forward, grabbed her by the arms, and pulled her close. "*This* is what a relationship is, regardless of whether or not it's a friendship, Armen. You can't hide for the rest of your life from the entire world. *This* is a part of life."

"Well, I don't like it!" She tried to free herself from his grasp. "Let go!"

"No." He tightened his grip. "I am not going to let you run and hide from this."

"Who says I'll run and hide?" She raised her tear-filled eyes to him. "And you can't dictate my life. He gave me free will, too."

Terry just shook his head. "I'm not trying to dictate your life, but for a Grigori, I'd think you'd know more about human nature than you seem to show."

Armen lowered her head and the well of tears fell. "I was a bit different than the others, besides being the only female."

Terry moved his hand to her face to wipe the tears from her cheek. "That was mourning hundreds or thousands of years old that came out in the room next door, wasn't it?"

She nodded, but kept her head low.

"My God, Armen, why couldn't you mourn for your only son before that?"

She slowly raised her tear-filled eyes to his. "I didn't have time, nor did I have closure like you had today." She nearly choked on the words. "They cast me into the Darkness before I could blink. You call it Hell. Well, you don't cry in Hell. You don't *feel* in Hell. It feeds off you if you do, and it drains you down to nothing, until you're just another poor soul, trapped there for eternity without hope until the End. That's how they keep you—barely a shade without hope." The last lines fell into a whisper and she lowered her head once more.

Terry sighed. "Then what you did for my mother . . . . Shit, Armen." He pulled her to his chest and held her in his arms tightly. "You and I have a unique relationship in that we tend to like to argue with each other, and it works for us. I love that you argue with me. I love your stubbornness. I love it when you giggle, and that I am one of the few people who can make you do so. I love your strength. And I love that you're an intelligent, beautiful woman who can dissect anything and kick a demon's ass all at once."

She laughed.

He ran his right hand up her arm and to the back of her neck. "I made a mistake. I'm sorry. Really, truly sorry. I'm only human." He ran his left hand up to her shoulder. "You have eons ahead of me, Armen. You're not as likely to make those mistakes."

"That's not true. I haven't been human all that long. And you weren't something that I can use against you."

"I promise you I will never use that again." He leaned forward. "He played me like a jealous boyfriend, and I fell for it. I'm not happy that I fell for it."

"Neither am I," she said softly.

"I know." He pressed his cheek against hers.

"You really need to learn how to distinguish their tones."

"I know," he repeated next to her ear. "My father said the same thing."

She pulled back to look him in the eye. "And you need to trust me, more than you say you do."

He nodded, then lowered his head and looked into her eyes. "Will those deep blue eyes forgive me?"

"How can I forgive you? I'm no angel. Not anymore." She lowered her gaze and stared at the stone floor.

Terry slipped his fingers beneath her chin and raised her head. "You've always been an angel to me." He slid his hand to the back of her neck once more and pulled her into a kiss. Then he rested his forehead against hers. "I love you, Armen. I know you don't want to hear it, but I *do* love you. I have for some time now."

Armen threw her arms around his shoulders, knocking him back and onto the stool behind him. The motion took him completely by surprise. He wrapped one arm around her waist to catch her and the other hand shot out to grab the counter to stop them from falling off the stool. His lips brushed against hers, and it was all she needed. She returned his kiss fiercely, biting his lower lip. He ran his hands up and down her back, traveling into her golden hair, back down to cup her ass, and he pulled her onto his lap.

Sean's voice traveled down the stairwell from the study: "Everything all right down there?"

Terry jerked his head away from Armen and cleared his throat. "Fine, Dad." He looked at Armen. "Damn, I feel like a teenager."

She laughed and moved forward to kiss him again, but he stopped her. "Not a good idea right now. House full of guests."

Armen pouted, and he chuckled.

"No, really, it's not."

"One more kiss?"

Before long, he had to push her away again.

"My, aren't you the little devil," he said and froze. "I didn't mean—"

She threw her head back with a laugh. "It's okay, Terry. I'll accept that."

He breathed a sigh of relief. "Lucky me. Come on, we need to get upstairs."

She slid off his lap and stood waiting for him, trying to figure out what happened and why she felt so damn happy. Had she really spent so much time in the void that she couldn't even recall what emotions were like? Apparently so. In Gehenna, they learned to turn off emotion, or wither into nothing as Hell sucked away their souls.

And that was all before Samyaza had Sariel pull her from the Darkness and gave her demon flesh.

When Terry got to his feet, he leaned over and gave her a peck on the cheek, took her hand, and they headed for the stairs.

"So, will I get to see that lovely little hidden tattoo of yours anytime soon?"

She lifted her shoulder and flashed a smile as she stepped through the doorway. "Maybe, if you're a good boy."

He let her go up the stairs first and slapped her ass at the top of the stairs. "I thought women liked bad boys."

She hopped into the study with a burst of laughter and abruptly turned. "Good boys can be bad when they want to."

He looked at her curiously. "Oh, got it."

"I wonder about you sometimes." When she reached the doors to the study, she heard the chatter and laughter of people coming from the two front rooms as she checked her face in the mirror. She turned to him. "Why are they so cheerful?"

He slipped his arm around her waist and pulled her close. "They're celebrating my mom and the life she lived."

Armen smiled faintly. "That's what they're supposed to do." Her eyes welled with tears.

Terry reached up to wipe a tear from her cheek and he nodded. "It's what she would have wanted."

She looked up at him, into his green eyes. "Terry, I'm so sorry about your mom. I wish I could have changed it."

Terry shook his head. "Don't. It's not your fault."

She knew he spoke the truth. "Come on, I think there are more people who want to welcome me into your family."

He laughed.

She led him through the kitchen, and Sean appeared in the entry before they reached it. He eyed them both.

"Everything all worked oot?" He headed for the counter with an empty tray. They both confirmed all was well, and Sean smiled as he set the tray down. "Guid. Noo, allow me to properly thank the lovely lady before you parade her off to the rest of the clan."

Armen chuckled and held out her hand.

Sean shooed her hand away and pulled her into a hug. "Thank you again. It's wonderful to have finally met you." Armen could only nod and smile when he stepped back, holding her hands in his. His eyes met Terry's. "Your mither would have loved her." Sean leaned forward. "She thanks ye too, for saving me, by the way."

Armen nodded once more. She wondered if Sean could hear his wife's voice, since she knew he could hear His.

"And for saving her, too," he added, his eyes focusing intently on Armen's.

Well, that answered that question. "You *can* hear her."

Sean gave her a big smile. "It's ma gift. Noo, go on, Terry. Take her to the rest of them."

Terry took her hand and tugged, but she pulled him back. "Wait," she said to Sean. "You said that He still loves me. Is that true?"

Sean's smile widened. "Of course it's true, dear. When does a father ever stop loving his child?" Sean took her hand again and patted it gently. "We'll discuss it when we dinnae have a house full of folk."

"Come on, Armen." Terry tugged on her arm again. "Let's join the crowd."

She let Terry lead her out of the kitchen, her mind going a million miles a second at the revelation that He still loved her—her Father. She supposed it wasn't so far-fetched. But why flesh? Was she on the path to salvation? Was this life her chance at redeeming herself, her soul? Perhaps she was here to work out her issues with Him, to prove her faith in Him. But her faith was different from a normal human's faith. Much like Sean, who heard His voice, she didn't have to rely on mere faith to know He existed. Armen had been in His presence, had bowed before Him and stood next to Him. She had once been in the Kingdom of Heaven and knew its glories before coming to Earth to watch over man.

What am I missing?

Terry led her around and introduced her to everyone, where Uncle Seamus greeted her with another big bear hug. She squeaked before he set her on her feet again. Armen met almost the entire Armstrong clan, and for the first time in her life of being flesh, she felt the warmth that radiated from their laughter and closeness as they held one another and reminisced about Lucille. When she looked up at Terry, he smiled and didn't look quite so aged any longer. He looked down at her, still smiling, and brushed his fingers gently across her cheek, and then he leaned over and kissed her temple.

At last, Armen didn't feel quite so alone in her flesh.

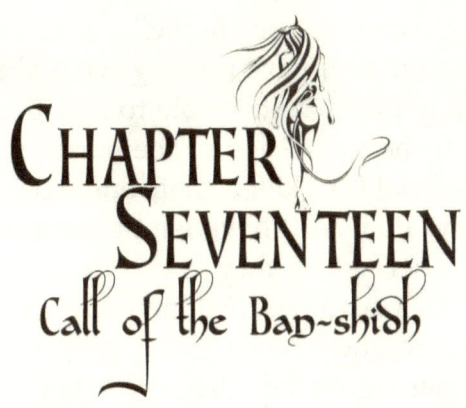

Chapter Seventeen

Call of the Ban-shidh

THE AFTER-WAKE LASTED UNTIL MID-EVENING with a tipsy Sean hugging everybody at least five times apiece until his brother finally got him to sit down. They'd had an actual wake prior to the funeral. Armen wasn't sure what this one was other than a party to remember her. Seamus and his wife planned to spend the rest of the week with Sean; they'd arrived a day before the funeral to help around the house, which made for a very grateful Terry and Armen because of the leftover mess. Demons were a messy bunch—all that damn ash; it was a wonder they didn't sneeze their heads off or choke on the dust. Sean had swept it into a pile, but hadn't disposed of it before they left the room.

Then there was all the blood in the master bedroom. Armen wouldn't let either of the men near the room until she collected what she considered useless evidence—orders from the captain—and cleaned the room herself. Who Brian thought he was going to convict with the evidence, she didn't know. But Brian couldn't handle anything outside of routine, which was another reason he didn't like her, so she didn't ask questions.

She was nervous about being in Terry's house alone with him after the funeral. Despite what happened earlier, and the fact that she now felt like she was a part of something, Terry scared the hell out of her. The idea that a man could love her knowing what she used to be was completely incomprehensible to her. Ezerah's father hadn't known she was Grigori. The horrified look on his face when Gabriel had killed their only son was enough to tell her how he would have felt about it. He wouldn't even look at her when they took her away; he'd just turned his back. Customary, but no less hurtful.

When Armen and Terry arrived at his house late that evening, Armen retreated directly to her room, telling Terry she was exhausted from the whole day and she was going to try to get some sleep. Terry only nodded when she looked briefly in his direction. She shut the bedroom door, undressed, and crawled into bed. Not long after, she discovered she truly was exhausted and fell asleep. At least she wasn't lying to Terry when she said it, and she turned over on her side, pulling the covers up to her ear because she could hear Terry rummaging around in his room.

Armen felt pressure against her body and she struggled to wake up, stuck between worlds, still dreaming. *Not again.* She opened her eyes in her dream realm to find a woman sitting on top of her, pale blue skin, hair stringy and black, and eyes as dark as an eclipsed sun with fire around the edges of the solid black iris.

"Banshi. Get off me."

Her dark blue lips curled up in a sadistic grin at Armen's recognition. She leaned forward, hovering over Armen's face.

"Sweet Azel," she whispered and drew in a breath.

Armen turned her face away from the demon's mouth and struggled to push her off. Banshi held fast, having the upper hand on fighting in this realm. Fighting in another plane of existence was completely different from physical reality.

She tried to push her off again, but she just didn't have the strength. Why did she feel so weak?

The demon pressed her cheek against Armen's. *"Come, my sweet Azel, do not struggle."*

"Get off me," Armen shouted and kept pushing. She had no power other than to turn her head to keep her mouth away from Banshi's.

The demon giggled. *"I do love this realm of the human mind."* Her lips moved against Armen's flesh, and she flicked out her tongue and drew a line up Armen's cheek. *"If they only knew its vulnerabilities."*

"Banshi, I'm warning you." Armen's impatience and anger grew. She'd had about enough of it all. Someday, she'd like to get a full night's uninterrupted sleep. Before the demons, her nightmares were of the life she had lived before her flesh. They were of things too gruesome to tell any human. Things that would make Terry turn tail and run, even as strong of mind and body as he was.

Imagining how nice it would be to see the demon fly off the bed, Armen worked her right arm loose and hit Banshi upside the head. The demon tumbled off the bed and hit the floor. Armen scrambled from the bed and stood to face the rising demon bitch who had invaded her dreams.

"Holy shit." She looked at her open hand, closed it, opened it again. *Okay, visualizing is the key. I can do this.*

"So you choose to oppose me, do you?" She pushed herself off the floor and glared at Armen from the other side of the bed, a twinkle in her eye at the thought.

Armen knew she rarely got a fight and relished in it when one presented itself. *"I have already made the call, my sweet. You are mine now."*

Terry. Given his Scottish lineage, he was sure to know what the call from the ban-shidh meant: Death had come. Armen looked at her indignantly and placed her hands on her hips. "You're not even the real ban-shidh and had no right to make that call. You are not taking me, not tonight."

Banshi stepped around the bed. *"Oh, yes I am."*

"Well, Sariel already tried and he's now dead . . . or no longer exists. Give it your best shot."

Banshi's tattered dress flowed behind her and wrapped tightly around her body, holes showing the flesh beneath. The dress was a shade or two lighter than her skin, making her look like the frozen dead wrapped in gauze. Her hand shot out, torn and tattered rags from her sleeves whipping through the air furiously and wrapping themselves around Armen's right arm in a tight embrace. Armen fought against them and they tightened, but then she twisted her arm around the cloth and yanked Banshi forward. When the demon fell into her, Armen threw a left upper cut. Banshi flailed backwards, landing hard with a loud thud. The house shook as though an earthquake hit. Armen stood, wearing only her underwear and a white tank she'd gotten from Terry, ready for the demon with her fists in front of her.

Banshi slowly pushed herself up from the floor and wiped her lip. Blue liquid smeared down her jaw and she scowled at Armen.

"A blue-blood, I see," Armen said. "I've killed many of you." She lowered her head, but her eyes remained on the demon. "It was fun."

"Perhaps so, but you were not flesh then."

"In case you forgot, this is a dream, which means I'm not flesh right now."

"True, but what happens to your body here will happen on the other side as well." Banshi lurched forward, grabbed Armen by the shoulders, and threw her to the floor too fast for Armen to react. Once on her back, Armen threw her legs up and kicked a charging Banshi in the stomach, sending her reeling into the wall. Her strength surprised not only the demon-wannabe-fairy woman, but Armen as well.

Banshi peeled herself from the wall, leaving a gaping hole behind. Armen got to her feet. The demon walked across the bed and dropped down to the floor. She crouched low, her head down, not moving at all. That worried Armen.

Banshi let out an exasperated sigh. *"You are making this difficult, Azel."*

"Tough shit," Armen replied and took a few steps back to make room.

"You shall pay for the trouble you are causing me."

"Bring it, bitch."

Banshi screamed.

Armen slapped her hands over her ears. The sound coming from the bitch's throat seeped between Armen's fingers to reach her eardrums. Armen dropped to her knees, shrieking in agony.

The demon rushed Armen once more, her hands stretched out to wrap scrawny blue fingers around Armen's neck and squeeze the life force out of her, to take her soul because a succubus she definitely was. Armen twisted to the side and fell to the floor, throwing Banshi off and breaking the demon's grip around her neck. She rolled away and hopped to her feet. Banshi hit the wall and started to turn around. Armen jumped forward, picked her up, and threw her to the other side of the room. Banshi hit the wall screaming, legs and arms flailing, before dropping to the floor in a heap of blue tatters.

Armen dropped to her knees again, covering her ears. Once the screaming stopped, she pulled her hands away and saw blood on them. She pushed herself up. She had to find a way to kill this bitch before she lost her hearing.

Hands touched her shoulders and she spun around in a circle. No one was there. Then she heard Banshi moving and groaning. Good, she'd hurt her. Armen quickly looked around the room for a weapon, but couldn't find anything that would destroy her. *Father, please, my cane, the scepter, ANYTHING.*

Banshi rose to her feet, hissing and seething.

A faint cry called her name. Hands once again applied pressure to her shoulders. *Terry.* The pressure grew and her flesh warmed in that area, as though he stood in front of her. It worried her because if she were to attack Banshi, she didn't know if she would hurt Terry, who seemed to be trying to wake her up. She brought her arms up in a motion to remove his hands from her by knocking them away, but the pressure remained. *Good.*

"Not yet," she shouted, hoping he could hear her.

She jumped toward the oncoming demon, held her arm out, and took a step to the side, catching Banshi at the neck and dropping her to the floor. Banshi yelled and vaulted to her feet, turning in a swirl of motion that created a whirlwind in the room for a brief moment. Armen grabbed the bedpost so the force of the wind wouldn't knock her off her feet.

"Weapon, please," Armen shouted and dodged the demon once more by ducking and turning to the side. She hoped Terry would understand her request. It was the only way.

"Can you bring it out?" Armen heard faintly. She frowned. How in the world was she supposed to do that?

"You little bitch," Banshi screamed when she turned around to face her.

Armen smirked when an idea came to her, and she summoned Banshi forward. "Come on, Sister, what about that pain you promised me?"

"Oh, you shall have it, Sister." Banshi lunged forward, feet leaving the floor as she flew at her.

Armen raised her hands, and the moment she felt Banshi's flesh against hers, she twisted to her right, pulling herself from the dream and Banshi along with her. Banshi soared through the air and rolled along the floor until she hit the wall in the spare bedroom of Terry's home.

"Holy shit!" Terry jumped forward with the scepter in his hand. He plunged the blade into Banshi's chest before she could get to her feet. She tried to shriek, but the scream was lost in her throat.

"You always were careless, Banshi," Armen said.

Terry held Banshi down and forced the scepter's blade in until she heard demon bone crack. The fire around her irises died, leaving only black to fill the void. The blue demon blinked a final time.

"Now I know how to fight in that realm." Armen tilted her head and ran her fingertips down the side of Banshi's face. "Too bad you can't tell the others." Armen stood up again and stepped back.

Embers rushed over Banshi's flesh, burning everything away.

Terry jumped back to watch her fade to ash, and turned to Armen and smiled. "Nice job."

"Thanks, you too."

He pulled her in tight against his bare chest, the scepter still in his right hand. His arm tightened around her until she could barely inhale. When she gasped for breath, he lightened his grip on her.

With eyes still closed and an arm embracing her, he finally spoke. "It seems I'm always asking you if you're okay."

Armen nodded into his chest and shoulder. "Yeah, fine." She didn't want to move from this comfort. Terry dropped the scepter to the bed and he wrapped the other arm around her waist. The form-fitting tank reached her hips. After the last wake-up call from a demon, she'd learned to wear something minimal to bed. It had nothing to do with modesty and everything to do with vulnerability.

"So, who's Banshi?" He moved his head just enough to kiss her temple. "You mean the actual ban-shidh?"

"Nah. Demon pretending to be one."

"Didn't expect her to look like that."

"She's a mean little bitch."

He chuckled. "Armen?" He gently combed through her hair.

"Hmm?" She was enjoying the warmth of his body against hers.

"I like your tattoo."

Armen's tattoo rested on her right hipbone, just below the rise of her hips: a Celtic trinity knot about the size of a silver dollar that looked exactly like the one he wore around his neck.

Armen opened her eyes and found him grinning from ear to ear. She looked down at herself. "How did you see it?"

"You moved a lot, but not really. It was weird." He chuckled again.

"So much for not moving while you sleep," she said, and then looked up at him with concern. "Did I hurt you?"

Terry shook his head. "You didn't really move all that much until the end, right before you brought her out. Kind of freaked me out at first. It wasn't like the last time."

"No, Banshi's tactics are . . . were different."

"So . . . bring it, bitch." He did a terrible job of hiding the grin as the corner of his mouth twitched. "Really?"

She laughed. "You heard that, huh?"

"I did." His hand drifted up and down her back, and he tilted his head toward hers. "I'm just glad you're okay."

Armen stared into his eyes with a smile. "Me, too." She wanted so badly for him to kiss her in that moment, to do more than that.

He lightly brushed a hand against her cheek. "I love you, Armen." He pulled her into his arms again. "When I heard the call . . . it scared the hell out of me. I haven't heard that call in ages. She's usually a bit more peaceful, though."

"Again, that wasn't the ban-shidh you know. I'm just happy you could hear me, *and* understand me."

"Me, too," he said right as his cell phone rang distantly from his bedroom. He sighed and took off after it.

Armen looked at the time. Technically, if they hadn't taken time off, she and Terry were on duty, as it was only five in the morning. *Yep, another night of interrupted sleep.* She walked out of the bedroom and into the hall. Her hours were completely out of whack now. It would be hell trying to get back into her routine again . . . assuming they lived through the hell that had only just begun. She never thought she'd see the day the War fell to Earth. Never thought it possible, it had been going on so long. And she certainly never thought she'd be flesh when it happened. Armen figured, given her human form, that her odds of survival might be in the low percentage range.

Extremely low.

A fair number of them, angel and demon alike, would want a piece of her.

Chapter Eighteen
The Book

HOT WATER SPLASHED AGAINST HER skin, little droplets forming and running down various directions. The heat felt wonderful and she stood under the hot stream for what seemed an eternity before she heard a knock on the door, distracting her aimless thoughts.

"What?" she yelled over the running water.

"I have to run out for a bit. Do you need anything?"

If only he could see the devilish grin that question produced when she thought about telling him to pick up feminine products. "Blended coffee, mocha, please," she answered after the long pause.

"Thank God," she heard him say, knowing full well he'd had the same thought she did. It was just uncanny how their thoughts linked. "I'll be back soon."

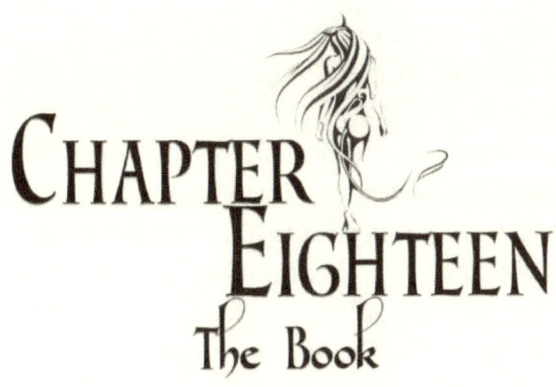

Armen didn't respond. She didn't need to. It was kind of like how he never said goodbye to anyone, with the exception of demons, of course. The habit had grown on her over the past couple of years. Hell, Terry had grown on her over the time she'd known him, much as she didn't want to admit it. She thought about all the times he helped her, took care of her, saved her from the wrath of the captain, and most importantly, the night he saved her life. That was a brutally fucked up night with what was thought to be a corpse, but ended up being a real nasty fellow who was damn good at playing dead before he put a knife in her multiple times. She ran her fingertips over the scars on her stomach and left side. She'd only been on the job for a few months, and had only known Terry for a short time when it happened. She'd heard that he sat all night in the hospital waiting to hear news about her. When they'd moved her into a room, he sat by her side for two days. Two. Days. She woke up to find him there one morning, sound asleep in the chair, and later on when Terry left to get something to eat, one of the other officers told her how long he'd been there.

She heard his voice in another memory. *Please don't make me say that word,* he'd whispered to her. *I can't say that word to you, Armen. I don't want to have to. You have to pull through this.*

Armen gasped and covered her mouth. "Oh my . . . ." Her mind raced through her memories, covering every moment of her stay in the hospital. They were vague to say the least. She abruptly turned off the water and stepped out of the shower, pulled on the robe, and left the bathroom. She stood in the hallway for some time, looking from her room to Terry's bedroom to the living room. Armen stood frozen with those words in her mind. He wouldn't have said 'goodbye' to her, would he? What if there was another word? Suddenly, she moved into the living room and headed right for his bookshelf, not certain for the reason but following instinct.

She scanned the spines of numerous books on law enforcement before discovering the section on religion. Interestingly enough, Terry had every book from each religion on the shelf, except the Book of Enoch. He even had a satanic bible on the shelf: a well-studied man is a well-prepared man, and his father likely had the same books. She passed over the Book of Mormon, paused briefly at the King James Version of the Bible, and stopped altogether on the Qur'an as her fingers pressed against the spine, so many memories attached to it. She vividly recalled the time in which it was written. Then she moved on, passing several others by, pausing briefly on a few from alternative religions and lesser known or welcome beliefs, before her fingers rested on a book she didn't recognize—one with nothing printed or written on the spine. She studied the aged leather and pulled it from the shelf after her fingertips tingled from touching it. This book held something powerful within its pages.

"What are *you*?" She stood up, flipping through the pages, and walked over to the sofa to sit down, curling her legs beneath her. Armen wasn't sure what she searched for exactly, but had a feeling something was about to reveal itself within the pages of this ancient tome. Even she hadn't possessed this one in her collection that burned up in the fire, and she'd owned some pretty rare books. Her Goya leered from the corner of the room as she fervently turned page after page, scanning each one with her fingertips so she wouldn't have to actually read the entire text—she still had a few traits leftover from her divine and not-so-divine forms—and she was so engrossed that she didn't hear Terry until he walked in carrying a couple of grocery bags and her coffee.

"Mocha coffee for the lady," he said in a light tone and handed it to her, and his eyes fell to the book in her hands. His light-hearted tone changed. "What are you looking for?"

The odd question startled her. "What? Why?" She took the drink from him and set it on the table next to her. "Thanks."

He stood upright and walked into the kitchen, then returned sans grocery bags and stood in the center of the living room staring at her. "Because someone doesn't pick up that book just to read it."

"Oh? It looked interesting."

Terry's brow dipped down, creating two vertical lines just above the bridge of his nose. He wasn't happy. He crossed his arms over his chest. "Armen."

She threw him an innocent look. "What?"

"Why did you pick up that book?"

"It looks very old. How did you come by it?"

"I don't recall."

"Liar."

He moved to sit on the sofa next to her. "You're lying, too." He dropped onto the cushion.

Armen looked down at the book, recalling those words again, and she finally turned to him. "Tell me about the time I was in the hospital."

Terry's body went completely rigid. He stared at the floor. "Why?"

She looked down and then back up to meet his eyes that wouldn't look at her. "You spoke to me while I was . . . sleeping. What did you say?"

The fingers of his right hand pulled at invisible threads on his jeans. "You were pretty much in a comatose state, not sleeping." He finally met her eyes. "How do you know I spoke to you?"

"I remember some of it, but I can't remember it all." She flipped the page of the book over to the next one. "Something about you not wanting to say *goodbye* to me."

Terry still plucked at invisible threads. "That's not the word I was talking about."

She stopped scanning the text and looked up at him. "So there *is* another word."

He nodded. "Did you even bother drying your hair? You're dripping all over the damn place."

"Don't change the subject."

"I'm not trying to change the subject." He stood to walk to the bathroom to fetch a towel. "Did you even dry off? There's a puddle of water in the hall."

Oops. She stifled a laugh and cleared her throat. "Sorry."

When he returned, he stood in front of her with towel in hand. "Come here."

She reached for the towel after placing the book down on the table.

He pulled it out of reach. "No, come here."

Armen rolled her eyes and stood up. He placed the towel over her head and worked it through her hair.

"I know how to dry my hair, Terry."

"That's debatable right now, but this way I get you close to me." A faint smile reached his lips. "Was it the memory that made you forget to do it?"

She nodded as he squeezed the ends of her hair into the towel.

"I don't like remembering that time, Armen," he whispered.

She smoothed down the robe with her left hand to 'feel' the scars. "Wish I could say the same, but I just plain don't remember a lot of it."

"That's probably a good thing. You don't want to."

She looked up at him. "I just want to know what else you said to me."

He slowly shook his head. "Not much else." He worked the towel underneath her hair and pulled the ends of it over her shoulders. Then he pulled her forward, using the towel, and he sighed. "I didn't know if you were going to make it."

"What word didn't you want to say?"

His nose touched hers. "I can't say it, Armen." He looked away, swallowing the frog in his throat before speaking again. "I had trouble saying it to my own mother." Tears welled in his eyes. "I tried, but it didn't work, not if you had to release her."

Armen's mind reeled through the conversation around his dead mother that day, trying desperately to find the word that he spoke. "Maybe it didn't work because of how she died," she said, not having a clue as to what she was talking about, but not knowing what else to say.

"Maybe." His eyes focused on her once more. "What are you looking for?"

"I don't know. Why don't you want to discuss what happened to me?"

He stared into her eyes for a long time before answering her question, and when he finally did, his voice trembled. "Because I sent you in there."

"Terry, it's not your fault. No one would have guessed that freak was still alive. Even I didn't realize it until he moved."

"I should have made sure of it."

"There was no way for you to do that," she insisted. "You *all* looked at him. You *all* thought he was dead. You *all* checked."

"There's something I never told you about that guy. I mean, what we discovered after he sta . . . did that to you and I shot an entire magazine into him because he wouldn't go down."

She was shocked beyond belief because Terry always kept his control. "What about him?"

"He was speaking in a tongue I never heard before when I shot him," he replied, and focused intently on her eyes. "The same tongue, I think, you were speaking to Sariel."

She frowned. "Possession?"

"Not quite. But not entirely demon, either."

Armen tried to remember all the legions that resided in the Darkness. His stating that the man wasn't entirely demon intrigued her. "Are you sure he wasn't a demon?"

Terry nodded. "Why?"

"Because there's one in particular who has attributes that would explain why everyone thought he was dead."

Terry's eyes grew wide. "Who?"

"Dumah. He represents silence and the stillness of death." She shook her head at her stupidity. "I don't know why I didn't think of that before. It makes perfect sense."

"Maybe because you were fighting for your life." He caressed the side of her face.

"I meant after that, like lately."

Her mind swarmed with thoughts about the attacks on her. Dumah, a chief in Hell over demons. Sariel and his wicked torture, seemingly to lure her—a Grigori as she had once been, then one of the Fallen chiefs who became Samyaza's hit man. Banshi, one of the first demon-born long before they fell who was also a hired gun, so to speak, and her invasion of the dream world and sounding the call of death. *What the hell?* The Shedim were coming out of the woodwork, each demon a notch up in the hierarchy from its predecessor. Banshi was higher than Sariel because she was more evil, though Sariel's victims would protest such a claim, but also because she was actually born a demon and Sariel had been an angel first.

"My word, Dumah was the first."

"The first what?"

"Demon." She bit her fingernail. "The first of seven, I'd bet." Armen pulled away from him and headed for the bookshelf. She ran her fingertips along the spines. "Each one is stronger, higher than the one preceding it.

They'll work their way up until they reach the seventh one, the strongest and highest one."

"Lucifer?" Terry asked, concern showing in his green eyes.

Armen gazed into those eyes then plucked a book from the shelf. "I don't think it'll go *that* high, but we need to figure out why they keep coming after *me*."

"I think they want you back."

"But they're attacking you, too, in a manner of speaking. I mean, Sariel's attack on your parents was about your dad and *you*, not me."

Terry shook his head. "I don't know about that one. Maybe they're pissed because you have redemption from Him, and they've seen me with you."

Armen bit her lower lip in contemplation. "What did your dad say? Something about they want the one who saved him. That's me. And the one related to him. That's you."

"But why?"

"You're an angel of death, Terry."

He frowned. "But I'm not an angel."

"Doesn't matter. You've been put on a path for a reason, and now it's being fulfilled. By the way, I don't have complete redemption."

He stepped closer to her and placed a hand on her shoulder. "Are you still a demon?"

"No," she replied.

"Then you're on the path, Armen. Name one demon who has met the same fate as you."

"I can't."

"See?"

She wrapped her arms around his waist and hugged him.

"This is going to be bad, isn't it?"

"Well, it certainly isn't good."

He kissed the top of her head. She pulled away from him, grabbed the ancient book, set the new one on the table, and sat down on the sofa once more.

Terry stared at her for a moment before sitting down next to her. "You may not know what you're looking for, but you'll find it in that book. It calls to you for a reason."

Armen stopped scanning the text and eyed him. "What *is* this?"

Terry smiled and patted her knee. "Find what you're looking for first, and then I'll tell you about the book." He rose from the sofa and headed into the kitchen to put away his groceries. "And while you're at it, figure out who the next demon is."

She repeated his last words in a grumble and scanned the text again. "Yeah, right."

Heavenly histories eons old lived within the pages of the book in her hands. She scanned the handwritten words, and memories long forgotten revealed themselves to her. For a brief moment, she saw the Light of Him and she rescanned the page to see it again, to no avail. She continued to search, moving along as Terry came into the living room once more and sat in a chair near the fireplace. He watched her intently, drinking a cup of tea, until she stopped, her finger pressed against the page. Terry leaned forward when Armen looked up at him. The word beneath her finger glowed around its edges.

"*Pax*?" She didn't understand.

Terry nodded once and sat back again.

"What, you couldn't give me the peace symbol?" She held up two fingers, but Terry shook his head. "It's a good thing you didn't live in the sixties."

"And was born after the era of disco."

Armen frowned. "Why that word?"

He took another drink from his tea, and then leaned forward again. "It's kind of like what you did for my mom, a release to the light, I guess, or into grace, rather. I can't really explain it. I don't know how it works."

Realization hit Armen. "You would have said that to me?"

"Yes."

"But it wouldn't have worked. Not for me."

"How do you know? Maybe you need someone to pray for you."

Armen blinked rapidly. "Have you prayed for me?"

Terry smiled. "Yes."

"Why?"

Terry's smile faded. "You really can't see the good in yourself, can you? Have you forgotten that you were once divine?"

Armen bit her lower lip and shook her head.

"Which question are you answering, or is it both?"
She nodded and stared at the book. Its voice among the words gracing its pages was unique, in that it spoke directly to the person reading it. She now looked at a sentence that echoed what Terry had just said to her. *There is good in you.* Armen flipped the page over to the next and her eyes widened. *Why do you question when you know the answer?* Armen moved her jaw forward and bit her upper lip. *What am I questioning?* She turned the page once more. Within the many words on the page, only four stood out, separately glowing like a beacon to form the answer:

When men began to multiply on Earth and daughters were born unto them, My sons saw how beautiful the daughters of man were, and so they took for their wives as many of them as they chose. And **My** *beautiful daughter saw how handsome the sons of man were, and perhaps she even fell in* **Love** *with one, and she took* **For** *her husband but one man unto herself and bore him a son. And after many years, when My sons had taken many wives, I sent Gabriel unto them and he said: "***You** *have sinned against the Lord, our Father, with taking so many children of man and creating the Nephilim, and you shall face punishment. You shall face the Darkness." My intention was never for My only daughter to suffer so greatly. My heart broke after discovering what Gabriel had done, and I washed away the filth from the Earth.*

When she returned her gaze to Terry, a smile beamed across his face. "What?"

"He's speaking to you, isn't He?"

The words had appeared in *her* story, written by . . . it couldn't be possible. "Who wrote this?" She held the book up.

"Certainly not my dad, but definitely yours."

"How old is it?"

Terry looked into his cup and ran a finger around the rim. "It's older than the Bible. That's all I know."

"But it's in English."

"I know. It was Latin before that, and Aramaic before that. It would be in Russian if so needed." His eyes met hers. "The language changes to that of the Keeper. That's the beauty of it, Armen."

She blinked one, two, three times. "How is that possible? I don't remember any book like this."

"Perhaps you weren't privy to that knowledge."

"Obviously. So then, this is . . . *His* book?"

Terry smiled again. "Yes. Ask it something else."

"Like what?" she said wide-eyed.

"Like, who's coming next."

She turned the page again and saw a name that terrified her to the core. "Oh shit." Her voice wavered and she met Terry's eyes with worry. "How did you come by this book, Terry?"

"My father gave it to me." He leaned forward. "What's the matter? Who is it?"

Armen looked down at the page again and felt a shudder run through her body. Would Terry know who it was if she said the name? She didn't want to say it aloud, for fear of invoking her.

"How did your father get it?" Her mind reminded her of the demon in vivid detail.

Terry sat on the edge of his chair, waiting for her to say the name of the next demon they would face. "To answer your question from that day in the apothecary, yes, he worked at the Vatican."

"He specialized in ancient relics, didn't he?" Her eyes remained on the page.

"Yes, ancient religious artifacts. Who is it, Armen? Why won't you tell me?"

She shook her head. "You really don't want to know and I can't say it aloud."

Terry abruptly stood from the chair and walked over to sit next to her. When he looked at the page, the word burned brightly with a hint of flame at its edges.

Judging from his facial expression, he recognized this demon.

"How far is this going to go?" he asked her, but the book provided the answer.

Until the End.

"Of days?" Terry asked.

"Yes." Armen looked at him again. "I told you."

"Shit," he said and stared at the name that still burned brightly amidst the other message on the page: *Ashtoreth.*

Chapter Nineteen
Proposal

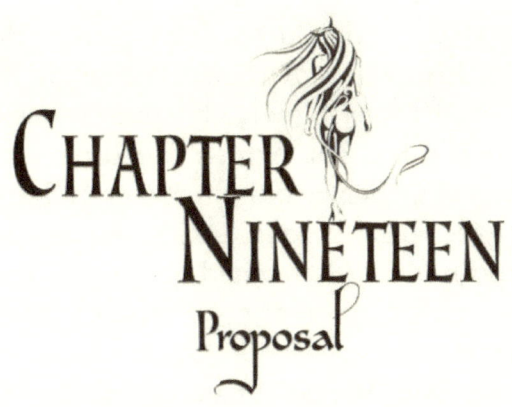

ARMEN CLOSED THE BOOK AND set it on the coffee table. She picked up her blended coffee and leaned back into the sofa, wrapped her lips around the straw, and drew the frozen beverage into her mouth. She batted her eyelashes at Terry and smirked around the straw.

"Why are you suddenly so calm?"

"I'm enjoying my coffee. It may be the last one I ever have."

"Funny." He moved closer to her. "Let me have some of that."

She held the cup away from him. "You want *me* to give you some of *my* coffee?"

"Well, I *did* buy it for you."

Armen stared at him a moment. "Okay, here."

He took the straw into his mouth. When he pulled away, surprise filled his features. "Hey, that's pretty good. I should've gotten myself one."

Armen nodded and took another drink. "Yes, you should have." Terry leaned closer, and she placed a hand on his chest. "And just what do you think you're doing, Detective Armstrong?"

"I'd like some more," he replied with a glint in his eyes. "Pretty please."

She eased up and allowed him closer. He took the straw again, his eyes remaining on hers as he sampled the coffee once more. Slowly, he pulled back from the straw and licked his lips. Armen licked hers in response, and he moved in, his face only inches from hers before he closed the gap. She allowed the kiss, having longed for it since the apothecary. He pushed his tongue past her lips, and she responded by pressing a hand to his chest again and holding him back.

"What are you doing?" She couldn't let him think it would be so easy, even if he'd held her in her near-bare skin recently.

"Trying to seduce the woman I love. I mean, it may be the last time I ever have the chance." His brow jumped and humor held his eyes.

She raised one eyebrow. "Does that actually work on women?"

"I wouldn't know. I've never tried it before." He pressed against her hand, her arm giving only a little. "Is it working on you?"

"Not even close." Of course it was working.

"Worth a shot," he said with a shrug. "How about another kiss then?"

"That, you can have." She set the coffee on the table and pulled him toward her.

His lips crashed against hers and the collision set her body on fire. In a series of swift motions, he had her pinned beneath him, and in all her years of seduction she'd never had a man turn her on the way he did with such simple moves. Terry hovered over her, bracing himself with his left hand near her shoulder, and the other settled next to her hip before he dropped to his left elbow and moved his right hand slowly down her leg. He kissed her again, and his warm lips trailed kisses along her jaw line to her neck. Her breath hitched.

"Terry?"

"Yeah?" He continued kissing along her neck and shoulder, his hand gripping her hip now.

"We should take it slow."

"Why's that?" He nibbled on her earlobe, which about drove her nuts.

"Are you *trying* to get me cast into the Darkness again?" She tried to make it sound funny.

He bolted upright. "What? Why would you say that?"

Apparently, it wasn't funny.

She propped herself on her elbows. "I'm sorry. I really do want this. It's just that . . . a part of me is scared shitless. It frightens the hell out of me not knowing which choice I made that might send me back."

He slumped. "Shit, Armen. I didn't even think about that."

"You don't have to," she said, sitting up.

"But I should." He ran a hand over his head. "When it comes to you, I should. I'm sorry."

She grabbed the sides of his head and made him look at her. "And this is why I love you." She let him go and reached for her coffee.

He sighed heavily, as though he'd fought an entire demon horde. "What if we were to get married? Would he reject that idea?"

Armen choked on her coffee and quickly covered her mouth. After wiping the liquid from her chin, she stared at him as he chuckled. "You haven't taken me out to dinner yet and you want to jump into marriage? Great proposal, by the way. I'm all aflutter." She placed her hand over her heart and batted her eyelashes.

"Fine, I'll take you to dinner tonight. Let's go buy you that little black dress." His eyebrows jumped.

"It's barely morning."

Terry looked at the clock on the far kitchen wall. "Okay, so we have some time to kill. What would you like to do?"

She shrugged. "At this hour?"

"How about breakfast?"

"I don't eat breakfast."

Terry laughed. "That's because you usually wake up just before dinner."

She couldn't argue with that one. He was right. Dinner *was* her breakfast. "True, but you do realize a quite nasty demon is coming after one of us soon, right?"

"Right now, I don't fucking care," he said.

"We should still plan for her. We can't go on like everything is just peachy fucking normal."

He cupped her face. "I'm not sacrificing any normalcy we might have to prepare for a demon I already know how to fight," he argued. "Life goes on, no matter what's coming."

Armen laughed. "You can't possibly know how to fight her."

Terry raised his face to hers and smirked. "She's a goddess of war, but I'd think you would know that."

"I do, and I've seen the bitch fight. I am *not* looking forward to facing her."

Terry pulled her head closer. "So let's have some fun. We have until Friday."

"What makes you think that?"

"Because that's her day." He kissed her before she could respond again. Smart man.

Armen's voice disappeared, as did her thoughts.

"I've been thinking about this, the days they appear, except for Sariel because there was some sort of link between you two—" Armen started to interject, and Terry quickly placed his hand over her mouth. "Which I am not upset about, so let me finish."

She nodded for him to continue.

"They are each connected to a day of the week. I don't know why, but it's in the texts. Yes, I've been reading the texts. I've read them all my life, and now I know why my father made me do so. He's been preparing me all this time. All the books he's made me read, the courses he'd told me to take in college, which made me think at the time that he wanted me to be a priest or a wrangler like him, but he never came out and said it. The relics he's shown me, the knowledge he's passed on to me about them, and that book." His eyes moved to the book on the table and quickly returned to hers. "*That* book. It's the Book of Secrets, Armen. He gave it to me a few years ago and told me to keep it safe. I wondered about that for a long time. Why would he give it to me when it would be much safer at the Vatican?"

Armen shook her head. "Damn, that was a mouthful."

"Armen, I'm serious."

"I know. I'm sorry." She laughed. "It's safer here than at the Vatican because anyone looking for that book will look at the Vatican first, among several other places. But . . . ." She scanned her memories for anything about a Book of Secrets. Wait, wasn't there an angel who guarded a book? What was her na—

"He gave it to me after a certain demon sacrificed her life for his."

She gulped. Shit.

"I think it's here for you." He sat back and stared at the book.

"It can't be. It's not my burden. I've never even heard of it."

"Maybe it has become your—"

She shook her head quickly. "No, that doesn't change. Ever."

"Well, it's here for some reason."

She sighed and dropped her head against the back of the sofa.

"Do you know what I am?"

She shifted her eyes to him. "Truthfully, I've never run across anyone like you before. I don't know what you are, other than human. And apparently Death to demonkind."

"Sariel kept calling me a knight."

"He was being sarcastic and condescending. Sariel was a Prince of Darkness. Don't be fooled by words. They'll be your undoing." Though if she really considered it, Terry *had* taken on the title and knights *were* higher than angels, which would have been the only way he'd been able to kill Sariel. *Shit. What the hell did that mean?*

Terry moved to the side and picked the book up from the table. He sat back again and flipped through the pages before finally closing it with a heavy sigh. "It never works for me."

"Why don't you just ask your dad?" Armen sat up and finished off her drink. "I mean, you said the book calls to a person. Maybe it doesn't need to call to you because you already have a way to speak with Him."

Terry placed a hand on each side of her face and kissed her hard. "You're brilliant! Let's go eat and then we'll go visit my dad. You wanted to talk to him about yours anyway." He jumped to his feet and went into the kitchen.

Armen sat in shock a moment or five. She finally got to her feet and wandered into her bedroom, walked over to the bed and sat on its edge, and stared into the picture that hung on the wall in front of her. It was a nice landscape painted by one John Constable, according to the signed name in the corner. England, she assumed, from the looks of it. She sighed heavily. *What is he*? She examined the painting more closely to see if it was real; Terry certainly couldn't afford a real Constable painting on a cop's salary, detective or not. Then she glanced to the corner of her room.

"Damn Goya," she said aloud, staring at the only surviving anything from the fire. *That* was an original, and it took quite a bit to procure. "I should go look at my condo." Armen stood, disrobed and pulled her jeans from the closet, along with a long-sleeved shirt she bought the day before the funeral, and a new hoodie. She dressed, fiddled with her hair until it was back in a ponytail, slipped on some Converse sneakers that she picked up that same day at the store, and walked back out to the living room. Normally, she'd be dressed much nicer, in more casual work attire, but with what had been happening lately, and the fact that they hadn't returned to work just yet, she felt the most comfortable in jeans. It sure as hell beat pristine white robes or scales any day.

Terry sat on the sofa and flipped through the book again. His frustration showed in his face until he noticed her standing there.

"Aren't you going to dry your hair some more?" He placed the book on the table and rose from the sofa.

"Why?"

"Because it's cold outside." He looked at her feet. "At least you're not wearing flip-flops. Want a coat?" He went to the front door.

"Nah." Armen grinned when she passed him and stepped outside. "I'll be fine." She waited for him to open the garage and back out the Lincoln. After they were both in the car, she turned her head to him. "It is a bit nippy out."

Terry slid his gaze to the side, but he didn't turn his head, and a grin crept across his face. He remained silent, however, and put the car in gear and backed out of the driveway.

"What, no smartass reply to that? I'm shocked."

He still didn't say a word, put the car in gear again, and then drove down the street, heading to Armen had-no-idea-where.

"Where were you born?"

"Here," he replied, keeping his focus on the road.

"Did you go to Catholic school?"

"Of course. Brophy Prep."

"Isn't that a high school?"

"Yes."

"Did you go to Catholic school before that?"

He turned his head to her briefly. "For someone who claims humans fill silence with needless chatter, you sure do ask a lot of questions."

Armen wrinkled her nose. "Questions are not needless chatter. They are information gathering."

He chuckled lightly and pulled onto the freeway. "Sorry, couldn't help myself."

"Where is this place?"

"Near my parent's house. I usually hit it on the way over after my shift. That is, when I'm not dealing with you."

"What's that supposed to mean?"

"Nothing, Armen." He chuckled. "Don't make something out of it. I enjoy the time I spend with you, even if we are working, otherwise I wouldn't have—"

"Proposed?" She leaned closer to him.

He cleared his throat. "Yes."

"So, you were serious with that."

"Yes, I was."

"Again, not very romantic." She may have only been human for a few years and was a workaholic, but it didn't mean she never saw a television commercial during Valentine's Day.

"Are you going to say yes?"

"No."

He snapped his head around to face her. "Why not?"

She casually pointed forward; he swerved slightly to miss the sidewalk. "Because of the context in which it was asked. It makes me think you only wish to marry me so you can have sex with me."

"Yeah, you would think that. Never mind that I've told you I love you countless times—"

"Three times," she said, and he laughed. "What's so funny?"

"I can't believe you're counting. No wait, yes I can."

Armen huffed out a breath and crossed her arms over her chest. "So happy to entertain you."

Terry laughed again. "I'm teasing you, Armen. That's what people do."

Silence filled the air of the Lincoln, and it was a long time before either of them spoke.

"The book said *Ashtoreth,* right?" Terry asked. "Not the other one?"

Armen slapped him. "Name! But yeah, I definitely don't want to deal with *him* yet."

"Shit, sorry." He took the off-ramp. "Pretty nasty fellow?"

"Horribly nasty," she replied and shuddered just from the mere thought of it.

"Okay, that's good."

"How is that possibly good?" She turned to face him again.

Terry's eyes briefly met hers before the light changed. "Because we know it's not him, and personally, if you're saying he's a nasty one, I don't want to deal with him yet, either."

"You haven't met Ash." Armen's stomach grumbled and she placed her hand over it. "Damn, I'm hungry."

"We're almost there." He drove toward Scottsdale, heading for the Arcadia district. It was one of the older areas, but certainly higher in station. Regardless, the land had belonged to others long ago, and they still lingered. Armen could see things there, in these older parts. Not always bad things, but things nonetheless. She had to laugh at herself because of the profession she chose. *Forensic pathology, what was I thinking?* Paranormal investigator might have been more fun. Not that that particular approach hadn't somehow taken over some of their cases. Speaking of which, she and Terry both were about due back to work. Seeing as how their sleep schedules were completely off, she could see that first night was going to be a killer, especially since their first night back on duty would be Friday night.

Chapter Twenty
Hidden Truths

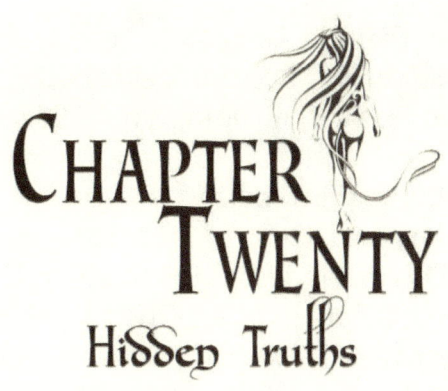

AFTER BREAKFAST, TERRY AND ARMEN made their way over to Sean's house, who greeted each of them with a big hug and a peck on the cheek before letting them inside. It was Armen's conclusion that Uncle Seamus and Sean were undoubtedly related to a clan of strong-armed men in the Highlands after he'd hugged her so tight she nearly squeaked yet again.

God, his family's going to kill me. The irony was not lost on her.

She stepped into the entry and braced herself for the next bear hug as Uncle Seamus walked out of the kitchen with a rather large grin spreading across his red Celtic cheeks.

"Armen." Seamus had a strong voice, too. "Guid to see ye." Those Armstrong arms wrapped around her and squeezed.

"You too, Seamus," she replied when he finally let her go. His wife, Beverly, appeared and stretched her hands out in greeting.

"Armen, sweetie, so delightful to see you." She took Armen's hands and pulled her forward so she could give her a dainty peck on the cheek. "Are you hungry? I've made muffins."

"Oh, no thanks. Terry took me to breakfast." She patted her stomach. "I couldn't eat another bite."

"Well, at least he's feeding you," Beverly said with a wink.

"Good thing I burn hot."

"I'm sorry, dear?"

Shit. "My metabolism, it's high-end. I ate enough earlier to fell a horse." She craned her head back to the door to see where Terry had gone. He stood just outside the door, talking quietly with his father. Seamus soon joined them, and Beverly pulled Armen into the kitchen, out of earshot.

"Let the men speak, dear. It's obviously something important."

Armen choked back the comment bubbling up because offending a family member of Terry's just wasn't in the cards. She closed her mouth and sat at the breakfast bar. She could act like a normal human being.

When she felt like it.

Most of the time, she didn't feel like it.

How did human women deal with this all the time? She blew her too-long bangs away from her eyes. It amazed her how little had changed over the centuries, and how long it took for the small changes they *did* accomplish, only happening in the last one hundred or so years. Much as mortal man liked to believe in the natural order of things, that they were above mortal females, the truth was that things weren't like that in her Father's Kingdom. She'd been treated every bit as equally as her brothers, the only exception being that she may have been a Daddy's girl and may have received special treatment for that and that alone.

Beverly smiled sweetly at her. "Coffee?"

Armen gave her a nod. "Thank you," she said when Beverly placed a cup of hot brew in front of her.

"You're welcome, dear." Beverly was not a small woman, but not large, either. She was about five-four in height, a little shorter than Armen, and of average build with a little extra to love. Her strawberry-blonde hair was cut short, just above the neckline, and she surprisingly did not share the accent of her husband. "My husband tells me you're a medical examiner. That must be a dreadful job."

Armen chuckled. "It's usually quite peaceful, actually, unless I have to go into the field."

"You mean on a crime scene?"

Armen could only imagine the thoughts going through Beverly's head, given her horrified expression. "Yes."

"Is that how you met our Terry?" She reached for a muffin and cut it open.

"Well, no, not really. The first time I ever saw him, he came into my lab with someone to view a body. He didn't speak to me, though, outside of an introduction and giving me the necessary information."

Beverly smiled, spreading butter over half the muffin. "Yes, well, Terry can be shy when it comes to women these days."

The comment reminded Armen of what Seamus said to her at the cemetery. She leaned forward and looked Beverly in the eye. "What happened with his last relationship?"

Beverly's eyebrows rose into her forehead and she blinked with surprise. "Hasn't he told you?"

Armen shook her head.

"Oh, dear, I don't think I should."

Armen sat back. "It's okay, I understand." She picked at an imaginary crumb on the counter.

Beverly buttered the other half of the muffin and raised it to her mouth. Her eyes darted toward the entryway and back to Armen. "It was a horrible experience for him," she whispered and took a bite.

Armen gave the woman her own look of surprise. "How horrible?"

Beverly chewed and swallowed, checking the front door again, and then leaned forward. "Poor Cassandra. She died in his arms."

"What happened?"

Beverly shushed her. "They'll hear you." She placed the muffin on a small plate in front of her and leaned on the counter, closer to Armen. "Well, I don't know the specifics exactly. He doesn't like to talk about it. But from what I understand, some perp—that's what he calls them—went into her apartment and killed her."

"How? Why?"

"Ex-boyfriend, or something of the sort, I think. Like I said, I don't know the details." She took Armen's hand in hers and studied her fingertips. Armen could tell she was listening intently for the men.

"Were they married?"

Beverly shook her head. "Not yet."

"How did Terry come to be there?"

"He was already there before it happened. He'd just gone to the store to get her something."

"Oh my." Armen's mind reeled with Terry's reaction to her almost dying and it all made sense now. The words he'd said and why he'd said them. He hadn't wanted to say it again to another woman he was interested in, not when he'd most likely said it to the woman he loved.

"At first, they thought he did it," Beverly added quietly.

Armen quickly withdrew from her thoughts and stared at Beverly. "They did? Why would they think that?"

"Because he was the only one there."

"The man had already left," Armen said softly.

Beverly nodded.

"Oh, poor Terry."

"It was very hard on him. It was hard on all of us, but we believed in him. Our Terry could never do such a thing."

Armen agreed. Terry could never hurt someone he loved. She met Beverly's eyes again. "How was she killed?"

Beverly still held her hand, studying each finger carefully. "Stabbed, several times."

Armen stilled. That explained Terry's reaction to Armen's stabbing even more. She bit her lower lip, thinking about the night she'd almost died and the strange coincidence between Cassandra's death and her almost-death. "How long ago was this?"

"Seven years. A long Seven years. That's why we were so delighted when he started talking about you a few years back." She looked up from Armen's hand and smiled.

Armen heard footsteps coming toward the kitchen. Beverly stood up straight as all three men filed inside, and she took Armen's hand and held it high, twisting it around so that Armen's palm was away from her. She feigned serious inspection.

"Oh yes, dear. You *do* need a manicure. We should go do that while I'm in town." She let go of Armen's hand and returned to her muffin.

Terry walked up behind her, leaned over, and kissed her lightly on the cheek. "Getting an inspection, I see." He sat down next to her and looked to Beverly. "Aunt Bev?"

"Coffee, coming right up." Beverly turned to grab a cup from the cabinet.

"Thanks."

She waved him off and poured the coffee. "There's nothing I wouldn't do for my nephew."

Terry smiled. "You're the best aunt a guy could ask for."

Beverly grinned. "I know."

Sean stepped to Armen's other side and placed a hand on her shoulder. "Armen, are ye ready fer that talk noo?"

She looked up quickly, a little surprised because she didn't think it would be so soon. "Yes."

"Follow me," he said and stepped into his office.

Armen followed, and he waited for her to enter the room before completely closing the doors.

"Please, have a seat." He waved his hand toward a chair on the other side of the desk. Sean pulled his chair back and sat, and then turned to her with a smile upon his lips. "He still loves ye, y'know."

Armen sat on the edge of her seat. "How do you know?"

"He told me." Sean's eyes sparkled with a smile. "An' he told me to tell you so."

Armen fidgeted, dancing her fingers on her lap, entwining them together and breaking them apart. "So, you really *can* hear Him?"

"Yes. What would you like to know?"

Lost in a sea of thoughts, Armen wasn't sure which question to ask first. Finally, she settled on the one burning question that bothered her most. "Why did they kill my son?"

Sean's smile faded. "You know the answer to that already."

Armen hung her head and nodded. "But I don't understand it."

"Aye, ye do. You're just choosing to deny it."

She looked up at him, tears welling in her eyes. "But he was my *child*."

Sean looked down at the desk. "Armen, I understand loss, and there is nothing I can say that will make the pain of losing your child go away. It pains me to know that ye watched him die, that ye watched Gabriel do it. I also understand that what is written is misunderstood. I know your child was nae a giant, nae in the Goliath sense. Even Goliath was nae the giant they made him oot to be. He was just a rather large man."

Armen nodded and wiped away her tears. His recount of what had happened proved that her Father had told him the true history, and for that truth, so was thankful.

"Please ask something else. I have no answers for you there."

"Meaning He doesn't wish to answer."

"No," he simply said. "Meaning ye already know the answer and you'll need to discuss the issue with Him because it's a personal matter between the two of you."

She drew in a deep breath and tried to think of another question, but was quickly drawing a blank. Her son was the main question that she wanted answers to, and it looked as though her Father wasn't about to let her have them. Maybe she just wanted Him to apologize for what He'd commanded of Gabriel. Another tear trailed down her cheek. She knew there were other half-breeds—angel and human—out there, still living. It was as if her Father had just stopped killing them after the first group of Nephilim. If that was the case, then why did her son have to die?

"D'you want to know why I summoned you that day?"

She looked up at him. "Please."

He smiled. "Because He told me to."

"But you didn't know my name."

"You go by many names, Armen." He folded his hands on the desk. "Armaros, Armoni, to name a couple. I believe the name Armaros means 'accursed one'."

Armen lowered her gaze. "I know what my name means."

"It's how I called to you—the accursed one. D'you still believe yourself to be the cursed one?"

She sighed heavily and shrugged. "I don't know. Why not? I mean, this life isn't much better than the last. It's still Hell; just a different plane."

"D'you think it's a curse to be flesh?"

"When you've experienced Heaven, yes." She tilted her head. "When you've been in His Light, yes."

"Don't you think that this is perhaps a chance to show your faith in Him?" Sean leaned back in the chair.

Armen snorted. "I don't need faith. Faith is a belief in something you've never seen, a belief in something greater than yourself. I *know* He exists. He's my Father in the literal sense."

"Aye, but perhaps ye have lost faith in *why* He does things."

Armen blinked rapidly. She opened her mouth to say something, but nothing came out, and she closed it again.

"It's okay, Armen," Sean said softly. "Sometimes we forget."

"Sometimes I wish I could forget . . . everything." She wiped yet another tear from her cheek. "You have no idea what's inside this mind."

Sean's mouth twitched, and he looked at his desk briefly before his sorrow-filled eyes met with hers again. "I do nae envy you the millennia of memories you must have and can never forget, especially since you've experienced three realms." He stood and walked around the desk, laying his hand on her shoulder. "I know the main answers you seek regard your son, but I can nae help you there. You *must* speak to Him if ye wish to know more on that topic."

She kept her head down and sobbed. Sean wrapped his arms around her shoulders and kissed the top of her head. It was an act of compassion her own Father hadn't shown her in eons.

"Just remember that He still loves you, Armen," Sean whispered. "Otherwise, ye would nae be flesh noo. He told me to call to ye that day because He was trying to save His daughter. What more proof do you need?"

That comment set the pinball bouncing through her mind, hitting memories, especially from that fateful moment when she'd saved Sean's life. But as much as she tried, she just couldn't remember anything past feeling Agares' sword slide through her torso.

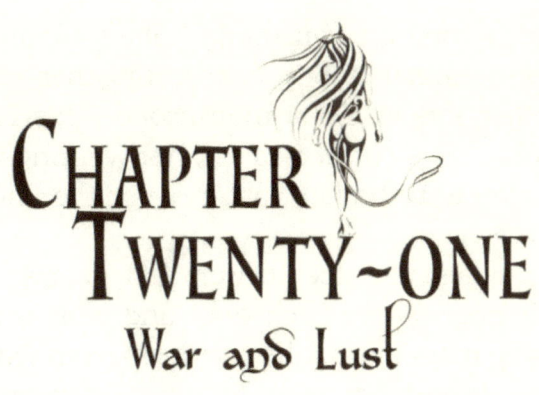

Chapter Twenty-one
War and Lust

THE FOLLOWING FRIDAY—ONLY A couple of days after her conversation with Sean—came too soon, and Armen found herself dragging feet to get through the day. Not a good situation when they had to work that night and might potentially face a demon. She and Terry both attempted to sleep through the daylight hours, but the impending doom of what they were about to face at any given moment held them fast and awake. She was completely on edge, as was Terry, and she jumped at every little sound.

Armen sipped on the coffee Terry brought her while flipping through the book once more. Its pages refused to speak to her this day, and she finally closed it with a heavy sigh. *Ashtoreth* clouded her mind. It worried her that Terry had said the name aloud that day on the way to his father's house. Just the mere gesture of a whisper could invoke a demon. On the other hand, it probably didn't matter much; the demon would come no matter what, as foretold by the book. And the book was, after all, *the* book of God.

The oven buzzer went off, startling her to the point of jerking the cup in her hand and spilling coffee on the table, narrowly missing the book. "Fuck!"

Terry chuckled. "Sorry. A bit jumpy?"

"What the hell do you think?" She took another sip, the divine caffeinated beverage hitting her taste buds, warming her tongue for a millisecond. "It's Friday, for the love of—" She cut herself off, not wanting to say the name she knew to be her Father's, nor the one humans called him by.

"If it makes you feel better, I'm experiencing the same." He opened the oven door and bent over to pull the bubbling mass of doughy goodness from within.

Armen shifted her eyes to ogle Terry and felt an overwhelming urgency to strip the man down and mount him. She slid her tongue over her lips and blinked, trying to expel the oncoming thoughts with a shake of her head, but the notions still lingered. Blinking again, she bit her lower lip, and shifted in the chair. Her breath staggered and heat overtook her body. Soon, she found herself pressing Terry against the counter, kissing him in a desperate attempt to subdue her desires.

Terry pushed her away at first, but soon gave in to her persuasive advances, letting her mouth attack his neck. "Armen," he said, nearly breathless. "Wha—"

She shushed him and continued down his neck. She yanked his shirt up and pulled it off.

"But—"

She pressed her fingers against his lips, and slid one finger into his mouth.

He pulled back, releasing her finger. "Armen, no."

She looked up at him and pouted. "It's okay, Terry."

"Are you sure? I thought you wanted to wait in case...you know, you get sent back." He struggled against her to keep his pants on.

She laughed, her hands fighting with his. "Oh yes, I'm sure."

Finally, he grabbed her by the wrists. "I don't think you're in the right frame of mind to be doing this." He studied her eyes intently.

A tiny spark of flame reflected from her eyes to his.

"I'm in a perfect state of mind." She moved her arms swiftly, twisting them down and outward to switch who had a grasp on whom. Surprise took over his face, and she pressed her body against his.

"Armen," he whispered as her face drew closer.

Her mouth took his, and soon he freed his hands and wrapped his arms around her waist, lifting her from the floor. He turned her around and sat her on the counter, running his fingers up into her hair. Armen locked her legs around his waist. He ran his hands down her back to the hem of her shirt. She helped him pull it off and grabbed his face, pulling him in for another heated kiss.

He broke the connection, breathing hard. "This isn't you."

The book flipped open, and brilliant light flooded the kitchen. Armen yelped and quickly unlocked her legs from Terry's waist, her hands over her mouth and her eyes wide. She pushed Terry aside and jumped off the counter, running for the table and dropping to her knees before the book.

"Father, please—" Her voice was a raspy whisper, hands clasped together, tears filling her eyes as she rocked on the floor. "Please don't send me back there."

Terry's phone rang, and he moved to answer it. "Hello?" He hummed an answer, and then paused.

"Please, Father, don't—"

"Yes, Dad," Terry replied softly. "I'll tell her." He hung up the phone, and the light from the book died down as he moved over to Armen. Terry knelt beside her fallen form and touched her arm. "Armen, sweetie, it's okay. He's not mad at you."

She sniffled and slowly opened her eyes. "He's not?"

Terry shook his head and sat on the floor next to her. He leaned over and pulled her into his arms and partially onto his lap, and he ran his fingers through her hair. "No, He's not." He kissed the top of her head. "You weren't yourself."

Armen shook her head. "No, I wasn't." Her body trembled involuntarily.

"And I'm too close to you," he added. "I didn't have the strength to stop you. I'm . . . I'm sorry."

"It's not your fault. You're only human."

He chuckled. "Why does that sound like an insult coming from you?"

She met his eyes, anguish filling her. "I didn't mean it to be."

He smiled at her and slid his fingertips down the side of her face. "I know." He kissed her forehead. "We're going to have to be extremely careful the rest of the day."

Armen nodded.

"I saw her in your eyes."

She looked up again. "You did?"

"Your irises were rimmed with fire, but I couldn't stop. And here I thought to dismiss the lust aspect of her." He sighed and shook his head. "I should know better."

"Yes, you should." She curled up in his arms.

"I'm sorry."

She ran her hand in a soft sweep up and down his forearm. "I wonder why me and not you."

He chuckled. "Probably because I'm a man. Lust is a given. It would be too easy."

Armen laughed at his attempt to joke, and he looked down at her with a smile.

"There's my girl."

She hid her face against his still bare chest.

"I still haven't taken you to dinner, have I?"

"No."

"Well then, how about Sunday night?"

"I'll need to go shopping."

"I've already bought it."

She jerked her head up to see the smirk on his face. "You have? Shoes too?"

"Yep," he said.

"You didn't have to do that."

"I don't *have* to do anything, Armen. I do things because I *want* to."

Armen lowered her gaze. "Aren't you afraid of being this close to me now?"

He smiled at her and kissed her forehead again. "I've never been afraid of you, Armen, and I never will be."

"Then why did it take you so long to talk to me?"

"That's different. You're talking about a different kind of fear."

She sat up and turned to face him. "Have you had a serious relationship before? I mean, did something bad happen?"

He raised his eyes to hers, studied her a moment, and he gave her a weak smile. "I see my Aunt Bev has let the cat out of the bag. It explains the manicure thing, which I can't picture you doing at all."

"She didn't mean to—"

He held a hand up to stop her. "It's okay. It's probably better that way. It's difficult to talk about."

"Even now?" After he confirmed her question with a nod, she drew in a deep breath and sighed. "Then we'll discuss it when you're ready."

"Thank you." He pulled her close again, wrapped his arms around her, and gently kissed her temple. "Armen, you're not wearing a shirt."

Armen chuckled. "Does that upset you?"

"Not at all. You can walk around shirtless anytime you want to."

"You're not wearing a shirt, either."

"Nope."

When she shivered, he helped her to her feet, grabbed her shirt from the countertop, and pulled it over her head. Once the shirt's hem was at her waist, he sighed and slipped his arms around her, pulling her close again.

"They didn't call the night Banshi attacked."

"True." He laughed. "I wonder what that's about."

"Ash . . . she's very powerful." She couldn't bring herself to say the demon's full name. They'd already said it once, and Armen was certain it was the reason for what had just happened. She'd never been taken over by one of them before. Demons didn't tend to possess their own kind . . . but Armen wasn't one of them anymore. She was human now. She opened her eyes and smirked at Terry. "You're still shirtless."

"Yeah, but I'm a man, so I can get away with it." He winked. "Come on, let's eat."

Three hours swept by, and they got ready for work and headed in. It was interesting riding to work with Terry, intriguing that they both wanted to listen to the same radio station, but what fascinated Armen most was when she pecked Terry on the cheek in the middle of the lobby in front of *everybody*. When she turned to look back at him, Terry had wandered off with a smile on his face. She quickly covered her mouth to hide her own, and stepped into the elevator.

"What was *that*?" a woman about Armen's height said when she walked into the elevator behind her. Armen turned to find long black spirals, one lock of which hung right over a bright blue-green eye. Both the hair and eye color were striking against her olive skin.

"Hi, Jasmine." Her face warmed with a blush. "What was what?"

Jasmine grinned, one crook of her mouth curving and signifying that Armen had been caught in something simply sinister. "Did I just see you kiss Terry Armstrong on the cheek?"

"Oh, *that*," Armen replied. "It's nothing."

"R*iii*ght. That smile of his sure said it was *nothing*. So, are you two dating now, or what?"

"Actually, I'm staying with him until I can find a new place to live." She quickly looked at Jasmine. "I'm staying in his spare room."

"Uh huh. Yeah, I heard your condo burned up."

"How'd you hear about that?"

"Oh, you know, the grapevine, since you didn't *call* me; news travels swiftly through these parts. Did you lose everything?"

Armen stared at the elevator doors, ashamed she hadn't called. Wow. She was really getting the hang of this human thing. "Everything but one painting."

"That's gotta suck. Is there anything I can help you with?"

"Nah, I'm good. I'm just waiting on the insurance company. That may take a while."

"No shit." The elevator doors opened and they both stepped out and headed down the hall. "So which painting was it?"

"Goya."

"Surreal, considering some of the gossip filtering through the vine."

"What did you hear?"

"Something about demons." She cocked a brow. "That true?"

Armen only gave a nod.

"Damn. Guess it's looking like Armageddon these days."

"You have no idea."

Jasmine stopped and looked around like she was lost. "Oh shit, I passed my own damn office."

Armen laughed and continued to walk. "Talk to ya later, Jazzy."

"Oh, you'd better believe it," Jasmine said and turned around. "Midnight snack?"

Armen waved a hand in the air. "Got a date."

"Don't start ignoring me for some man," Jasmine shouted.

"I would do no such thing," Armen shouted back and turned the corner to head to her office. She walked through the double doors and smiled. "Good evening, Art. How's business?"

A short, balding man looked up from his desk and peered over the top of his wire-rimmed glasses. Her boss, Arthur Spisany, Forensic Section Supervisor straight from New York City, and damn good at his job. A half-eaten sandwich sat on top of a file and he looked at it as if he'd won a jackpot. "There you are."

Armen wasn't sure if he was talking to her or the sandwich.

He picked up the sandwich. After taking a bite, he looked at Armen again. "Business? Well, I keep getting some weird shit through here. Anything to do with your little spree lately?"

Armen frowned. "What spree?"

"The one you and that detective who looks like a goddamn Navy S.E.A.L. have been on. You know, with the *demons*." He, of course, used his fingers to draw quotation marks around the last word.

Armen wrinkled her nose. "Funny, Art." She walked over to her desk to look at messages and discovered quite a pile of them. "Well, that's what I get for taking so much time off."

"Yeah, thanks for that, by the way." His sarcasm bit at the air. "I just love pulling double duty."

She looked up at him wide-eyed. "They didn't bring in someone else?"

Art shook his head. "City budget, or some shit. They're starting to drop the axe. You might want to watch your neck." He took a big bite from his sandwich and chewed slowly. "And that assistant of yours is a joke. He'll be the first to go."

She ignored the last comment and focused on the former pre-bite one. "They're cutting people?" She sat down in her chair and stared at him.

Art nodded and took a big bite of sandwich again. "Left and right," he said around a mouthful of food so that Armen could barely understand him. "But maybe you could become the city's resident demon hunter, or some shit."

"Ha, ha," she replied.

He jumped to his feet so fast, it surprised her. "C'mere, you have to see this." He opened the door to the "icebox," the frigid medical examiners' laboratory, and stepped inside. She quickly followed. Art stepped up to number seven and grabbed the handle, the sandwich still in his other hand. He pulled it open and reached for the tray. Armen looked down at the sheet-covered body and Art motioned for her to pull the cover back. She grabbed the top and pulled it down.

"What d'ya think of that?" He took another bite and chewed slowly, watching her.

Armen turned around and grabbed some gloves. "Tell me." She pulled the gloves on and shook her head at Art's atrocious habit of eating while in the lab. She never could understand it. Not that it bothered her to eat in the lab herself. It was just that food and dead bodies did not go together well.

"Well, obviously murder." He pointed to the now sewn up slit throat—a slit that was not made during an autopsy. "Cut him right open, but"—he pointed again, telling her to pull the sheet down more—"looks like he's missing a couple of things."

When Armen pulled the sheet down further, the man's hands were missing. The left and right comment must have reminded Art about the body. She took one arm and lifted it to view the wrist. "That's a clean slice."

Art nodded. "Not only clean, but hot enough to cauterize it. He was still alive when it happened. Weren't you looking at some torture cases?"

Armen nodded, recalling the man nailed to the wall. "When did this one come in?"

"Last night," Art replied.

She looked up from the body as Art finished off his sandwich. "Was he dead when they found him?"

"Yep. He's been dead about two days. He wasn't alive for long after his hands were removed. He'd only been missing for twenty-four hours then."

The demon's name jumped into her mind again, and she dropped the arm and stepped back. Ash had a specific sword she liked to use, one that would sear through the flesh of man or demon or angel. After all, she was the demoness of war. That sword just happened to be a fire sword.

"You all right there, Armen?" Art pulled the sheet up to re-cover the body. He pushed the tray back inside and shut the door.

"Yeah, I'm fine," she replied, not very convincing.

"Uh huh," he responded. "You've seen a lot of shit this last week, haven't you?"

She pulled the gloves off and turned toward the door. "You have no idea." She tossed the gloves into the trash on the way out.

Art followed her back into the office and gathered his things. "I can't say that I'm not happy you're back, but damn, Armen, what the hell is going on around town?"

Armen looked up at him and smiled. She shifted her eyes to his desk and the multitude of family photos and knick-knacks cluttering up the space. He even had little origami figures scattered about that he'd made. "Art, go home to your wife and kiss her, and be happy."

He quirked a brow at her and then grabbed his jacket. "Have a good night, Armen." He headed for the doors. "Be safe."

She found that last bit odd coming from Art, especially with his demon cracks, but no matter how much he made it sound like the current state of the city wasn't a big deal, she knew Art was concerned. At the very least, he didn't want to pull double duty again for a while.

Armen stared at the phone for a long time after Art had gone, trying to decide whether she should call Terry about the body that sat in number seven. She chose to wait until he came to get her for their midnight snack, also known as lunch to the graveyard crew. Graveyard shift was usually quiet and sometimes boring as hell. It was why she didn't mind going into the field . . . until recently. Right now, she'd really dread getting one of *those* calls. From the looks of Mr. Jones in number seven, Ash had been a very busy little demoness of war from the moment Terry uttered her name. Armen wondered when the next body would turn up.

Chapter Twenty-Two

A Corpse is a Corpse

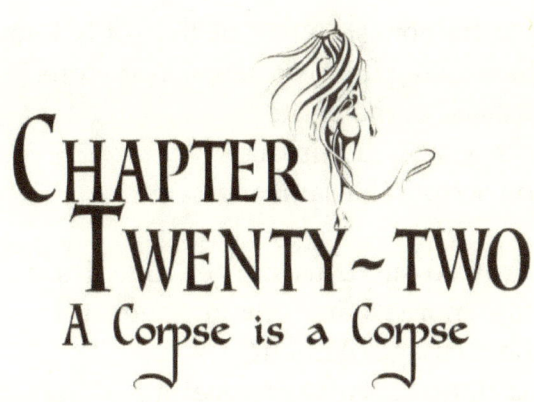

A TAP ON THE LAB door's window caught Armen's attention, and she turned away from the body to find Terry peering through the glass. She held up a finger, telling him to give her a minute, and turned around to finish up her work. When Armen stepped through the doors, Terry sat at her computer, getting ready to do a criminal record search on Mr. Jones, whose file was open in front of him, the pictures from the crime scene all laid out.

"I've already looked."

He turned his head up to her. "What's it say?"

"Thief. It would explain why his hands are missing." She closed the file, pushed it aside, and then sat on the desk. "Common practice in ancient traditions; still used in some countries today. Demons love it because it ties the soul to them."

Terry's wide eyes met hers. "How?"

"Well, they've taken a part of him away. No doubt Ash has those hands hidden somewhere." She smiled at Terry's confusion. "Demons like to hide things."

He sat back and stared at her. "What the hell for?"

"Well, like I said, it ties the soul to them. If the soul can't find the missing item, it will remain subordinate to the demon forever with no chance of escape. It's really pointless, to be honest. None of the souls know to even look for the missing item, or items, as it were."

Terry looked at the photos.

"Yes, it's what you think it is."

"Demon script. The same message?"

"Yes."

He narrowed his eyes on her. She'd seen the stern look of his more than enough over the past week. "What's the message, Armen?"

"I'm having difficulty translating it into English so that you'll understand it." She then noticed a bag sitting on the desk. "What did you bring me?"

"Your favorite—food."

"Smells yummy." She reached for the bag and pulled out two large sandwiches, and handed one to Terry. Then she peeled the wrapper back and took a bite. "Oh, this is good."

"Glad you like it." He took a bite of his sandwich. Then pointed at the picture. "So, this is Ashto—"

Armen waved her hand quickly and shook her head. She swallowed the bite she'd been chewing on. "Don't say her name!" She inhaled deeply and released it slowly. "Just call her Ash. That way she won't appear."

"She'll appear if I say her name?"

"Did I appear when your father summoned me?"

"Well, yeah, but she didn't appear when I said it the other day."

"Not to us, but you invoked her by saying her name. Mr. Jones there has been dead for two days, and was missing for twenty-four hours before that, so yeah, she appeared."

"Meaning what, she wasn't hanging around the planet somewhere?"

"No, she wasn't." Armen started to take another bite.

"Where was she?"

"On the edge of Gehenna," Armen said and took the bite.

"Where the hell is that?"

"Gehenna? The void, the Darkness, where we were all cast. Not a pleasant place to sit around in, especially if you're one of the Fallen. Even demons skirt the edges of it and stay the hell out. It's dark and dreary. That's the place I was telling you about, where you lose yourself. Sariel got me out of there somehow. Still haven't figured out how he did it or even got out himself."

Terry blinked rapidly and stared at her. "You can't be serious."

"I'm very serious." She picked up her water bottle, twisted the cap off, and took a drink.

"What about Hell? You said you were in Hell."

"Yeah, I've been there too." She could tell he didn't quite understand what she was talking about. "What do you think happens when you die?"

"You go to Heaven or Hell."

"Not exactly." She placed the water bottle back on the desk, folded her hands on her lap, and leaned forward. "If you've lived a good life, like your mother did, you go into the Light. If not, you go into the Darkness. You wait there, in either place, until the End of Days or Judgment Day. Some souls don't go to either place, but wander the Earth in spirit form. Some call that Limbo, or even Purgatory. Some of it is by your own choosing; some, not so much. It's in the texts, Terry. I'm surprised you don't know that."

He shrugged. "Well, religious teachings have altered over the years."

Armen let out a short laugh. "That's the damn truth of it." She could practically see the wheels turning inside his head before he focused on her again. "Wait, but your dad speaks to Him. Why don't you know that from your father?"

Terry chuckled. "If you were God, would you tell every little secret you had to a human?"

"I suppose not," Armen replied.

"Even with my dad, it's still about faith, Armen. We don't tell our kids everything, and we are *all* His children. I vaguely recall that no one's in Hell yet, but didn't realize it worked the same for Heaven. I remember that the fires of Hell would be *after* the End of Days." He paused, fidgeting, picking at a crumb on the desk. "Did you find out what you wanted to know from my father?"

"Not really. Well, I guess I already know the answers, buried deep within my mind. I just haven't reached the point of discovering them yet." She bit her lower lip to keep from crying. A breakdown was the last thing she needed at work.

Terry nodded. "You'll figure it out."

"I know," she said, and picked at her sandwich.

"So, is there any clue you can give me about this message?" He pointed to the photo.

She sighed. "Well, it's not just that I'm having trouble with the translation, but it doesn't make any sense to me."

"Try me, then. What'cha got?"

She focused on the photo and moved to point out one of the symbols. "This one, it means birth. Outside of Jesus, no one's been born in any realm for roughly two thousand years. But it has nothing to do with him because this symbol"—she pointed to another figure etched in blood—"means female. It's been a while since I've seen this script, so I'm not certain about that one. This one near the end means death, and this one over here means reborn. It's like it all points to the Lamb of God and a sacrifice, with exception to the female aspect.

But even without the female aspect, it can't be correct because, as we all know, Jesus was roughly two thousand years ago . . . unless He's coming back. Holy shit."

Terry chewed slowly, contemplating her words. "Interesting."

"Confusing is more like it."

He shrugged. "Maybe it's talking about you. I mean, my dad did say something about you."

"Well, if that's the case, then apparently I was born, which would mean I have a Mother, and I do not recall ever hearing a word uttered about Her." She paused, staring at the photo. "And that last one—death—means that I'm not going to survive this thing, if what you're saying is true."

"Then let's pray it's not about you. Unless *death* is referring to the moment when you sacrificed yourself to save my father."

"Doubtful. This biblical shit is so damn cryptic. It could be like a tarot card and mean something that has nothing to do with actual *death*."

Terry continued to eat, and she stared at the photo, tilting her head to view it better from a different angle. She pointed to the final symbol. "That one means Darkness eternal."

"That doesn't sound good." His phone rang, and he detached it from the leather case on his belt and answered it. "Detective Armstrong." He listened carefully and hung up the phone. "Got one."

"Shit," Armen said with a shake of her head. "I was hoping to get through the first night back without a call."

"Yeah," he replied somberly and stood up. "Coming?"

"You'll be calling me anyway." She hopped off the desk, rewrapped her sandwich, and placed it on the desk before grabbing her water bottle. Then she reached for

Terry's pea coat and flung it over her shoulder. "Let's go."

"After you, sweetie." He held the door open for her.

She hit him in his hard-as-a-rock stomach when she walked by. "Don't call me that at work."

Terry laughed and stepped out after her. They ran into Jasmine in the hall, who was entirely too delighted to see them together, judging from the broadening smile across her full lips.

"Where are *you* two going?"

"Corpse," Armen said and walked into the elevator.

"How romantic," Jasmine quipped, and Armen flipped her off before the doors closed completely. She heard Jasmine's laughter as the elevator started to move, and it took all she had to stifle her own.

"What was that about?"

"Nothing."

"Mmhmm." He shook his head. "Women."

Armen carefully inspected the body as Terry watched.

"Wow, she doesn't even leave them alive." He knelt next to her. "At least they're not suffering."

This one's throat was slit as well, but he didn't appear to be missing anything that Armen could see right away. There also weren't any signs of a struggle, which Terry likely found odd, but Armen didn't.

"No. It's not her style. She prefers to get the suffering in up front and then go for the kill. Sariel enjoyed—" *Shit.* "Never mind."

Terry shrugged. "At least we don't have to worry about triggers then, right?"

Armen shook her head. "No, just the fact that she's building an army."

"Shit."

"Exactly." She ran her gloved fingers over the man's chest, stopping abruptly just below his ribcage. Beneath the flesh and bone felt different than it should have. Hardened where it shouldn't be. "I need to bag this one and get him back to my lab."

"What's the rush?" Terry looked at her hand as she pressed it firmly against the body.

She looked him in the eye and moved her head closer to his. "Because there's a present inside him and it wouldn't be good for anyone else to see it."

"I'll help." He reached for the bag she'd brought with her. They bagged the body, lifted it onto the gurney, and wheeled it out to her van.

Once they had him inside, Armen closed the doors. "Thanks."

"I'll meet you there."

"Terry, I'm sure you have work to do."

"And this is part of it."

"To help me dissect a human being? I don't think your stomach can handle it."

"You'd be surprised what my stomach can handle," he replied with a smirk. "Stop arguing with me for once. I'll follow you." He turned and headed to his squad car before she could reply.

Armen sighed and walked around the side of the van. She opened the door and climbed in, then shut out the cold quickly. More fickle Arizona winter-time weather. At night, the temperature generally held around 50 or 60 degrees, but she could feel the frigid air tonight and knew that it would hit freezing.

As she drove through downtown Phoenix, she reached over to adjust the heat. For some reason, it just wasn't heating up inside the van. She'd have to remind herself to let maintenance know about it. The radio hadn't worked in a long time, either, and tonight she wished it did because it was too silent, aside from the unhealthy rumbling of the engine. Armen hated the silence. It reminded her of the Darkness, never gave her a good feeling, and her nerves were already on edge, especially after feeling that lump inside the corpse in the back of her van. She had an idea of what it might be, but she needed to be certain.

Her ears perked at a distant cry and the sound of a thick plastic bag rustling—from the inside—as though fingers were clawing at it to find the opening. When she stopped at the next light, she turned around and stared at the body bag. For several seconds, it didn't move, and she told herself to stop worrying. The light changed to green and she moved forward. The noise came again, and she stopped at the next traffic light and turned to view the body bag once more. She focused intently on it, but it sat perfectly still. Armen shook her head. *You're letting your imagination get the best of you.*

Vibrant sound burst through the air, cutting the silence and making her jump. Her hand went to her waist and she pulled her cell phone from her pocket, which was one hell of a struggle with the seatbelt attached. It continued to ring until she touched the screen and answered with a hasty hello.

"Wow, are you okay?" Terry asked.

"No, I'm not. The silence in this damn van has my mind creating all sorts of noises."

Terry chuckled. "You're fine, Armen."

"Why are you calling me? Aren't you behind me?"

"Yeah. I was just wondering if you were ever going to go on this green light."

"What?" She looked up. The light was green, and from the looks of the flashing "Don't Walk" sign, it'd been green for a little while. "Shit." She started to move again and held the phone to her ear. "Sorry."

"It's okay. You want me to hang on so you have some distraction from your imagination?"

"That would be nice."

"Okay." She could faintly hear his radio in the background. "So, dinner Sunday night. I was thinking about the Salt Cellar. You like seafood, right?"

"Isn't that place expensive?" She stopped at the next red light. She hated driving through the downtown area. The traffic lights were all a quarter of a mile apart. They'd found the body at one of the new condos. That would really bring up the value of them now.

"Don't worry about how much it costs, and answer my question."

She rolled her eyes. "Yes, I like seafood."

"Don't roll your eyes at me, either."

Armen laughed. "Damn, you know me well."

"And don't you forget it," he said with a chuckle.

Something mimicked her laugh and she froze. Dropping her voice to a whisper, she said, "Terry."

"What is it?"

"I don't know." Driving the van made her vulnerable and Armen didn't like feeling vulnerable. She cursed her assistant for calling in sick. That boy had better be in traction or something along those lines; otherwise, he was bound to be when Armen got hold of him. "I just heard an echo of my laugh, but I'm not hearing an echo of my voice."

"Pull over."

"Maybe it's just because the van's so quiet." She knew it was wrong. She viewed her mirrors to see if there were any cars around her. There was traffic everywhere. It was the weekend—and one in the morning. The bars were still open and the downtown area held many attractions for people.

"Armen, pull over now," Terry demanded.

"I can't. Not here. There are too many people."

"Fine." He flipped on his lights and siren. He pulled around her, sped up and eased through traffic at the next red light. "Follow me."

She flipped on her lights, pushed down on the gas pedal, and kept up with him as he wound his way through traffic. The plastic shifted again, loud enough for her to hear it over the sirens. Her eyes went to the rearview mirror. She couldn't see anything but the back windows.

"Talk to me, Armen."

"Nothing's happening yet." She continued to follow him. "Where are you taking us?"

"Away from the public."

A loud thud hit the floor of the van, and Armen sat up straight to see in the mirror. "You'd better hurry." She still couldn't see anything, and it would be too dangerous to turn around while driving. "Maybe we should've stayed at that place with it."

"Yeah, I'm thinking the same thing right now." He eased through another red light. He drove to the other side of the ballpark and arena, past the federal building, courthouse, and their building, and through the train yard.

"My bad," she said, and tried to get a quick glimpse behind her when Terry slowed down. The body bag had fallen off the gurney and to the floor. Hadn't she strapped it down? "Shit, Terry. The bag's on the floor."

Armen turned her eyes back to the road and slammed on the brakes. She'd nearly rear-ended Terry's squad car. Terry took a quick turn into a garage. "Are you crazy?"

"Just follow." He swerved his way around the corners of the garage as quickly as possible.

Armen tried to keep up with him.

The phone went dead and she abruptly stopped the van on the fifth level due to the clawing and scraping and plastic tearing in the back. In the distance, she heard Terry's car squeal to a stop not long after. The sound of his car door slamming shut thundered through the garage, even over the hissing coming from the back of her van.

She moved out of her seat, but lost precious time trying to untangle herself from the seatbelt, as she was no match for the thing crawling out of the body bag.

"Armen!" Terry's voice bounced off concrete blocks and walls.

The last she saw of him, he stood twenty feet away from the van, his Glock drawn and aimed directly at the windshield.

And her.

"Armen!"

She picked up the nearest thing to a weapon she could find and stood in the cargo compartment just behind the front seats, facing off with the creature. It hissed again.

Armen pulled the ring and depressed the lever to activate the fire extinguisher.

Chapter Twenty-Three
Warrior

THE WINDSHIELD CRACKED, BEGINNING AT a small dot, and then slowly spider-webbed from there, each line of webbing cracking one millimeter at a time in a jerk-stop motion. As soon as one would stop, another would jump again from elsewhere on the web.

Armen struggled for breath after slamming into that windshield, but she still managed to hit the demon upside the head with the fire extinguisher. She saw Terry move behind the van through the windows—barely—and swung at the demon again.

The demon retaliated—hitting Armen hard in the chest with both hands—and she flew backward again.

The windshield shattered this time, and Armen hit the garage floor with a thud, a roll, and a grunt. Terry jumped around the side of the van again. Armen lay on the concrete in a crumpled heap, groaning, and he ran to her side.

"Are you okay?" He knelt to help her up.

She let out a frustrated growl. "I *hate* being human."

Terry chuckled. "Well, I suggest you get over it. You're going to be human for a while. Also, we weren't meant to fly."

She glared at him, but her attention soon moved to the van that shook violently. "Shit."

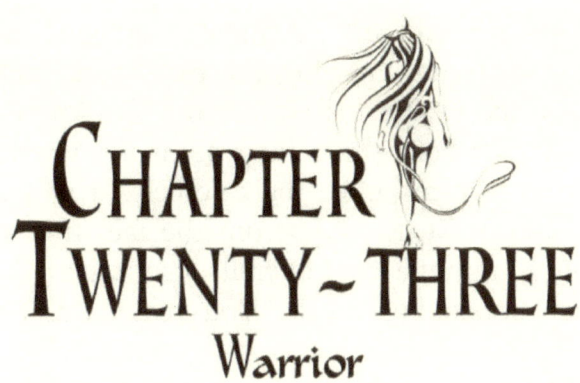

"What's in there?" Armen watched as Terry alternated between checking the exits and tracking the activity of the creature in the van. She knew he was concerned that before too long someone would surely enter the garage to get to their vehicle. It was Armen's primary concern too, aside from the fact that a demon was about to remove itself from its steel cage.

Armen shook her head. "You really don't want to know."

"If I have to fight the damn thing, I want to know," he said and pulled her to her feet.

"Really, must you manhandle me?"

Terry looked her in the eye, the serious, no bullshit expression on his face. "Tell me what I'm about to face, Armen."

"Warrior demon," she replied and yanked her arm from his grip. "A nasty one." She brushed herself off and stood straight, albeit painfully. She really didn't want to resort to using her cane again.

Before Terry could respond, the demon came to the front of the van, climbing onto the dash. It perched in the open windshield.

"Okay, *that* is something I've never seen before," Terry said, staring at the creature.

"Not surprising." Armen moved to his side. "They don't appear much in this realm. It's usually by accident. I don't think this one was, though."

It was small, perhaps about three or four feet in height, no eyes, and several sharp teeth. But the size of a demon didn't really matter. They were all equally dangerous, especially when they had several sharp teeth and claws, much like this one did.

"Was *that* inside the victim?"

"Yes, and there isn't much left of the victim. Do you have silver loaded in that gun?" Armen kept her eyes on the demon.

"Yes." He raised his gun and aimed at the intended target. It snarled at him.

Someone screamed. Armen didn't look away from the demon, but it switched its attention to the screaming woman near the elevators. It leapt forward.

"Shoot it!" Armen ducked out of Terry's way, running parallel to the gunfire as it rang through the garage. Terry succeeded in taking out a car window, a light, and a tire as the demon sped toward its target, crawling over and under cars and along the wall sideways. Armen just hoped it didn't decide to jump in her direction; she didn't want to get inadvertently shot.

"Shit!" He fired once more and the demon dropped to the concrete right in front of the woman, who despite being petrified managed to continue screaming relentlessly. The demon writhed on the floor of the garage, hissing and cursing them both in hoarse whispers suitable only for Hell.

"I thought you never missed."

"Shut up."

Armen ran over to the demon and stomped on its head, which immediately burst into embers and ash. The woman continued to scream.

"Would you shut the hell up?"

The woman closed her mouth and stared at Armen wide-eyed, unblinking, and trembling violently. She asked, "Wha . . . what was . . . that *thing*?"

"A demon. What did it look like?"

"Armen, don't be so cruel." Terry walked over to them after retrieving his radio from the squad car. "Most people haven't seen a demon." He observed the woman briefly after watching the demon disintegrate. "Are you all right, ma'am?"

"I . . . I . . . think so," she replied, her voice just as shaken as her body.

Terry grabbed his radio and called it in. When he finished, he looked at the woman with soft eyes. "I'm having someone come down to speak with you, ma'am."

Her eyes widened again. "What . . . for?"

"Just a precaution, ma'am." He held out his hand, pointing to his car. "Here, you can wait in my car. It's safe in there." He gently took her by the elbow and led her over to it. "Just wait here. Someone will be along shortly." Once he closed the door, he returned to Armen, who crouched over the ashes. "Honestly, you need to learn some people skills."

Armen huffed. "I don't have time to cater to fragile people when there are demons running around looking for hosts." She poked a finger into the ashes and lifted it to her tongue. "Ugh, you reek of Ash." She raised her head to Terry. "This was the first of many."

"Look, I get it, I really do," he said calmly, "but you need to have more tact. That woman was scared to death and you snapped at her as her world just crumbled because a creature that's not supposed to exist charged her."

She dragged a hand over her face with a sigh. "I'm sorry. I'm just . . . I'm focused on the bigger picture here because I don't know what's happening or why, and I'm afraid that it's too big, that it might involve humanity, the whole of the planet, or maybe even the universe."

Terry crouched beside her and touched her arm. "Am I not by your side right now, through this? Armen, I'm here. Talk to me. Tell me what's going on when shit goes down. I'm your partner in this."

She quickly rose, pulling her arm from his grip. "More will come soon. I can't be weak. Not *now*. Do you want a polite, tactful woman or a warrior? Because let me tell you, the warrior is the one you fucking need right now, even if she isn't pleasant."

He stood up and stared at her, and gave a short nod. "How soon?"

Armen saw the horror in his eyes before he returned to cop mode, that he saw the warrior angel she once was before him now, that cold-hearted bitch of a demon she'd never truly be rid of even with her flesh, and *not* the human woman he fell for. "It's not Friday anymore, you know."

"So? What's that have to do with anything?" His words were cold, clipped, as though he'd shut down all emotion.

She grimaced. "It means we're in for a long damn night, that's what." When he frowned, she sighed. She shouldn't have to explain this to the son of a priest. "Saturday, the day before the Sabbath." His frown remained, but comprehension started to seep in. "This is going to be a 24-hour rollercoaster ride to Hell."

He stared at her a moment before finally saying, "Shit."

"Ah, now you get it," Armen said. "Welcome to the end of the world."

"How many more demons are coming?"

"Don't know." She looked at the ashes again. "It depends on how many she already has, and how many she's taken besides these last two." She headed toward the back of the van.

"And the host thing?"

She clucked her tongue. How to explain that one? "The warriors . . . plant a seed in a human body—dead, fresh kill—and it produces more of them."

Terry blinked at her before responding. "How in God's name are we supposed to fight this?"

A patrol car pulled up behind the van as Armen rummaged through the mess. Bits of human flesh covered the inside of the van, and she had to pick them off to get to what she needed.

"I honestly couldn't tell you." Terry, she knew, would be more concerned with keeping it out of the public eye in order to keep the public safe. Armen wasn't sure that was entirely possible. If Ash wanted to make herself known to the world, she would, and if the End of Days lurked around the corner, there'd be no stopping those residing in Gehenna and all of the Underworld from coming into open view for all the world to see. She headed back over to the demon.

"Great," was Terry's reply as an officer approached. He took in the van's condition, then his eyes moved to the woman sitting in the car with her face in her hands, and finally, his eyes fell on Armen and Terry.

"Detective Armstrong, Dr. Leza," he said with a nod to each. "Are you in need of assistance?"

Terry nodded to his squad car. "Could you take that woman in for counseling?"

"You know the doc's not in at this hour," the officer replied.

"Call her in, Peterson," Terry said. "This woman needs her attention immediately, and Dr. Whitewolf will know exactly how to treat her."

"Whitewolf, huh?" Peterson's eyes lingered on the pile of ash. "Another demon? Who was it this time?"

"Just a warrior." Armen scooped a small sample of the ash into a vial she'd plucked from the van when he pulled up.

"Warrior for whom?"

Armen peered up at him, surprised. "If you're asking that question, then you know damn well her name can't be spoken aloud."

Peterson nodded. "Give me the shorter version, if she has one."

"Ash," Armen replied.

"Wow, really?"

Armen nodded.

"Damn."

She pointed a finger at him. "How do you know that?"

Peterson shrugged. "Catholic school and college theology and anthropology classes."

He might be of use to them if he knew about demons. "What else do you know?"

Peterson smiled. "Enough to possibly help, if you need it."

"Do you know how to defeat her?" Terry asked.

Peterson frowned. "Perhaps. Let me think on it while I take this one in and call the doc." He walked over to Terry's squad car and opened the door. "Ma'am, if you'd come with me, please. I'll take you somewhere safe." The woman shakily climbed out of the car, and Peterson took her by the elbow. He turned back to Terry and Armen. "I'll be right back. You want me to call someone to come for the van?"

"Yes, please," Armen replied. "Thanks."

"No problem," Peterson said, and waved. "Investigators should be here shortly to close off the scene."

Terry turned to Armen and eyed the glass vial in her hand. "What are you going to do with that?"

"Study it, what did you think I was going to do with it?" She walked to her van once more to gather a few things.

He followed her. "Study it for what?"

"There's got to be a better way to get rid of them. Exorcism and banishment just sends them away for a while, but won't kill them. The scepter kills them, but we only have one scepter, and silver bullets only work on the lesser ones." A sudden thought hit her and she bolted upright, turning to face him. "How many demon wranglers are there?"

"Several. They're placed all over the world."

Armen bit her lower lip in thought and stared off for a moment before she jerked from her trance and looked up at him. "Would you know if there's been any activity with them lately?"

Terry shrugged. "I suppose I could ask."

"Yeah, do that." She pulled a duffle bag from the mess in the back of the van, opened it, sifted through, and pulled out a small satchel. She placed the vial inside the satchel, seated the satchel safely inside the bag, and closed the bag. Then she looked up at Terry again expectantly.

"Right now?" Terry looked at his watch.

"No, on Monday during normal business hours," she replied, the sarcastic twang ringing through her words.

"Fine." He pulled his phone from his belt.

Armen opened the trunk of his squad car and placed the duffle bag inside. She spotted the scepter hidden partially beneath a blanket. *Smart man.* But she wondered how they would get to it quickly if needed. It'd have to sit near them, one of them holding it, perhaps. Before closing the trunk, the twisted putrescent odor she'd always linked to demons before their arrival invaded her nostrils. She looked to Terry, whose nose wrinkled; he could smell it, too. Terry's eyes widened with acknowledgment and shifted to meet hers. She gave a quick nod. He ended his phone call and walked over to her.

"No activity elsewhere. Guess we're special."

"Scepter or gun?"

He looked briefly into the trunk. "Gun. You're probably better with that thing than I am."

She reached down into the trunk. "I doubt that." *Something* slithered through the garage. "Oh, that's a big one."

"Armen, I really don't need your commentary. It's not helping me."

She chuckled. "Fine, it's not a big one."

"You are so not funny right now." He drew his weapon, checked the magazine, refilled it, and slid it back into the Glock with a snap. "Do you have any idea how long this damn report is going to be?"

"A small novel?" She pulled out the scepter. "As I said earlier, it's going to be a long night."

The sound drew closer, coming from one of the upper levels. Armen listened carefully, distinguishing between the normal sounds of the city and those that were otherworldly. The sounds shifted in her ears and otherworldly became prominent with its beats and winds. A hot breeze blew across her flesh. She leaned closer to Terry.

"It's not alone," she whispered and thumbed the trigger on the scepter. Its blades swept out with a ring of metal scraping metal just as a car alarm went off on the level above them. A loud crash echoed, and Armen figured the demons had flipped the car over. "That doesn't sound good."

"No shit." Terry raised his gun.

Armen followed the ramp on the other side of the wall with her eyes, peering through the shrinking gap. Several feet appeared, running down in a stampede, shaking the entire concrete level. She heard Terry mutter something under his breath before he took aim and fired. A prayer, perhaps, which she thought wasn't such a bad idea at the moment.

Father . . . .

Chapter Twenty-Four
Ashtoreth

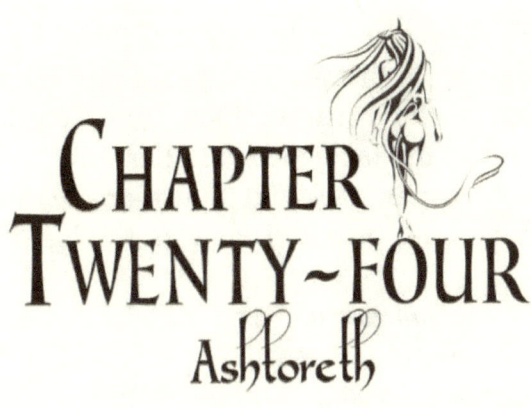

AN ARMY OF WARRIOR DEMONS rounded the corner. Terry took out several on the front line, but he would be out of bullets soon. Just as the thought occurred to Armen, she heard a click signaling he'd released the magazine. He reached for his utility belt and pulled another loaded magazine from it as the empty one fell from the gun, the plastic clacking against the concrete. The demons drew closer. He slid the magazine into place and drew the barrel back, firing once more at those nearest to them. Several of them moved around the squad car. Armen sliced through one with the scepter when it came from behind. It crumbled into ember and ash with a garbled scream that barely left its throat before that too disintegrated. She jumped to the opposite side of the car from Terry, blades cutting through the air with viciousness and speed. Her body responded almost as though it remembered her days as a warrior. The demons dwindled in number as Armen cut and sliced and decapitated, and Terry fired upon them one after another.

The air in the garage filled with ash, but it was the woman standing at the top of the ramp looking down at them with a grin upon her pale face that concerned Armen. Two small horns protruded from her forehead, framed by deep burgundy hair that flowed to her waist. A lightweight cloth barely covered her almost human body, rich with crimson blood. She stood poised in observation of the tableau before her. In a long sweep of her blades, Armen took out five more warrior demons before they could attack. That was the last of them, for now.

"Azel, you impress me," the Red Queen said, a smile twisting the corner of her ruby lips. *"Had I known it would be so easy for you, I would have brought forth Leviathan."*

"What do you want, Ash?"

Ash's grin grew wider, revealing four fangs among the otherwise perfectly human white teeth. *"You, my dear."*

"What the hell for?" Armen had long grown tired of this game.

Ash laughed, almost a giggle, but not quite. *"We know He favors you; that He still loves you."*

"What does that have to do with anything?"

"Absolutely everything, my dear."

"Why are all of you after me?"

Ash raised one shoulder casually. *"Why not?"*

Armen frowned at the Red Queen, wondering what in the hell the endgame was. Demons were never forthright with their answers. "I'll not be your prisoner in your war against Heaven."

Ash threw her head back and uttered a short bark of laughter. *"Who said anything about imprisoning you, dearest Azel? We, who shared the Darkness with you after your Fall, would never imprison you as He did us."*

Armen cleared her throat. "I think you placed yourself there, Ms. Lust."

Ash pointed. *"Pot, kettle."*

Armen growled. "Don't you *ever* try that shit with me again."

A witch's cackle came from Ash's throat. *"I thought you should enjoy yourself with such a fine human specimen."* She eyed the muscle-bound cop next to Armen. *"But, of course, if you do not care for him, he should make a wonderful playmate for me."* She winked at Terry.

"I don't think so." Terry held his aim on her.

Armen's anger flared. "Don't you *dare* touch him."

Ash arched a fine-lined brow. *"Is that jealousy I hear, dear Azel? My, you are one step closer to coming home to us, then."*

"I will never go back there," Armen spat.

"Oh, but you will not need to, Azel." Flames lit her eyes. *"Here, my pet shall help you bring it forth."* She gracefully waved her hand toward the ramp the warrior demons had come down.

"What are you—?" The garage shook again, but this time only four footsteps sounded. It was large, whatever it was. Armen's mind raced to recall Ash's pets. She had several: snakes, scorpions, spiders, felines, canines—all taken from Earth the first time she came to this plane and all larger than those residing on Earth because she had manipulated her pets to their larger size. One particular four-legged beast jumped into her mind and she shot a look at Terry.

"Cerberus," they said in unison, the creature's most common name. Armen didn't have time to ask how he came to the same conclusion.

"Get in the car." Terry ran past her to the driver's side.

Armen thumbed the trigger on the scepter, and its blades promptly retracted. She threw a glare at Ash before climbing into the squad car. As Terry threw the car in reverse and backed up to pass the van, Armen saw Cerberus round the corner and stop next to Ash. The dog stood taller than the demon, whose height was close to a human's. He lowered one of his three heads to Ash, who stroked his fur and whispered in his ear. A lip on each head curled in a snarl, and all three heads barked viciously. Ash gave Cerberus a command and stepped away, and he started after them. Terry turned the car around at the end of the ramp.

"Go, go, go," Armen yelled, hitting the dash, and Terry slammed his foot on the gas pedal, sending her flying to the back of the seat. She snapped her seatbelt into place; this was going to be one hell of a ride.

Terry took a sharp turn. The rear end fishtailed into a parked SUV, setting off its alarm. He sped down the ramp and made another neck-snapping turn. Armen hoped the corners would slow the beast down. They drove past a car coming up the ramp, and Armen cursed herself for letting Terry lead them into the garage in the first place. She should have known better. Cerberus barreled into the car as it skidded to a stop, crushing the side of the vehicle with his weight. Screams from the tires and from the people in the other car echoed off the concrete walls and floor of the car park. Armen could only hope that the people inside were okay as Terry took the next sharp corner, heading to the third level.

"How in the world are we supposed to kill *that*?" He sped down the ramp.

"I'm thinking." Armen faced forward again. "Watch out!"

Terry mashed his hand against the horn to get the pedestrians that suddenly appeared ahead of them out of the way, but Armen had a feeling that their scrambling, along with screaming, had nothing to do with Terry's horn blaring.

They sped past the small group with the Hound from Hell right on their tail.

"Shit! Tell me he didn't hurt any of them."

Armen looked back. "No, he's still coming after us." Cerberus snapped at one man who was too close. "As long as they stay out of reach, they'll be fine."

"I did not want to hear that." He cranked the steering wheel, screeching the tires around yet another sharp corner.

"I know. It's like a bad werewolf movie." *Two more levels. Come on.* The bars would be closing soon, and she worried that they'd encounter more pedestrians. Drunk ones, at that, which would be ten times worse.

Terry zoomed down the ramp to the second level and spun the tires around the turn, narrowly missing another car's tail end. Cerberus took care of it for him when he shoulder-checked the vehicle. Its alarm sounded, which made the beast angrier, and he stomped his large paw on another car, causing it to crash into the one next to it.

Once around the last corner, Terry sped up. *Almost there.* Armen could see the street below. A short round woman with straight brown hair appeared in their path, and Terry laid on the horn once more. The man with her quickly pulled her back, and Terry sped past them and onto the street.

Armen hastily turned around to see where Cerberus was. Unfortunately, the woman was too close, and with a snap of his jaws from the nearest head, Cerberus decapitated her.

"Oh . . . wow."

"What? What happened?" Terry swerved around traffic.

"Yep, bad werewolf movie." Armen turned in her seat to face forward again.

"Okay, we need to think about where we're going to lead this thing." Terry reached forward to flip on his siren and lights, but Armen grabbed his hand.

"Don't. That sound will just make it worse. It'll draw more attention than we want."

"How am I going to get around this shit, then?" He yanked the wheel to the left to stop from hitting a car, and then quickly jerked it to the right. "And FYI, a giant fucking three-headed dog running through the streets is going to draw some damn attention."

Armen growled, mostly because he was right. "You're just going to have to navigate through it and get us away from all this damn traffic." Armen turned to look back and saw Cerberus barreling into cars left and right, knocking some of them over and running over the tops of others. "And quickly, before he destroys everything and hurts more people." She faced forward again and placed a hand against her forehead. "Oh, this is so going to end up on the morning news."

"I don't give a rat's ass about the morning news. Maybe it'll wake people up." He flipped on the lights anyway.

Armen nodded absently, thinking about how to destroy Cerberus. The main concern, of course, was not getting hurt in the process, which seemed impossible considering the three heads with very large, sharp teeth. How do you kill a three-headed dog? There was decapitation, which instantly brought back the image of the woman at the garage entrance. That would mean three in a row and would be too damn difficult. She looked in the side mirror and watched the destruction taking place behind them, and she sighed before looking at the scepter. Its blades weren't long enough to remain out of reach of the beastie's snapping jowls. Then she looked at Terry. Would silver bullets work on Cerberus? He was much larger than the minions. She supposed it was worth trying. She shifted her eyes to view Terry's fiercely focused face.

"We need to trap him. So he can't move around too much."

"He's as big as a truck," Terry replied. "What do you suggest?"

"Well, think of a place that a truck can't fit through that will hold him still so we can kill him."

"This isn't Rome. We Americans like big open spaces for our gigantic automobiles."

"That's because you're all over-compensating for something."

"What was that?" He took a sharp right down Van Buren, which was only two blocks away from their starting point.

"Nothing," she replied.

"We need backup, or *some*thing." Terry grabbed his radio and told dispatch what was happening. The woman didn't believe him at first, until Peterson called in after hearing the all-call. After running a few red lights, which was dangerous enough with the lights *and* sirens, the next intersection they approached had a police car on each side blocking traffic, which relieved Armen to no end because it meant they wouldn't T-bone someone. She hoped.

"Tell me what you've got," Peterson's voice called over the radio.

Armen grabbed the radio and held it up to speak. "Cerberus."

"Get the f—" Static garbled his words, and then he came back clearly. "How big is he?"

"About seven feet at the shoulder. And probably wider than Armstrong's squad car."

"That's about the shuddering truth of it," Terry said.

"Holy crap, really?" Peterson asked, his voice crackling. "Does he really have three heads?"

"Yes, and very large teeth." She leaned over to get a look at the speedometer. "We're going about sixty right now and he's having no trouble keeping up."

"And he's not going to wind down, either," Peterson said. "I hope you have a full tank."

"Three-fourths. We need to trap him. Any ideas?" They whizzed under the overpass for the I-10 freeway.

"Go faster." He chuckled. "Give me a minute. I just heard where you are."

"Well, hurry it up. We haven't got all night," Armen replied with her own unique tone, the one that implied she was just razzing him.

The radio remained silent except for the chatter from other officers witnessing the event and giving information on their whereabouts. Armen noticed that their speed had increased. Now they were going seventy, and Cerberus was only about four or five car lengths behind. He showed no indication of slowing down. One officer had the bright idea of pulling out quickly behind them when they sped past and placed his car as an obstacle for Cerberus to overcome. Shouts over the radio came next. Cerberus sailed over the top of it, taking the lights off with his back paws.

"Peterson," Armen said firmly into the radio.

"Head up to McDowell . . . . That idiot, I can't believe he did that," he said in the background, not really talking to Armen. He returned to her. "There's a National Guard base over there. They know you're coming and they're ready. Cooper, what the hell were you thinking? Did the three heads not clue you in to the danger?"

Armen interrupted the tirade. "What the hell are they going to do at the National Guard, blast him with a tank?"

"If they can get him positioned right, yes," Peterson replied.

Armen could hear the smile in his voice when he said that. "You're enjoying this." Truth be known, she was kind of enjoying it herself.

"Damn straight. It's not every day you get to take down a mythological creature. Just wish I could see him. I'm on my way to the base now, but I don't know if I'll make it in time."

"Be careful. I may need you later to help me get rid of Ash."

"You bet. I've got some ideas on that one too."

"She was still in the garage when we left."

There was a pause, and then Peterson cleared his throat. "I know."

Armen closed her eyes tight. "Damn it."

"How many?" Terry asked, and Armen repeated the question into the radio.

"Five," Peterson replied.

"Bitch," Terry muttered. "I'm going to cut her dog into several little pieces for that."

Terry made a hard left turn onto 40th Street and sped up again. Armen told Peterson where they were, even though he likely already knew via the GPS tracker. It gave her something to focus on. The turn Cerberus made was much shorter and he nearly took out the traffic light with it.

Armen looked back at Cerberus to see how far back he was. "Terry, we're going to need more time between us if they intend to blow his ass up."

"I'm working on it."

Patrol cars littered the streets, keeping traffic at bay so they could escape the beast. A news van appeared ahead of them and she laughed.

"I told you it'd be on the morning news." She turned in her seat to face Terry so the camera wouldn't catch her face. Terry turned sharply to the right, sending the back end of the car fishtailing again. Armen hung on for dear life, trying desperately to not have her head end up in Terry's lap. "Don't spin us out of control."

"Would you like to drive?" Terry snapped. "I'm trying to not kill us."

"On McDowell, right?" Peterson's voice came over the radio. "Oh wait, I see you . . . *and* him . . . Holy Hannah!"

"Big and nasty, isn't he? Where are you?"

"About a block back. The gates are open. When you get inside, turn to the right and hit the dirt, round up near the mountain— "

"That is not a mountain," Armen replied.

"Mountain, hill, whatever, just round up to it. They're positioned so that if they miss, it'll hit the *mountain*."

"Smartass."

"Is she always like that, Armstrong?"

Armen grinned. "He can't answer that right now. He's trying to drive."

"Yes," Terry shouted before she let go of the button.

Peterson's laughter came across the airwaves. "Lucky man."

"Not so lucky if I get us both killed," Terry replied.

Terry floored the gas pedal to create more distance between them and Cerberus, who was now about nine car lengths back. Of course, there was nothing safe about traveling nearly one hundred miles per hour down a city street. He moved the car to the right lane, intending to take a very wide left turn without losing much speed.

And then there was the semi-truck coming over the mountain that would block his path to the gates if he didn't time it just right.

Armen was pretty sure her life was about to flash before her eyes as she braced herself.

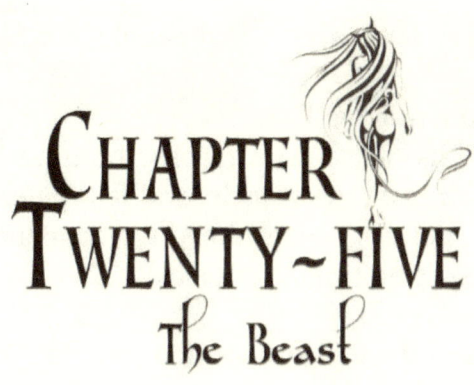

Chapter Twenty-Five

The Beast

THE GUARD AT THE GATE watched with ever-widening eyes as Terry maneuvered the car, cutting across the path of the semi-truck, whose driver panicked and locked up his brakes. The semi skidded along the asphalt, tires bouncing on the trailer, making it swerve to its right. Soon, the trailer skidded and bounced on only four tires on one side until toppling over, taking the rig with it.

"Damn it!"

"I'm sure he's fine," Armen said.

Terry took a sharp right upon entering the gate, headed into the dirt and toward the mountain. He drove along the fence, rounded the tank, and neared the top of the hill at the mountain's base. Armen felt queasy and crossed an arm over her stomach. Terry zoomed past the tank's aiming point as Cerberus leapt over the skidding semi-truck and barreled through the gate opening. Armen had no idea if the guard was out of reach of the beast's snapping jowls, as the world had suddenly blurred on her. Soldiers directed Terry to stop at the base of boulders, their shouts heard amidst the chaos, and the car slid sideways when he slammed on the brakes. Armen clutched her belly with both arms as Terry jumped out of the car. After a pause, he ran around to the passenger side, and opened the door. She started to fall out, but Terry and the seatbelt caught her before she hit the dirt.

"Come on, move it."

She fumbled at the contraption holding her hostage, pulled herself from the vehicle, and fell to her knees.

"Armen, get up." He grabbed her arm and quickly let go. "Shit, this is no time to get sick."

"Fuck y . . . ehhk."

Terry leaned over and pulled her hair back. "What was that again?"

"Shut up." She wiped her mouth, sat up, and teetered to the right.

Terry held her steady. "Armen, sweetie, I'm extremely sorry for this, but there's a very big three-headed dog that wants to eat us coming our way. We need to move . . . NOW!" He picked her up and popped her over his shoulder.

She screamed at him, but her cries were lost in erupting gunfire. Cerberus had entered the field.

Terry carried her around the boulders and leaned her up against one. She lurched forward and he jumped out of the way.

"What the hell is wrong with you?" He propped her up against the large rock again and asked for some water. A canteen headed his way and he made her drink from it. "You've seen the worst shit there is to see out there."

Armen groaned. "Motion sickness." She took another swig from the canteen and the coolness of the water penetrating her body ran in a wave over her. She shut her eyes tight in an attempt to quell the on-coming headache.

Terry peeked around the boulders and Armen took in slow concentrated breaths between water relief and clenching eyes. "So, how exactly does that work with wings?" He looked back at her before returning his gaze to the spectacle on the other side of the boulders.

"Not then. Now," she snapped.

"Cover your ears." He slapped his hands over his ears.

Armen dropped the canteen and had her ears covered a mere second before the blast. The ground quaked and the boulders shook. Terry peeked around the boulder again to view the heavy dust cloud. Silence fell on the air and they waited to see what had become of the beast.

Gunfire resounded again, at close range.

"Shit."

Armen watched his face, studying the expressions as he concentrated on the field. Finally, after his last colorful word, she spoke. "He needs to be killed with the scepter." She knew it all along, but a small part of her had hoped, prayed, for something else to work. Either she or Terry would have to get close enough to kill him, and it was highly doubtful in her mind that whichever one of them it was, it wouldn't be an easy escape from Death. She leaned over and picked up the canteen. The nausea had gone now, and she had a job to do.

Terry grabbed her arm when she walked by. "Where are you going?"

"One of us has to do it. It might as well be me."

"Excuse me, but why you? The scepter belongs to me."

"Actually, it belongs to *my* Father, but you can have yours call Him to ask if you can use it." She pulled her arm from his grasp and continued walking. "Besides, I'm the warrior, not you."

"Damn, you're a bitch when you want to do things your way." He trotted to catch up to her.

She walked up to a soldier, eyeing his canteen. "Is that full?" When he nodded, she smiled and asked,

"Trade?" His brow quirked up, but he nodded once more and exchanged the canteens with her. "Thanks." She turned and headed toward the car to fetch the scepter.

"What do you need that for?" Terry asked, following her.

Armen mumbled, her fingers moving over the open canteen. Then she lifted it over her head and dumped its contents onto herself.

"What are you doing? You'll freeze now."

"Hush." She looked toward the not-so-quickly clearing dust cloud and leaned into the car to pick up the scepter.

"Armen, I can't let you do this."

She stood with the scepter in hand and eyed him. "What do you suggest, then? We keep trying to blow him to Kingdom Come?"

Terry cocked his head to the side. "Funny, and no, it's obviously not going to work."

"Then what? He needs to go bye-bye and this scepter is the only way to do it."

"We work together. If you want to be the one to slice him open, fine, but I'm helping you slay that godforsaken thing."

"Then I suggest you find a full canteen." She walked to the back of the car.

A soldier overheard their conversation and tossed him a canteen as he turned around. He nodded a thank you and ran over to Armen. "Now what?"

She looked down at it. "Open it." He opened the canteen and she mumbled once more, moving her fingers over the top. "Now pour it over you."

"Was that a blessing?"

"Don't question, just do it. We don't have much time on our side here."

Terry did as she told him to. The icy water soaked his head, shoulders, and shirt. "Jes—"

Armen glared at him briefly, but relaxed when he didn't finish the name. Good. He was finally learning. She moved forward. "Come on."

"What are we going to do?" Terry walked alongside her, drawing his weapon out of habit.

"I want you to try and shoot him, since you have the silver bullets." She pointed at his gun. "That might distract him so I can sneak around."

"He has three heads, Armen. He's going to be hard to sneak up on."

"Oh, you don't have to tell me that." She quickly placed her fingers to her lips.

The dust was still thick, and Cerberus couldn't be seen. Armen wondered if he'd escaped the field and would pounce on them from above. She immediately turned to the boulders, searching them. He wasn't there. The CO had ceased all gunfire while she and Terry were in the field at the base of the mountain. Her apprehension increased for several reasons, one of which included the likely itchy trigger fingers of frightened soldiers who'd never seen anything like Cerberus before. She heard a moan coming from ahead. Terry moved forward, but she quickly stopped him. When he looked at her, she shook her head and then pointed to her ear.

Moaning, brief and soft, and then loud again. Bones crunching the next second, followed by a scream of sheer pain and terror. Those were the sounds she wanted him paying attention to. Unfortunately, she couldn't block out the whispers from the guards behind her, or the screams rising from Hell. Two shooting stars caught her eye, and she closed her eyes and swallowed her fear.

Terry froze. "Holy shit," he mouthed to Armen.

Armen pointed to herself and then pointed across the field. She then motioned to Terry and pointed down for him to stay put. He raised his gun, aiming into the dust, and nodded. Armen walked carefully across the field, going as wide as possible, veering from the beast's location.

A snarl sounded, a low growl, and Armen stopped walking. She focused intently on the space between her and the evaporating dust cloud. It was still thick enough to hide Cerberus well, though the dust should have mostly settled by now. The low grumble sounded once more, and Armen's thumb found the trigger on the scepter, ready to release.

Armen thought for a fleeting moment that it might be a trap. After all, Cerberus wasn't your run-of-the-mill canine. She peered into the dust. Her ears twitched, listening intently to pinpoint his location, and she took a careful step forward. She could see Terry's apprehension at her moving closer, but she ignored him and continued. The damn dog wasn't going to kill itself.

Armen stood near the edge of the cloud, barely breathing and holding the scepter ready in her right hand. She tilted her head and turned to the right, allowing her left ear to close in on Cerberus. *Oh, you are not going to catch me in your little trap, beastie. I hear you.* With a quick jerk of her hand, she popped the scepter up in the air for a different grasp on it. When the weapon landed in her hand again, she held it like a spear. She knew she'd need to spear the center head in order for this to work. All creatures of the Darkness were like that, if they had three or more heads. If there were only two, one had to aim for the left head, as it was the dominant one. And one head . . . well, that was fairly obvious. Four or seven heads was a bit more difficult.

A low grumble came from the center, and Armen yelled. Cerberus lurched forward, leaving the confines of the dust and exposing himself, but still far enough away from her. Terry fired several rounds into him, which didn't faze the beast, nor did it draw his attention to Terry. Armen didn't hesitate, and before his front paws hit the dirt, she thrust the scepter's blade at the center head, piercing his skull between the eyes. Cerberus' center head yelped, and the other two followed. His right head snapped viciously at her, and she ducked and rolled to her right. Then his left head snapped in her direction when his front legs gave as he fell to the ground. She narrowly got away from his large teeth before the head flopped to the ground.

Terry ran to her side and stared at Cerberus. "Damn, that's one big dog."

Armen let out a short burst of laughter and leaned forward to pull the scepter's blade from Cerberus' head. The right head rose and snapped at her, catching her arm in its teeth. Armen screamed, but dared not pull away from him. Terry pulled at Cerberus' mouth in attempt to release her arm from the beast's jowls. Steam billowed into the air as Cerberus tried to tear through her flesh with his teeth, but the barrier of the water on her skin prevented it. With her other hand, Armen yanked the scepter out of the great beast's center head and quickly plunged its blade into the right head, puncturing his red eye. His grip loosened and he yelped once more before the head dropped to the dirt.

Terry pulled her away. "You *did* bless that water, didn't you?"

Armen wiped the beast's drool from her arm with disgust. "Sort of."

"What's sort of?"

She placed a hand on her hip and stared at him. "You really don't get the whole *enchantments* thing, do you?"

He stared back. "So, what, you're a witch?"

"Basically."

Peterson ran up behind them. "Can that thing slice through his necks? You should take all three heads."

Terry slowly turned to him, and Armen eyed him curiously. She wondered how a human would know such things. She inspected the scepter. The blades weren't long enough to cut through the neck of something so large. The minute trigger only seemed to work one way. She thumbed it and the blades retracted within the two-foot long cylinder, its track completely disappearing so only someone who knew how to use the weapon would know which direction to push or pull the trigger. It was Divine, after all. She thumbed it again and the blades shot out each end.

"Try reading the inscription," Peterson suggested.

Armen shifted her gaze to meet his. He quirked his eyebrow, and his lips turned up just slightly on one side of his mouth. She thumbed the trigger once more, sending the blades inside, and she looked at the scepter more closely. There it was in the tiniest of lettering—an angelic language; her Father's language. Her eyes brightened, widening with each word. She quickly turned the scepter in her hand as Cerberus continued to struggle against Death, his breathing becoming shallower by the second. She rested her thumb against the trigger and smiled when she looked into the beast's eyes. The interesting thing about the scepter's trigger was that it wasn't very large and it was generally unnoticeable as it sat amongst other similar shapes. First noticing that the track disappeared as the trigger moved was a clue that the weapon held more than one function. Armen had held many weapons like the scepter before she fell from

His grace. Each one had its own idiosyncrasies. Her smile slowly diminished and she held the scepter before her.

"Poor pup." She looked down at Cerberus. "I enjoyed your company a long time ago, but now . . . ." She pushed the trigger to the side instead of up, and a damn near three-foot blade formed at one end. "Goodbye, dearest Cerberus." Armen raised the blade over her head, and sliced through the center head's neck, then the right head, and finally, the left one. Cerberus lay in a headless heap and gradually started smoldering.

"Dearest Cerberus?" Terry questioned with a cocked brow.

"Poor pup?" said Peterson.

Armen turned to them. "What of it?" She turned to Peterson, who had a curious expression on his face, too. Damn, he didn't know what she once was. "Mythology, you know."

"Yes, I know. That was a bit more sentimental than the love of ancient stories, though."

Armen shrugged and stepped away from the large dog, in case he went up in a heap of flames, which wouldn't surprise her. She turned to Terry again. "Can we get back to my lab so I can study that sample?"

"Are you going to get car sick again?"

"Funny. It was the ride through this shit." She pointed out the rough terrain around them.

"No four-wheeling for you." Terry turned to head back to the car.

"I think it was that sandwich you brought me."

Peterson caught up to her and walked with her to Terry's squad car. "So, what does it say?"

"What?" Armen replied.

"The inscription?" He gave her a full right brow raise. His eyebrows were thick and black, much like the hair on the top of his head.

"You don't know?"

"Of course not. It's certainly not in any human language."

"How many languages do you know, Peterson?"

He smiled. "More than you'd believe, but I've never seen *that* one."

"Oh, well, then I can't tell you." She stepped around the back of Terry's car.

Peterson turned to Terry, who stood in the open door of his car. "Your woman's a tease, Armstrong."

Terry let out a short burst of laughter. "You have *no* idea."

"Shut up and get in the car," Armen said and climbed into the vehicle.

"Demanding, too," Terry said. "You heading back to the station?"

"Damn straight. I want to see what she's got. I'll follow you."

Terry got in and started the engine, but his phone rang loudly from his pocket before he could go anywhere. He quickly picked it up after seeing the caller ID. "What's up, Dad?"

Armen watched the blood drain from his face. "What is it?"

Terry shook his head. "On my way," he said finally and put down the phone. He placed both hands on the steering wheel and stared ahead.

"Terry, what's happened?"

"The Bishop has been crucified . . . in the church."

Armen quickly covered her gaping mouth with her hand. "The Basilica?"

Terry nodded and focused to put the car in gear. "Tell Peterson we're heading there first."

Armen reached for the radio, but her hand went to his arm first. "I'm sorry, Terry."

Terry gave a quick nod and turned the car toward the exit gate.

Armen picked up the radio and informed Peterson of their new destination. Once she finished, she stared out the window. She didn't know what to say to him regarding the Bishop. Armen was certain his father knew the man well, considering Sean's profession and that it stemmed from the Catholic Church. *Oh dear Father, why?* No answer came to her, though she wasn't really expecting one. She hadn't spoken to her Father in quite some time, aside from that little word game with His book. She turned the scepter in her hands and found herself reading the angelic inscription in its base. If Sean couldn't speak to her Father, she'd have been surprised at his knowledge of how to use it. She wondered if Sean ever questioned her Father and why He let things happen the way they did. But then she remembered her conversation with Sean and tossed the thought aside. *Faith in* why *He does things.*

Crucified. In the Basilica. There was no damn good reason for a priest to die in such a horrible way. She wondered if her Father did *anything* at all worthy for her to have faith in.

Why?

Such a simple question, but one with too many answers to ever be simple.

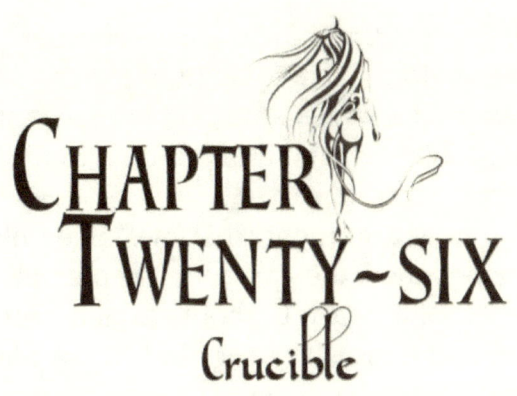

Chapter Twenty-six

Crucible

THEY PULLED UP TO THE Spanish-style church on 3rd Street—St. Mary's Basilica. According to Terry, Sean had always liked this particular church for several reasons. The people were always very nice, the neighborhood was in the heart of Phoenix and quite old, and he could often find the Bishop there. Terry had mentioned before that he had come here a lot in his youth.

It was close to three in the morning. Terry parked his unmarked squad car and turned it off. He sat silently for a moment, concentrating on the top of the steering wheel as he took in slow breaths to steady himself for what he was about to witness. Armen could only guess that losing his mother had been the single worst thing that ever happened to him; and that losing his fiancée or girlfriend may have been the second worst thing he'd experienced. He looked worn out. Lack of sleep and constantly moving were beginning to show in lines on his face and dark circles under his eyes. Losing the Bishop would be another huge blow. During the drive over, Terry divulged that he'd known the man since birth. Armen was surprised he even said a word.

"Terry." Armen reached for his arm. He closed his eyes briefly before turning to her. She tilted her head, blonde locks spilling over her shoulder from her ponytail. "You don't have to do this."

He attempted a smile, studying her face intently. "I'll be fine." He took her hand and pulled it to his lips. "Let's kill this bitch so this'll be over."

"You'll get no argument from me." She unlatched her seatbelt and opened the car door, scepter in hand, and climbed out. She wasn't about to tell Terry that it wouldn't be completely over, but it would end the current situation of sacrifices. The only way to know for certain if or when this insanity would be over was to ask her Father, and she doubted He would give much detail concerning it, though she was beginning to add up everything. Literally. For instance, the number of demons—the high-ranking ones—encountered thus far. By her count, there had been three. If one counted Dumah, it would make four.

A police cruiser pulled into the parking lot and stopped next to them. Peterson climbed out.

"What's up?" he asked on his approach.

Armen hadn't given him any information other than where they were heading. "The Bishop's been crucified," Armen replied so Terry didn't have to.

Peterson stilled and blinked from her to Terry and back to her again. "Bishop Thomas?" His voice trembled. Terry gave a quick nod. "Shit." He took a deep breath. "What are we dealing with, Ash still?"

"Yes," she replied. "She's a particularly nasty little bitch."

Peterson agreed. "I hope to hell she doesn't have any more of those pets."

Armen looked at him. "Oh, she does, but Cerberus was the worst of the bunch, depending on your definition of worst."

"Wonderful," he responded with a good amount of sarcasm. Armen found herself admiring the man for more than just his wealth of knowledge.

"Check your gun, Terry, and give some of those bullets to Peterson."

"Dante," Peterson replied.

"What?" Armen asked.

"My first name, it's Dante."

Armen snorted. "Oh, that is priceless."

"Yeah, rather fitting, don't you think?"

Terry shook his head, but a small chuckle left his lips. "You two are seriously demented." He handed Peterson a handful of the silver bullets. "Hope these will work on her. They only seem to work on the lesser demons, though. Make sure they're solid before shooting them."

Armen cleared her throat. "Yes, well, shall we?" She waved her hand toward the entrance, and then clicked the scepter's trigger to the side. A single ferocious blade shot out from the hilt.

Dante admired the piece. "That's just freakin' cool." He loaded his magazine with the silver bullets.

Armen smiled. "I know."

Terry turned around and headed toward the entrance. "You two coming?" He'd already withdrawn his gun.

Armen started moving, with Dante Peterson following closely. "Where's Virgil when you need him?" she muttered, so quietly only Dante could hear her.

"No shit," he replied in a near whisper. "Especially since we're about to enter the mouth of Hell."

"Trust me when I say this isn't even close." Armen knew what the mouth of Hell was like. The Darkness teetered on the edge of it, tormenting all who had fallen within its fires.

"You don't know that."

"Yes, I do. Maybe someday you'll find out why."

"Doesn't look like you're too happy to be going inside, regardless of what lies within."

"There's another reason for that."

Terry stopped at the main door and peered through the crack. His knuckles turned white from his tight grasp on the door handle. Behind them, another car pulled into the parking lot. Armen turned to see who it was, and as she did, she noticed Dante's eyes widening as she listened to Terry open the door.

"Christ," Dante whispered under his breath.

Armen cringed and shook her head at him. "Don't say names like that." She rushed past him to greet whoever pulled up. Once she reached the parking lot's edge, Sean was climbing out of his car. "Sean, what are you doing here?" Her mind and body wanted to go into hysterics, knowing Terry would flip over this one, but she managed to control her reaction. "You can't be here."

"Och!" Sean walked up to her, his expression grim. "I'm a demon wrangler. 'Tis my job."

"But Terry—"

"Terry'll just have to deal with it, won't he?" His voice was no-nonsense fatherly firm and she knew he wasn't about to budge on the matter. "I'm his father an' I taught the boy all he knows." He looked at the scepter in her hand. "Are you using that?"

Armen nodded.

"How'd you get it to do that?"

Armen flicked the trigger to the opposite side and the blade sheathed. Sean's eyes lit with delight. Then Armen pushed the trigger back, bringing the single long blade out once more. "It's written in the script."

"Script?"

"This." She pointed to the cylinder, showing him the angelic script engraved in it.

"O' course," he said softly, shaking his head. "You'd have the ability to read such text. What else does it say?"

Armen looked over her shoulder briefly. "Later. I need to get back over there before Terry gets himself killed." She turned and headed back.

When she neared Dante, Terry stood just inside the entrance to the Basilica. Dante was frozen in his stance, but he quickly moved when Terry ducked.

"Look out," Armen shouted and jumped backwards with Dante when Terry rolled out of the entrance and jumped to the side.

"Shit," Terry spat.

A scream sounded from within the Basilica.

Armen turned to Sean. "How'd you know the Bishop had been crucified?"

"Dad, what the hell are you doing here?"

Sean pulled an ancient relic from his leather bag, ignoring Terry's question. He sure collected quite a few ancient pieces. This one in particular had ancient Celtic runes carved within the wood. "Father O'Malley called me." He pulled at both ends of the wooden piece, and it stretched and elongated, slowly forming into a staff. "He must be in there somewhere."

"And probably in pieces now," Armen mumbled. Only Dante heard her and he nodded subtly in agreement. Armen took in a deep breath and stepped forward cautiously. "Okay, let me see what we're dealing with."

"Armen," Terry said in that tone of his that was hard and father-like.

"I'm not going to sacrifice myself to this bitch, so quit it."

Sean spoke up before Armen could reach the entrance. "When the two of ye fight, it gives them more power."

Armen spun on her heel. "When Terry and I argue, it's not a *real* argument, Sean."

Sean looked at his son, who nodded. "It sounds like it, and thas all they need."

Armen turned again, ignoring him because she knew better than he did that it wasn't true, and peered around the edge of the door. She drew in a deep breath, barely picking up the scent that usually traveled with demons. Ash was good at masking hers. Then she focused her eyes, shifting them to that otherworldly vision of light and dark. The light image at center stage was fading. *The Bishop.* She caught movement of the dark variety in the shadows along the edges of the pews. Shadows didn't look the same as the minions. The shadows where no light fell were darker and impenetrable, whereas the shades of minions were lighter and translucent, and they moved. Shadows only moved when the light source moved. There were no light sources inside tonight, aside from the moon shining through the stained glass windows, which threw all sorts of other weird effects into the mix if she wasn't looking through gifted eyes. She pulled her head back briefly from the doorway and looked from Terry to Dante, who both looked like white visions to her, hardly distinguishable from one another if it weren't for their specific signatures of color swirling around them and the white. Terry's was a brilliant blue, and Dante's, sea-foam green: both quite good in nature.

"You'll need those bullets, boys," she said and looked back at Sean, whose signature revealed only brilliant white. She quirked a brow. "I hope you have something good to fight with."

"I do." He held up the relic, which had a white signature of its own.

Armen smiled.

"Why do your eyes look like that?" Dante asked.

"Like what?" She turned to Terry.

"They're white," Dante replied.

"She can see things we can't with those eyes," Terry said.

"Dante, look through that door and tell me what you see." If he couldn't see what they would be fighting, he'd be useless. This wasn't like seeing Cerberus. Everyone could see that damn dog, even the news crew that filmed him barreling down the street after her and Terry.

Dante leaned forward and quickly withdrew. "A hell of a lot of moving shadows."

"Shades," Terry corrected.

"Minions," Armen re-corrected.

"Lesser demons," Sean further corrected.

"Whatever," Armen snapped. "As long as you can see them."

"I can," Dante replied with a nod.

"Good. Don't shoot them until they materialize, otherwise the bullets will go right through."

"Got it."

Terry took a step forward. "Armen, I can't smell anything."

"Neither can I. What does that tell you?"

"She's pretty damn high up in the hierarchy?"

"Yes." She peered around the door again. "The trigger's been thrown. It's now or never."

On Terry's nod, Armen jumped forward, with the others following closely.

Bishop Thomas was a horrific sight to see, nailed upon a large wooden cross behind the altar. Ash stood beneath him, turning what looked to be a dagger over in her hands. She smiled when Armen entered.

"Hello, Azel, I figured this would get your attention." Sweet sadism lent a razor-sharp edge to her voice.

Armen stopped in the center of the room, taking in her surroundings, before finally resting on Ash. "You're one sick bitch, entering a church and crucifying a Bishop."

Ash giggled. *"I know, is it not wonderful?"*

"Um, no, it's not." Armen held the scepter's sword ready in her right hand. "Why in the world would you need to crucify a Bishop? There are other ways to get my attention."

"Eye for an eye, dear," Ash said smugly. *"You slaughtered my Cerberus. I slaughtered a man of . . . ."* She looked up to the ceiling.

"Why won't any of them say it?" Terry asked his father.

"Because they can nae say His name. It can nae pass their tongues."

Minions tackled Armen from the left, pulled Dante back from behind, and knocked Sean to the ground. Terry just stood turning rapidly in a circle waiting for one of them to materialize so he could shoot. Ash's horrid cackle echoed throughout the hall. Armen had been fairly certain it was another trap, but what other choice did they have? They needed to get near the bitch to kill her, and it was quite possible that Armen would be the only one who could achieve it with the scepter.

Armen jumped to her feet and sliced through a few minions before gunfire erupted. Terry took aim at those materializing before him. Armen knew he had a full magazine, but he only had fifteen rounds, and there were more than fifteen shades closing in on them.

A lot more.

Chapter Twenty-Seven
The Fall

ARMEN HAD FREED HERSELF OF another attacker, and the minions lay in a bubbling fiery mess at her feet.

"Try to not do too much damage to the church." Terry moved closer to her and fired at the minion nearing him.

"I'm not the one crucifying a Bishop here." Another gunshot echoed through the cathedral, telling them Dante was alive and kicking. Armen quickly scanned for Sean and found him thrusting his ancient relic into the chest of an oncoming minion. The creature shrieked and dropped to its knees. "Okay, how does that thing work?"

Terry looked around and saw his father. "The shillelagh? It belonged to St. Peter."

"No shit?" Armen swung her blade up over her head and dropped it onto the neck of a nasty little bugger with perfect precision, taking its head in a clean sweep.

Terry fired into a few more shades as they solidified. She'd been trying to keep a count on his rounds so she'd know when he had to reload, but she was losing track. There were just too many shades surrounding them.

Five more shots sounded across the church. Dante. That didn't help.

"Hey, I'm going to have to reload soon."

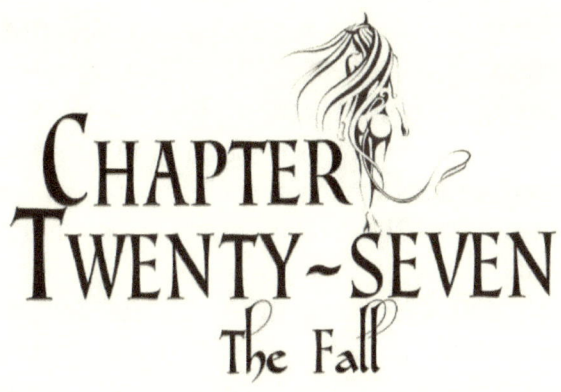

"I'm right here," she replied, her voice floating just over his shoulder.

Another gunshot sounded near Sean. Dante had made his way over to him. *Good.* The less she had to worry about anyone, the better she could concentrate on the minions. Terry fired three more bullets and then she heard a click.

"Duck down," Armen said. She needed a full 360 degrees clear to work with.

"Down." She and Terry worked well together when fighting demons, much like their arguing.

Armen scanned the room; shadows peaked intermittently like waves over the pews.

Terry reloaded at a rate faster than Armen had ever seen a human move. "Coming up." He stood and soon had a blade at his throat.

"Terry, really, you should wait at least three seconds after stating something like that." Armen lurched forward, moving the blade swiftly past his neck and around, to spear the minion in the face. She looked up at him, felt his breath on her cheek, and she smiled as he craned his head back to look over his shoulder.

"Nice move."

She brought the blade back over his shoulder and lowered it with a snap to cut the minion rising from the floor in half. "Thanks." She looked to the front of the church. "We need to get closer."

"I know. How do you propose that?"

After scanning the room, she realized there just weren't a lot of options. As much as she hated to admit it, coming here had been a good move on Ash's part. "Just move forward, cutting down anything in our path."

Terry shrugged. "Beats standing around."

"It has to be quick so she has less reaction time."

"Go," Sean said from ten feet away. Dante fired at another rising minion. "We'll cover ye as best we can."

Armen looked up into Terry's vibrant green eyes.

"You heard the man." He grinned at her. "Move your ass."

She spun to her right and ran down the aisle, Terry right on her heels. Gunshot sounded directly behind her and a minion fell to her left amidst the pews. She sliced through the air to her right, cutting another in two. Terry fired three more rounds into approaching minions when they materialized before they could reach Ash. Armen rounded the corner of the first pew and slid wildly on the slick floor until she came to a teetering stop. Once she straightened with Terry's aid, and her body wasn't making an attempt to prove gravity wasn't always on her side, she was able to take a look at the liquid that caused her to slip. The hardwood steps to the altar ran in red rivers; the wood stained with the Bishop's blood. There was also a priest lying at Ash's feet, still and pale as Death.

"You've killed two men of God, Ash," Armen reprimanded.

"So I have," Ash replied with a giggle.

"It will not please Father."

"He's no Father of mine."

"He is the All-Father, and He'll be displeased with your . . . creativity."

"As it will displease Him when I take you, Azel."

"The hell you will." Armen took a step closer. "Try it."

"Puppet." Ash snapped her right wrist over the body lying at her feet. The dead priest twitched, and Armen widened her eyes as he slowly sat up on the steps.

"Shit." Terry stepped up behind her. "I didn't know she could do that."

Armen just shook her head, unwilling to respond in voice, watching the priest stagger. She really didn't want to behead the man, even if he was dead, but it'd be the only way to stop him.

In her distraction, a small minion snatched the scepter from her grip, and she leapt after him to retrieve it. The imp scurried up the stairs and around the pulpit. Soon, it cowered behind Ash and raised the scepter to her.

"Good boy." Ash patted its head.

Armen stepped carefully backwards to Terry.

Ash studied the scepter's base for a moment, and then pressed the trigger to the side. The blade sheathed, and a large grin spread over her ruby lips.

"Armen, what are we going to do?"

The priest finally stood upright, and his hollow eyes stared past them. *"Bring her to me."* With a jerk, he took a step forward.

"Shoot him in the head," Armen whispered.

Terry took aim and fired. The priest stumbled back and fell onto the steps. Ash giggled and flicked her wrist. The priest twitched again and sat up.

"Okay, so that doesn't work," Armen said.

"He's obviously not a zombie."

"Oh, no, they're quite different," Armen replied with a quick shake of her head.

Terry turned to her. "I don't even want to know."

"I'd heard of the puppets, but I've never seen one until now." Armen thought hard about how to get the scepter back. Facing Ash without a weapon was a good way to die, and Ash would make the death slow and painful. Terry was still shooting minions occasionally, mainly keeping a path open between them and his father, who neared the front of the church with Dante.

"Shoot that one, behind her." The little varmint deserved to die for leaving her weaponless. Terry took aim and fired. The minion screeched when it fell back, leaving Ash to look briefly at it as it suffered before turning her attention back to Armen.

"Would that be vengeance?" The corner of her mouth curled.

"No, only you will feel the wrath of my vengeance," Armen replied.

"You forget my duties, dearest Azel."

"You have nothing to do with revenge, so don't try to play it off like you do."

Ash giggled and the priest stumbled forward again. *"You forget that revenge and lust are quite the pair."*

Terry touched Armen's arm, gripping her gently, and he leaned closer to her. "How can she stand on consecrated ground? My property burned Sariel's feet."

Armen shifted her eyes to view Ash's feet, which were covered by her long red dress. "If she's not burning, she's not standing." She quickly tracked one of the shades to watch it materialize. Once it did, the faint smoke rising from its feet when they touched the floor sparked an idea. She jerked away from Terry.

"Ar—men!"

She headed straight for the priest, jumped up onto a pew, launched herself as high as she could, and slammed both of her feet into the priest's chest as she came down. Ash stood on the second step, just below the cross holding the Bishop at center stage. The priest sailed backwards and slammed into her, which released the scepter from her hand, popping it away from the demon and toward the pews. Armen hit the blood-soaked floor on her left side, her jump a little off due to the slick blood, but it had worked, and Ash was now lying on the floor with her puppet priest on top of her. She shrieked, the consecrated ground burning her flesh, and she pushed the priest off. Armen slid over to snatch the scepter from the floor. When she looked up, Ash's face was directly in front of her, hissing. Ash wrapped her fingers around Armen's throat.

"You shall die by the blade of that weapon, as was meant to be!"

Behind her, Terry shouted to his father and Dante as Ash lifted Armen into the air by the throat. Armen held onto Ash's forearm with one hand to keep from truly hanging.

"You were always His favorite, made in His image. You even have His eyes."

"It's not my fault you look like a fiery Medusa," Armen choked out. "But hey, you *are* a demon."

Ash's fingers tightened around her throat, and she gasped for breath. *"You even have His pathetic wit. I look nothing like that bitch."*

Armen hooked her left hand over Ash's arm and brought her right hand up to clutch Ash's throat. "You're . . . just . . . jealous," she forced, squeezing her fingers around the demon's neck.

"Me, jealous of you, who has been turned to flesh? Ha! I could snap your little neck right now if I wanted to." Ash struggled against Armen's tightening fingers. *"But . . . I . . . will not . . . because it is not how you . . . must die."* She grasped Armen's left bicep with her right hand. They drifted upward, attempting to strangle one another. Armen still held the scepter, the cylinder forming an effective hook holding her in place, and she wrapped her legs around the demon bitch and tightened.

The grip on Armen's neck loosened a bit, and she drew in a breath before speaking. "I'm in His favor again," Armen replied hoarsely. "A place you will never be, and that's why you're jealous."

Ash snarled. *"I do not need Him, dear, or to be in His favor."*

"Then why seek me out?" One of them was bound to tell her eventually.

The right side of Ash's mouth curled up. *"You are the only angel He fathered, dear."*

Armen sucked in a small gasp of air. Her Father never told her of her creation. She assumed she was like all of the others.

Ash chuckled. *"And you are the key to all that exists."*

Armen frowned at that point. "What does that mean?" She knew demons held no truths on their tongues, and if they did, it was something usually spoken in cryptic idioms, much like the message scrawled in blood.

"If you die, you shall enter the Light, correct?"

"I suppose so." Armen held back on her grip. She needed answers.

"However, if one of the Dark kills you, all of your precious existence shall vanish."

"One of the Dark *did* kill me," Armen stated.

"Ah, but you were one of us then."

"If all existence would vanish, then why in the world would you kill me? You would disappear, too."

"Hmm, shall I tell thee all?" Her red eyes brightened as Armen's fingers tightened on her throat again. *"All existence shall fall into the Darkness."*

"I've conflicting stories. I think you'd better be certain before one of you kills me," Armen suggested, the scepter turning in her left hand, searching for the trigger with her thumb. Generally, she was right-handed, but there wasn't time to squabble over which hand was better suited for what she was about to do.

"I am certain," Ash said, the grin stretching over her ruby lips. *"The Namseer tells me it is so."*

"Oh?" Armen arched a brow. "Can you hear him right now?"

Ash smiled, her fangs appearing as her lips parted.

"Tell him to mind his own fucking business, and then tell him to leave me the hell alone." When Ash's wide eyes returned to calm, Armen knew a reply was on the tip of her tongue.

"He says he cannot do such a thing."

Armen shoved the end of the scepter between Ash's ribs, just under the breastplate. "Then say goodbye to him." She pushed the trigger to the side and the scepter's blade unsheathed into Ash's body, ripping through her black heart and out of the top of her skull. Surprise manifested on the demon's face for a mere second, and then rage ruptured with a silent scream as her mouth opened wide. Black blood flowed, gushing down her chin, and her grip on Armen tightened, fingernails digging into Armen's skin. Armen let go of the demon's neck and punched her in the face. Ash flew backward, forcing Armen's legs to let go. It took only a second for her to realize how high in the air she was.

"Shit." She plunged to the floor, rapidly leaving the fiery demon behind, and sheathed the blade. Knowing Terry wouldn't be able to save her from this and there was nothing else she could do, she closed her eyes tight, awaiting the impact and her death.

The hardwood floor of the church never came, and she bounced back up before realizing someone caught her. The insanity of anyone attempting such a feat, and the fact that it had worked, made her open her eyes.

His fiery blue eyes cast down at her as she rested in his arms. His lips slipped into a sly grin, black hair fell in cascades over his shoulders. He gently set her on her feet, but still kept his arm wrapped around her shoulders.

"Samyaza," she whispered, shocked. He had no doubt saved her and he would never let her live it down. She would owe him.

"Armaros," he replied, the corners of his mouth twisting into a sinister grin at her realization.

"Shit," was all she could say. Terry bolted for her, but it was too late to say anything else. Samyaza raised his hand, palm facing Terry, who froze in place with a yell.

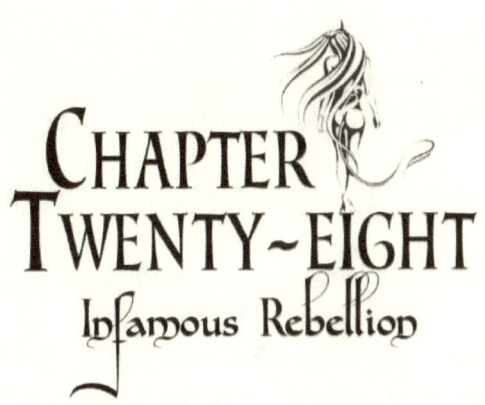

Chapter Twenty-Eight

Infamous Rebellion

ARMEN JERKED AND TRIED TO remove herself from his arm, but found she couldn't move much. Terry let out a shriek of agony, and his father and Dante couldn't take a step near him to help.

"Stop it," Armen shouted.

Samyaza's eyes met hers. *"Why?"*

"Because you're hurting him," she replied, her voice shaking at what *he* could possibly do to Terry with just a mere flick of his wrist. *That* was the kind of power this one held. The Leader of the Rebellion, the most powerful of the Grigori, the reason she fell from Grace. Stupid, gullible, naïve girl. She wondered if her Father had any regrets, if such a thing affected Him. She certainly did.

Samyaza lowered his hand and Terry dropped to the floor, the spell broken. That would cost her, too. Sean and Dante rushed to his side.

His eyes sparkled when they returned to her. *"That is twice now."*

As if he needed to remind her. He always was an arrogant bastard. "And I'm sure you'll try to collect." Agitation at his holier than thou attitude rolled through her. "However, I don't recall asking for help the first time."

He smirked. *"As if I could watch you die like that, Armaros."*

Didn't they want her dead? She turned her head to face him. "What are you doing here?" She hadn't seen any smoke rising from his feet when she glanced at the floor.

He chuckled. *"The ground here does not offend me, Armaros,"* he said in a delightful tone unbefitting the Master of the Darkness. Which he definitely was. Lucifer was the Prince of Hell. Really, he was King, but no one ever called him that. She wondered if it had anything to do with her Father. Maybe even Lucifer wouldn't disrespect her Father's Throne on that level. Which sounded absurd, considering.

To say he was complicated didn't begin to scratch his surface.

Armen bit the side of her lower lip as she stared into Samyaza's eyes, something a human should *never* do. "You didn't answer the question." His powers apparently didn't affect her, as she was able to maintain her mind.

"You are destroying my Highest." His grin smoothed into a fine line.

"They're killing people." She pointed to the crucified Bishop, never removing her eyes from the Fallen holding her hostage.

"It is their duty," Samyaza replied. *"Those souls already belonged to Lucifer."*

"I doubt the Bishop belonged to him."

He frowned as he stared at the man hanging on the large wooden cross. *"Correct. He did not belong to him. But since you killed Ash, we do not have to punish her for it."*

"They keep coming after me, too."

"You keep interfering," he replied, the grin reappearing, a slight twitch at the corner of his eye.

"Not on purpose."

He raised a brow as he peered down into her eyes. *"Is that so?"*

"Look, when they invade my dreams, it's an entirely different ballgame."

"I did not tell Banshi to do so. I will not hold that one against you. Sariel on the other hand – "

"Sariel killed his innocent mother" – she pointed to Terry – "and tortured his father."

Samyaza raised his head. *"Ah, the demon wrangler. There was a purpose to that one. But as I said, I shall not hold Banshi against you."*

Armen gave a short nod. She knew better than to say 'thank you' to him, or to question the killings further. But that didn't mean she couldn't change the subject a little because the son of a bitch was lying. "Tell me the truth; what's really happening?"

A chuckle rose from his chest and shook her in his arm. He moved his lips next to her ear. *"Why don't you ask Him?"*

"You know I can't talk to Him, not since the Fall," she whispered.

"And this, dear Armaros, is what makes you so entertaining," he replied, his lips gently brushing against her flesh.

She pulled back and met his eyes. "Is that what I am to you, mere entertainment?"

Samyaza smiled widely. *"Not entirely. Sariel had other plans."*

She grinned smugly. "Not anymore."

"True." He dipped his head down again, closer to her face. *"Do you intend to destroy me as well?"*

Armen shook her head. "I honestly don't think I have that kind of power."

He chuckled again. *"You are a terrible liar, Armaros."*

"Do you *want* to be destroyed?" She turned the scepter in her hand.

"Where's the fun in that?"

She shifted her gaze to Terry, who was now kneeling and staring at them.

Samyaza took notice. *"Tell me something, do you love him?"*

Armen nodded.

"Then say it."

"I love him." Her eyes met Terry's.

"Why do you love him?" He focused on Terry, his eyes studying him intently.

"He's intelligent, strong, and he makes me laugh," Armen replied. "And he cares about me."

Samyaza's smile broadened. *"Do you know why Lucifer had Eve eat from the Tree of Knowledge?"*

"To piss off our Father."

A short burst of laughter came from him and he shook his head. *"Not exactly."*

"Then why?"

"To give humans a chance to grow, evolve, to become enlightened. Father would have been content with their ignorance. Our Prince thought it not fair to them, never to know of their potential. Would you not agree?"

"I am not stepping into that argument," she quickly replied.

"Do you think your Terry would be the person he is today had Lucifer not enlightened humans?" His vibrant eyes met hers again. *"Or would he just be another mindless drone?"*

"Don't try to justify what he did," she said. "Father was pissed when he wouldn't bow before Adam."

"Then he should not have made us what we are," he replied. *"Lucifer is the Angel of Light, of music and beauty. You are the Angel of Enchantments, of magic and sorcery. I am*

the Angel of Knowledge, of learning and creativity; all of us with free will."

"We *were* that," she reminded him. "Now we're all just Angels of the Darkness. Even angels fade over time, Sam. We are no exception."

"You know I hate that name." He tightened his grip on her shoulder and leaned closer. *"I could kill them all right now,"* he whispered, eyeing Terry, Sean, and Dante.

"And you will surely face a war if you do," Armen firmly replied.

"As if one millennia-long war is not enough? It is already falling to the human realm."

"So I've noticed."

He grinned. *"You cannot lead a war against me if you are flesh."*

"That could easily change."

"You would be a worthy opponent, Armaros," he said with admiration. *"I would welcome it, but for now, we shall let it be."*

She gave a nod. "Of course."

He removed his arm from her shoulders and let it drop to his side. She took a step forward, heading toward Terry. Six steps into her walk, Sean launched his shillelagh at Samyaza. Armen caught it with the yell of a warrior, leaping to the side to snatch it mid-air.

The shillelagh's tip hovered at the edge of Samyaza's chest, barely brushing the fine silk shirt he wore. His fiery blue eyes shot up to meet Armen's, and she grinned.

"That equals twice, I think," she said with a smirk.

"The debt has been repaid." He winked at her and vanished in a cloud of black smoke.

Armen quickly turned to Sean. "Bad move, Sean, but thank you."

His bewildered eyes stared at her. "Och! That was Satan. Why'd ye save him?"

"That was Samyaza. He and the one you call Satan are two separate beings. I would think you'd know that." She handed him the shillelagh and knelt down to Terry. "Are you okay?"

"Yeah, I think so," he replied, rubbing his chest. "That hurt like a bitch, though."

"I'm sure it did," she said, helping him to his feet. "It's not every day you get tortured by that one and live. He's not kind."

"Sounds like you speak from prior experience," Terry grunted.

"Nah, he's got a soft spot for me."

"How so?"

"I'm like his little sister."

"Aren't you *all* brothers and sisters?"

"I'm his Grigori sister, the only female Watcher. Remember? Each group is bonded and bound to one another, like siblings, or lovers."

He shook his head. "I don't think I'm ready to hear more on that just yet."

"Probably not."

Dante made a call to get a clean-up crew down to the church. Sean inspected the dead priest to be certain he was dead and not likely to jump up at any time. After giving last rites, Terry stood in front of the Bishop for some time before turning away. Armen knew there was no way for her and the others to get him down from the cross.

She and Terry stepped outside as dawn approached. It was early Saturday morning, which meant they still had another nineteen hours before Constantine's venerable day of the sun, or the Sabbath. Armen looked Terry over for open wounds as policemen and crew walked briskly past them, heading into the church. Not long after, one or two ran back outside, retching the remnants of their latest meal. She sat Terry in the garden near a small fountain and ripped off the lower half of her t-shirt not covered in blood from underneath her hoodie and dipped it in the water.

"You really do love me." His words were heavy with the understanding of what it meant to voice her feelings to her brother.

Her eyes met his and she nodded, running the cloth over his right arm, eyes scanning for scratches and cuts. "I do."

He stopped her hand from cleaning and touched her cheek with his other hand. "I love you." He slipped his hand around to the back of her neck and pulled her forward. Their foreheads touched. "And I'd die if I lost you."

She moved her head up and kissed his forehead. "I know how you feel."

Dante cleared his throat. "Sorry to interrupt, but Captain's heading this way. Thought you might want to disappear before he gets here." He winked and smiled, then turned around to head back inside.

Armen turned back to Terry. "Should we?"

"What do you think?"

She shrugged. "How long do you think it'll take?"

"Depends on his mood," he replied. "Maybe an hour, maybe three."

"It's not Sunday yet, you know."

"So?" He met her eyes and worry spread across his face. "Do you think it's over?"

Armen shook her head. "It can't be."

"Samyaza shows up after you kill Ash, has a chat with you after saving your life, and then disappears after telling you the debt has been repaid, and you don't think it's over?"

"It's too easy, too simple, too quick. Something isn't adding up."

"Who else could be coming?" He quickly turned his head. "Dad!"

Sean peered through the doors and found Terry. "What is it, my boy?"

"Could you please ask *Him* if anyone else is coming, to put Armen's mind at ease?"

"Aye, o' course," Sean replied and closed his eyes. A split second later, they opened. "He wishes fer Armen to ask Him."

"I can't!"

"Ye mean you will nae do it," Sean suggested with a cocked brow.

"No, I mean I *can't*," she replied.

"He says then ye dinnae need to know."

Armen growled and crossed her arms over her chest. "Smartass."

"Dinnae call yer Father names," Sean reprimanded.

"Dad, seriously, it'd be good to know."

Sean looked at him and nodded. "He sees not a ting."

"That doesn't mean anything," Armen mumbled. She looked at Terry, who was eyeing her with that look of his, the scrutinizing one. "What? I'm sorry, but I don't trust Sam. He let that go way too easily. And just because dear old Dad doesn't see it, it doesn't mean nothing will happen. The Grigori were down here for years before He finally noticed what we were doing."

"She has a valid point," Dante suggested when he walked through the open doors past Sean. "I mean, you can't trust a demon, right?"

Terry looked from Dante to Armen. "What are your thoughts?"

Armen sighed heavily. "Don't you feel it in the pit of your stomach? I know you trust your instincts. What are they telling you?"

Terry stared into her eyes long and hard before answering. "It's not over."

"Thank you," she said.

"Can we talk about the fact that Ash flat out stated that Armen has to be killed with *that* blade?" Dante interrupted, pointing at the scepter.

"Right," Terry replied, turning to Armen. "What the hell is that about?"

"Like I know," she answered, raising her hands up. "It's news to me, too."

Terry gave a short nod, indicating they'd figure it out later, which she had no doubt would be right before the blade plunged through her chest. "So who's left then?"

"Take your pick."

"You know them. Narrow it down."

"You have no idea the chore I'm undertaking with that." She thought about it, nibbling on her fingernail, considering those that had already come forth and her past with them. Only one came to mind through all of the others; one who held a grudge against her; one who, above all else, had been partly responsible for her becoming flesh. Her eyes met Sean's, and she knew from looking into those green eyes of his, that he knew exactly who was on her mind—the one who had hunted him.

Chapter Twenty-Nine

Agares

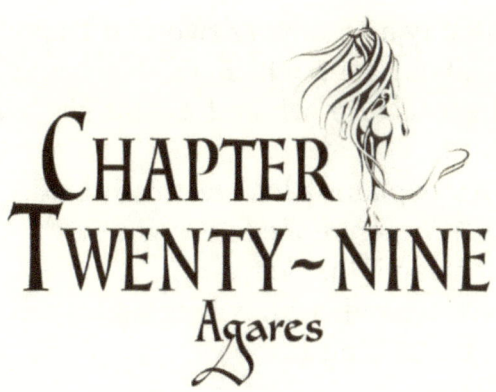

After exchanging glances with both of them, Terry shook his head. "You can't be serious."

Armen nodded. "I'm afraid so."

"Why's he comin' back?" Sean asked.

"To finish what he started, I suppose," Armen replied, more than a little nervous about facing this one. "I'm afraid you're in serious danger, Sean."

"That so? He seemed so calm."

Armen wasn't certain if that was sarcasm or not, as she hadn't quite learned Sean's inflections yet.

Terry touched her arm to get her attention. "You're talking about the one who hunted my dad and killed you, aren't you?"

"Yes. Deception is his specialty, along with great storms and the ability to make you stand still when you want to run."

"Thas why I summoned you. I could nae move."

The corner of Armen's mouth hitched upward. "Good thing his gift isn't silence."

Dante waved his hands back and forth. "All right, you guys want to let me in on the secret now? What's he talking about, Leza?"

"Ah hell," she muttered. "Terry, explain it to him." She stood at the edge of the garden and stared out into the breaking day as the other two told Dante everything they knew about her, which in the grand scheme of things really wasn't a whole lot, and she was just fine with that.

"Well, that explains a lot," he finally said.

"Thanks," Armen replied.

"I didn't mean it that way."

She waved a hand, acknowledging his comment.

"Don't go blabbing it to everyone you know," Terry firmly told him.

Dante cocked an eyebrow. "Like anyone would believe there's an ex-angel, ex-demon working at the police station." He paused briefly before the corner of his mouth lifted. "Well, except for the captain. He'd probably believe it. Man, he does not like you."

"Yeah, I know," Armen said, brushing the comment off.

"Well, I'm sure it wouldn't be all that difficult for people to believe considering the news van we saw when Cerberus was chasing us," Terry replied.

Dante's thick eyebrows popped up. "Oh shit, really?"

Terry nodded.

"I'll keep my mouth shut."

"Good." Terry walked over to Armen and placed a hand on her shoulder. "Any ideas as to where this one will show up?"

Armen slowly moved her head back and forth. "I think he'll find us."

"Great. Let's hope it's an unpopulated area."

"I still need to get to my lab."

"We'll go as soon as the captain gets here and finishes with me."

Armen turned her head. "Well, I suppose that'll be soon." She nodded to the front gate.

Terry touched her arm before turning and walking over to Brian. Their conversation was short, and soon he was back standing next to Armen. "Ready to go?"

"That was quick." She raised a brow.

"I gave him the short version."

"I'm certain he's not happy with the 'short version'."

"Probably not, but he'll have to deal with it until I get a chance to write it out."

"That's a lot of writing you've got ahead of you."

"It'll be a damn book by the time I'm finished. Let's get you to your lab, doc." He gave her a once-over. "You're covered in blood, by the way."

Mostly dried by that point, the blood ran down her entire left side from her landing after kicking the priest and the front of her after crawling after the scepter. "I've got scrubs at the office."

Armen walked into her office, duffle bag in hand, and Terry, Sean, and Dante following close behind. She set the bag on her desk and stepped over to the lab doors to peer through the small window. Art was wrist-deep in someone's abdomen, beginning his shift with pleasantries as he whistled along to a 50s song playing on the radio.

"If you have a weak stomach, you might want to stay out here," she said and pushed the doors open. Considering what they'd just seen and their chosen professions, she doubted any of them had a weak stomach, but it was something she often said to people entering her office. "Hey, Art."

He looked up, surprise capturing his more than middle-aged face. "What the hell are you doing here?" His eyes took in her appearance. "And why are you covered in blood?"

"I haven't finished my shift yet," she replied and stepped up to the table.

"More demon chasing?" he queried, a hint of a smile reaching his lips. "Is that demon blood?"

"Funny. And no, demon blood is black, sometimes blue, depending on the breed."

He chuckled. "I heard about some big damn dog or the like chasing a squad car through downtown."

"Was it on the news?"

He shrugged. "Haven't had a chance to watch, but it's all over the radio." He viewed the clock above the doors. "Might be on right now, though."

Armen turned toward the doors, cupped her hands around her mouth, and yelled, "Terry, turn on the television."

"Must you yell? You'll wake the dead." Art waited for a response, but received none. "You've lost your sense of humor, Armen. Must be serious."

"Since when have you known me to have a sense of humor?" She folded her arms over her chest.

He nodded with a chuckle and withdrew his hand from the corpse. "That's right, you call it sarcasm." His eyes met with hers briefly before returning to the body. "Wanna know how this one popped up?"

Armen arched her right brow. "Is it unlike the normal dribble?"

"These days? Not really." He summoned her closer but held up a hand. "Wait, you'll contaminate it. Go change first."

"Fine." She wandered off to their small locker room and changed into a spare set of scrubs before returning to the table. When she took a step toward the body, she looked down into the gaping hole. Art had marked the original opening before beginning the autopsy.

"See anything?"

Armen leaned forward and searched the specimen by eyesight only. Noticing something, she reached for a pair of nitrile gloves and pulled them onto her hands with a snap. She pulled back on the flesh carefully.

"He's a fresh one."

Art nodded with a hum.

She peered closer, inspecting the incision not made by Art's scalpel. "Sword?"

"That's what it looks like, doesn't it?" He studied the wound through his bifocals. "But it's not the same sword as the last one."

"Honestly, who dies by a sword these days?"

"I can count two people so far. So it's not all that far-fetched."

She looked up at him and arched her brow once more, and he chuckled. "When did he come in?"

"'Bout twenty minutes before you got here."

She tried to hide her expression, but Art's eyebrows rose higher.

"What's up, Armen?"

She shook her head and peered inside the body again, slipping her hand through the layers to feel around. "His liver is missing."

Art smirked. "Good job. But the question is how was it taken out? Aside from the wound, he was intact when he got here. There's no evidence that someone reached in and cut it out, and a liver just wouldn't fit through the original opening. Not without liquefying it, and I don't see any evidence of that, either."

Art was correct. No one would have the ability to pull a liver out of such a small opening—except demons. "I'm more concerned with where it's gone."

"You would be."

Armen frowned.

He chuckled again. "You never cease to amaze me, Armen. I mean, emotion? Wow."

"Glad I could amuse you." She withdrew her hand when the doors opened.

"Anything important?" Terry asked from the doorway. "Because that shit on the news is a mess we can't clean up."

"Definitely." Armen looked at Art and pulled the gloves off. "I need to use the lab to test a specimen I picked up in the field. Ice this guy. Don't examine him anymore."

"Since when did you become my boss?" Art asked with a snort.

Armen looked straight into Art's eyes, not faltering for a second. "Art, trust me, please, just this once."

He stared at her for a few heartbeats, and then finally gave a short nod. "With all the weird shit going on around here lately, I'll trust you." He pulled up the sheet to cover him, and then wheeled him over to the open box.

Armen headed toward Terry.

"You wanna help me with this before you head to the lab?"

"Of course," she said and turned on her heel as time slowed. "Sorry abou—"

She barely caught the transformation of Terry's face: his eyes going wide, his jaw growing slack, and the twitch in his hand before it moved to his side, reaching for his weapon of choice. Then as she turned, her eyes fell on Art, who had stopped the gurney and reached for the tray inside the box. He hadn't noticed the sheet move, or the one standing behind the gurney. Before her hair settled from her turn, before her lips could part to shout a warning, the blade of the one who had taken her demon life seared through Art's neck.

Time caught up in a rush.

Art dropped to his knees, headless, before she could take a step forward. His head fell onto the tray and rolled inside. Her shout came as gunfire rang through the chilled room. A hand grabbed her arm and yanked her back, but the demon already held his hand up, palm facing them. All that traveled to Armen's ears was a loud pop, and she and Terry flew backwards through the double doors. Terry clipped Dante's shoulder before bursting through the office door and hitting the wall in the corridor. Dante dropped to his knee and went for his gun. Another strident pop and Dante slammed to the floor unconscious. Armen and Terry lay in a tangled heap in the hallway. She dared a peek inside the room. Agares walked forward, slow at first, then with inhuman speed, alternating back and forth in a jerky motion that screamed Japanese horror movie.

She jumped when Sean slammed the tip of the shillelagh against the floor, cracking the linoleum. "I have a weapon this time, demon."

"And I am much stronger than when we last met, wrangler." Agares' deep voice rang through the corridor, stopping the influx of officers that ran down its wide walls for a brief moment of speculation. Soon, the sound of cautious footsteps made their way to Armen's ears, rounding the corner not thirty feet away. Two officers scuttled over to her and Terry, and got an eyeful of the demon standing inside the room. Agares mocked their widening eyes before his hand shot up and sent them tumbling back to their co-workers. His quick movement

made his still form look like only a lingering shape that made one wonder if he moved at all. His laughter ensued shortly thereafter.

"Stay back." Sean focused on the demon. *"By the Light of God, you shall leave this place, demon."* He slammed the tip of the shillelagh to the floor again, cracking the linoleum even further, a bright white light going super nova in the small room.

"Do you think yourself a wizard with that stick, wrangler?" Agares took one long lazy step forward that measured the equivalent of three human steps toward the office. His bright yellow eyes, contrasting his red armor, slowly swept the floor, taking in Dante first, and then out to the corridor where Terry and Armen remained motionless. A smirk unnaturally hitched the right corner of his mouth. *"Your son, perhaps?"*

"I have no son," Sean spat at the young-looking man who stood before him. Those yellow eyes moved rapidly to meet with Sean's.

Terry carefully turned his hand in Armen's until he could grasp a few of her fingers to let her know he was conscious. She returned the squeeze.

"You try to deceive, wrangler; however, you do not accomplish your goal."

"I have no son."

Armen tapped Terry's finger three times, telling him she was able to move and ready to do so, and he returned the tap once.

"I am a master of deception, wrangler," Agares said. *"You fail miserably."*

Armen tapped again three times, and Terry jumped up to one knee when she pushed herself off. Terry brought his gun up and fired at the demon. Agares took a jolted step backwards. Terry rose from the floor, gun still aimed at the demon, and fired again. Agares jerked back. Terry fired again and again, and each shot forced Agares further into the dismal, chilled room. The fluorescent lights overhead flickered briefly before sending down a shower of sparks and going out while Sean yelled his incantation. Armen crawled around the corner of the broken door to Dante's side. She looked him over and tried to wake him, but received no response. Terry continued firing, edging closer to the doors.

"I hope you're keeping count." Armen scooted across the floor to her desk. Sean stood in the center of the office, holding his shillelagh as though he were some grand wizard. She reached for the duffle bag she'd brought in earlier.

"Out soon," Terry responded between shots.

"Any more?"

"No," he replied.

She pulled the bag to the floor and slid back over to Dante, who remained unconscious. Then she grabbed his gun and slid it across the floor. "At your feet."

Terry squatted to the floor with a click of his gun and snatched the other one up quickly. "Scepter!"

"Working on it."

Neither of them knew how many bullets were left in Dante's gun.

"Hurry."

"I'm trying," she muttered and unzipped the bag. She dug inside and searched rapidly. It wasn't there. "Shit." She pulled everything out, throwing her gear aside without thought, as well as the small satchel with the vial inside. "I can't find it."

"What?" Terry fired again into the darkening room. Agares let out an angry yell. The lights flickered once.

"It's not here." Armen looked around in the mess, picking up coveralls and dropping them in a different spot. "Where the hell is it?"

"The car," Terry shouted.

Armen slapped her thigh. "Damn it." She crawled to Dante and pushed him under her desk as best she could. Then she jumped to her feet. "I have to go get it."

The hammer clicked into silence. "I'm coming with you." Terry dropped the gun, turned, and grabbed his father's arm on the way out the door. Armen ran with him. "Go, go, go!" he shouted to the officers blocking their path, waving his free arm at them. The blockade broke into many feet running down the corridor.

Chapter Thirty

Vial Magic

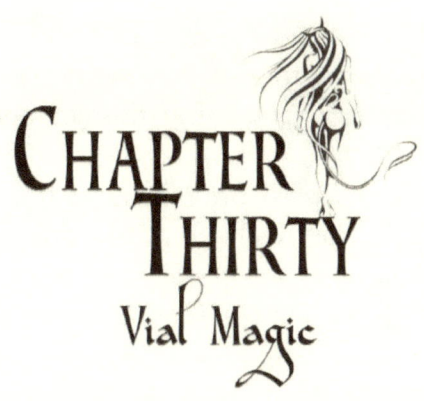

ARMEN RAN PAST JASMINE'S OFFICE hoping Jazzy had already left or was out in the field. "We'll have to take the stairs," she yelled and ran toward the stairwell door. She slammed into the door, flinging it open just as the other officers ran down the hall. When Terry pushed his dad forward, she yanked Sean into the vestibule. A few officers hung back, taking cover in open doorways, their weapons drawn. Gunfire erupted when Terry jumped inside the stairwell. Before the door closed, one officer was thrown past them.

Armen stared through the door's window, captured by the scene.

"Armen," Terry shouted from halfway down the first flight of stairs, grabbing her attention, and she quickly ran down after him. Once they reached the garage level on the next flight down, Terry flung the door open and pushed his father and Armen through. The door from the first floor exploded into the stairwell.

"If he's a demon, why doesn't he just appear in front of us?" he asked, running through the garage.

"He enjoys destruction," Armen said gruffly. She ran up to the passenger side of Terry's squad car and yanked on the door handle. "Unlock it!"

Terry pulled his keys from his pocket and fumbled for the remote. Sean took a few steps away from him. Terry hit the button, unlocking the car before noticing. "Dad?"

Armen looked up to find Sean in the center of the garage. Terry spun on his heel, prompting Armen to scan the area. All shadows were still, but her gut told her to stay sharp, and she had a feeling Terry felt the same thing.

"Armen, hurry up." His tone quieted and his eyes scrutinized the landscape.

Armen pulled the scepter from the car.

"He is here," Sean said.

"One of these days, Armen, I'll have to start lis—"

Armen let out a yelp when Agares clutched the back of her neck.

Terry quickly spun around again. "No!"

Agares laughed and squeezed harder, and Armen whimpered. Her grip on the scepter loosened and it slipped in her hand.

"I shall not toy with her as Sariel so enjoyed."

Several seconds passed before Terry responded. "Good, it'll save us a lot of time."

Sean stepped up next to his son and glared at the demon. "It's me you're after," he said sharply. "Leave them be."

Agares chuckled. *"You are not the only one I am here for, wrangler."*

The scepter slipped until Armen held it with only her fingertips.

Terry dismissed him with the wave of a hand. "Yeah, yeah, something about eternal darkness."

"Do nae provoke him, son," Sean whispered.

"It's the only way," Terry replied out of the corner of his mouth. He stared at Armen and once she made eye contact, he looked down at her feet, attempting a signal. When she lowered her gaze to the ground before him, he shifted his foot. "You wouldn't happen to have any of those ancient religious daggers on you, would you?"

Sean shook his head. "Naw."

Terry leaned into his father and spoke words unheard by either Armen or Agares, but Armen was able to read their lips after Terry pulled back enough that she could watch his mouth moving.

Sean shook his head.

"Why not?"

"Ye can nae run in his presence."

Terry frowned. "Then how in the hell did we get down here?"

"Ye injured him temporarily. 'Twas enough to dispel his power for a short time."

"Then use the shillelagh—"

"Enough!" The echo of Agares' yell reverberated throughout the garage, setting off car alarms. Agares' distraction caused him to loosen his grip on Armen.

"Well, now he's pissed," said Terry.

Agares leaned closer to Armen, his unnatural flesh brushing against her ear. *"Who is he, Azel?"*

"Knight," she whispered.

"A knight?"

"Yes." The scepter was about to slip away. She tried to gather it back up into her hand, but it was sliding from the tips of her fingers.

"For whom?"

"Father. He killed Sariel."

"Sariel is the Angel of Death."

"Well, now he's a dead demon," Terry replied, watching the scepter closely.

"Ask Samyaza," Armen whispered, looking up at the side of his face.

Agares closed his eyes, and Terry widened his as a signal. The scepter slipped from her fingers. It hit the lower part of her shin, and with a quick enchantment, the cylinder rolled down her pant leg to the top of her foot, and she swung her leg forward, launching the weapon into the air.

The jolt from Armen's body disturbed Agares' concentration. He lost his hold on Terry and Sean, and his grip on Armen weakened.

Terry bumped his father's arm and jumped forward. Sean lifted the shillelagh and threw it at Agares. Terry caught the scepter in his right hand, brought it down in a roundabout motion, and clicked the trigger forward when Agares stepped to the side, away from the staff as Armen twisted out of his grasp in the opposite direction. The scepter's blades shot out at both ends, and Terry landed in front of the demon. He leapt once more, bringing one blade forward as the other blade rested near his arm.

Armen scrambled away from the car and ran over to Sean, who stood watching his son. "You good, Sean?"

He replied with a nod. "Look at him," he said after a few seconds. "My boy."

Armen turned her attention back to Terry, who had successfully administered a nice slice to Agares' left arm. "Yeah, he's pretty amazing." Then she saw Agares going for his sword. "Terry, switch the scepter's blades."

He jumped back, pulled the trigger down and pushed it to the side. The blades regrouped inside the cylinder and shot back out in one long sweep of silver-coated steel. Terry smirked at Agares. "I'm willing to bet you think you can't die. Sariel thought the same thing."

Agares chuckled and swept the air with his sword. *"I am not ignorant, such as my brother was."*

"Of course you are; otherwise, you wouldn't be standing in front of me." Terry countered Agares' low position with his own sword, and then raised the weapon, keeping the blade hovering above and pointing at Agares. Terry summoned the demon forward with a smirk spreading across his lips and a quick upward nod.

"Boy, he really knows how to win them over," Armen whispered to Sean.

The only sign of Agares' temper shone in his eyes, which flickered with flame around the yellow edges of the iris.

"He's usually as slow as a corpse," Armen said loud enough to reach Terry's ears. "But can move swiftly when he needs to." Terry already had him backed into a corner at the start of this, between car and wall. It was a good advantage.

Agares engaged Terry's sword high overhead, and the clanging metal echoed in the garage. Once more their swords connected, low this time, and Agares deflected Terry's blade, redirecting it into his car so it sliced into the tire. The rubber hissed when Terry withdrew his sword and he jumped backwards to avoid the point of Agares' blade as it traveled in his direction.

Then, the demon vanished.

Terry spun in a frantic circle, and he scanned the garage. "I don't like this so much."

"It's different when they have a weapon and can disappear on you, huh?"

He turned to her, disbelief layering his face. "Is that supposed to be funny?" He stepped away from the car, moving closer to Armen and Sean.

Armen nodded once. "Behind you."

Terry turned quickly, bringing his sword around to block Agares' bold thrust. The demon made one more jab at him before vanishing again.

"For your information, I knew that."

"Ri*iii*ght," she replied. "Don't get too far out in the open. He'll be able to come up on you from anywhere."

"Then I suggest you and Dad do the same."

"Good point." She grabbed Sean by the arm, walked over to the shillelagh and plucked it from the garage floor, and then pushed Sean up against the concrete wall. "Stay put."

"I *am* a demon wrangler, ye know."

"Oh, I know. But experience isn't what's going to get us out of this."

Sean arched a brow, and he opened his mouth to speak, but closed it and nodded, as though hearing an answer Armen never spoke.

She tilted her head. "Dad?"

"Aye."

"Is He going to help?" She examined the shillelagh.

"Naw," Sean replied.

"Figures. How's this thing work?"

The left side of Sean's mouth hitched upward in a half-smile. "Well, hit the bloody bastard with it an' find oot."

Armen grinned when her eyes met his. "Is that so?" She turned to Terry, who'd just finished another scrape with Agares. "Get him between us if you can."

"Oh, sure, no problem."

Armen detected something else in the garage—shadows moving like waves over the concrete. "Minions."

"Ah, hell." Terry turned slowly in a circle.

Agares suddenly appeared to their side as they stood back to back. *"It shall be your home soon."*

Armen swung to her right, and Terry brought his blade around to the left. Agares stopped Terry's blade, but Armen was successful in hitting him on the leg with the shillelagh. His yellow eyes met hers and he smirked with the blades locked.

"Nice weapon, Azel." He forced Terry's sword down and jerked in a motion to vanish. He jerked again, and his eyes widened with the realization of what Armen had just done to him.

"HA! Nice weapon, indeed." One hit from the shillelagh grounded him to this plane.

Fury built in his eyes, the fire burning brightly, and he roared. The shadows darkened and slithered along the floor.

"I hope you're ready for this," Armen said, keeping an eye on Agares. He wouldn't get too close now, which would make him easier to kill once they finished with the minions.

Terry grabbed her by the arm and pulled her away from Agares. "You, too."

The shades rose from the floor and neared Armen and Terry.

"I'm really wishing for silver bullets right now," Terry said.

"Then you wouldn't have to be so close to them."

"Exactly." He looked at the scepter. "One blade or two?"

"For these guys, I'd go with two."

Terry agreed by rapidly switching the blades. "Two it is, then."

Armen's eyes flicked to Sean. "I really hope your dad has something in that satchel to defend himself."

"I wouldn't doubt it. I don't even know all the shit he carries with him." Terry quickly sliced through the shade materializing before him. "One down."

"Make that two," Armen said after shoving the end of the shillelagh through the chest of the oncoming minion. Its flesh sizzled and popped when she withdrew her weapon, and she wrinkled her nose in disgust. "Nasty, I'd much rather have a cleaner kill."

Terry chuckled, taking out two more before answering. "I'd give you the scepter, but I'm kind of using it right now." He swiftly decapitated the next materializing minion.

"That's okay," she replied and clubbed another with the head of the shillelagh. "You were meant to wield it."

"Then why are you so good with it?"

Armen glanced at him. "Duck." She swung the shillelagh over his head and sent the minion flying into a concrete column, where it exploded into a shower of embers. "Because all angels of old were warriors, and I am most definitely an angel of old."

"Och. Nae all angels of ould were warriors," Sean said, throwing a fine powder around himself as a barrier against the minions coming toward him.

"In a manner of speaking, they were," Armen argued. She scanned the area to find Agares hiding behind one of the columns. "Don't even think you can hide from me," she shouted at him. She brought the shillelagh around and took out three minions, sending them to the floor in a burst of fiery dust.

Sean tossed a handful of powder at a brave minion, who retreated, screaming in agony. "Naw. You have those who helped with creation. They certainly were nae warriors."

Terry lurched forward to take on two more minions, beheaded them, and jumped to the side to take three more.

Armen laughed. "They are when you mess with their creations."

Surprising Armen, Agares actually chuckled before he briefly engaged Terry for a few rotations. Then he slipped around one of the columns again. He was testing

Terry's distractibility level, she figured. Good luck with that, she thought, because that man was on constant point when it came to focus. Hardcore was an understatement.

"Do we really need to have this debate right now?" Terry asked in the midst of spearing a minion through the chest. "I mean, we're in the middle of a fight." He yanked the scepter back and the minion dropped to the floor and burned.

"Next, he'll want my witty comments to stop," Armen said and took a quick headcount.

"Only you think yourself humorous, Doctor Leza." Terry lunged for two of the remaining minions.

"You find me funny on a regular basis, Detective Armstrong." She swung at the last minion. "You even said so before my condo burnt down."

After killing the two he'd lunged for, Terry straightened and held the scepter at his side. "I found your avoidance issues amusing at the time, Armen, and I still do."

"Same difference." She turned on Agares, summoning him with her finger. "Come on, we'll make it quick before the next wave."

Agares walked around the concrete column with a sneer. *"Do you think it wise to destroy me, Azel?"*

"I'm gonna let him have the honors, since you tried to kill his dad twice now." She pointed to Terry.

"And my woman," Terry added.

He studied the two of them. *"You fight well together, but I would like this one-on-one."*

"As you wish." She walked a few paces over to Sean. "I've already done my part."

"That, you have, Azel," he grumbled and stepped forward.

"It'll really suck for you if you win." She turned to face him again. Terry switched the scepter's blades out.

"Why is that?" He turned his blade in his hand as he neared Terry.

"Because you'll be stuck here forever if you can't dematerialize." She beamed when his eyes darted to her. "At least, until I kill you . . . because I *will* kill you if you take his life."

"She kind of likes having me around," Terry said.

"I can't possibly see why."

Armen slammed the shillelagh to the floor.

Terry thrust at him in his moment of distraction, and Agares redirected the blade and pushed him back. He slowly wagged a finger at Terry. *"Ah, ah, ah, Knight. Do not make the mistake of thinking I am not aware of my surroundings."*

Terry grinned. "Just testing."

Agares thrust his blade forward and down. Terry blocked, stepped to the side with it, and immediately turned his own blade back and down for a lower hit. The silver sliced into the demon's leg. Agares yelled and swung his sword wide at Terry. When Terry blocked, the force of impact sent him stumbling backwards. His eyes locked with Armen's briefly.

"You didn't tell me he was that strong!" He quickly blocked the next attack, which sent him tumbling to the concrete floor.

"Don't worry about his strength," Armen replied, hoping her worry didn't show. "Find his weakness."

Terry rolled, Agares' blade narrowly missing him, and he jumped to his feet. "Easy for you to say, you know him better than I do."

Armen turned to Sean. "Do you have anything in that bag he can use?"

"Possibly." He searched his satchel and pulled out a small vial. "Here, this might do the trick."

Armen took the vial and examined it. "What is it?" The vial appeared to be empty.

"Angel's breath," Sean replied.

She lifted a brow, surprised. "You're serious."

Sean nodded. "Absolutely."

An idea came to mind. "Terry." When he turned to her, she tossed the vial at him, but Agares snatched it from its path.

"Remind me not to ever play catch with you," Terry said.

So predictable. "Certainly, after you kill the demon."

Agares held the vial up to his nose and sniffed. *"What is this, Azel, something magical?"*

"There's nothing magical about it." It was the truth.

"It looks empty, but I know there are things invisible to the eye." The flame in his eyes flashed brightly and his vision changed. *"And yet, I still cannot see it."*

"There's nothing for you to see. I just want a sample of your blood." She glared at Terry. "Get the vial from him. You *need* it."

Terry nodded subtly and attacked Agares with force. The metal clanged and echoed in the garage when their swords clashed. Agares held tightly onto the vial, even when Terry's blade cut into his arm. It was a deep gash; one that had him step back after throwing Terry to the ground again. He growled upon inspecting the wound that shouldn't be there, or should at least start healing right away. Silver didn't allow such luxuries. He opened his hand, revealing the empty vial. Terry got to his feet once more, and Agares positioned his thumb to open the vial.

"No!" Armen tried with all her might to withhold her eagerness for Agares to open the glass cylinder, but she waited patiently through seconds that felt like hours. The top of it popped off and she slammed the tip of the shillelagh to the floor. Its thunder reverberated all around them, and Agares' eyes widened with surprise as he froze in place.

"What is this?"

A whisper came forth, touching their ears like a soft breeze. Agares' horrified expression frightened her at first, for the sound feathering around her was unexpected, though Terry and Sean seemed to show no indication of hearing the voice. Armen somehow knew the voice that breathed in her ears, and she knew from whom it came. It had been so long since she'd last heard that voice, though she couldn't recall hearing it at the same time. It was familiar, yet strange to her, as though she'd only ever heard it one time.

Agares dropped to his knees, his sword supporting his body, the vial falling from his hand and shattering on the concrete. He closed his eyes tightly and shook his head violently. Finally, his body calmed and he knelt as still as a statue. Only one word passed in the silence between them, and Armen whispered it with him.

"Mother."

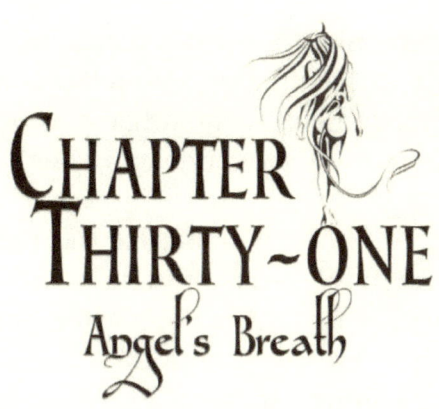

Chapter Thirty-One

Angel's Breath

ARMEN STARED AT THE KNEELING demon, not sure what to think. Was the breath upon their ears actually her Mother? Did she and Agares share the same Mother? Ash suggested that Armen was the only one conceived, but it could have been a lie. Demons lied a lot, but then, they also liked to exaggerate fact, so there could be some truth to what Ash said.

"Kill him, Terry," she said softly. "He can't move now."

Little did any of them know, she couldn't really move, either.

The tip of the scepter's blade rested lightly against Agares' chest just above the heart, over his armor.

"Do you think there is life after death for you, demon?"

Slowly, Agares' eyes lifted, the vibrant yellow showing half-circles mimicking the sun as it dips just into the horizon. His lips curved back to reveal a sliver of his demon teeth.

"I'll take that as a yes."

Armen could sense the strength building in his arm in order to force the blade through the red armor.

Mother, please, let me move.

"Terry, wait." She forced her feet forward, though it was extremely difficult, but she felt the energy shift, allowing her movement. If she'd had a moment to think, the weight of emotion at experiencing her Mother would crumble her.

Terry relaxed only a fraction. He didn't trust that the demon couldn't move, nor should he.

Armen stepped up to Agares, placing her hand on his shoulder. "Why were you after me?"

Terry's eyes shifted to her. "You stopped me to ask *that* question?"

"I need to know." She returned her attention to the demon.

Agares' grin remained, but he said nothing. Armen squeezed his shoulder, digging into a wound left by Terry's sword during their fight, until he shrieked.

"Why do you seek me, Agares?" she snarled in her ancient demon tongue as a gust of wind blew through the garage.

A short laugh left his throat and he roared once more when Armen put pressure on the wound. A curse in a thousand languages old and new flew past his lips, and he glowered at her. Armen punched him in the face and his head jerked back. He still knelt, unable to move. Another gust of wind, stronger this time, swept the underground structure.

"Answer me," she demanded.

"Why, shall you let me live?"

Armen bit her lower lip in contemplation.

Terry frowned. "Armen, what did you just ask him?"

She leaned over Agares. "Tell me the truth, or you *will* die, slowly. Sariel's death wasn't pretty."

"Because you are Father's only true child . . . who is flesh."

She leaned forward, closer to him, her lips next to his ear. "I don't believe you."

"Nor should you have reason to. However, it is the truth . . . for once."

"And why does fetching me hold any importance?"

"Because you are the Light, dearest Azel, O fallen angel."

"So, if you douse the Light, only Darkness shall remain."

"Darkness shall come."

"Gehenna," she whispered as the wind tossed her hair around, its ends whipping her cheeks.

"No. All of it."

"Gehenna what?" Terry asked.

Armen became leery of the wind within the concrete fortress. It wasn't normal by any means. She looked over to Sean briefly, who made his way gradually toward them. The creak of metal sounded, reverberating off the concrete walls. Terry snapped his head around to see what it was, as did Armen, but nothing came into view.

She returned her gaze to Terry. "Gehenna is where all the souls of sinners go to wait until the End of Days."

"Yeah, we've covered that already."

"Yes, but if they extinguish the Light, *all* souls will fall into the Darkness," Armen added. "And I believe we covered that as well."

Terry stared at her a moment. "Shit."

"And why were you after Sean?"

"He is on Samyaza's list."

"What list?" Armen saw the sinister grin reach his eyes. "Oh, *that* list. Oh my." *That* list held the names of those who were the top enemies of the Angel of Darkness. Armen shifted her eyes to Terry and Sean. "Basically, *that* list is Samyaza's FBI's Most Wanted."

"Shit." Terry averted his eyes from Armen and Agares to the other end of the garage. Armen followed his gaze. The gale of wind forcing through the garage rocked the cars. A car alarm sounded, making them all jump, and Terry shifted the blade, accidentally cutting Agares just at his neckline between the collarbones. Agares drew in a hiss as the silver burned his flesh. The wind picked up.

"What the hell is going on?" Terry asked.

"The Angel's Breath is weakening," Sean said from behind Terry. "Take him noo."

Armen stood back so Terry could complete his task. The cars rocked harder. Those at the far end lifted from the ground, and the farthest vehicle lifted tail end first and slammed on top of the one next to it. The bumper fell off and the wind picked it up.

"Look out," Armen shouted, and they all ducked when it sailed overhead and slammed into the wall near the door they came through previously.

Agares' hands moved to the blade, grasping it tightly though it burned his flesh, keeping the silver from gliding through him. He raised his knee and secured his foot to the ground.

Go, the voice floated around her.

Her Mother, again.

"Terry," Armen yelled.

Terry held the scepter with all his strength, struggling against Agares, unwilling to let the blade go. Cars moved forward into the aisle between rows. Armen wondered, not for the first time, if the cost of stopping the Darkness would be their lives.

Blood trickled down Agares' hands as the silver-dipped steel blade cut into his flesh, and he forced himself to stand. A Ford Mustang patrol car hurtled toward them, sirens blaring and lights flashing. They all ducked again, Agares bending back, and the car tumbled over their heads and into the wall, coming to rest on top of another car. The siren made an awful screech before whining into silence.

"Is that a tornado?" Sean yelled over the wind.

Armen scanned the ramp of the garage and she grabbed Terry's arm. "We need to get the hell out of here!"

Terry still struggled against Agares, the scowl on his face matching the glare on the demon's. He tugged on the blade, cutting Agares' hands deeper, and once he pulled it free of the demon's grasp, he held it up and sliced diagonally through Agares' armor. More debris flew past them, and Armen pushed Sean toward the stairwell door.

"Terry, now," she shouted over the wind, hoping he could hear her.

Agares' breastplate fell to the floor with a loud clang amplified by the carrying winds. He fell backwards, and Terry turned and ran after Armen and Sean.

"Go," he yelled, and they ran through the doorway. He slammed the door behind him once he was through.

Armen looked back at him and Sean was already halfway up the first flight when Terry stepped back from the door. It shook and rattled, the bolts on the hinges rising up.

He ran up the stairs after them, shouting, "Run!"

Armen burst through the first floor doorway opening into complete chaos, and ran directly into Captain Brian McNeil. They tumbled to the floor, and Armen scrambled to her feet in the midst of Brian's obscenities.

"Shit, Brian, stay the hell out of the way."

"No time for arguing." Terry grabbed her by the arm and pulled her along. "He's coming."

"Who's coming?" Brian said, getting to his feet. The garage door clanged and echoed in the stairwell. "That freak who killed Art?"

"Yes," Armen and Terry answered.

"Well, kill the son of a bitch."

They all ran toward the lobby.

"We're trying," Armen shouted.

"He's a real pain in the ass to kill. Of course, I could have if *someone* hadn't stopped me."

"Oh, shut up," Armen snapped. "You would have done the same." She slid to a halt on the marble floor in the center of the lobby and scanned the area. "Sean!"

Sean stopped in front of her. "What?"

"Is there any way to stop his weather control?" She really didn't want to take this outside. The tornado would be much larger and too big to run from, although tearing a building apart from the inside wasn't an ideal situation, either.

"The only way would be to destroy him," Sean replied.

Terry ran back toward the hall upon hearing this.

"Son, what're ye doin'?"

"Sneak attack," Terry replied a mere moment before the demon's entrance into the hall sounded with the train echo of a tornado. Terry slammed up against the shaking wall. His eyes quickly met Armen's, and he mouthed his command to her. She nodded and pushed Brian toward the front doors.

"What are you doing?" Brian asked, resisting being forced out of his own station.

"Keeping you safe. Go!" She gave him a final push, and then placed her hands on Sean's shoulders and whispered in his ear. "You're the bait, Sean. Call him out." With that, she scurried over to the front desk and jumped behind it, leaving Sean standing in the open and without a weapon.

Silence fell on the station, but Armen could hear human breath within the small offices surrounding the lobby, which meant Agares would hear it as well. She carefully crawled over to the edge of the large front desk and peered around the corner. Sean stood perfectly still; Terry pressed himself against the wall near the corner with the blade sitting just over his right shoulder, but she could see nothing in the hall past either of them. An eerie silence took over, the proverbial dead calm before the storm. Even the officers still inside the building held their breath for that moment in dreadful anticipation. Life stopped all around them.

Thunderous footsteps echoed in the hall, but there was no wind. Armen was thankful for that. Suddenly, the thought of Samyaza popped into her mind, and she slid back behind the desk. She nearly screamed when she discovered him sitting next to her, leaning casually against the desk, one leg stretched out with the other bent at the knee and his arm lazily draped over it. His blue eyes met hers and he winked.

"What on earth are you doing here?" she whispered.

He smirked, and then jacked his thumb backwards, in Agares' direction. *"He has gone a bit mad."*

"No, really," she returned, her renowned sarcastic twang evident even in a whisper.

"He is hell-bent on killing you and the wrangler." He grinned.

Armen glared at him. "Was that supposed to be funny?"

"It is to me," he replied with a shrug.

"So you're not here to help him?"

"Who, Agares?" When she nodded, he sighed. *"Armuros, sweetie, what fun could we have if all realms fell into the Darkness?"*

"A great deal, I imagine."

He chuckled soundlessly. *"I am certain you could imagine quite a bit."*

"Please, let's not go into my past."

He leaned toward her. *"It is who you are."*

"It's who I *was.*" She scooted over to the edge of the desk again, peering around the corner carefully. It was entirely too silent. Terry was still pressed against the wall, waiting for Agares to enter the lobby. Armen turned her eyes back to Samyaza.

"Is what they're saying about me true, then?"

His head stopped in the midst of a nod and tilted to the side as he eyed her carefully. *"I did not set them upon this task. It is of their own will."*

"Well, certainly, if you don't wish this realm overcome by the Darkness," she replied. "But they do, apparently."

"Yes, they do."

"You can't stop them?" She turned her eyes on Terry and Sean once more.

"You and your plaything back there have stopped three of them already." He grinned, awaiting her response, but she chose to not give him the satisfaction. *"But I suppose I shall have to if you and your friends cannot stop Agares. He is a tough breed."*

Armen sat back on her feet and glared at him. "Samyaza, innocents are dying."

"Better they die as innocents than as sinners, princess."

She cringed upon the declaration of her status, but thought the rest an odd statement coming from one of the princes of the Darkness.

"Otherwise, they belong to him anyway, so what is the difference?"

"That's not to say that none have sinned," she said abruptly. "They are innocent of the situation."

"True," he said with a nod. *"Do you wish me to stop it?"*

"Oh, I know better than to ask anything of you."

He smiled. *"I do so miss you, Armaros."*

"No offense, but I really don't feel the same." She peered around the desk again. Agares stood just around the corner from Terry, waiting patiently for the right moment. "He knows Terry is there, doesn't he?"

"Yes," Samyaza replied.

There wasn't anything she could do to attract Terry's attention without also attracting Agares' attention. She could only hope that he would look her way.

"A father's eyes give the child away."

She sat back again and looked at him. "Tell me something; am I the only one Father conceived?"

Samyaza beamed beyond what Armen could imagine possible. *"No. There were two physically conceived."*

"Who's the other one?"

"Not Jesus," he replied with a snicker.

"So we have a Mother, don't we?"

He nodded. *"You heard Her voice."*

Armen dipped her brows. "Mother was created before *him*, wasn't She?"

Samyaza nodded with delight, a quick motion, quite childish in nature. *"Oh, yes. I see you are figuring it out, albeit a little late in the game."*

"Then he, the Angel of Light, was the first. Not the first to be created like the others, but the first of all created after Mother, and the first actually conceived."

"And the first of our happy little family to fall," he added. *"Father was so distraught when you fell with us."* He watched her reaction, and she lowered her eyes to the floor. *"And the guilt has consumed you ever since."*

Her eyes met his again. "Why have I not known of Her?"

"She died after giving birth to you." Sorrow crept into his eyes, and it was the first time Armen had seen such an emotion stir within him.

"How?"

Samyaza shrugged. *"She was not strong like you or him, or Father. She had a weakness."*

Armen couldn't imagine her Mother having any sort of weakness, but then again, she couldn't fathom her Mother dying, either. Not if She was created before *all* they who were immortal. "What weakness?"

He reached up, pinched her arm, and grinned. *"Flesh."*

She pinched him in return. "You're flesh right now."

He nodded. *"It is because of Her that a few of us can appear in this form. The* others *try to mimic it, but it never looks natural, does it?"*

Armen shook her head, and then peered around the corner again. Everyone stood still. She frowned at the inactivity. "Did you stop time?"

"You know I do not have that ability. Big brother did, for the moment," he replied with a nod. *"I felt it best for our conversation."*

Such power frightened her, especially if it were to be used against her or the others. She sat back on her legs and looked at him. "Why did Her voice work on Agares?"

"They all have a small amount of Her in them," he replied. *"She is the Mother to All—angels, demons, monsters—though She did not physically give birth to all."*

Mother to all, repeated in Armen's mind. *Mother of all . . .* "How is that possible?"

"Father," he said, and he held up his hand and brought his thumb and forefinger together until she could see only the tiniest of space between them. *"A microscopic particle of Her was embedded in every angel ever created."*

"Before humans."

He nodded.

"But He created many angels before I was born."

"Yes, He did. Agares is one of them," he replied. *"But not in the same way you and the Angel of Light were created."* He

leaned toward her again with the grin stretching across his face. *"You were like a mid-life crisis child, Armaros."*

Her brow went up. "You can't be serious."

"Oh, I am," he said with a chuckle. *"You were the last of Her, you know, before He created humans."*

"Why?"

"She knew She was going to die, and since she had already birthed a male, she wanted to give birth to a female."

"So Luc and I are Her and Father's only true children?"

He gave a nod. *"It is why you are Father's favorite. You are Daddy's little girl, Armaros. He holds you much higher than the rest."*

She closed her eyes as guilt and sorrow filled her. *No wonder He was so devastated.* "And that makes me the last of the Light, doesn't it?"

Samyaza nodded. *"Because Mother* was *the Light, and you are the last of Her. It is much different from when you fell. Then, you did not die; you only fell into Gehenna and into the Darkness. Now that you are flesh, if you die at the hands of one of the Fallen and your Life taken by a specific weapon, the Light will extinguish completely, and take all who have it within them, bringing about a new age."*

"Damn, that's a lot of pressure to put on a girl."

His lips stretched. *"Not if you bear children."*

"They killed my last child," she snapped.

"You disobeyed," he responded rather bluntly.

"Excuse me, but whose idea was it to descend unto the mountain?"

He held his hands up quickly. *"Not that I am against disobeying, and yes, I led us all down here. It was mostly my fault, for which I have taken full responsibility."*

"Mostly? We *all* know how you like to break the rules."

He chuckled silently once more. *"True. But other factors were at play when we descended, which we will discuss another time after I have learned more."*

She bit her lower lip, contemplating just what in the bloody hell could have been a factor in their dissension, and she planned to ride his ass about it later. Providing he wasn't actually present to kill her like the others had been. "What was Her name?"

Samyaza laughed and let his head fall back against the desk's cabinets. *"Armaros, you know Her name."*

"Does She still exist somewhere?"

He shook his head, but stopped short. *"Well, I suppose She does if you count yourself and every angel before you out there."*

"Seriously, Sam, stop beating around the bush."

He frowned. *"Do not call me that."*

She pushed herself to her feet and walked around the desk, heading over to Sean. Samyaza followed at a leisurely pace, content with the questions he'd brought forth in her mind, no doubt.

"Come on, Armaros, say Her name," he pushed, draping an arm around Sean's shoulders. He fiddled with the cross that rested against his shirt and smiled. *"I love that they think these symbols work against us, but it is interesting that they work against the minions, do you not think?"*

Armen turned on her heel to head over to Terry, who stood as still as a weird cop statue. It was creeping her out. Samyaza was quick to follow her, and he stood in front of Terry with his arms crossed over his chest.

"Really, what do you see in the man?" He raised his hand to his face, studying him more intently, as though he studied a sculpture at an art gallery.

She smiled. "He loves me for who I am . . . angel, demon, flesh."

"Well, that is a plus, is it not?"

"You're so not funny," she said and walked up to Terry. "Do you think I can move him?"

His brow rose. *"Where to?"*

"Behind Agares."

A sparkle glistened in Samyaza's eye. *"Well, are you not the sly little devil?"*

"Shut up and help me."

"Why would I help you?"

She smirked. "Because it'll be fun to see the look on Agares' face."

He chuckled. *"I must admit you have a good point there."*

"And I saved your life from Sean's shillelagh," she added.

He growled low. *"After I saved yours."*

She shrugged and wrapped her arms around Terry's waist, trying to lift him, but he was too heavy. Samyaza laughed aloud at her efforts before she turned to glare at him. He held up a hand, telling her to let him have a moment, shaking his head as he laughed quietly, keeping the laughter muffled only briefly before he barked it out.

She placed her hands on her hips. "I'm so glad you find this amusing."

He gathered himself together. *"All right, fine, I shall help you, but really, Armaros, you are going to hurt yourself if you do it that way."*

"Then what do you suggest?" She cocked a brow at him.

"Say Her name first."

She blew out a frustrated breath and growled at him. "Fine, it's Lilith."

Samyaza clapped his hands together and grinned. *"Very good. How did you know?"*

"You had said Mother to All. Only one name in all of history goes with that title."

He snapped his fingers and Terry disappeared from where he stood.

Armen jumped around Agares to find Terry standing behind him. "Nice. Now move Sean."

"No. He must remain in order to deceive."

"Oh, his eyes, right." Armen walked back to Sean and forced his hand to take the shillelagh. "Okay, shall we go back to our places now?"

"Of course," he replied and headed back to the desk.

Armen stopped and went back to Sean for a moment to rummage through his leather bag. Within it, she found a small shiny object and quickly pocketed it before returning to the desk. Once she reached the desk, she knelt on the floor next to Samyaza and sifted through the drawers.

"What are you looking for?"

"Don't worry about it. Release time."

He nodded once and peered over the top of the desk as Armen continued to rummage through the top drawer looking for anything to use as a discreet weapon. Soon, movement began and Armen heard Terry's confusion. Sean yelled. She peeked over the top of the desk to find Agares, with Terry's sword in his back, heading right for Sean. It concerned her for a moment until Agares stumbled. She resumed her search for specific items as Samyaza watched them. The shillelagh slammed to the floor. Lights around the building flickered, giving her pause. When she looked again, Terry pulled the sword from Agares' back, who spun around, his own sword lancing through the air, and came down on Terry, who moved in time to block the demon's attack. Agares' momentum forced him to the floor. Armen squeaked with panic and moved to the other side of the desk to search more drawers. By the third drawer, she found a wide rubber band. *Slingshot, it is.*

"What are you doing, Armaros?"

"You just never mind," she replied and took a pair of scissors from the pencil jar. She cut the rubber band in two and tested its length. Next, she grabbed two pens from the jar and tied each end of the rubber band to one of the pens.

"Is that a slingshot?"

"Hush," she said, taping the two pens together in an X. "It worked on Goliath."

"Do you intend to take him down like Goliath?"

"Just tell me what's happening." She sat back on her feet to tinker with the object.

Samyaza looked on and smiled. *"Agares has your plaything trapped on the floor . . . no, wait, the wrangler has just hit him with his mighty stick."*

Armen shook her head and tried not to give him the satisfaction of a smile. It would only make his commentary worse. "Be serious, Sam."

He growled at her, and then she heard Sean's yell. Sam winced after something hit the floor nearby. *"Agares has thrown the wrangler across the room. Nice hit. A homerun, I believe."* There was a brief pause. *"The wrangler lies motionless and your plaything still duels with Agares."*

"Stop calling him that," Armen said. "He has a name."

Samyaza chuckled. *"The Detective is down."*

"What?!" Armen jumped to her feet, and then quickly glared at Samyaza. "You're such an ass."

They were no longer hidden from the others, and Agares craned his head around to view them from the side. *"Samyaza?"*

Sam waved his hand in a motion to carry on, flitting it lightly, but without interest. Agares' brows dipped in displeasure, and he attacked Terry ruthlessly with a growl and aggressive thrusts.

Armen sprinted over to Sean to check on him. After she found him breathing and checked his pulse, she snatched the shillelagh from him and ran toward Agares, the makeshift slingshot dangling from her back pocket. While in motion, she threw the shillelagh up in the air and grabbed the lower end of it. Then she swung it like a baseball bat with all her strength and hit Agares hard enough upside the head that it sent him careening to the floor some thirty feet away from Terry.

"Double play," Samyaza shouted.

Terry grabbed her arm. "What's that about?" He jerked his head toward Sam.

"Oh, he's in baseball mode. Just ignore him. He doesn't even know what he's talking about." She looked to Agares. "Go kill him, before it's too late."

"On it," Terry said and ran to the demon.

Armen kept an eye on Sean and Samyaza, especially since Sean was on his list. It was a fairly exclusive list, and one had to have either sold their soul to her dear brother Lucifer or had to have killed an awful lot of his minions.

She was pretty certain Sean hadn't sold his soul to the devil, but as much as she hated to admit it, the possibility did exist. Of course, then Sean wouldn't be able to talk to her Father, so the minion-murdering theory seemed much more likely.

Terry struck Agares, plunging the sword into his chest, and the demon screeched when the blade seared through his flesh.

"Brother," Agares shouted.

Samyaza only stood and watched, his hands set in a prayer-like pose, fingers closed together, the tips of his middle fingers touching his nose.

"Brother!"

Samyaza shook his head, the motion slow and guarded.

"Brother, please." Agares choked on his words, his body reacting to the silver blade.

Terry withdrew the sword and in a swift motion, brought it down on his neck. The garbled screams stopped, and Samyaza closed his eyes for a brief moment.

He wasn't the only one on guard. Armen stood poised and ready. She didn't know her brother's plans. Not helping Agares hadn't surprised her. With Sam, one had to stand one's own ground. Asking him for help was as big a no-no as one could commit.

Samyaza opened his eyes, looked at Armen, Terry, and then the wrangler lying on the floor nearest him. Within two supernatural steps, he stood at the wrangler's side. The shillelagh hit the floor, but not by force this time. When Samyaza looked at Armen again, she held the makeshift slingshot in her hands, its contents aimed at him, the grin stretching his face as true as she'd ever seen.

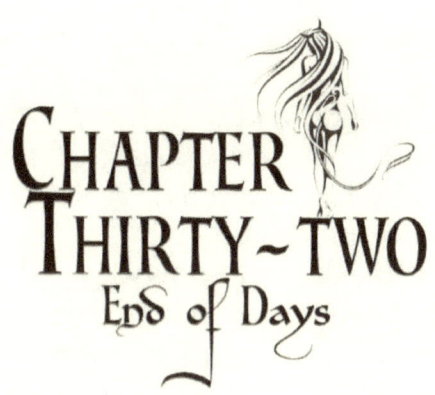

Chapter Thirty-Two

End of Days

SAMYAZA TILTED HIS HEAD TO the side and back, and he watched Armen adjust her aim. *"So it was for me. I you were lying,"* he reminded her of their previous discussion within the Basilica. *"You do not doubt your power to destroy me, nor the will to carry it out."*

"Sue me."

Terry stood frozen. "Armen?"

Samyaza straightened his head and looked at Armen dead on. *"I could have him stop time again."*

"You could, but you won't. It wouldn't be fair, and I believe Father would enter the game. Besides, who's to say Luc would do that for you again?"

"Wow," Terry said softly. Armen then knew he'd caught up on what had just happened and how he came to be behind Agares.

Samyaza gave a short nod. *"You do know me well, Sister, but perhaps our dear Father will turn a blind eye once again."*

"Call it a hunch, but I don't think that's going to happen this time around." She held her aim steady. "Step away from him or I *will* kill you."

He chuckled. *"And what would the world be like without me, Princess?"*

"A hell of a lot better, I'm sure," she replied with a smirk.

He shook his head and took a step away from Sean. *"Doubtful. I have given them knowledge. I have taught them* how *to learn what Luc opened their eyes to. I am the reason they better themselves."*

"Or become the dregs of society."

He chuckled. *"Ah, but those were already on their path to us. It is because of our temptations, however, that mankind ventures toward the Light."*

"Damn, you're an arrogant son of a bitch. If Luc heard you talking like this, he'd slap you out of existence." Armen held her aim on him with each step, keeping the silver ball locked on his head.

"You call your own Mother a bitch. Nice."

"It's an expression, Sam."

"DON'T CALL ME THAT!" He swung his arm low, backwards, rounded up from behind, and when he stopped, his hand spread open, in the form of a baseball pitch. A fast-pitched sonic wave traveled across the room until it slammed into Armen and Terry. Armen had just enough time to close her hand around the silver ball seated within the slingshot before barreling backwards into Terry and the wall behind them. The impact forced all of the air from her lungs and she gulped in gasps to force it back in.

Terry fell next to her, a pain-filled yell coming from him before he reached for her leg. "I hate being human, too." He sucked in a breath when he attempted to move and gave up shortly thereafter.

Armen couldn't help herself, she laughed, and it hurt . . . bad. She leaned over and kissed the top of his head. "Anything broken?"

"My leg, I think," he grunted.

"No more demon fighting for you. Not today, anyway."

"You okay?" He attempted to sit up again, but failed and fell to the floor with a grunt. The fact that he wasn't still yelling in agony with a broken leg was a testament to his strength, and Armen admired him a great deal more.

"Stay put. I'm fine." She moved her hand to his cheek and rubbed her fingers along the stubble. "I love you, Terry."

He attempted a smile. "I know."

"I just wanted you to know that."

"I love you, too, Armen." He clenched his teeth to bite back the pain. "Finish him off."

"Will do." She slid her right leg beneath her to stand and casually searched for the scepter with only her eyes. If they needed to kill her with that weapon, she wanted to know where it was at all times. She spotted it on the other side of Terry, between him and the wall. "Keep that hidden until necessary," she whispered. Thankfully, he'd had the good sense to retract that blade before she'd slammed into him.

Terry nodded and squeezed her leg. "Don't let him take my dad."

Armen frowned. "I'll do my best, Terry, but he's strong."

"I'm just asking that you try."

She nodded once and pushed herself to her feet by sliding up the wall, pausing a moment to gather her energy before pushing away. Armen needed a prayer answered right now. *Father, if you can hear me . . . .* It was worth a shot. She stepped forward. This was something she would have to do without the divine weapon. Truly, it was the only way.

Samyaza stood near the desk and Sean, his long black hair resting against his shoulders and his blue eyes brightening to the color of a true flame. Armen did *not* have the stamina for this fight. Her energy had all but drained completely out of her by the time she stood and walked a few feet from Terry and the wall. A heavy sigh left her.

"I told you once, *Sam*, that taking the wrangler or his son will start a war between us." She was rather surprised he hadn't vanished with Sean already.

He grinned. *"You are still flesh, Sister."*

"I won't be for long." Her voice sounded tired and at its end.

"What?" Terry said in the background.

He scanned her body. *"You are not injured."*

"Not on the outside." Armen continued her path to him with painful steps, and each of those steps felt as though someone poured sand into her legs, making them heavier every time she lifted a foot.

"Armen?"

She ignored him. There was nothing left to say.

Samyaza arched a brow. *"And yet, you still seem willing to fight me. Not surprising, I suppose. You always did find strength when you needed it the most."*

"I can't allow you to take Sean," she said, still moving toward him. "And I simply *won't* allow you to take the man I love." She paused in her step to catch her breath. "They're good people who don't deserve Hell. If that means I have to fight you, then so be it."

"I cannot kill you, Armaros," he said. *"I do not wish to end it all. You can keep the detective."*

"You've already killed me, Sam," she replied. "I'm just not dead yet."

Concern creased his face. *"Then the war would take place in Gehenna."*

"Yes, it would." Armen kicked the shillelagh up with her foot and caught it. He knew she could kick his ass in that realm. Being a princess had its perks. "So why not begin it up here, where Armageddon seems to be starting?"

He pointed a long finger at her. *"I had nothing to do with that!"*

"I don't care."

Sam stared at her for a long time, and Terry attempted to make his way over to her by dragging himself along the floor. Sean stirred and his eyelids fluttered. Silence filled the air as the sky outside turned red and black; lightning filtered across the sky, clouds darkening and swirling, thunder roaring, but not from brewing storms. As much as Armen wanted to know what made the thunderous sound, she couldn't concern herself with finding out . . . not yet.

"Think about what you are doing, Armaros."

"It's no longer my choice, Sam." Cries in the distance made their way to her ears, but she didn't remove her eyes from him. "You've brought this upon me now, finished what the others couldn't. You know that even without the weapon, my dying at the hands of one of the Fallen will take me back to Gehenna, not Home, regardless of the fact that I'm in the Light now."

She could see the changes taking place outside from the corner of her eye, and it perplexed her. Perhaps she'd misinterpreted the demonic graffiti. Maybe Armageddon didn't rely on her death to begin its reign because the war had already started falling to this realm a little at a time over a much longer period than the time frame in which they had been attempting to kill her. Perhaps it was just that her death coincided with the End of Days, or it was the perfect time to kill her as a way for Hell to win the war without a fight. Kill the Fallen Princess with her Father's weapon; everything falls and the Darkness wins. Earth would become Gehenna, everlasting

Darkness, and all the things that came with it. Samyaza and the others would have all of humanity readily available to torture, no matter how they lived their lives. A harpy flew across the sky, followed by several scattered human screams from people running to get away.

Armen stood still, staring into her brother's eyes, fighting the weakness that was about to overtake her human body. Her breath hitched and she coughed. It made her stumble forward and she tightened her grip on the shillelagh for support. She coughed again and found blood on her hand when she withdrew it from her mouth. Questions arose in her mind of why her Father made her flesh. She reminded herself of Sean's words: *Faith in why He does things.*

"Armen," Terry called to her, fear catching his voice as he crawled across the floor. "No."

Samyaza closed his eyes, the regret showing on his still angelic features.

Sacrifice. Armen knew the Fallen despised it, and she had apparently just done the deed, not for the first time, by stepping in front of Terry before the sonic wave hit and casting a spell that wouldn't get him killed. She'd forgotten to include herself in that spell.

Oops.

Sean tried to sit up, but fell back to the floor with a grunt, catching Armen's attention.

Samyaza's eyes shifted to him, and then quickly back to Armen. He moved fast, twisting in a whirlwind over to Sean, and picked up the demon wrangler. He held Sean in front of him like a shield.

Armen hadn't moved. She only stared at him. "Father won't let you keep him," she growled. "You *know* that."

"Father will have to look for him if he wishes to save him, and by then, there will not be anything left."

"He belongs in the Light." She fell into a coughing fit and dropped to one knee, leaning forward, her fist pressing hard against the cold floor, the silver ball still confined within. "You cannot take . . . that which . . . belongs in the . . . Light." She coughed again, spitting blood onto the floor.

"He is not the golden child you think, Armaros."

"I don't c-care. It's not my pl-place to judge him." She raised her head and glared. "He still belongs . . . to Father if he can hear Father's v-voice."

Samyaza cocked his left brow, as though he didn't know that information. He shifted his gaze to the side of Sean's face. *"Is this true, Wrangler? You can hear and speak to our Father?"*

Sean nodded.

Samyaza's wide grin reappeared. *"Tell him you are fucked."*

A scream came from within the offices and a door opened. Jasmine ran into the lobby, chased by a one-headed hellhound much smaller than Cerberus. It was nonetheless horrific, however, as it had no skin. Nothing but muscle and tendons and bone; the creature didn't even have any eyes, but it still had very sharp teeth.

"Here," Terry shouted, and when Armen looked behind her, he slid the scepter across the floor to her. She dropped the shillelagh and snatched up the scepter, then thumbed the trigger for the full blade. As the beast ran by, Armen beheaded it from her crouch on the floor after Jasmine ran past her. She didn't have the strength to stand any longer.

"Jazzy, go to Terry," she shouted as best she could. Jasmine skidded to a halt and turned to look at Armen, her eyes bewildered, and then she eyed Terry and ran over to him after seeing the events unfolding outside.

Armen couldn't blame her. Things walked the earth that didn't belong on it.

A ball of fire shot across the sky. Damn, she hated being wrong about the fire and brimstone shit.

"That was my favorite dog." Sam growled.

"Sorry, they all look alike to me."

"You are such a bitch."

Her eyes tightened with pain and she grunted. "Get over it." She collapsed, and the scepter clinked against the floor, but the silver ball remained within her left hand.

Terry's shouts echoed across the lobby. "Jasmine, get the scepter!"

Armen turned around in her spirit form and stared at the small group nearing her body. She stood twenty feet away, and Samyaza's eyes shifted from her spirit to her body, but he said nothing.

She wasn't dead yet.

Jazzy ran toward her, picked up the scepter as she slid across the floor, and she positioned herself in front of Armen's body, shielding her, pointing the blade toward Samyaza.

"Armen!" Terry finally made his way across the floor, dragging himself over to her. He turned her over, cradling her in his arms. "Come on, Armen." Terry patted her face lightly, but her eyes remained closed, even when he shouted her name again. "God, please, no. Don't let this happen." He whispered into Armen's hair.

Jasmine didn't move.

Terry looked up at Samyaza, anger raging in his green eyes. "What have you done? Look at what you've done!"

Sam stared at him, uncertainty evident in his gaze. *"I did not intend for this to happen."* He briefly looked at her spirit again.

"Well, it did happen."

Armen watched as Sean reached into his satchel and withdrew the powder he'd used on the minions earlier. He carefully opened the container during Samyaza's distraction, and threw it over his shoulder into the Fallen's face. Samyaza roared and let go of him, and Sean stumbled away from him as quickly as his legs would carry him.

Gunfire erupted in the lobby, and Samyaza jolted a step back. Smoke billowed from the wound in his right shoulder and he stared at it, shocked. Another shot hit his left shoulder, throwing him back two steps.

"How?" He scanned the lobby for the perpetrator.

Dante Peterson stepped out of the shadows with a Glock pointed directly at Sam's head. He smirked. "I was a priest before I became a cop; therefore, I blessed the few silver rounds I still had before loading the gun." He glanced at Terry. "Thanks for dropping it in the lab."

Terry nodded. "Figured you'd need it when you woke."

Dante fixated on Sam again. "Now, fix it before it's too late."

"I did not mean for this to happen." He regarded Armen's body, which looked rather pale, and then glanced at her spirit once more.

"That's why I'm telling you to fix it," Dante said. "You may not wish to go back to your Father, but I know you don't want all of this. It's the only reason I haven't taken the shot to your head."

Sam pointedly arched a brow and tilted his head. *"Do you really think you can kill me with a mortal weapon?"*

"I know exactly how to kill you, Samyaza," Dante said. "You've already killed your lord's only true sister. You've already brought forth the Darkness."

"That is not the Darkness." He gestured to the window. *"I cannot stop* that *because it has nothing to do with* her *death."* Rather than pointing at Armen's body, he pointed at her spirit, which, of course, no one else could see. *"That outside is the War falling to earth."*

"If you won't fix it, then my killing you will."

Dante wasn't budging on his view of things, and Armen had no way to communicate with him that Sam wasn't lying. For once. Maybe twice.

Sam's eyes dawned with comprehension. *"If you think the Exchange will fix things, be my guest. It will not save her. It will not stop Armageddon. She and I will return to the Darkness, where we will likely fight until one of us is dead now that I have completely pissed her off."*

"You're talking like she's still alive."

"No, that vessel is dying, but she is right there." He pointed in her direction again, but Dante looked right through her.

Silence swept the room as Dante considered his words. "You have to do something. You know He'll be here soon."

"Too bad I beat Him here," a newcomer answered. *"It would be interesting to see what He'd do with you, Sam."*

Sam flinched. *"Shit."*

The newcomer leaned against the front desk casually, one leg crossed over the other while tapping the tip of his cane against his foot, long black hair pushed to one side and flowing over his shoulder. He scratched his bearded chin before dropping the tip of the cane to the floor.

"Would someone like to explain to me just what in the bloody fucking hell is going on?"

Armen gasped, covering her mouth before finishing his name.

He looked right at her spirit and shook his head. *"Now, there's a name I haven't heard in quite some time."*

She placed her hands on her hips. "What, Lucifer?"

"I thought you were going to shorten it like you always have."

"It got cut off by my shock at your arrival."

He laughed. *"Pity, you're the only one who's ever been allowed to say it."*

Terry cleared his throat. "I don't mean to interrupt the crazy session, but the love of my life is dying—"

"Oh, right, you can't see her." He pushed away from the desk and walked over to Armen's spirit, taking her hand. *"Sam did this?"*

She nodded.

"I'll take care of it."

Terry stared at Lucifer. "Who the hell are you and who are you talking to and just what exactly are you going to take care of?"

"Don't see the family resemblance?" Lucifer smiled at him as he strolled away from Armen. *"I am the King of all demons, the Angel of Light, the First created and the First of the Fallen, the King of Hell, the Prince of Darkness, and I was speaking with the love of your life, the princess, who is standing right fucking there."* He pointed at her without averting his eyes from Terry. *"Now, if you'll allow it, I can save her. Otherwise, I'll have to arrange to have her pulled out of the damn Darkness again."*

Armen gasped again, and Lucifer gave her a wink.

"Why should I trust you?" Terry protectively pulled Armen's body close.

"Because she is my one true Sister, and I cannot allow her to die and leave this world like this. It needs her." Lucifer pointed at the windows and what lay beyond them, behind the glass. *"Be glad you're on this side of the glass. Her death will speed it up."*

Sam brought his hands up. *"Fucking hell. Are you going to save her?"*

Lucifer sliced through the air sideways with his hand, and Sam flew back and hit the wall, sticking there. *"I will deal with you later,"* he growled. Then, Sam was sucked into the stone wall, completely vanishing beneath its surface.

"What did you do to him?" It was Terry who had asked as he still clutched Armen's body to his chest.

"I sent him back, Knight. Not all that dissimilar from how you do it." He smiled then and continued toward the little group huddled together.

"But I don't send them anywhere."

"Don't you?" He glanced back at Armen again. *"Dear Sister."*

She nodded.

Cries suddenly sounded behind her and she turned, thinking they came from outside, but she ended up facing darkness in the shape of a doorway. "Oh no!"

"Don't go near it, Armen," Lucifer said in the ancient language as he neared her body while pointing at her spirit. *"We must hurry."*

Jasmine pointed the scepter in his direction. "Stay away from her."

"Do you want her to live or not?" His voice bellowed through the lobby, echoing off the walls.

Terry stared hard at him, his hand shaking with anger. "How are you going to bring her back?"

Lucifer sighed. *"Don't ask about things you don't understand."*

"Terry, please . . . ."

Lucifer looked back again. *"She's asking you to allow me to do this."*

Terry looked around. "Why can't I see her?"

"Because you're burdened with emotion, dear boy. Now, if you please . . . ."

He watched him cautiously. "If you try anything—"

"Your friend shall kill me, Detective." Dante's gun was now pointed at him, and perhaps within his vast array of knowledge, Dante knew exactly how to kill the Devil. Lucifer paused and stared into Terry's eyes. *"And so shall my Father, considering He'd saved her for a reason, which has not yet come to pass."* The sky continued to darken outside as Lucifer knelt next to Armen's body. He looked at Terry's leg and smiled. *"Trust me?"*

"Absolutely not," Terry replied. Armen lay in his arms between the two of them.

Lucifer shrugged. *"Too bad."* He held his hands over Armen's chest and stomach, moving back and forth in a slow sweep. Then his eyes met Terry's once more. *"Would you die for her?"*

"Stop stalling," Dante commanded.

Lucifer chuckled. *"I'm not stalling, Dante. I merely wish to know the man's feelings for my Sister. She IS my Sister, after all."* His eyes returned to Terry. *"Well?"*

"Am I not sitting here, staring you in the face?"

Lucifer smirked. *"You're sitting here because you're sworn to protect the innocent. That has nothing to do with Armen. So when I ask you if you would die for* her, *I mean, would you truly DIE for her?"*

"Yes," Terry replied.

"Not good enough. Would you place her above all others?"

"Stop fucking around, Luc," Armen said. Sean looked directly at her and she gasped. Then she felt something pulling on her essence. She looked back at the dark doorway. "Luc, hurry."

"I need to know, Armen."

Terry growled. "What the hell are you saying in that language?"

"I'm merely speaking with Armen. Now answer the question. She doesn't have much time."

"I don't know what you want me to say."

"You have said it once before, I believe."

Terry looked him squarely in the eye, his own eyes piercing, shimmering with light. "A thousand times, yes."

"Much better." Lucifer grinned and leaned over Armen's body until his face was within an inch of Terry's. *"I do not ever want to hear the word 'demon' said in anger, in reference to my Sister, come from your mouth again."*

"Luc, stop it!" Armen slid backwards a few feet. "Hurry!"

Terry looked at Armen's face, and he nodded. "It won't happen again. I already told her that."

"If it does, you shall see me one last time, Knight of Death," Lucifer threatened in a low growl, *"and you will not enjoy it."*

"Understood," Terry replied with a nod.

Lucifer waved his hand over Armen, clapped them together, and hopped to his feet. He turned his head to her. *"Get your ass back in there."*

The pull on her vanished right before she reached the doorway. "That was too fucking close."

"Yet you're still here." As Armen moved toward her body, he looked at the small group again. *"Interesting group, aren't they?"*

"Yes, they are." Terry, whom her brother apparently felt would take good care of her, or Terry would be dead; Jasmine, surprising her with the warrior princess action;

Sean, the demon wrangler Samyaza had most regrettably lost; and Dante, the second surprise of the evening. Armen had feared him dead.

"Well, children, I'd love to say it's been fun, but I must be going."

"She's not alive," Terry said.

Lucifer smirked. *"She will be, whenever she decides to get back inside her damn body."* He glared at her. Then he ducked to the side. The silver ball flew past his head and he stood straight again. *"And this is the thanks I get for saving your life, Princess."* He leaned forward. *"We're even now. Until we meet again, dearest Sister."* He bowed, looked up, and smiled. *"Dante."*

Dante nodded once, and Lucifer disappeared in a cloud of black smoke.

"Crap, I missed," Armen said hoarsely.

Terry looked down at her. "Damn, you've got an arm on you for someone who was mostly dead."

"I didn't want him trying to take your dad with him." She attempted a smile and only halfway pulled it off. "Sorry if I hit you."

Terry chuckled, until she moved and bumped his leg. "OW!"

"Sorry again," she said. "Why didn't you let him fix it?"

Terry just shook his head. "Should I have trusted the Devil?"

She smiled at him and placed her hand on his face. "When it comes to me, yes, and you are a part of me."

"What's going to happen to Samyaza?"

"He'll torture him. Poor guy."

"You're awfully forgiving of a man who killed you," Terry said.

"He didn't mean to. If I wasn't human, that would have been a light slap on the cheek, much like our little fights used to be. You wouldn't even believe the havoc we caused in Heaven and in Hell when we'd fight."

The shuffle of feet made its way to Armen's ears, and they both looked up to find a small elderly man standing next to Sean. They conversed briefly in hushed tones, and then the man looked over to Terry and Armen. His vibrant blue eyes sparkled and focused on Terry's broken leg. Then he looked outside, and sorrow filled his eyes.

Smoke filled the red skies as buildings burned. People ran through the streets, chased by hounds of Hell, harpies, and the like. Armageddon had begun and her death only seemed a coincidence, not prophecy.

Armen didn't really believe in coincidences.

The old man spoke quietly with Sean again, drawing their attention, and when they looked back outside, a rising sun had replaced the burning sky.

Terry looked back again to find the man gone. "Where'd he go?"

Sean smiled. "Home."

Armen swallowed the lump in her throat after realizing who the man was. "Father," she whispered, and Terry pulled her close. "Why didn't He talk to me?"

Sean stepped closer to them. "He will, dear, when you're ready to hear Him."

Dante holstered his gun and started for the front doors.

"Where are you going?" Terry asked.

He stopped and turned to them. "Home. Facing three powerful demons and then the damn Devil is about all I can handle for one night."

Terry moved suddenly and was shocked to discover no pain. "Holy shit, my leg's not broken. I hadn't even realized . . . ." He slid it beneath himself, and moved to stand, bringing Armen with him. "Home sounds really good right now, but I think I need a drink first."

"So does sleep," Armen suggested. "A lot of sleep."

"Agreed. And a drink."

"Okay, I got it. You need a drink." Armen looked back at Jasmine. "You okay?"

Jasmine stared at her wide-eyed. "You all are crazy! But thanks for the save." She blew a stray curl away from her eyes.

Armen smiled at her. "Go home and rest, Jazzy. Everything will be fine tomorrow."

"I sincerely doubt that."

"Or you could join us for a drink."

"Bars are closed."

"Pretty sure the one across the street is open," Dante shouted from the doors.

Jasmine finally shrugged. "Why the hell not? This is all a dream, right?"

"Sure," Armen said. "If that's what you want it to be." Who was she to destroy the woman's fantasy?

A disheveled-looking Brian stepped through the doors, passing Dante as he walked out. "Where's everyone going? What happened?"

"We'll explain it at the bar," Terry said, pointing at the doors.

He met Terry's eyes and shook his head. "I don't even want a report on this fire and brimstone shit."

"Good, I don't feel like writing it," Terry replied. "Join us?"

Brian looked around the lobby. "To hell with it, I think I will."

They stepped outside, surveying the destruction caused by the very brief apocalypse. Considering how much damage there was, Armen was glad it only lasted a short time. She followed the others across the street, toward the still-standing sports bar—imagine that—but she stopped just shy of going inside. The hairs on her arms stood on end and a tingle ran up her spine. Something was off. When she glanced down the street, her eyes rested on a tall blond male leaning against a light pole. His long hair whipped around lightly in the still-present breeze, and his black leather trench coat flapped against the light currents.

It was not one she recognized.

He smiled at her and licked his ice cream, never once taking his eyes off her.

She feigned a smile, but wondered who he was because he certainly seemed to know her with the way he looked at her.

He pointed up and to his right before licking the ice cream again.

Armen looked up, following his direction, and saw a small disturbance in the southern sky. She shifted her eyesight, and realized it was a shooting star, though not your normal shooting star. This one had a glowing vibrant orange tail. When she returned her eyes to him, his aura stunned her as it swirled in light *and* dark.

"What the hell?" She started walking toward him. "Who are you?" Someone grabbed her arm and she spun around to find Terry, switching her eyesight back to normal.

"Hey, who are you talking to?"

Armen looked down the street again and the man was gone. "Apparently no one."

"Then come inside," he said with a long stroke down her arm that brought her skin to life.

She agreed and followed him into the sports bar, taking one last look down the street before she stepped through the door, feeling a little rattled. It wasn't as though she hadn't seen any shooting stars recently, but they weren't generally good, especially when they had a tail like that one on them. It made her wonder who had just joined the Fallen.

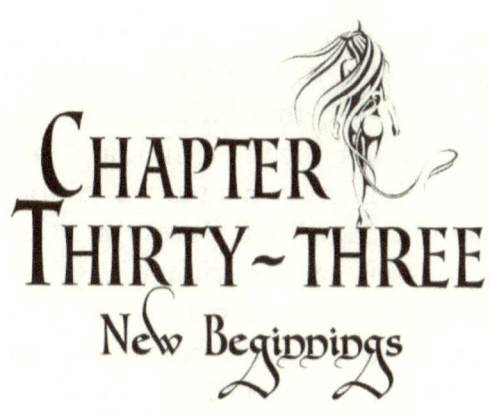

Chapter Thirty-Three

New Beginnings

ARMEN SAT ON THE EDGE OF the bed and stared at the John Constable landscape painting hanging on the wall in her room, still in Terry's house. She'd stared at it before, but never really looked at its detail. What captivated her so about the portrait, she had no idea. Perhaps it was the solitude of the piece with its English countryside, a little cottage with smoke rising from the chimney, and the trees, so lush and full of life.

As she continued to stare at the picture, leaves from the trees' branches moved, slowly swaying in a non-existent breeze. Armen sat up straight and leaned forward. She focused her eyes so she could see in a more ethereal plane and noticed something else not seen by normal human eyes. A little man who appeared to be lit from within, or perhaps surrounded by an incandescent aura, walked along the narrow path, the glow suggesting something divine. Armen jumped from the bed and stood before the painting. She touched the protective glass Terry had placed over it, and the little man turned to face her. He was so small that she couldn't make out any details. His tiny hands rose up in the air and the colors of the portrait brightened to the point that Armen had to squint. When the colors died down again, the landscape had changed. The little man now stood before

Mt. Hermon, the summit where she, Sariel, and the others had descended to take the daughters of man—or son, in her case—at the bidding of Samyaza. She frowned; she didn't need reminding of what had happened. The little man held up a hand, seeming to know her thoughts. She lifted a brow and tilted her head, and she could barely see the smile that graced the man's lips. The landscape changed once more, diving into the depths of Hell as flame and embers rose to the top of the portrait. She looked for the little man within the fire and finally found the man at the top of the picture, standing on a ledge that the fire couldn't seem to reach, on the edge of the Darkness. She frowned again and the little man looked at her, still smiling as she was next shown the day she became flesh.

"Sacrifice," she whispered, and the little man nodded, but the smile faded. He stood over her fallen demon body and the image grew enough for her to see the tear that fell down the man's cheek while lifting her from the cold ground.

A tear fell down Armen's cheek and she pressed her hand against the glass in an attempt to touch the man's face. "Father." The word nearly caught in her throat and she croaked it out in a whisper.

He rested a hand against the wound in her abdomen and a brilliant light shone beneath it before her flesh began its change. Armen never knew how it had happened; only that she awoke in her new human flesh in a Catholic hospital.

"Why?" she asked when He laid her on the hospital bed.

He waved a hand and showed her the image of an infant girl with blonde hair and blue eyes, a male holding her and rocking her slowly, with joy and sorrow emanating through the image.

Her thoughts returned to Terry.

"What is he, Father?"

He turned to her and smiled brightly, and then He pointed directly to her.

"Who, me?"

He shook His head.

"Like me?"

He nodded.

"But how? He has human parents."

He only smiled, and the landscape changed again. She now saw Terry's mother, Lucille, as the others welcomed her into the Light, and then into Heaven. He nodded to her once more as she watched. She knew this one to mean approval. Lucille turned around and waved to her, and wings unfolded behind her. Lucille was an angel.

"Of course." Armen closed her eyes briefly and opened them to find a new landscape. Ashtoreth's face appeared before her and she jumped back from the portrait. The demon suddenly disappeared and Armen was staring at Him once again.

"Really, must you be so dramatic?" she said, and received a disapproving look. "Don't look at me like that."

He threw His head back in silent laughter, and she sighed.

"What's the point of all this?"

He placed His hand over the center of His chest and beamed.

"You love me, I get it. I saw it in the book."

He waved a finger at her and shook His head.

"I don't get it?"

He shook His head again and pointed toward the bedroom door.

"Yeah, Terry loves me, I know."

He smiled and pointed at her, then at the door.

"Do I love him?"

He nodded.

Armen let out a deep sigh and turned to sit on the bed again. "I do. But I'm afraid, Father, after what happened the last time."

He nodded once, His features still not clear, and changed the landscape. The picture filled with sand and soon, a stick drew coarse lines through the grains. *You are human now. It is entirely different.*

"You're kidding me," she said and stood to go to the picture again. Water washed the words away and He was soon writing more. She had to giggle at this method of communication, but then, He couldn't actually speak to her right now. She'd closed her mind to His voice long ago.

Three simple words formed in the sand. *Go to him.*

"Really? I can?" She soon saw His face again. It filled the entire frame. She'd nearly forgotten what He looked like, it had been so long, and it was nothing like the small elderly man they'd encountered after Lucifer left. His hair was salt and pepper gray, and His vibrant blue eyes, reflective of hers, gleamed at her with tiny crow's feet around the edges. He didn't look as old as humans portrayed Him. He was a handsome man with not-so-pale flesh. He looked like He'd been on that beach for some time. It wouldn't surprise her. He loved the beach. His lips curved into a smile surrounded by a moustache and goatee, also salt and pepper gray. In fact, Lucifer was the spitting image of their Father. She stepped closer to the portrait and touched the glass above his cheek, and her mind opened.

"Go, Armen," He whispered. *"You have my blessing."*

"May I . . . see my Mother?"

His eyes welled with tears before He changed the image.

She stepped back in awe of the image before her. As Luc was the spitting image of their Father, she apparently was the twin of their Mother.

"I love you, my Daughter."

Armen leaned her head against the portrait and tears fell when she closed her eyes. "Thank you, Father," she whispered in reply.

When she opened her eyes again, the Constable portrait had returned. She turned to face the bed, looking at the black dress Terry had bought. Her mouth curved at its corners, and she slipped out of the robe and held the dress up. It had been a hellish three weeks, cleaning up the aftermath brought forth by an Armageddon they weren't certain how to stop but seemed contained for the time being. She'd buried herself in research on the message left by those who had tried to kill her, but had yet to turn up anything. McNeil promoted Terry to Sergeant after the unfortunate discovery that his superior had died at the hands of a nasty zombie-like puppet. She hadn't found out who controlled it, but it didn't matter now because the demons, minions, and their ilk were all back in Gehenna where they belonged—for now. Dante had been promoted to Detective, making him a very happy man, and Jasmine still twitched occasionally whenever she was surprised by an unexpected sound. It made Armen sad to see Jazzy like that, and she was the one who suggested Dr. Whitewolf speak with her. Dr. Whitewolf worked with her daily. The doc just had an uncanny knack for dealing with it.

Armen found herself filling Art's shoes in the forensics department. It was a big jump, and she wasn't certain she could handle it, but Terry quelled her doubts whenever she brought it up.

She was, however, now delighted to have Terry take her out to dinner, even if it wasn't the day he'd promised. Once she was ready, she opened the bedroom door and walked into the living room.

Terry sat on the sofa reading a book, and he looked up when he heard her enter the room. His eyes twinkled, lighting up his entire face. He stood and walked over to her, leaning over to kiss her cheek. "You look beautiful."

She thanked him and they walked to the front door, but first, Terry stopped at the closet. He pulled out a black shawl, and draped it over her shoulders.

She fingered the silky material. "Very nice."

"The Salt Cellar awaits, madam," he said, and she stepped outside.

On the drive to the restaurant, Terry cleared his throat. "Armen, I've been thinking, about everything, and well, with what we've been through, and more specifically what you've been through, well, I, we, as in my dad and yours, we think that you deserve to have these back." He slid a hand across the seat, pushing a black velvet box next to her.

She beamed with excitement and snatched up the box. "Oh, what is it?" She opened the box, and inside was a beautiful silver cuff bracelet with wings sitting one above the other. She blinked at him. "Wings?"

"You don't like it."

"No, I do," she replied. "I just thought—"

"That it would be a ring?"

"No," she said with a shake of her head. "I just didn't expect *silver* wings."

"Liar," he replied.

"Okay, maybe I thought there would be a ring in there, but the size of the box threw it off." She pulled the bracelet out and slipped it on. A wave of energy ran up her arm and continued throughout her body. She gasped. "Oh my."

Terry smiled. "It's special."

"I can see that," she said as she stared at it. "Like the scepter is special?"

Terry nodded. "You have to figure it out, though, because I don't know how it works."

"Nice, and my Father is probably the only one who does." She brought her wrist closer to view the details. "What's with the diamonds?" One large diamond sat at the top of each wing.

"Hardest substance on Earth," he said. "I guess it's supposed to protect you."

She glanced at him. "Did you get anything?"

He nodded once more and smiled. "You."

"Not without a wedding," she said with a smirk.

"I can do better than that," he replied. "I have your Father's blessing. Now I just need yours."

She lifted her brow. "Is that so?"

"Yep." He returned the smirk. "So what say you, Angel Armen?"

She let out a small sigh. "I'll have to think about it."

Terry laughed. "You're such a tease."

"Better a tease than a demon," she replied with a playful lilt in her voice.

Terry reached for her hand. "See? I forget sometimes."

"When I'm with you, Terry, sometimes I forget too," she replied and entwined her fingers with his briefly. "And I'm very thankful for that."

They pulled into the parking lot of The Salt Cellar. Terry put the car in park and killed the engine.

"Here," he said, reaching into his jacket breast pocket. "Try this one." He gently placed a small box on her lap.

She opened it and a brilliant diamond ring sparkled at her. "Wow! That must have been some raise."

"Just give me an answer."

She turned to him, smiling. "You're so romantic."

"I know. Wait till the honeymoon." He waggled his eyebrows.

Armen laughed.

"Well?"

She reached around to the back of his neck, pulling him to her. "A thousand times, yes."

FINIS

About the Author

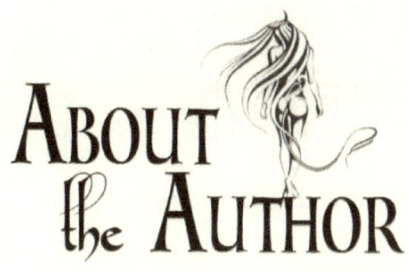

N.L. "Jinxie" Gervasio is a creator and destroyer of worlds. She is both editor and author, and has discovered she's quite good at the romance thing—writing it, that is—with vampires, werewolves, zombies, angels, and demons. Jinxie spends most of her time—when not working in the IT industry—chained to her laptop writing, editing, gaming, or watching movies. But mostly editing.

Born on Friday the 13th, her dad wanted to call her Jinx; her mom said no. After 34 years, she discovered the nickname, and she's grown quite attached to it, thereby choosing the moniker as her interwebz handle. She lives in Tempe, Arizona with Umi (her mother), whom she cares for. She enjoys riding her beach cruiser "The Betty" around downtown Tempe when it isn't being used as a clothing rack, loves a good pub crawl on occasion, and has had the pleasure and the heartache of experiencing a love far greater than she could have ever imagined.

She welcomes you to her worlds.

Jinxie is the author of the Kick-Ass Girls Club series book *Nemesis,* and the Prophecy series books *The Dracove* and *Gods & Vampyres,* as well as co-author in anthologies *Into the Darkness, Undead Uncensored,* and *The 434 Revolution.*

You can find Jinxie in cyberspace here:

Website: http://jinxiesworld.com/
Twitter: http://twitter.com/Jinxie_G
Facebook: http://www.facebook.com/Jinxi3G
Tumblr: http://jinxiesworld.tumblr.com/
Newsletter: http://eepurl.com/bBo7or
Goodreads:
https://www.goodreads.com/author/show/584192.N_L_Gervasio
Instagram: http://instagram.com/jinxie_g
The ZSC: http://zombiesurvivalcrew.com/fearless-leaders/brigade-leaders/jinxie-g/

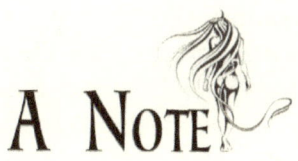

A Note

Dear Reader,

Several years ago I wrote a short photo essay for a college English course, and a few years later, posted it on a writer's website. My friend, James, read the piece, commented on how he enjoyed it but wished it had been longer. I read his comment and thought, "I can make that longer." And thusly, Armen sprang from my mind.

I'd like to share that inspiration with you. I hope you enjoy it and Armen's story, and that it helps you understand where exactly Armen came from.

Sincerely,
N.L. Gervasio

Skin

I am a tortured soul of times long past, centuries old and lost in a world unknown to me. Such anguish I feel, such sorrow. Heartache, I am, that I break my own flesh and feel discontent with the world, so I hide beneath my quivering wing in hopes to block the malevolence from my vulnerability of reality. Even my ancient wisdom cannot save me from the agony mounting inside, swelling beyond its boundaries, growing into regret of things long lost to fate and destiny. The same wing arm that braces me from falling prevents my soul from diving into the pits of Hell, while my tail wraps around me to form a circle none are to enter. Wings shroud me with protection like a cloak of invisibility to hide my ache from this unknown land. Blonde locks spill like rivers over arms too tired to move.

My skin is tight with the *act of atonement,* yet ripe for destruction while I tear at the flesh with sharp nails. Blood trickles slowly down, as though teasing me with the *dawn of life* rather than the *dusk of death,* and I ask myself if I am worthy of this grief I bear. I ask myself if I am worthy of the life I live and the blood that flows through me. I ask myself if I wish to continue on, or give up as I lie in this ball on the ground. I must remind myself that my pain is only temporary and that tomorrow will be a new day when I hold my head high and spread my wings. I am not the skin that covers these ancient bones. I am not the flesh that beneath lies a beating heart. I am the soul within, a soul not broken, a soul reborn from this torment. I will not bow to this pain, but I cannot promise my skin will feel the same.

FOOTNOTE

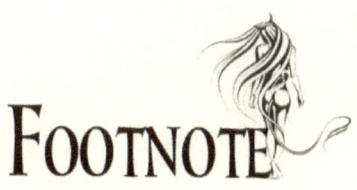

1 - In Chapter Five, at the bottom of page 57, Armen talks about being "pressed." This is a state called hypnagogia. I have experienced this state myself and it can be extremely frightening if you're not aware of what's happening. The site listed below gives a pretty decent explanation, but I'll cite the basic concept:

> *"Hypnagogia (also spelled hypnogogia) is a disorder usually described as sleep paralysis, although this definition does not indicate all possible symptoms. In the transition periods of waking up or falling asleep sufferers of hypnagogia feel awake in the mind but paralyzed in the body. These episodes can be quite frightening and hypnagogia is thought to be the origin of stories of demonic or extraterrestrial visits. Studies performed in sleep labs show that while a patient with hypnagogia is awake and aware of their surroundings, instruments measuring brain waves record their brain as asleep"* (2016).

"Quick Links." *Hypnogogia,* Sleepdex, n.d., Web. 25 April 2016

http://www.sleepdex.org/hypnogogia.htm

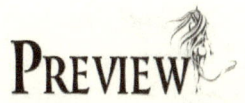

Preview

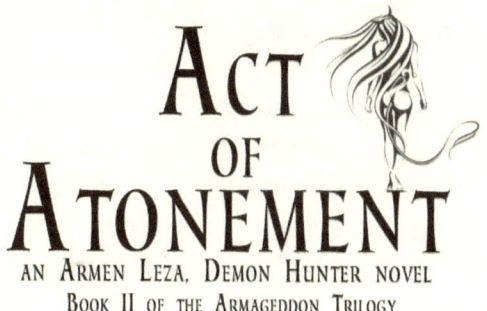

Act of Atonement

An Armen Leza, Demon Hunter novel
Book II of the Armageddon Trilogy

by
N.L. Gervasio

Chapter One
Book of Secrets

Enoch had been a sorcerer. Few knew of it, and it never made history. Of course, they'd sidelined his book and labeled it Apocrypha, but parts of it had resurfaced and become quite popular in recent years. His book was a journal filled with half-truths and spells; some tales were true, some words powerful, and some were just his vivid opiate-induced dreams.

Enoch had called his book *Kitab 'Asrar*, or Book of Secrets. It wasn't the true Book of Secrets—not her Father's book—but for Enoch, it was filled with many wondrous things.

Truly, the man was batshit crazy.

But that was just Armen Leza's opinion, though she may have been biased against him. What did one expect after he'd cursed two hundred of them to descend upon Mount Hermon that day? She'd recently discovered that he was the reason she and the other Grigori fell. And anyone who'd truly been given a tour of the heavens would have known the Sun didn't revolve around the Earth. She'd cut Aristotle some slack; the man hadn't toured the holy canopies with the Divine, and never claimed to.

The spells in Enoch's book were not things to be trifled with, though an unfortunate few had. While they may have been the ramblings of a crazy old man, they were still dangerous spells, and the words within the pages of that book could bring down the heavens piece by piece if one knew how to use it. As far as Armen knew, Enoch had been the only one who knew the order of the spells to bring about the End of Days.

Since Armageddon had begun, she could but guess that someone had found the book and pieced it together.

The true Book of Secrets, though, the one that was even more dangerous than Enoch's book? Armen knew exactly where that book was—tucked neatly between the spines of many religions. After what had happened most recently, she'd needed to keep it safe, to keep it a secret.

JUST INK PRESS, LLC

Anthologies

Into the Darkness
The 434 Revolution: Volume I

N.L. Gervasio

Nemesis
The Dracove
Gods & Vampyres

Coming Soon

The Devil of Dating
Gemini: Book III of the Prophecy series
Assassin: Book 2 in the Kick-Ass Girls Club series
Quattro: an anthology

justinkpress.com

Want to hear about upcoming books? Sign up for the Just Ink Press Newsletter (http://eepurl.com/bBo7or). We do not share emails with anyone.

www.ingramcontent.com/pod-product-compliance
Lightning Source LLC
Chambersburg PA
CBHW050911250626
47155CB00001B/183